Nothing in Particular

By Kate LeDonne

With love to all misfits, outcasts, weirdos, mavericks, punks, Goths, geeks, nonconformists, free thinkers and true individuals. I wrote it for us.

· Acknowledgments ·

Big thanks to my husband, Alex LeDonne, who has helped every step of the way with layout and production. You've always been so great at weathering the storms that come with me of the creative temperament. Good practice, I guess!

Gigantic thanks to Anna Maxted, editor and writer extraordinaire whose talent and patience are unsurpassed. Your guidance whipping this book into shape made all the difference in the world! You're the best.

Anna Maxted's Book Clinic:
http://annamaxtedbooks.squarespace.com/book-clinic/

Big thanks to Tiya Marshall, the best Beta reader and typo detector a writer can have. You're the perfect match, and I'm so grateful I stumbled into you in writer world.

Tiya Marshall's web site: http://www.proofeditcheck.com/

Thank you to my Grandma and Grandpa, Dot and Raymond, for teaching me Latin roots of words, giving me my first dictionary, teaching me how to sew, how to bake, and how to nurture friendships.

Thank you to my grandfather "Pappy". Your example taught me persistence, perseverance and DIY are the way to go. Everything I know about true generosity I learned from watching you when I was little.

Thank you to Mrs. Rose Mahern, Mrs. Jean Burns, Mr. Glenn Linneman, and Mrs. Mayme Stump. My first English teachers who created the foundation, pushed me to do better, and who took the time to encourage me early on on my life. It means the world.

Thank you to my first French teacher, Mr. Richard Stokes for being the best first French teacher to a kid who always dreamed of learning the language and culture. You are the most patient, kind teacher and are the yardstick by which teachers should be measured.

Thank you to Donita Parrish for sticking around these 15 some odd years. How did it go by so fast??!

Thank you to Jennifer Goldstein for reminding me in word and deed — screw fear. Just do it anyway! Dance on, you clown.

A giant thank you to all my Twitter peeps! Your words of encouragement and the constant stream of humor got me through some tough times. One day, you shall all have cake!

Thank you to all artists, writers, and musicians who have gotten so many of us through what felt like endless despair. Music was the friend who held my hand when I was alone, in the dark. Thank you.

· In Memory ·

Bryan Audrey (BSA) Dude — it sucks that we never got to trade pages while I was doing this edit. You are sorely missed. Thank you for always telling me I was good enough. You always backed me up, even in our last conversation you were telling me to "Tell them to go pound sand". Thank you for being my friend and helping me drown out the negative voices.

Jeremy Bowers — You deserved better.

Andy Hale — This was all going to be a fun surprise for the old gang. I can't believe you're gone. Love always, my red-headed friend.

Jamie Duffy Coldwaves Memorial festival http://coldwaves.net/

Don't end your story before it has even begun. Get help. Stay here. http://coldwaves.net/hope-for-the-day/ http://hftd.org/

Nothing in Particular

By Kate LeDonne

· One ·

Red pen slashes a bloody trail all over the journal that lands in front of me. Mrs. Starling continues tossing journals onto everyone's desks. Muttering and groans are heard throughout the room. Over the murmur of grumbling, the wall clock ticks loudly as though mysteriously amplified by our desire to escape both the room and the obnoxious teacher. We all impatiently watch the second hand as the end of the day approaches with all the speed of a rainforest snail. I look at my shoes and perch on the edge of my chair like a crow about to take flight.

"Class! Settle down! You're still mine for the next three minutes. I must say, I was very disappointed in your efforts so far, as you can see by your lousy marks. You must apply yourselves more productively next time," chirps Mrs. Starling with a condescending smirk. Apparently, if one is not inclined to be all flowers and kittens and fluff, one is not going to get good marks in Mrs. Starling's class.

Mrs. Starling is a pouffy, gray-haired nitwit, who seems to have a seriously twisted reality. From the first day of class, I knew she was going to be trouble. The big, stupid, geese and duck sweater she was wearing clued me in from the get-go. What kind of person looks at that and says to themselves, "Oooh! This is a good look for me!"? Now I have my answer. She is the kind of person who believes that the only valid ideas or thoughts are nice, pretty, frilly ones. In her world everything is light, clean, and fluffy. There is no darkness or ugliness, although I beg to differ after seeing her clothing choices. There is also no truth.

Anyway, the assignment was to write at least half a page about *anything*, once each day. I completed and surpassed the required length of the assignment. According to the red-inked objections all over my journal, I should have known better than to write a story about a kid suffering at the hands of an unmerciful, cruel family. "I hardly think this is realistic," is just one of the criticisms. Lady, I'm writing fiction. School corporations care about test scores, not the kids taking the tests. Message received, loud and clear. We're just here to bark edicts, not care who or how you are. The idea of writing in a style she likes brings bile to the back of my throat. And they lived happily ever after, right?

The bell rings at a deafening volume. I throw my books and folders into my big, black bag and mercifully escape before Mrs. Starling can catch me. Behind me, her obnoxious braying at me is lost in the din of the chattering students converging in the halls. I speedily slip into the crowded hallway. It seems I have narrowly avoided yet another lecture on what she deems inappropriate material.

As I head down the hallway, a group of younger, trashy girls smacks right into me, knocking me into the lockers. A blonde girl with fried, permed hair and loads of purple lip liner with light pink lipstick yells, "Fucking freak! Why don't you go back where you came from?"

Regaining my balance, I turn as they walk past shouting insults and retort, "I've been *here* since I was eleven, you fucking genetic experiment!" This is nothing new. I get crap from just about everyone, just about every day, because I "don't fit in". Even though I grew up here, I still can't see why I should be a vacant, brainless wonder like these knobs. I am guaranteed the right to be exactly who I am, according to The Constitution of The United States. No inbred, brain-dead hayseed is going to change that, no matter how hard they try. I am also guaranteed an education, something these dumbass hillbullies couldn't care less about.

I collect my stuff from the dusty floor and continue down the crowded hallway to my locker. Lucky for me and the rest of the student body, it's Friday. For the next two days, we are free from this gunmetal gray and beige hell that was obviously designed sometime in the early 1970s. The fluorescent lighting gives the hallways the distinct look of a prison, washing away all of the color. This place sterilizes everything within until it is one beige, boring blob.

I need to be sure I have all my homework for the weekend. Reaching my locker I hear, "Dude, you look like an elephant crapped on your head or something. What's the deal, bitchy kitty?"

I roll my eyes at Mandy, my best friend, who has sidled up behind the locker door. Mandy and I have been friends ever since the sixth grade, when she and I discovered The Dead Kennedys . She is a teeny puckish girl with black hair cut in a bob and shaved in the back. Today she is sporting ripped fishnet stockings, a purple plaid skirt and a black Skinny Puppy t-shirt. My locker is usually neat and organized, but lately I haven't had time to straighten things. My books and folders are all haphazardly crammed in the bottom of my locker. Siouxsie and the Banshees and PiL postcards adorn the interior, along with a flyer for a Ministry concert we missed.

I turn to my friend, "Well, we got our journals back in Mrs. Starling's class and the bitch gave me a D minus. I can't even deal with another lecture from her about how come I can't write something more upbeat, and realistic." My French book, a folder and some papers slide out of my locker onto my foot. Mandy ducks out of the way as I violently shove the escaped items back into the locker.

"Maybe some rubber cement and some Edgar Allen Poe Xeroxes are what she needs on her blackboard...." replies Mandy, a mischievous twinkle in her eye.

"I doubt she would even notice she's so oblivious. Apparently, it's something that's going around. These total retards tried to flatten me in the hall on my way here. They were under the impression that I'm from somewhere other than this dump. Ha! I wish! I mean, granted, I wasn't born here, but I've been here since the sixth grade, so what the hell?" I slam the locker closed, glowering menacingly at the small group of freshman girls whispering in a cluster just across the hall.

Mandy rolls her eyes with a bored sigh and begins to stomp over. The twittering dimwits disperse as if someone has set their gigantic, permed, blonde hair on fire. "Sorry you had to deal with a crowd of the brainless today. Just remember, we only have the rest of this year and next year — then we are off to college where we will be among intelligent life!" she replies with a manic grin. Together we trudge out to the parking lot, climb into her silver hatchback, and throw in a mixed tape.

My mood improves on the drive home with a little blast of Public Image Limited. I adore John Lydon, a.k.a. Johnny Rotten. His venom toward the inanely stupid gives me more pleasure than a vibrator ever could. Mr. Rotten screams, bellows and wails that talking to these people is a waste of time, and they need to crawl back in their own dustbin. Screw Mrs. Starling. Screw them all.

I climb out of the 1985 Ford Escort that is plastered with Oingo Boingo, PiL and Skinny Puppy bumper stickers and a random sticker that states, "The religious right is WRONG".

"So what do you feel like doing this weekend?" Mandy asks, leaning over from the driver's seat.

"Hmmm — I dunno. I have a lot of housework to do. I'll call you tomorrow and we'll see then, OK?" I mutter, knowing that a dreary weekend of chores surely lies ahead.

"When is your mom going to start acting like a mom?" She yells out the driver's side window in exasperation as she pulls out of the driveway.

"Five past never!" I holler back.

I walk through the blue-and-white checked kitchen and start heading up to my room when I am summoned.

"Kiiiieeeerrraaa! Get in here!" screeches Mom from the living room.

Oh crap. I just got here. What could possibly be a problem already?

"Kiera!!" Her voice pierces my thoughts like a hundred tiny daggers.

"I'm coming! Geez, give me a sec…" I reply, rolling my eyes and wishing I had a magic wand to transport myself far away, or into a different life.

"I need you to get dinner going right now. Your father has had a rough day and I haven't had time to do a thing. You know how he gets..." she slurs. As usual, she is sprawled in her La-Z-Boy with a half empty scotch and soda in her hand and some soap opera on TV.

"Got it. Is the food already in the fridge or do I need to go to the store?" I say, already guessing the answer as I run upstairs to my room to drop my things inside.

"Don't get smart with me, young lady! Take my car, and get the meat and salad," she snaps, her finger stabbing in the direction of the key rack hanging on the kitchen wall.

My mother, Dana Graves, has never worked a single day in her sorry, drunken life. She was raised a privileged debutante in Kentucky. She is accustomed to Cadillacs, servants, country clubs, the whole nine yards. Her parents, Leo and Cleo Gold, weren't thrilled when she married my father, but who could blame them?

My brother, Brett, has the car that we supposedly share and isn't home from school yet. He drives it whenever and wherever he wants. He probably has basketball practice or something. I make sure I have my driver's license, grab her keys, slam a mixed taped into the stereo, and take off. It's 4:20 P.M. I have to get the groceries and get dinner cooked and on the table by 6 P.M. or else.

Just my luck. There's a train. I sit there praying to anyone to help me pull this off before all hell breaks loose. The train thunders and squeals along at a good clip, but I'm anxious.

I close my eyes, listening to Johnny Rotten shrieking about how someone's problem is themselves and asking what they're going to do about it.

After what feels like three days, I fly into the parking lot and scurry into the store. Snatching a cart, I hustle through the produce section. The fluorescent lights drain the life out of the fresh fruit and vegetables. Even the clerk stocking the apples appears to be a lifeless shade of gray. Seems to be a trend in this part of Indiana — everything is drained of color and substance. People are staring at me as if I have horns sprouting out of my head. Could be the hair, could be the clothes — I never know. I don't have time for explaining anything. I race through Kroger grabbing everything on the list and dash to the cash register. It's almost 5 P.M. when I fill in the amount on the check my mother has written. My heart picks up its pace as I face the bleak reality that awaits me at home. Dread overwhelms me and I steel myself as I zoom into the driveway.

I walk as quietly as possible into the tacky, country kitchen, ignoring the duck and geese motif on everything. Quiet as a mouse, I gently put the groceries down on the counter and start putting things away. I hear heavy footsteps heading my direction. The hairs on my neck stand on end and my body instantly becomes rigid. He's home early. I close my eyes, cringing, waiting for what comes next.

"Kiera! What the hell took you so long? Get your fat ass in gear and get my dinner now!" My father screams in my face as he rushes at me, grabs my arms, and starts shaking me. Interesting choice of insults, really, being that I am 5'8" tall and weigh around 120 pounds. I see the familiar psychotic fury in his eyes. I am so screwed.

"I'm going as fast as I can. There was a train and I…"
WHAM!

He smacks me so hard across the face that I hit the linoleum floor, skid about a foot and slam into the oak cabinets. I cringe against the vicious onslaught, my arms held feebly over my head as I attempt to protect myself.

"SHUT UP! I don't want to hear your bullshit excuses!! What are you waiting for you stupid, worthless bitch?!" He kicks me hard in the thigh, luckily just once this time. There is a dull crunch as he grabs my wrist and hauls me upward, dragging me across the room and throwing me against the stove. Lady Luck smiles on me. It isn't turned on yet.

My head is throbbing. I glare at the floor, stoic. I give him nothing. No tears. No pleading. I wait.

Crying or pleading never helps. He appears to enjoy causing pain, especially if it's me. I have learned how to hold it all in so that he doesn't get the satisfaction…so that he doesn't "win" if I can help it.

My mother is standing in the doorway that leads to the family room with a half full glass of scotch and soda in her hand. She just stands there watching and does nothing. She turns away and returns to her chair to continue watching TV.

I wait in silence, painfully holding back tears.

"GET YOUR DUMB ASS IN GEAR NOW!" He is about an inch away from my face. My father, Peter Graves, is a fifty-year-old assistant principal in the middle school here, and is accustomed to giving orders. His breath smells like scotch and whatever he had for lunch; which must have been rancid manure and fish heads. He looks like a normal, white businessman: crisp, buttoned-down shirt, suit and tie, wingtips shined to glossy perfection. But in a blink he gets that sick, deranged, inhuman look in his eyes, and unleashes such rage, hatred and violence– I know one day I'm going to die.

I stand up, get the groceries and begin preparing dinner. My brain is still playing the Sex Pistols song about having a problem, and the problem is you.

I smile to myself and fantasize about slitting his throat ear to ear, my leg throbbing in pain where he kicked me. In my mind, I watch his blood cover the kitchen floor, a pool of crimson spreads slowly across the pristine blue and white speckled linoleum. I envision the shock in my father's eyes as he topples. My thoughts are my own. I can think anything I want and I am not actually hurting anyone.

After dinner, I load the dishwasher and retreat into my fantasy world where someday I will go to Paris. I want to see all the art, eat French food, maybe even start a Josephine Baker record collection. I have been drawing since I was old enough to hold a crayon. Art, books and music are my life. I hide most of my work because I just can't handle any more criticism than I already get. I gave my mother a painting for her Christmas gift last year and she threw it away. I worked on that portrait of her for a week solid. It was over 45 hours of work. They don't get it. "Art isn't a real job, Kiera." I dream of going to Paris and Milan, maybe working for a magazine or in a fashion house. I think I'd be happy pushing a broom if I could just get out of here.

I have two large portfolios full of drawings and a few paintings. They are carefully hidden behind my clothes in the closet. As a kid, I used to hide behind my clothes in the closet when my brother or father was hunting me. I learned that if you controlled your breathing, they couldn't hear you and, therefore, couldn't find you. I was really good at playing hide and seek. I've always known how to hide really, really well— almost instinctively. I try to just slink past people at school, mostly anyway. On days when I am completely fed up, I put on a black crinoline, black tights, a Salvation Army thrift store men's suit jacket, along with my Skinny Puppy t-shirt underneath, and Doc Martens on my feet. This ensemble is reserved for when I want a really wide berth in the hallways. The crinoline sticks out a bit and people seem to be afraid of me, which suits me just fine. It's my "get the hell away from me" outfit.

People here are always giving me a hard time about how I look and who I am — so it isn't like it matters what I do. I don't drink, do drugs, slut around, shoplift, cheat on tests or vandalize anything. The jocks and preppies do all that stuff. My crowd basically consists of freaks and outcasts. We are mostly honors kids and, on the whole, a mixed bag. Some Goths, some Punks, some Hip Hoppers, and some just plain old normal kids. We have all been rejected by the rest of the school because we are too much of something that has been deemed bad. Too smart, too weird, too ugly, too something. Fuck 'em. They are all too stupid in my opinion. I don't understand people who don't get that there is a whole world out there with LOTS of different people who have completely different cultures, religions, music and ways of life than those witnessed around here. Different isn't wrong. It's just different. I guess this mentality is part of what got me thrown out of the confirmation class my father forced me to go to. I asked too many questions that they couldn't or wouldn't answer. I got one hell of a licking when I got home that day, but it was worth it to not have to waste any more Sunday mornings on that crap. Like I need more people telling me to shut up, not think for myself, be a good girl, and just swallow whatever they're trying to shove down my throat. I was obedient and tried their way. Seems to me that for a guy as meddling and nosy as they purport God to be, he's been awfully busy looking the other way.

Rolling over and yawning, I stretch out like a cat, blinking as a sliver of sunlight pierces the window blinds, catching me across the face. I roll out of bed in my rumpled t-shirt, and cotton undies. As I shuffle around the room looking for some pants, my leg is killing me. I have a huge, ugly, purple bruise in the shape of a wing tip on my thigh- one of his usual signatures. My father loves the entire Bush family, all things Republican, scotch, beer, football and Playboy. He is anti-anything-or-anyone-different. Period. He was in the Army for a while and behaves like we are his own little platoon. He has absolutely no impulse control whatsoever. He says and does *anything* he wants to anyone he wants, and he doesn't have the foggiest idea that some of the things he does are wrong. The weirdest thing is how everyone typically stands around watching him do whatever to whomever, and nobody says a word. I locate a pair of paint spattered gray sweats and tug them on. I take a deep breath and hold the doorknob in my hand for a moment. Maybe I can hide today? Maybe they won't notice if I just don't come out of my room?

My mother screeches up the stairs, "Kiiiiiiiierrrraaaa! Get your butt in gear!"

"Coming!" I holler back. Oh goody. My presence has been detected.

Wandering downstairs to forage for breakfast, I cringe as my mother begins to belt out orders. The volume of her voice is tough to take right when a person first gets up. It's like the racket of blue jays fighting, but louder.

"You will be outside today raking and bagging, and when you're done you can clean the fireplace," she squawks, jabbing her finger toward the door. "Make it snappy, your father's in a mood today and I don't want any problems because of you!"

I scarf down some cereal and hustle back upstairs to put on a sweatshirt and socks. I don't want to end up getting locked outside without enough warm clothing. They did that once when I was about nine and I got frostbite; granted, it was January then. I just hate being cold, and that incident taught me the hard way about being prepared. I grudgingly plod outside to begin my enslavement for the weekend. Checking for witnesses, I put on my headphones to hopefully make time go faster.

Jello Biafra yowls into my ears about a terminal preppy who wants a grinning pair of tits. I mean, a wife. The thrashing guitar and Jello's acid words bring a smile to my lips for the first time today. The flavor today is the Dead Kennedys' "In God We Trust, Inc.", among others. Nothing like a little hard core to blast your worries clean out of your head. After a few hours of raking and bagging leaves, I notice my hands are starting to blister. With a loud growl, my stomach informs me that I'd better eat something soon or it may digest my internal organs. I slide my Walkman back in my pocket and trudge into the house.

"What do you think you're doing?!" my mother shrieks, sprawled in her chair as usual.

"Um, having some lunch? I'm about to fall over," I explain.

"No time for you to have lunch, missy. Get your ass back out there and finish before your father gets back from the store, or else!" she snarls, flopping back into her chair.

I ignore her and grab some bread and peanut butter.

"I said, get back outside NOW!" She stomps into the kitchen and grabs at my half-made sandwich, but I am too quick for her. Apparently, she isn't aware that being a drunk slows your reaction time. I am also a good deal taller than her at this point, and can easily hold things out of her reach. She grabs the back of my sweatshirt, nearly strangling me.

"You little shit! I told you what you had to get done and if you had finished, it wouldn't be a problem. Now give me that and get back outside!" she snaps.

I wrestle myself out of her grip and turn to glare at her.

"I don't care. I am hungry, so I'm going to eat," I get really tired of her irrational behavior at times. This is definitely one.

I have to push her away with my foot while I finish making my sandwich. I lock myself in the bathroom to eat it. Most of the other locks in the house have been removed or broken due to violent outbursts from my parents and sibling. This is one of the only ones left that works. Wishing for milk, I cup my hand under the spigot and get some water so that the peanut butter doesn't permanently cement my throat closed. Unbelievably, the entire time she is outside the door screaming, threatening, and carrying on.

BANG! BANG! BANG!

She scream through the door, "Kiiiiiieerra!! Open this door, goddammit! You open this door or I'll thrash you so hard you'll never sit down again!!"

It's like being cornered by some warped version of Elmer Fudd in "Looney Tunes". One... two... THREE. I open the door quickly, and my mother falls into the small half bathroom, smacking her head on the door as she tumbles in continuing to screech a mixture of swear words and orders at me. I flee outside to resume the nearly completed yard work. I am disgusted that I have to fight this hard with my own mother to meet my basic needs. It's just ridiculous. When I get to the rake and piles of leaves I was working on, I discover that someone has jumped onto the bags of leaves, tearing them open and scattering leaves all over.

"Hey dildo-brains," my brother says from behind me.

"You fucking PRICK!"

Brett and his friends laugh their butts off before running off toward his buddy's house. They have been over there most of the day playing video games. Typical.

Brett Graves is tall, athletic and a vicious little fucker who will, no doubt, grow to be a vicious big fucker, just like our father. People are only nice to him because they know if they aren't, he'll humiliate them until they'd wish they were never born. He starts rumors about people, calls them names, makes fun of them until they cry or try to hit him, and then he beats them to a pulp. He's your typical baseball-hat-wearing, beer-guzzling, cheerleader-chasing asshole who is totally incapable of independent thought. He graduates this year, which is fortunate for me, from the viewpoint of — fewer beatings and less torture. He'll be in college somewhere far enough away that I'll be safer…until the holidays, anyway.

I try not to cry as I furiously stuff leaves into bags that don't have holes in them. I start having a sneezing fit and my eyes begin to swell. Autumn sucks for people like me who are allergic to mold and ragweed. I have snot all over the place and I feel like someone has shoved me into a tiny box — I can't move and I can't breathe. It's times like this that I just want to scream and throw a real tantrum, but I don't have the time.

I soothe myself listening to the Sex Pistols rage and seethe about a liar, demanding why they couldn't tell the truth.

This is such total bullshit. I re-rake, and seethe, wondering why my parents had children at all. I have no idea how to fit in and be "normal". I have no idea how to stop being a constant moving target. Other people seem to have perfect little lives, free from static. Yet they are the ones with the least tolerance for those less fortunate. I don't get it.

Later that night the phone rings as I'm putting dishes in the dishwasher and cleaning up after dinner.

"Hey lard ass! Phone!" hollers Brett from upstairs.

I roll my eyes in disgust, and don't reply as I walk over to pick up the phone hanging on the wall in the kitchen.

"Hello?"

"Hey! It's Mandy. What do you say to a movie tonight?"

Somewhere on the line there is a snicker followed by —

"No one wants to be seen anywhere with an ugly freak like you!" Brett snipes with a predictably childish put-down.

"Get off the phone shithead!" I demand.

click

"Sorry about that. The inmates have no privacy," I sigh.

"No problem. I don't see how he thinks is he just sooooooo hilarious," she replies. "His mentality is so fourth grade. But, I digress. A movie? You, me? Tonight?"

"Wish I could. I'm so beat after doing manual labor all day and I'm sure they have plans for me tomorrow. I gotta get some sleep or I am going to be an even more miserable being," I groan.

"OK, but only because I know you are such a blast when you have no sleep. I guess we'll just try again next weekend. Maybe you can stay over, huh?" she suggests, trying to cheer me up. Mandy knows the whole deal with my family, so she's always been really easy on me when I can't do stuff. Most other people get pissed off when I have to stay in for whatever reason and they take it personally. The thing is — I'd love to be like them and not have any understanding of what life is like without all this static. I really would. Ignorance is bliss I have heard. I'd love to see what that's like, just floating along in life with no major problems. Will I ever experience calm normalcy? It seems so far away from where I am right now.

"Yeah, we have to keep trying because I desperately need a social life!" I tell her.

"Kiiiiiiieerra! Get off the goddamn phone! NOW!" my father yells from the family room.

Uh oh.

"Shit, I gotta run," I stammer, my heart picking up its pace.

"Yeah, I heard. What the hell is up his ass?"

"No clue."

"KIIIIIIIIEEEEERRAA!! Get in here NOW!!" he screams.

"Fuck! See you Monday. Bye!" I immediately hang up and rush to the family room.

My mother is totally wasted and sprawled in her chair. She gazes at me with her drunken, unfocused eyes, a smug look on her face as she exacts her revenge.

"Did you disobey your mother today?" he asks, holding a glass of Scotch like he's the King of BFE.

"I don't think so," I reply trying to buy some time to think, "I raked the whole yard, bagged the leaves and re-bagged them after Brett and his buddies jumped on them and made a huge mess…"

"I'm not talking about your brother. I am talking about YOU! Now, did you or did you not disobey your mother?"

"I did everything she told me to do today," I say looking at the ceiling.

"Wipe that snotty little smirk off your face you little shit!" he snarls, setting the glass down on his side table.

In one movement, he stands up and comes at me. I brace myself knowing that I am IN TROUBLE.

"If your mother tells you to do something, you better do it!" he rages, grabbing my arms. I feel like someone is filling me up with hot water, super fast. I look at the floor. My feet are just barely touching the carpet. He has lifted me off the floor, shaking me like a rag doll.

"She told you that there wasn't time to have lunch and you ate lunch anyway. WHAT *shake* DO *shake* YOU *shake* HAVE *shake* TO *shake* SAY FOR YOURSELF?!!" He shakes me so hard I think my eyeballs are going to pop out of my head and roll onto the floor. My arms are being crushed and searing pain is shooting up them. I try not to cry or let on that he is hurting me. I can't let them know that they have successfully inflicted pain, or they win. My feet dangle two inches from the floor.

"OK Peter, that's enough," my mother drawls softly. She looks over at me, with an unfocused gaze and smiles.

"I was really hungry. I really needed to eat!" I plead.

"I don't care if you starve to death! You will do what we tell you, when we tell you to do it while you live under this roof!" He is foaming at the mouth like a rabid possum.

I am always astonished when they show me how much they loathe me. They have never once acted like they even liked me — unless you count the act they put on in front of other people.

This is the way it has always been. I just can't figure out why. I don't understand .

I lay on my twin bed under my ancient white comforter and stare at the ceiling. My room is small, with one small closet, cream-colored shag carpet and white walls. I have a poster of the Eiffel Tower on one wall and an art poster of a woman with a dark bob smoking a cigarette on the other. My furniture is the same I've had since I was six. My father chose it. White with little flowers. It's for the daughter he wishes he had, not me. Closing my eyes and sinking into the bed, I roll over onto my side, curl up, and try to create a lovely dream. I envision myself outside in the sun on a campus somewhere hot and miles away from here. People are smiling and greeting me. I am accepted here. I belong here. Now if I can only find somewhere like it in the real world…

There is a man in the blackness standing over me. He tells me he is going to kill me and he puts a pillow over my face, smothering me while I scream for help. I sit straight up in bed screaming a piercing horror movie scream. I am dripping with sweat and shaking like I've chugged ten thousand pots of coffee in about a minute. I look around the room. Nobody here but me. I have this dream all the time. I feel like there's something I need to remember. There are pieces of a memory that fade as soon as I reach for them, like ice chips melting through my fingertips. There is a flash of being on my parents' bed when I was little. There was pain and then…I can't quite see it. I can almost remember. I have these fragments that resurface now and then. It's always so foggy and out of focus that I'm just not sure. I feel like I'm putting together a puzzle. I keep thinking if I can figure it out, maybe I'll sleep better. Maybe I won't be afraid all the time. My mother stumbles down the hall and opens the door.

"Kiera!" she whispers, thoroughly annoyed that I woke her up, "What is going on in here?"

"Sorry. Had a nightmare again," I mutter.

"Well, shut the hell up and go to sleep! If you wake your father up, you'll be sorry!" she slurs.

"I know," I sigh.

I can never sleep. It takes me around three to four hours each night just to fall asleep, and, even then, I almost always have nightmares. Mostly, there's a man either smothering me with a pillow or I am drowning. Then, there's the wonderful new one where I am being chased. Sometimes a man is chasing me, sometimes dogs. Either way, I end up screaming bloody murder and pissing off my family. I sleep with my eyes open a lot. It scares the crap out of my mom and she yells at me. Like I do it on purpose. I've heard war veterans do that too. I only do well in school because most of the work isn't that hard. The only classes that I actually have to work at are the honors classes I'm in. Otherwise, I'd be bored the whole time. Like typing class, for instance. I get in trouble with the fascist teacher for finishing too fast and then writing notes to my friends. It's the most stupid, remedial class ever, but everyone is *required* to take it. After all, girls aren't anything more than baby makers and secretaries, right? I'll never understand why being smart or doing something well is a cardinal sin in their eyes.

I roll over and stare at the ceiling. What do these dreams mean? What is this fragment that I keep remembering? It's like looking in a broken mirror.

I lay there on my back and work at slowing my breathing. I pray silently for a dreamless, peaceful sleep. Two hours later, I finally drift off and get some restless sleep. I dream of being chased somewhere that is dark…a shadowy man is trying to kill me.

· **Two** ·

October 5, 1987
B.F.E., Indiana

I shuffle out of bed and throw on whatever clothes I can find. I am exhausted, and my brain is still totally asleep. I figure as long as I don't go to school naked, I can't get into too much trouble. I slog down-stairs, grab a few granola bars and hear Mandy's car pull up. I race out the door and flop into the passenger's seat.

"Wow, you look like total hell. Are you OK?" Mandy says, looking at me with concern. Her eyes slide down to my arms. The Oingo Boingo t-shirt I have on evidently doesn't cover the bruises that daddy-shit left all over my arms.

"Holy fuck! What did they do to you?"

I wince at the volume of her shock and fury. I twist around to get my jacket on while she pulls out of the driveway.

"The usual insanity. I ate lunch, which was disobeying mother's orders. She whined to my father, and he knocked me for a loop. It's the usual fun at the Graves' residence," I croak sleepily.

"How is eating a crime with these people? They are your *parents!* What the fuck is wrong with them?" She pounds the steering wheel with her hands, livid with my family.

"If I knew that, I'd be omniscient and I could rule the world," I respond. I'm so bored with the whole thing, I don't want to talk about it.

We look at each other briefly and speed along to school in pensive, frustrated silence.

From the stereo Ogre growls how life shifts up and down, and everybody knows it wrong.

Skinny Puppy in the morning is a beautiful thing.

This weekend we will be going to go to a school dance. My parents are actually letting me go because it's a school thing. They aren't particularly fond of Mandy, because she doesn't hide the fact that she hates them and thinks they are total shitheads. Whenever they try to talk to her, she glares at them and only replies with a closed-lipped "um hmm" or "uh uh". I find it all very amusing, because she's about five foot three. My father could throw her like a discus, no problem. He refrains from throttling anyone outside the family to sustain his "upstanding citizen" status. I can always tell when he wishes he could haul off and deck my friends. Sadly, they aren't complete strangers to bullying.

We have to be careful around school. My friends are a small group of smart weirdos. We like it that way. Andy is an artist. He gets crap from the jocks because he has red hair and wears a pin that says "Nazi punks Fuck OFF!!". He's the comic relief of our group and is damn good at it. Andy is a super sweet guy with a great disposition, unlike the rest of us. He's super hyper and we all harass him for being spastic, but he knows it's out of love. The most colorful one of our group, he often wears stuff like shocking pink pants with neon blue paisley shirts.

Max used to get beat up all the time until he had a growth spurt. He went from like, 5'2" to 5'10" almost overnight. He's now around six foot three. It was Karmic poetry the day Max unceremoniously stuffed the asshole who used to chase him headfirst into a trash can. People rarely mess with him now. He's super quiet and really shy, except around me, Mandy and Andy. He wears black perpetually, which we lovingly tease him about, but it suits his serious demeanor.

There's nothing to do around here except drive around and go to movies. There are cornfields, a K-Mart and one movie theater. What a metropolis! We get crap from people because we listen to bands like, what we wear, and generally dancing to the beat of a different drum. The hicks around here constantly say garbage like, "Whut the hail is that? Yew ahr weird. Yew all ahr in service to Satan!" We like being individuals, therefore, not exactly the same. Those little brainless wonders who dress up like Robert Smith really get on our nerves. We are equal opportunity smart asses. It doesn't matter which end of the spectrum you're on. If you're fake, we'll make fun of you. It isn't that hard to pick a personality and stick with it.

The worst intimidation in town was last year when someone started a rumor that the "freaks" are Satan worshippers. Drinking blood and sacrificing virgins on Halloween– the whole nine yards. We have a pretty good idea that the source was the self-appointed head of the local pseudo-vampire clique, a halfwit extraordinaire. It became a major problem when even the *adults* around here bought into the rumors. Life became extremely difficult for us. Things got really out of control, with people making death threats, and bringing guns to school to "blow those goddamn freaks' heads off." There was even a story in the newspaper. We were all questioned by the cops and hunted like rabbits during school. Then the very worst happened. Some hillbullies saw this kid in my French class talking to me about our homework. They followed him home, and beat the living shit out of him with baseball bats. The cops told his mom to control *her* child. The thing is, he's Mormon and doesn't even drink soda, let alone fool with the occult. The cops treated all of us like we deserved everything that was done to us. The whole thing scared the shit out of us. We learned to always look over our shoulders, and trust no one. It's a heavy load on your shoulders when a whole town comes after you the way they did. I thought adults were supposed to know better than believe a bunch of stupid rumors.

The best way for us to retaliate against the hillbullies is to go to the dances. This is our school, too. We have every right to be here and participate. If it makes the perfect, popular people uncomfortable, that's just too damn bad. The world doesn't belong to *them.* Last month we actually got the DJ to play "Grey Matter" by Oingo Boingo and "Everything Counts" by Depeche Mode. All the jocks and cheer-leaders cleared the floor in horror while all the so-called freaks ran out to mosh and pogo with each other and the floor. We can't usually get them to play *anything* that we listen to. Alternative music is too edgy for most people around here. At school dances, we congregate in a corner and make fun of people until something resembling music comes on and then we go thrash around until it is replaced with drivel. We generally don't bother anyone, unless they come looking for trouble. Then all bets are off. It's not like we have anything to lose.

Mandy knows how to turn on the charm and bat her eyelashes and do the "I'm cute" thing. She's not easy or anything. She just knows how to push people's buttons. I'm basically her sidekick. She's the gregarious one. I am the quiet one who only talks when I have to. The last few years if I am talking to someone, it's to issue a threat of disembowelment for picking on someone they shouldn't have. I caught some burnouts one time and stopped just short of pounding the hell out of them single-handed. They had cornered a little freshman kid with glasses and were verbally terrorizing him when I came walking by and saw them going after this poor, trembling kid. He was small for his age, wearing floods, and a long sleeved golf shirt. The kind of kid who is generally invisible and tries hard to stay off the radar so that he doesn't end up stuffed in a locker or beaten black and blue. I decided on this occasion it would be worth the pain if I got caught. Nerds are cool. I love smart people and couldn't care less what they look like. I am skinny, but when I am pissed you better clear out. They didn't screw with that kid again and they are afraid of me now. Just the way I like it. Fuckers.

It's Friday night and I actually got permission to stay at Mandy's for the first time in months. I can breathe for the first time in weeks. We are getting ready for the dance, listening to Siouxsie and the Banshees. Andy and Max wait for us in the living room, playing "Dig Dug" on the Atari. Clickclickclickclickclick. The joysticks are being pummeled relentlessly as the guys flee dragons.

"So, what do you think?" Mandy asks, finishing putting on her mascara.

"I think I'll be happy with just about anything. If it's the usual guy, he goes to Wax Trax regularly, so he's not totally out of it," I reply, putting on some deep red lipstick. I can breathe for the first time in a long time, and I smile broadly at my dear friend. It's so hard sometimes, trying to jump through all these hoops. I have the coolest friends. They are always here. Warped, twisted, and dorky just like me. The outcasts. The weirdos. Freaks. I prefer being myself than being a conformist lemming who has never had an original thought. It's worth the pain. I look in the mirror. My tired face stares back, looking worse for wear. Tall, pale, thin and fairly awkward– I am not exactly a pillar of confidence. Black skirt, black tights, Skinny Puppy t-shirt and Docs. It's tough wanting to blend in with the wall and not be stared at, but also wanting to be who I am.

We walk the few blocks to the school in the misty, chilly night. Andy and Mandy are having an animated discussion about which bands should be played more regularly as the streetlights' amber glow casts our shadows onto the wet, sparkling street and sidewalk. Max and I walk along in observant silence, absorbed in our thoughts and listening in amusement to our friends' conversation.

"…they have to start playing more Depeche Mode, I mean, in most places it's not really considered alternative because everyone listens to them!" Mandy says, Andy vigorously nods in agreement.

We tromp up to the open doors that lead into the gym and hand over the dollar admission. The blonde cheerleaders by the door roll their eyes and whisper. Mandy and I look at each other and grin. As we walk by, heading toward the cafeteria, she turns to them and asks, "Think much?" Max and Andy are walking behind us, and we are all laughing our butts off at the confused expressions on their vacant faces.

"I think that went right over," Max snorts, giggling and cuffing Andy lightly on the head as Andy starts prancing down the hall with his hands on his hips like he's holding pom-poms.

"Like, ready OK! We- have- no- brains- cuz they went down the drain!" Andy's voice turns falsetto as he mimes another cheer, "One- two- three- four- I am such a stupid whore!" To finish the act, he jumps in the air and hops around waving invisible pom-poms. Max, Mandy and I are doubled over laughing. People are looking at us like we are from another planet. And they wonder why we loathe them?

The strains of some Bon Jovi song come drifting out of the cafeteria. We stay just outside. Crappy songs like that are just too harsh to take full blast. Some other metal song fades in and Mandy bravely heads in to chat with the DJ. Max and Andy head in to mosh and screw with people. I hang by the door and watch. I hate having my ears polluted with garbage. But I love watching Max and Andy pogo all over the floor and into each other. People are looking at them, totally pissed that they are out there. The jocks are all performing their best air guitar routines while the cheerleaders are bouncing around and singing. I start cracking up. Out of thin air, the assistant principal walks over to Andy and Max. They stand there arguing for a minute and then come back out to join me.

"What did the old bat want?" I ask, glaring at a whispering group of burnouts who seem to be talking about us.

"She told us to get off the dance floor because we were being 'disruptive'," says Andy in disgust, as we watch a random jock slorping on his girlfriend's face like a starving remora.

Max nods and looks at the floor, as we all turn our backs to the nauseating display.

We go to the dances because we have as much right as all the "normal" kids to be here. It's a battle every time. The jocks and fluffballs show up drunk most of the time, and never get into any trouble. They start fights and get off scot-free. We get in trouble for just taking up space.

Mandy returns from her chat with the DJ, peers around Max and says, "I think you're going to be very happy in a minute."

I hear a familiar beat begin and scurry quickly to the dance floor.

Depeche Mode fills the room as we spin around the nearly empty floor. Only one sullen mini-Robert on the floor. Yay! Poseur free zone. Max and Andy are actually really good dancers. It's so cool to have guy friends who aren't wallflowers. The DJ fades into "Papa Don't Preach". Odd choice, but OOOO-K. We all start bouncing around. Mandy and I slam into each other, while Max flips forward and lands on his back, thrashing around like he's having a seizure. It's a favorite Max dance move. It scares people. Boo.

We have an audience. There is a clump of mini-Robert Smiths and girls wearing black lipstick standing nearby watching us. It's the pack o' poseurs who we associate with being the pseudo-vampire king's little minions. I dislike them on principle– they almost got us killed with their attention seeking bullcrap. We collectively turn our backs to them, and continue dorking around on the dance floor. Suddenly, for no apparent reason, Max is being shoved by some thick-necked wrestler guy. Max puts his hands up palms facing away in the universal "oops, sorry" signal. But the lame-o jocko doesn't care and shoves him again, hard enough to get Max off balance, and sends him careening into some girls dancing nearby. A science teacher comes flying over, "Break it up! Break it up!" He grabs Max and hauls him by the scruff out into the hall. We glare at the blockheaded wrestler who is laughing it up with his buddies and follow Max and the teacher into the hallway.

Mr. Worley is reading Max the riot act. Max is standing there looking at the floor, visibly and understandably angry. We race over, "Sir? Why didn't you grab the guy who shoved Max?" says Mandy, trying to wedge herself between Max and the universally hated Mr. Worley.

"You stay out of this, missy," he snarls. "And watch your mouth, or you will get detention every day for a week!"

"Pardon me, but that guy started it. And watch my mouth for what? Asking a reasonable question?" she calmly replies, still edging between Max and Worley.

"You kids think you can do anything you want! Blue hair! Skateboards! You need to stop causing all this trouble!" he yells in Mandy's face, spit flying everywhere. She winces, blinking at the spittle Worley has sprayed in her face. Disgusted, she wipes it off on Max's trenchcoat. Max glances down a moment and shrugs.

"We can look any way we want, according to the Constitution of the United States," Andy chimes in, now standing near Mandy's shoulder.

"Look, Max accidentally danced into that guy. He didn't do anything on purpose," I add very quietly.

Mr. Worley looks at me with such contempt, I can't comprehend it. "I'm letting you off this time, but if there are any more problems, I'm banning you all from any more dances," he bumbles off with a sinister grin. He walks away to pry couples apart as they slow dance to some lame Chicago ballad.

Mr. Worley teaches biology and freshman math. He wears brown pants and a brown and white striped shirt *every* day, complete with pocket protector. His wife left him for an investment broker a few years ago. We heard rumors that he beat her, which given his behavior wouldn't be a huge shock to anyone.

"Just what we need, a vendetta with Mr. Fuckly," Mandy groans to no one in particular.

"Thanks you guys. I'm really sorry..." says Max, morose that we have yet again unintentionally landed on someone's radar.

"*You're sorry?* They're are total shitheads," I say gesturing around to the pinheads who are now all playing air guitar. "Don't even worry about it. The only reason we go to these stupid things is to remind them that this is our school, too. It isn't like it's the social Mecca of the world. We need to expand our parameters anyway," Mandy and Andy nod in agreement and we slink off to a nearby corner to lie low for a minute. It sucks getting screwed with by almost everyone in this town. It's like a hobby for these losers.

Someday very soon we will all have served our time and be free to go. College professors *have* to be more intelligent than the majority of these assholes. Now, don't get me wrong. There are a few teachers that are really good, just a select few though. The rest are mostly power-tripping poop schnozzles.

Toward the end of the night we slide onto the floor and the DJ gets bonus points for playing a song that has Mandy begged for every time. Al Jourgensen growls about how he lives with snakes, lizards, and things that go bump in the night.

For us everyday *is* Halloween. Personal expression in this place is all we have. We don't expect other people to be like us, why do they expect us to be like them? What, exactly, is so dangerous about a hairstyle? We groove ourselves into that zone where you stop being totally in your body and are somewhere else. Somewhere good. The thing that nobody gets about me, except possibly my friends, is that I am actually an introvert. A healthy dose of fuckitis can apparently masquerade as confidence. I seem to have everyone fooled, but it doesn't mean I want to "put my self out there". Each day I wake up with such dread and terror that some days I am paralyzed into total lethargy. I never know what triggers my parents — the dishes "put in the washer *wrong*" or a B minus on a test. Maybe just sitting there will be enough. I got my clock cleaned for sitting on the wrong cushion on the couch, so why not die for something that actually *matters*. I tell the truth because it's the right thing to do. I won't give in just because that's what would be easier. This is me. I am no one's enemy, unless they come looking for me with trouble on their minds.

Al wails about why can't he live his life for himself and why should he take the abuse?

Why indeed.

We collect our jackets and tumble out into the night, walking back to Mandy's to hang out.

"I hope you know that this will go down on your *permanent record*," drawls Andy doing his best "school administrator" impression.

"Oh yeah?" grins Mandy.

"Well, don't get so distressed… Did I happen to mention that I'm impressed?" we chant together loudly running down the sidewalk before someone comes out to tell us to keep it down. Max and Andy sing the rest of "Kiss Off," while Mandy and I jitterbug in the street as we progress to her house. It's a cold, foggy autumn night; not quite cold enough to freeze. I am thankful for the warm, yellow light from the streetlights. I wouldn't walk anywhere around here in the dark. The bare trees glisten with moisture, the streetlights' reflection turning the droplets into tiny fairy lights.

We reach Mandy's front porch and bustle inside. We take off our shoes and pad downstairs to the basement. Andy pops in a tape.

Ogre snarls acidly from the speakers, and my mind begins to unclench. We find industrial soothing, for whatever reason. It drives our parents nuts. I hide my albums and listen to tapes on my Walkman. Mandy has slipped me many a contraband mixed tape. Mixed tapes are a hobby with us because there isn't much to do around here once you're done doing homework. I scramble to repay the favor whenever I have a free moment from slave labor. We live to go to Chicago and blow our savings at Wax Trax Records, *the* best record store *ever.* They sort of specialize in hard core punk, but they have just about everything that's worth listening to: Bauhaus, The Dead Kennedys, The Cocteau Twins, Skinny Puppy, Front 242, Siouxsie and the Banshees. All the stuff you can't find at the local record store in Indiana because it's too obscure, you can get at Wax Trax. It isn't obscure in the rest of the world, just in the microscopic little world of hillbullies we are currently stuck in.

We sit around gossiping about who was at the dance and who was the biggest doofus of the evening. We, of course, all agreed that it was Mr. Lame-o Jock-o buttface who started trouble involving Max. The next contestant being Mr. Fuckly, oh excuse me, Worley. That whole situation was unbelievable. The final contender was the dingbat cheerleader, who approached Mandy and me in the restroom and said, completely seriously, "I hope you find Jesus someday."

We explained to Little Miss Cheerleader, in very small words, that the violence directed at all the so-called "freaks" was based purely on rumors and lies. Then we suggested she and her little friends check the facts before condemning us, and sending their boyfriends after us to beat us up. She made a sniffy, huffy noise, turned on her heel, and flounced out of the girls' room, followed by her cheerleader pals.

Everyone within earshot was cracking up. I don't think anyone had ever called Miss Perfect Senior Cheerleading Captain on her bullshit before.

"You're messing with us," says Andy.

"Nope," replies Mandy.

"Do you think we can get through the next couple of years without being lynched, burned at the stake, or shot?" Max chimed in.

"Doubtful, but we can try, I guess," I say, wishing I could actually click my heels together and get the hell out of here.

It's completely backwards how people around here think we are troublemakers. We're part of the student body that makes them look good on paper. We take turns getting straight As. The worst thing we ever did was whip a gumball machine toy called a wacky wall walker at the glass library wall where it stuck, motionless. We had no idea this would happen. So, there is a bright yellow octopus-looking thing permanently adhered to that window, distracting all who see it and usually causing hysterical laughter because it was positioned on the window to the Library Head's office. The Assistant Principal actually asked the school to help bring forward "the fiends behind" the permanently affixed wall walker. We sure as hell weren't going to hang ourselves for something stupid like that. Besides, it was an accident. Nobody saw us do it, so they are pretty screwed on ever finding the culprits. We have several plans for mayhem and pranks that we are currently discussing. Nothing really destructive or harmful. Just something to say "fuck you" to some people who need to be taken down a peg or two. There are plenty of total fuckwits around here who deserve a good verbal lashing, but we wouldn't waste our time physically harming anyone. That would just put us on their level. I'll leave that to the über-perfect jocks and cheerleaders who rule the world and try to squeeze everyone else out. The Fellowship of Christian Athletes members who think Christianity is the only religion in the world. It's the only one that counts in the good old U.S. of A. We're sick of them trying to shove their bullshit about school spirit, patriotism, and religion down our throats or in any other handy orifice. Besides, everyone knows FCA meetings are just excuses for the jocks, pseudos-jocks and cheerleaders to get sloppy drunk and grope each other. Prayer works as birth control, right?

Max and Andy gather their stuff and head for the door. It's around 1 a.m. and time for us to crash. They clomp down the sidewalk heading for Max's house a few blocks away. Mandy leans heavily on me, "Dude, I am so beat."

"Me too," I yawn.

We meander into the bathroom to remove makeup and brush our teeth. We start laughing because we're slaphappy and tired. We fall into bed; I'm on the pull out trundle bed that's under her twin.

"We'll have some fun tomorrow," she says pulling the covers under her chin.

"What a novel concept," I mumble rolling over onto my stomach and passing out from blissful fatigue.

It is night and I am running though people's backyards. There is a man running after me; he is trying to kill me. He is going to catch me and slit my throat. I reach a dead end and start yelling for help. Someone is shaking me...

"Kiera, wake up! Kiera..." I hear Mandy's voice calling me and I sit straight up, soaking in cold sweat and breathing hard.

"What the hell?" Mandy whispers, leaning over to peer into my face in the inky darkness of her room.

"Sorry," I whisper back, "I was having a nightmare...."

"You were thrashing and yelling for help," she tells me, her voice slow and calm with concern.

"I was being chased by this man who was going to cut my throat," I am shaking, and curl into a ball.

"Jesus, Kiera!" she hisses. "Try to think about college or going to Paris…"

"I do," I whimper, still shaken from the horrific circumstances of my nightmare.

I hear Mandy snore and know that I am alone in the dark. It's not her fault. It's some ridiculous time of morning and we *should* be asleep. I wish she understood that I ardently wish all the nightmares and drama would just go away. Sometimes I feel like she just doesn't understand that this isn't my choice. I feel terrible that she ends up dealing with it. I know sometimes it gets on her nerves. She should try being me though. I roll over onto my stomach, pull the covers over my head and try to think of blue skies and sunny fields.…

· Three ·

I wake up alone in Mandy's room to the heavenly scent of hickory-smoked bacon and coffee. Pulling on my sweats, I shuffle out to the kitchen, my tummy gurgling the whole way.

"Hey Kiera! I knew this would get you moving," Mandy grins at me.

I nod sleepily and flop down at the kitchen table.

"Do they ever feed you properly? Like, Ever?"

"About once every blue moon," I reply, sleepily rubbing my face. "Can I do anything to help?"

"Nah, I've got it," she says good-naturedly, flapping her hand at me to sit down at the kitchen table.

She brings over two mugs of hot coffee and has added milk to mine, because she knows my preferences like the back of her hand. Did I mention how much I love Mandy? She's the sister I always wanted, even though sometimes we are at odds. She slides two plates full of bacon and hash browns onto the table and reaches for the ketchup sitting in the middle of the table.

"Dude, you are so awesome!" I exclaim, loving my friend for being an amazing cook.

"Can't help it! I gotta be me!" she laughs, shaking her head.

We leisurely eat our delicious breakfast, chatting, drinking coffee. I collect the dishes and put them in the washer, then we flip for who gets to shower first.

"So, what shall we do today, eh?" Mandy asks as she combs through her wet hair.

"Hmmm. Maybe first call Max and Andy and see what they're up to?" I volunteer.

"You get to wake the beasties," she giggles. "I did it last time."

I pick up the phone and dial the number with no thought. It's automatic. We've been hanging out with these two for *ages*. I don't actually remember when we all met or how. It's like we've just always been friends. There's an unspoken rule that we don't date each other, because that would screw everything up. We fill in as dates for events when needed, but just as friends. Once, Max started developing a crush on Mandy, but she slapped him really hard and told him to cut it out or she'd "cut them off" and make him a eunuch, thereby eliminating the source of the hormones causing the problem. There's nothing wrong with Max or Andy. It's just that there are so few intelligent life forms in this town that we can't afford to complicate things. Besides, they're like our brothers. Mandy and I agree, boyfriends are a dime a dozen, but friends you keep — no givebacks.

"Hello?" says a very groggy Max.

"Hey there," I reply.

"Hey. What's up?" he sighs sleepily.

"We're trying to figure out what to do today and thought we'd see what you guys are doing. So, what are you doing?" I razz, knowing full well they are barely if at all conscious.

"Um, I dunno. Hang on," he says.

I can hear a muffled discussion between he and Andy in the back ground. There is a loud thud followed by a loud expletive. Max starts laughing his ass off and gets back on the phone.

"What the hell?" I ask.

"Andy fell off the bed because he was tangled in the sheets and he landed on my guitar amp kinda hard," Max said quietly, trying not to start laughing again.

"Ooooo! Ouch! Is he OK?" I wince.

"I think so," Max says. "So, maybe a movie followed by Chinese at the Foo Dog?" he suggests.

"Sounds good. So you guys get fed and dressed and meet us here, okay?"

"Cool. See you in about an hour," says Max, yawning.

I hang up the phone and parrot the conversation back to Mandy.

"What a goob. Falling out of bed and creaming oneself on a guitar amp takes some real talent," she giggles.

"Hey, it could have been any one of us. You know what Max's room is like. It would take archaeologists ten years to find the damn floor!" We laugh our heads off, and ferret out a newspaper to see if there are any movies worth watching. Mandy has "Treasure" by the Cocteau Twins playing as we mull and discuss the meager pickings in the area. We settle on "The Lost Boys." We've heard it's really good, but since it takes a million years to get movies here, we never see new ones until months after people in say, California, do. The theater is nearby and only costs one dollar, so it's affordable weekend fun for us. The Foo Dog is a Chinese place a couple blocks from the theater that has really cheap, good food. We usually order several things and then share. It's kind of a tame weekend I guess, but we are poor high school kids who live out in the middle of nowhere. It isn't like we'd go to keggers even if we were invited.

Eventually, the doorbell rings, we turn off the lights and stereo and head out to walk the few blocks to the ancient cinema. Mandy practically lives alone because she is an only child and her Mom works all the time. Her dad took off right after she was born, so she doesn't remember him. She doesn't care either. Her Mom is supremely cool. Mrs. Goebel works as a legal secretary at Pratt, Sinn and Broker. It makes her life interesting since her employers' kids are all members of the elite popular group at school and her daughter is one of the so-called "troublemakers". Their house is an average one story with a basement, located downtown— the thriving metropolis that it is. I live out in the boonies, while Mandy, Max and Andy all live in town. It sucks for me, but I get to stay at Mandy's every now and then. It keeps me from going totally crackers.

"I think we should start planning our next Chicago trip," says Andy skipping down the sidewalk.

"Yeah, it's been like, three months or something," chimes in Max.

"Actually, it's been four months and two weeks," I correct him gently.

Mandy looks at me with a pained expression, "You really do live for those trips, don't you?"

"Well, for those and you guys," I say smiling and gently slamming into her so I don't knock her on her ass.

She elbows me and shoves me into the grass, "I'm soooo flattered!"

We reach the glass ticket window and pay our admission. One buck each, gotta love it. We clomp into the theater with "Lost Boys" on a marquee over the door.

"I'll get us a snack," volunteers Max.

We find seats in the middle easily as there are only five other people in the theater. Max jumps over the back of the seats and flops into the chair to my left.

"Twizzlers?" he offers.

"Nah, the movie hasn't even started yet," I decline.

Andy and Mandy grab a twizzler each and start gnawing. The lights go down and for the next hour or so we are transported to a California town where blood drinking fiends who fly are terrorizing people. The poseur squad at our school actually think vampires are real and some even dress accordingly. I can't stand that crap. It's beyond stupid. Besides, why the hell would anyone want to live forever? I guess if you're undead, at least you can't get a cold or bronchitis every winter, but finding a date would be a drag — and you'd eventually watch all your friends die. Forget that.

We stroll out of the theater and hastily make our way to the Foo Dog. We are good and ready for lunch, and I've been dreaming of crab Rangoon and egg rolls. We grab a booth by the window and order tea.

"That was gnarly when the Grandpa skewered the head vampire, wasn't it?" says Andy, his face alight with interest at the gore we had witnessed on-screen.

"SPLAT!" remarked Max.

"You guys, we are going to have food now, so be nice," I chide.

Mandy makes a face, "Yeah, I was planning to order sweet and sour pork, but not if you're going to bring up the image of fake blood squirting everywhere while I'm eating, ugh!"

We eagerly dive into the food when it arrives, Andy inhaling his egg rolls with Hoover-like efficiency. We thoroughly enjoy our meal and chat about the movie as well as other various and sundry subjects. The usual — music, road trips to Chicago, graduating, and finally leaving this hell hole.

"So, when are we going to go to Chicago next?" asks Andy.

"I'd say November could be good, unless my parents invent some chores or random punishment," I say.

"Or lock you in your room," Mandy snarks. Max and Andy sneak a look at each other, and there is a moment of awkward silence. I'm stung by her insensitivity, but remain aloof, and the moment passes.

We have to plant the seeds early with my parents or execute a foolproof plan and alibi, just so I'll live to graduate and not be scattered in four states. It isn't like I ever do anything bad. Fun isn't bad. Sometimes my father is really irrational and says I can't do something just because. It's a control thing. It has nothing to do with "protecting me for my own good." My parents seem to keep me isolated on purpose. Possibly so that no one will figure out that there's something wrong with the picture; or simply to retain their live-in servant. I can only guess.

"I hear there's a kick ass after-hours club now," says Mandy, eyes aglow.

She and I share a passion for dance. We both took tap and jazz when we were kids. Now we just go to school dances and aspire to go to nightclubs. Of course, the other lure of this nightclub idea is finding an actual boyfriend. The pickings around here are slim and none, and slim went home, as Granddaddy says. Mandy dated a guy for about a year and a half, until she found out he was cheating on her and lying his sorry ass off. She kicked in his dashboard before dumping him. What a total scumbag. His excuse was that "men aren't made for monogamy." She informed him that she wasn't created to tolerate abject stupidity, got out of the car, and walked home. Luckily, they weren't far from her house and it wasn't winter. She's still stinging from the whole thing because she was really, truly smitten with him. So, she and I hang out and avoid contact with the local pool o' retards.

"Do you know the address and the hours?" I ask, thoroughly giddy at the idea of finally going out dancing somewhere *real.*

"I'll ask my cousin Sandra. That's who told me about it. She went last week and said I'd love it," she replied.

We laugh and high five each other. The boys look at us with mock disgust, as if they are above such things as scamming on the opposite sex.

"We'll have to get dresses at Wax Trax for the occasion. My mother would die on the spot if she ever saw me in one of those vinyl numbers," I guffaw mischievously.

Mandy's eyes widen in mock horror at the suggestion and then she cracks up.

"Ooooo! Or there's Bizarre Bazaar," she offers, "they have some of everything there and I need a new hat."

"We'll just escort you for safety, I take it?" Andy sniffs sarcastically as if his ego has been wounded.

"Well, that and Max is the one who has a big enough car that he can fit in comfortably," Mandy replies punching on his arm lightly, "We'll be helping out with gas, of course."

Max has an old, black Lincoln Continental that has a glow-in-the-dark skull hanging from the rear view mirror. It looks like a hearse. There are about a zillion tapes piled in the glove box and in a box on the floor in the back seat. Max is so tall that he has a tough time when we all pile into Mandy's little Escort. His Lincoln fits him much more comfortably. Max could totally "score a chick" if he wanted to, but he's the perfect gentleman. He's so shy that I think he'd implode if a girl ever talked to him.

We have finished devouring our feast, and are stretched out in the booth like spoiled, overfed cats. The total bill was $15 and we are stuffed. That's why we love this place. So good! And sooooo cheap! Besides, they let us hang out after we're done eating and don't throw us out. It's nice to have someplace to go and something to do around here.

The bell hanging over the door jingles cheerily and in walks my brother with his cronies. My heart drops to my stomach. Brett started hanging around these beer guzzling jock hillbullies after his freshman year and now he is one. I hunch down and try to hide.

"Hey birth defect," says Brett ambling over with tweedledumber and tweedledumbest in his wake.

"Fuck off," I mutter shrinking as far back into the seat as I can. I can feel the heat coming off my face. He'll beat the bloody hell out of me if I defend myself at all. I stare at the plate in front of me, silently praying he and his little buddies will just go away, and leave us alone.

"What was that?" he swings his fist through the air at my face and laughs. "Ha ha, made you flinch."

"Why don't you guys go sit down and leave us alone?" says Max standing up and lengthening like a periscope to his full height.

"Why don't you make us, freak?" retorts Brett.

It's like his new friends have sucked the intelligence right out of his head. Brett is as smart as me, but because he doesn't want anyone to think he's a dork, he hides behind the jock, hillbully façade.

Max is as pissed as I've ever seen him, his face darkening by the second. As he starts to fully extricate himself from the booth, Brett looks up at Max and realizes he might have made an error in judgment. Max stands up, glowering in my brother's face, fists clenched at his sides, waiting for Brett to make a move. Fear flickers over Brett's face briefly as he backs up, away from our table, his cronies shuffling after him. He's nothing more than a sexist, greedy, selfish, lazy, spoiled little white boy who gets everything handed to him on a silver platter because he's a good boy and does what he's told.

"Let's get out of here you guys," I whisper.

We pay our bill and leave a generous tip. That's probably another reason why they let us hang out at The Foo Dog. I rush outside and feel the tears starting to well up. I kick the brick wall in frustration. I'm so embarrassed and ashamed of my family.

Mandy comes up and puts her arms around my shoulders to comfort me, "It's OK, Kiera, it's OK. It's hard to believe you guys came out of the same gene pool."

I wipe my tears on my sleeve and try to laugh. "You're telling me."

I miserably whisper to her, "How much longer?" I try to stem the flow of tears that just won't stop leaking out of my eyes.

She shakes her head, "Not soon enough. I wish I could magic you out of that goddamn house and out of here, but all we can do is dig in our claws and hang on."

Max comes up behind us with Andy so we are in a sort of huddle. "Hey, don't let that fucker ruin such a perfect day," he says.

"Yeah," chimes in Andy, "or I'll have to kick his ass," he says imitating the voice of "chicken hawk" from Looney Tunes as he balls up his fists and hops around, taking swings in the air like a boxer.

We are all laughing, partially at his impression and partially at his 5'6" frame that Brett would easily stomp into a paste. And yet, I know Andy probably would risk life and limb to help me out — or any of us. He's a true blue friend.

"Max," I say tugging him to the side, "thanks for stepping in there," I say with gratitude.

"No biggie, Kiera. Glad the growth spurt is paying off!" he grins.

I swallow a flood that threatens to break loose and throw my arms around his neck, "Thanks for being my friend, I don't know what I'd do without you."

He awkwardly pats me on the back and blushes. "Well, you know, I had to pay you back for the tutoring sessions somehow," he says as he grabs me and starts swinging me around.

"Yiiiiii! Put me down put me down!" I am slightly breathless as he gently sets me on my feet.

"Me next! Me next!" Mandy says hopping up and down.

Max leans over and she puts her arms around his neck and he stands up. Mandy's feet are dangling a good six inches of the ground. He starts to whirl her around.

"Wah-hooooooooooooo!" she hollers with glee.

We wander back to Mandy's house and clomp into the basement, our usual lair. It is a dark, paneled, brown carpeted, dank place with one lamp and one window. The window doesn't really count since there is a bush just outside of it, blocking any sunlight that might eke its way in. On Mrs. Goebel's salary, remodeling this 1965 throwback isn't an option, so we have plastered the walls with enormous posters purchased from Wax Trax. Bauhaus, Siouxsie and the Banshees, and New Order grace the walls, covering up the dark, bland, gray paneling. There is an old console stereo down here that houses an assorted collection of records and tapes. Against one wall is a huge old television. Luckily, it is hooked up to cable and doesn't need an antenna. On the opposite wall is a beat up red velour couch that threatens to leak its contents onto the floor if it is put through much more stress, and two black bean bag chairs. In the middle of the various seating is a large, round coffee table. There are concert flyers, kneadable art erasers, a sketch pad, and some paintbrushes on it. There are stacks of canvases leaning against the wall and a couple of folded easels. In one corner resides Mandy's typewriter on an old desk with a stool in front waiting for her next spewing of hilarity. She is an awesome writer and an avid fan of "Saturday Night Live." Max, Andy, and I often use this place as a creative haven, too. It's our little clubhouse, our den, our sanctuary. I flop onto the couch and Mandy flumps down next to me, almost on top of me and laughs.

"Oof! Dude! You aren't *that* teeny!" I complain in jest, because really, she is that small.

"Fuck off," she retorts with a wicked smile.

Andy and Max have deposited themselves on the bean bags. Max resembles a large spider with his long limbs dangling out of the bean bag. Mandy pops over to the stereo and soon the strains of "Addiction" by Skinny Puppy emanate and fill the room. Ahhhh. This is one of my very favorite songs, if I could pick a favorite. It makes me want to purr.

"So what do you guys think about the whole journal project with Starling?" Max asks.

I snort and make a face. Mandy makes an even worse one.

"That cow wouldn't know a good batch of writing if you shoved it up her ass and lit it on fire," offers Mandy.

Andy is shaking with laughter at this illuminating response.

"I couldn't believe just how slanted she is. I mean, clearly, unless you write *exactly* like *her,* you're totally screwed," I respond. "I can't wait for the next round. My father doesn't know about this yet, but he will when he sees my grades for midterm." I say apprehensively.

My friends look at me with wide eyes. They know about the thing with my father and grades. Anything less than a B is an F to him, resulting in pain beyond pain and punishments so severe, you'd think I murdered his mother. He actually thinks he's perfect and expects us to follow suit. My brother and his little friends all cheat on tests and papers. It's what allows Brett to have the social life that he has. I wouldn't be caught dead cheating. If I can't get my grades on my own brains and talent, then I don't want them at all. I'll take the major ass kicking instead. I will probably have to face a pretty horrific one since that D minus is going to be showing up any time now. But I'd really prefer to just ignore that for now.

"What did she give you?" Andy demands, furious with our idiot teacher.

"A D minus," I say looking at the floor in embarrassment. I never get grades that bad, except for sometimes in math.

"No way! I read through what you wrote! You were dead on!" exclaims Max in protest.

"Thanks. I guess in her world, not being all fluffy and flowery and pink makes a person a criminal. I don't care. We'll be done with her forever in just a few weeks and then we'll have an awesome teacher," I say, determined to find the silver lining.

"Is your dad going to be mad?" Andy asks, barely looking at me.

"What do *you* think?" I say with a sigh.

"Man, that sucks. You need to call the cops this time if the psycho starts thrashing you like he did last time," urges Andy. "He beat the shit out of you for that Algebra grade last year. He almost killed you, remember?"

"True. It's hard to keep him away from me..." I trail off, blankly. "It's a matter of keeping the phone cord in the wall," I whisper to myself. I realize no one heard my muttering, and listen to my friends talking about Starling, and their other classes. I remember the wood splintering as he kicked in my door last year in a rage because of a C plus in Algebra that I'd worked my ass off for. The horrendous crunching sound of wood and horrible metallic sound of the doorknob exploding into bits is burned in my memory. I thought I'd come a long way. But not far enough for him. So supportive and loving, my father. I stuff these thoughts back down, like it happened to someone else. Like it isn't really my life.

"When is your mom going to tell him to knock it off? What does she do, sit there and watch?" fumes Max.

"Actually, yeah. She does. I doubt she'll ever get off her besotted bum and tell him anything except, 'Yes dear'," I shoot back with disgust. "Sorry, Max. I don't mean to be all pissy. It just really bugs me that she doesn't give a crap at all."

"Well, we do," chimes in Andy, "We love you Kiera, no matter what."

We put our hands all together and start laughing —

"Wonder twin powers activate!" giggles Mandy.

"Form of… an ice dildo!" caws Andy gleefully.

"Shape of… a boa constrictor!" laughs Max.

The boys dive on top of us so we are a tangle of arms and legs in a heap on the couch. Mandy is screaming for them to get off and we are all laughing our butts off. We have many inside jokes and this one kills me every time. Andy is really good at being the comic relief at the perfect time. We figure Mandy writes the comedy and Andy performs it, while Max and I are the very appreciative audience.

"Hey! SNL is coming on!" Mandy squeals.

"Cool," we all respond in unison.

Mandy flips on the tube and we settle in. It's a repeat from May with Suzanne Vega. We think she's cool in a mellow, hippy kind of way. She just released a new album with this funky song on it called "Tom's Diner". It's like hippy rap jazz. Odd, but good. My friends are into every kind of music you can think of. We agree that good music is good music. Period. We like Ska, Reggae, Punk, Goth, Classic Rock, Classical, Jazz — everything. Metal glam rawk is the only variety we truly shun. We don't think being closed-minded about people, ideas, or music is very smart. Discerning is the word. We don't open up and swallow whatever current trend the media is spoon feeding the masses. You have to think for yourself — especially around here.

We are all dying of laughter at this skit about using Einstein's space-time continuum to deliver packages. It's like Federal Express, but they can get it there yesterday. Mandy is turning bright pink and gasping for air. She loves the intellectual jokes more than the fart jokes. The boys, of course, love the fart jokes. Not that they don't also appreciate the intellectual types of humor, they just seem partial to slightly grotesque bodily function jokes.

At the commercial break, Mandy and I go upstairs to make popcorn and some drinks for everybody.

"So when do you think you'll be committed to prison?" asks Mandy.

"Well, midterms will be out in the next two weeks, so we'd better get a move on," I groan.

"Maybe next weekend?" she asks tentatively.

"I don't know if they'll go for two in a row," I sigh. "They seem to hate it when I have fun."

"Hmmmm. We'll figure something out," she replies, dumping popcorn into a giant bowl.

We return downstairs and the boys quickly demolish half the popcorn. They seem to be going through a growth spurt where they are hungry *all* the time and they eat everything in sight. It's quite entertaining to us. I am still growing too, but not like a couple years ago where I grew almost two feet in less than two years. I've always been huge. I don't mind. People stay the hell away from me because they think I'll stomp them into a paste if they talk to me. Doc Marten boots and intelligence frighten the inbred, apparently — or maybe it's because I tell them to "fuck off" with monotonous regularity.

There is a news brief that breaks in the show. There's been a lot of bullshit going on this year with our government, but what do you expect with weasels like Reagan and Bush in office? The Iran-Contra thing is still spewing crap and people are scrambling to cover it all up. Basically, our government covertly supported insurgents in Nicaragua and Iran by selling guns to Iran and giving the cash to the soldiers in Nicaragua. The funny thing is that no one is holding the *President* responsible for any of it, nor is the Vice President being held accountable. Just another day in the Republican party. Lying, cheating, killing, and covering up. It seems to be a hobby. What I really don't get is why anyone votes for fuckers like these guys. They are old, white men who don't give a shit about *anyone* but themselves and their little circles of elite. The main thing we have a problem with is this arrogant idea that everyone else in the world should be just like us. Don't get me wrong, I adore my country and the freedom it affords me. My problem is that there are so many religious zealots and right wing kooks who keep forgetting that ALL people are afforded the right to have their own thoughts and opinions about things. The Constitution doesn't just apply to right wing, old, white men — it applies to everyone born in the U.S.A. This bullshit Republican agenda is going to get us all killed someday if someone doesn't make them knock it off. I thought that Congress was elected to serve the people, but I must be mistaken because all they're doing is kissing the President's ass. Anyway — I digress, I could talk all day about politics since I am in Mr. Deiter's class. I excel at ferreting out facts and prefer dealing with facts rather than someone else's warped perception of the truth. I've already got enough warped reality at home to last my entire life.

"Fuck OFF!" Andy yells at the screen as they flash a picture of Vice President Bush.

"What a shithead. Every time I see him talk it's just so insulting," seethes Mandy, "He acts like people are so stupid that we'd buy the pile of crap that he's trying to sell, 'We didn't know, ask Ollie North'. What a weasel."

"I just hope they don't elect him next or we're screwed," Max adds.

"Don't worry, they will," I grouse. "With assholes like my father, and there are a bunch of them out there, he'll be elected. White men like other white men and the right wingers are gaining momentum."

"The right wing SUCKS," says Andy with venom.

Saturday Night Live is now over and we send the boys on their way. I'm starting to feel the dark fingers of depression sneaking in to grip me. When I'm here, I'm so happy and relaxed. I don't want to go back to that house.

"Hey, you're not going home yet, so don't think about it yet," says Andy as he hugs me. "See you Monday."

"Hang in there and don't let them kick you, Kiera," says Max squishing me in his long skinny arms, "We'll figure out how to get Starling, too," he says with a wicked smile. You gotta watch out for Max.

"Thanks you guys," I say smiling at my friends as they head down the sidewalk smashing in to each other. Boys.

We go in and start removing our make-up so that we don't have huge zit farms in the morning.

"I love those guys," says Mandy with a smile.

"Me too," I answer.

"We're so lucky to have each other, you know? This place would suck SO bad without our little bubble of sanity and reason," she says as she wipes off her eye makeup.

"I have that thought several times a day," I respond quietly, squirting some toothpaste on my toothbrush.

We lay down in her bedroom chatting about possible Chicago trip plans until heavy, velvet darkness submerges us and we sink into the realm of sleep and dreams. Here I am safe and I am my own. Sometimes, in my dream world, I have my own place, my own car, my friends and my own life — and I am happy.

I am silent on the way home. Mandy looks over with sympathy, "This'll be a good week. Who knows? Maybe they'll lay off of you for once…" she says trying to convince me and herself of this unlikely probability. She's been around too many years to really believe it. Of course, we both want to. Without any faith in anything going right, you might as well just go right ahead and blow your damn head off. Death is easy. Living is the hard part. I figure eventually it'll get easier. It has to, right?

Morrissey croons about being the son and heir of nothing in particular.

The weather is getting to me. Cold, gray and rainy, and nothing but fields of dead corn stalks and bare trees everywhere I look. Gray, dead, cold, and icky. We pull into the driveway and I slouch out of the car with my bag. The cold drizzle, and returning to this house, has washed away all traces of happiness. Mandy looks at me desperately, "I'll see you tomorrow. And don't forget to bring your homework. Only one more year after this one, dude. We're going to make it."

Morrissey wails about being human and needing to be loved like everyone else.

I nod and force a tiny smile, "Listen, thanks for everything. I had a blast, as usual."

"You know you're always welcome, Kiera," she says with a pained expression. Her mom has offered more than once to let me stay with them. I am just terrified of what could happen if I tried it. Daddyshit doesn't abide by the rules and I really don't want them getting hurt because they tried to help me. Besides, this is a small town and Mrs.Goebel can't afford to lose her job. My father is well connected. It's sort of a network of assholes around here. I miserably slink out of the car to the house as Mandy pulls out of the driveway. I hesitate at the door, getting pelted with freezing raindrops. My instincts scream to turn around and leave, but I force myself to slip quietly into the house.

· Four ·

I try not to breathe. I barely make it halfway up the stairs before…

"KIIIIIEEERRRRAAA!" yells my mother.

I squeeze my eyes shut and take a deep breath, willing myself to keep moving farther into the house. My heart turns cold and drops into my boots. I feel hollow and numb. This is what my existence has been as long as I can remember.

"I HEARD YOU COME IN!! GET YOUR ASS DOWN HERE NOW!!" screeches my mother.

"I'm just putting my stuff away, hang on! I'll be right down!" I yell back, shoving my stuff in my closet.

It has always been made distinctly clear that I was born unwanted. They had me by accident because some idiot told them it was harder to get pregnant after you have a baby, when in reality, it's the opposite. So, ta-da! Instant servant! Lucky me.

I scurry downstairs to see what has my mother screeching at me the instant I return to the house.

"Kiera! You were supposed to get the laundry done this weekend. You didn't do it yet and I need clean underwear. Get it in gear!" she squawks.

"Sorry, I wasn't aware that I have sole ownership of all laundry duty," I mutter as I stalk away.

"Watch your mouth young lady, or I'll let your father know you were being rude." she threatens, her eyes narrowed slits as she follows me around the house. "Your grandparents are coming over, so you'd better hurry up and get things spic-n-span."

My mother makes me ill. She sits around drinking booze and watching TV all day and then makes a mad dash right before my father comes home to tidy up and look pretty. Sometimes she cooks dinner, but most nights I do it because she's too drunk to complete the whole meal without burning the house down. She burned up a pot holder last week making stew. Luckily, I was home and doing my homework upstairs when I smelled the smoke. I smothered the flaming pot holder before it burned the hell out of the cabinets. She told my father that I did it and then watched him kick me up the stairs and beat the daylights out of me in the hall. It's like she wants me to know just how much she hates me. I have no idea why. I used to adore her when I was little. I look a lot like her. I just hate her for letting him treat me like this. I always tried to please her and went to great lengths to try and get her to love me. I tried to be perfect. Perfection is not an attainable goal, especially not when you're two years old. She always told me to "go away and quit bugging" and she told me to shut up every time I tried to talk to her. She would be watching TV or talking on the phone and get really pissed whenever I "interrupted" her. She should have gotten a dog. She started locking Brett and me out in the yard all day when we were three and two, respectively. She'd shove some sandwiches out around noon and let us in around 5 o'clock so we'd be ready for when our father came home from work. I used to try and hide behind the coats and vacuum cleaner in the hall closet so that if he was in a bad mood, he wouldn't be able to find me. I have no choice. I can't run away because all that would happen is that they'd bring me back here and then I'd really be in trouble. Someone would know there was a problem.

My relatives, teachers and neighbors should be able to see that there's a major problem. I mean, one kid who goes everywhere and can do anything he wants and one kid who is always at home, doing chores and yard work. They see me in the yard and in the driveway, and raking and sweeping and shoveling and whatnot. I used to hope that someday someone would speak up for and protect me. I don't know why they seem to be indifferent — but I don't dare ask.

It's like last year when we went to Chicago on one of our first excursions — there was a man standing in the crowd we were in to cross the street. He was wearing a very nice Brooks Brothers navy suit and tie, and he was carrying a briefcase. He suddenly fell on the ground and cracked his head on the pavement and lay totally motionless. I was so shocked I stood there for a few seconds before I came to my senses and realized that this was really happening. I watched several people step on the man's hand and then keep going. I pushed through the throngs to get to him and shield him. People were barely stepping over him, not stopping or looking. It was like they were totally oblivious to what was going on right in front of their faces. I began calling for help as I stood sentry over his body trying to spread myself out like a human fence, so that he wouldn't be stepped on any more than he already had. Mandy and Max who were with me at the time, had taken off like shots to find a phone and call the police. Mandy had gotten into an argument with the server at the Pizza Hut about the definition of an emergency because the woman wouldn't call the police for us. The whole thing was incredible to us and still is. The man eventually woke up and informed us that he was a narcoleptic and thanked us for helping him. I was so glad and thankful that he was OK. The police and an ambulance finally showed up to help him, at which time we proceeded on our journey. I sat in a café with my friends and sobbed over a cup of decaf at the indifference and coldness that I never thought possible from my fellow Americans. I thought we were bigger-hearted than that. I guess it wouldn't be the first time I was wrong about something like that.

You have to defend yourself, and it seems like a bad idea to rely on someone else to help you. I love my friends with all my heart, but I know that it is all me when you strip away everything else. A leg up would be appreciated, but being a charity case is not my goal. All I have to do is figure it out. Someday it will be different. I will work my ass off to drastically improve my reality, or I will die trying.

I gather everyone's laundry hampers and start sorting. Brett's room always smells like feet and farts. It's so gnarly and gross, not that my parents' laundry is fun to handle. Majorly nasty. I troop down to the laundry room and fill the washer with soap and clothes. I feel like crying, but the tears rarely come anymore. I am so numb. This is just how is it every goddamn day. My grandparents actually call me Cinderella, but they never say anything to their son about how he treats me or my mother.

I love my grandparents. They are the only people I am related to that ever act like they are glad I was born. They love me in their own way. They choose to live in a reality where their son isn't really an evil bastard. Too bad it isn't true reality. Dale Graves is my grandfather. He's about six feet tall, with steel gray hair and periwinkle blue eyes. His hands are big and rough, but gentle. They are the hands of a working man. He is a retired plumber. He was one of eight kids and the only one to go to college. He couldn't get the kind of job he wanted because of the Depression, so he got what employment there was and then he stayed because he made a good living. He reads all the time and does crosswords. I have only heard him raise his voice once. He speaks with a low, deep voice that is so soft you have to strain to hear him. He has always been gentle, patient and loving to me. He is my favorite male human. Lucille Graves is his wife and my grandmother. She is four feet eight inches of spunk and wit. She has mouse brown hair that she gets done once a week, usually Friday, at her beauty parlor. She has a kind face and sparkling hazel eyes that seem to look right through to your soul. My Grandma makes the best desserts you've ever tasted and she sews all of her own clothes. She is a homemaker, but once worked as a secretary. That's how she and Grandpa met. The sink in the executive bathroom flooded and she called a plumber and voilà… she and Grandpa became an item. She is highly intelligent, but she never had the opportunity to go to a university or have any secondary education. She wanted to be a nurse, and as much as she fusses with people, I think she would've been great. She feeds absolutely everyone and loves to talk. She's a little bit of a gossip, but mostly just because she is interested in other people. She is the hostess with the mostess. I adore them to my detriment because they can manipulate me really easily. I always feel so guilty if I say "no" to them. They force me to hug and kiss my father, which I resent. They always have because they know that otherwise I won't. I was always afraid of him as long as I can remember — and I remember being a baby.

I return to my room as the washer chugs along and de-funkifies our clothes. I straighten things up after unpacking my overnight bag and I get my school crap ready to go. I slip a mixed tape in my walkman to keep me company as I vacuum, dust, polish, clean and straighten each room.

Siouxsie's voice purrs as smooth as silk about putting your head down to the ground and shaking it all around when you slowdive.

I go to my desk, flip open my photo album and glance at the pages. The only pictures where I am smiling are the more recent ones. The ones where I'm a kid, my smile is screwy because I didn't know how to smile when people with cameras exclaimed, "Smile!". It's more like a grimace and I am always looking off to the side. I am certain that the little girl in the pictures is checking to make sure she hasn't displeased a parent. In the ones from last summer, I am laughing and so is Mandy. We are just outside of Wax Trax and laughing like loons because I had just scored Cocteau Twins "Garlands". We had so much fun that day. Mandy, Andy and I had jumped in Mandy's car one hot summer afternoon and sped off to Chicago. Max was forced to mow the lawn that day, so he missed out on that particular trip. We walked all over the city and got yelled at by some yuppie for running through sprinklers in front of a condo. We spent hours at Wax Trax and made mental lists of every record we intend to get our mitts on. It was total euphoria. This perfect moment is frozen in time in this picture and is one of my all-time favorites.

I unwillingly slide back into my current and grim reality. I finish cleaning the house, finish the laundry and change clothes before the arrival of my grandparents. Brett wanders in at the last minute and is being assaulted by our mother to get his clothes changed and hair straightened out before they get here. My father thunders downstairs in a cloud of after-shave, and starts pouring martinis as the doorbell rings.

I rush to answer the door. "Kiera!" my grandma exclaims, reaching up to hug my neck and plant a big kiss on my cheek. "Hi, Grandma." The splinters of fear that were creeping in dissolve and I hug my Grandpa, my main man. "Did they have you working like a dog again, Cinderella?" he asks, bringing a hot flush of humiliation to my face and ears.

"No," I lie, seeing my father glowering angrily from the doorway. I studiously avoid eye contact with everyone, hoping this will slide.

"C'mon in Dad," my father says, a smile lightning up his face, all traces of the glowering threat disappearing like a shadow. I take their coats and hang them in the closet, awaiting my instructions. Ice clinks in the glasses as drinks are handed out, and my grandparents settle on the couch for a visit.

"Kiera, come on in here, Mom wants to ask you something," my father calls into the kitchen as I check the roast that's cooking in the oven. I nervously go in and sit on the floor in front of the couch near the lobster trap coffee table. I have no idea what she's going to say.

"Helen's granddaughter has been going to all kinds of school activities and I was wondering why you aren't?" she bubbles. Helen is her next door neighbor who has coffee with Grandma everyday. I look at her, then to my father who rolls his eyes and takes a sip of martini. I stammer for a moment, while I try to think of the right answer.

"Well, I guess I study a lot..."

"Obviously not enough with those Algebra grades you've been coming home with," interrupts my father. "She needs to be here with us, to do her chores and get this pigsty clean." My mother opens her mouth and quickly closes it. I sit silently and wait, looking from my parents to my grandparents. Brett sits silently by my mother's chair, looking distractedly at the ceiling. I don't think he's even here.

"Colleges these days want the kids to have extra-curricular activities, Peter," my Grandpa scolds. "She should be going to French Club or Art Club."

A miniscule spark of hope ignites in my chest. I look at my grandparents gratefully. Grandma winks at me slyly. She knows me like nobody else. I have always told her everything. I don't get to spend time with them as much as I used to, but it's my doing. It's clear to me that she's trying to have me at their house more.

"Art?! That's the stupidest thing I've ever heard! You can't make a living by painting pretty pictures. I don't give a good goddamn! Like those idiots at that school know anything about the real world anyway," my father hollers, flying into a rage. I cringe and scoot closer to the red, floral patterned couch. I could swear my mother just smirked at me, as if to say, "so there!" I look at the carpet.

"She's a great artist, Peter. She could do so many things," murmurs Grandma to her son, looking hurt at his outburst. "I don't know why you're like this..."

"Mom! Why don't you just worry about yourself instead of everyone else? She's my daughter, and I decide what happens to her."

"Well, I think she'd get in somewhere better if you let her work on her French," grumbles my Grandpa.

I get up to take the roast out of the oven before it turns into shoe leather. "Where the hell are you going?" my father yells, grabbing my wrist violently as I attempt to walk to the kitchen.

"I was going to take the roast out," I respond, trying to wriggle out of his grasp.

"Let her go, Peter" my Grandpa says louder than most people ever hear him speak.

I scoot to the kitchen while the battle rages on. My Grandpa's voice is like thunder, low and resonant. He hardly ever raises his voice, so I know he's really angry. Grandma seems to enjoy being a pot stirrer, but this time I'm actually grateful. I'd love to get to do stuff with Art Club. My parents refuse to allow me outside of the house and it sucks.

"What's the matter with you? She's a good girl, she gets good grades. She should be allowed..." my Grandpa yells.

"It's a bunch of malarkey and a waste of time," my father yells back.

"But Peter, we miss seeing our little girl, can't you let her stay with us sometimes? Staying after-school for activities would be good for her, and I want to see my girl," my Grandma pleads.

"You see her plenty, and that's the end of the discussion," Peter barks, the ice clinking loudly as he drains the last of his martini.

I keep my head down, and place the salads at each place at the kitchen table. I set the roast by the head of the table for my father to carve. I set the canned peas, mashed potatoes and boiled carrots in the center of the table with serving spoons in each bowl. It looks like a photo from "Better Homes and Gardens". My heart starts to race as my mother pours huge glasses of wine for the grownups. Brett sits across from me, aloof, with his hands folded in his lap, just like we were trained. My mother pours herself into her chair and I help my Grandma scoot her chair in before sitting down. My mother says grace, which we only do when there's company, and starts digging into the mashed potatoes.

"You have to pass everything clockwise, dammit!" yells my father to my mother, who flinches and takes the potatoes out of my hands to pass them to Brett. My father proceeds to almost cut his thumb off while drunkenly carving the roast and yells at me. "These goddamn knives are dull! What, do you want me to get hurt? Next time make sure it's sharp!"

"I thought it was, sorry," I mutter.

"Well you didn't think," he snarls, forking roast onto everyone's plates.

"Peter! You stop that," scolds my Grandma, patting my leg under the table.

"Oh you be quiet Mother, she's so stupid. How worthless do you have to be to bring home grades like that? And these knives are so dull, only an imbecile would miss that," he growls, shoving a huge bite into his mouth.

"Don't tell your Mother to be quiet, Peter," says my Grandpa, glaring at his son. "Kiera isn't stupid. You're her father, it's terrible the way you talk about like that. She's a good girl."

I hold my breath, trying not to cry. My mother takes a big glug of wine and Brett mouths "Don't" to me. Two big teardrops fall into my lap, and I excuse myself to go to the bathroom. I sob silently, curled in a ball with my back against the wall, my hands covering my head like during a tornado drill. I try not to make any noise, and I turn on faucet to mask the sound of blowing my nose. The discussion rages on in my absence, and I am terrified to leave the haven of the bathroom. But, I splash cold water on face, and return to the table. I see everyone is mostly done eating and I sit quietly, inhaling my dinner before it's time to clear the plates. Brett shovels the rest of his food down like it's the end of world, and says, "I need to go study for a history test."

"Go ahead lovey," says our sloshed mother, excusing him with a pat on the shoulder. He hesitates, looking at our father who dismisses him with a hand flap. I chew, and stay silent, listening to the banter of my family. They talk about Brett, his friends, how popular they are. My father slams me some more for my poor math grades, and starts in on my friends. I feel like the worst friend in the world for not defending them, but I have to stay quiet. My mother watches me in amusement as I struggle to keep my cool, and keep my mouth shut.

"How about sherry in the living room, Mom?' my father asks, hauling my grandma out of her chair.

"Straighten up in here, Kiera," says my mother, grabbing glasses for their "dessert". I clear dishes, put away food, fill the dishwasher, wipe the counters, scrub the sink, clean the kitchen table, and wipe off the refrigerator door for good measure.

"Kiera, get the coats," my father directs from the doorway, making me jump as I put the final touches on the cleaned, straightened, and wiped down kitchen. I hustle to the closet, and help Grandma get her coat on. As my parents are distracted, talking to Grandpa, she pats my face, "Well sugar, I tried. You'll get there someday. Ooooo, I love you!" she squeezes me in a tight hug. I nod, feeling like my heart is a piece of paper curling up and burning to bits. I hand my Grandpa his hat, "Peter is your father, Kiera. You've got to mind him and do better in that math class. Then he'll back off," my Grandpa says gruffly. But he won't. They seem to be laboring under the delusion that he will ever be reasonable. I know better. I miss them. I don't know when I'll get to see them unsupervised again. Lately, he doesn't let me out of his sight.

I go to bed praying for early sleep. I want this week to start as well as it can. My heart breaks as I lay in bed, remembering all the good times I had with my grandparents. I miss them terribly, and they miss me. It feels like I've lost them forever.

In the morning, I realized that I managed to finish the laundry before 11 P.M. last night and got to bed at reasonable hour for once. Mommy Dearest passing out around 10:30 P.M. was helpful, because she couldn't keep me up with other chores or get me in trouble. Daddyshit was already asleep, the only way I like him. So, today I am feeling pretty good. I'm dressed and am ready to go. All I have to do is sneak downstairs and snag a bagel before I end up on anyone's radar. I move silently down the stairs and pad through the kitchen slowly, barely breathing. I slide open the bread box and get a cinnamon raisin bagel. I do all the shopping, so I get the kind I like the best. I forgo the cream cheese to avoid making any noise and slip silently out the door to wait for Mandy. I really hope she's on time today.

Chapter Four

Right on cue she pulls in the driveway and I meet her halfway.

"So… how are you doing?" she asks apprehensively, looking me over.

"Actually, today was a miracle. I got out without anyone screwing with me at all! So, hurry up and get us out of here!" I tell her with glee, as I chuck my bag into the backseat and flop into the passenger's seat.

"Your wish is my command," she grins and carefully backs out so that no one is disturbed.

"Har dee har," I yawn, smiling at her.

We smile at each other and listen to Depeche Mode singing about taking a ride with your best friend. We drive past acres of dead fields covered in frost. The gray sky looks like a muddy water color and the trees are all bare and dead-looking. Inside the car, we are warm and enjoying the comfort of each other's presence. Sometimes we can just hang out and don't have to talk. It's great to have a friend like that. I feel so lucky, because I have three friends like that. We pull into the parking lot and shuffle quickly inside before we become frozen to the pavement. There's no snow yet, but it is effing cold out here in the morning. We separate and go to our respective lockers. I see Max's head bobbing down the hall toward me above the crowd of students. It's handy that he's so tall, it makes him easy to spot at a distance. Max is very protective of us, and is sort of our "guard dog." I smile at him, he smiles and waves back, pushing his way through a stubborn wave of people. I see Andy next to him as they get closer. His red hair is a bright spot of color among the beige lockers, gray walls and dark winter coats. I finish getting my stuff situated and close the locker door with a metallic bang.

"Hey you guys, what's the latest news?" I say knocking into them with my shoulder in greeting.

"Nothing so far, which is good. I don't want to get detention for that crap at the dance," says Max.

"I hear that," I reply, nodding in agreement.

We head in the direction of Mandy's locker so that we can walk to class together. Mandy, Andy and I all have French, while Max has U.S. History. We catch up to Mandy as she closes her locker. Inside are pictures of the two of us standing outside of Wax Trax, a picture of Siouxsie, and a flyer for a Ministry show that we missed.

We hustle down the hallway so that we aren't counted as tardy. There are some teachers who try to delay us on purpose so that we rack up enough tardies for detention. Like Mr. Worley, for instance. He is a math and biology teacher with a major attitude problem. He gossips about students, spreads rumors and has some kind of weird vendetta against my little group of friends. He actually physically blocks us from passing his room in the hallway to try to make us late. He makes up student handbook violations and stands there, berating us until the bell rings. Then he slips happily into his classroom with a satisfied smirk knowing that he has scored once again in his screwing-with-the-weirdos game. Luckily, he has a really obnoxious voice, and we can hear him before we get to that section of hallway. We go out of our way to avoid him as much as possible. Andy got into trouble once for pushing him out of the way as he tried to get by him when Worley kept blocking him. Mr. Fuckly needs to get a life and quit picking on teenagers. Luckily, we're in the clear right now.

Max takes off to go up to U.S. History. Mr. Deiter is very cool, but none of us want to push it. We want him to stay cool with us. We only have a few teachers that are rooting for us and we need all the help we can get! Mandy, Andy and I slide into our seats as the bell rings.

"Bonjour classe! Comment allez-vous?" Mr. Green greets the class. He is a middle-aged man with a very sweet demeanor. I have never heard of him losing his temper, which for a teacher, is a miracle. There are students in his classroom I'd like to slap into eternity, and I don't have to deal with them for eight hours. Some of the kids are rude to him because they aren't very good at French. They want to make Monsieur Green look stupid as revenge for when they look stupid for incorrect answers or being so retarded that they are incapable of answering at all. A jocko jackass is draped across a chair in the back of the class like he's a french aristocrat.

"Bon-jer Mon-see-er Ver-tee," declares the jock at full volume, making those of us who actually speak French cringe. He destroys the language on purpose and doesn't even try, so he makes fun of us for doing well.

"Bonjour. Taisez-vous s'il vous plaît," responds Monsieur Green calmly walking to his desk so that we can listen to the morning announcements. It's usually crap about the next "big game" and the like.

I put my head down for a short rest, I take catnaps any chance I get. This soporific droning would put even the most enthusiastic pompom girl into a coma. I open one eye and look around the beige tiled, beige walled, drab institutional looking room. Snore. Mandy and Andy are snoozing like me, and the rest are either finishing homework or staring into space like zombies. I return to my meditation until Monsieur Green's voice stirs me to consciousness. Begrudgingly, I open my book and repeat the sentences along with the rest of the class.

"J'ai besoin," for sure there are plenty of things that I need.

"J'ai faim," I'm so hungry all the time. I've gotten used to not getting what I want or what I need, so I just live with this constant ache.

"J'ai soif," I am thirsty for exposure to the world. I feel like a wilting flower. My mind drifts back into the dismal present...

We whip out paper and pens to take a vocabulary quiz, which I complete in less than ten minutes. I am really good at French, mainly because I love it. I also figure it'll come in handy when I finally journey overseas. The plan is to take part in the foreign exchange programs that are available through most schools. Every college and university I've looked at has at least one semester overseas available, and France is always on the list. I am so there. The farther away from my family and this stinking place, the better.

I look over at Mandy and raise an eyebrow. She sticks out her tongue and gives me the finger. She finishes her last two questions and hands in her quiz. I stick my foot out in the aisle to block her way and she flicks me in the head. We laugh quietly as she sits down at her desk.

"Mesdemoiselles, taisez-vous, s'il vous plaît," murmurs Monsieur Green, scarcely glancing up from his desk.

We scrawl notes to each other during the last few minutes of class since there is nothing else for us to do. A paper wad hits me in the back of the head. I turn around and Andy waves at me, grinning like a loon. He quickly looks down at his desk when Mr. Green looks up from the quizzes he's grading. I turn back around and finish my correspondence to Mandy. The bell rings and with a rumble of a hundred rhino on an African plain, the class stands, gathers books and belongings and departs.

"A demain, mes étudiants!" exclaims Monsieur Green over the din of the chattering group as we exit the classroom.

There are groups of people wearing hula skirts, leis and straw hats in the hall.

"Oh for Pete's sake!" I exclaim, thoroughly annoyed. "I guess it's that time of year again."

"Puke," adds Mandy venomously. "I hate Spirit Week."

Spirit Week is the week before homecoming when everyone is supposed to follow along and wear the assigned wardrobe on different days of the week. Apparently today is Hawaiian day. There is always an orange and black day, since those are the school colors. Whoever made that decision must've been smoking some funny tobacco because absolutely no one looks good in that particular combination of colors. The ironic thing is that we get messed with by students and teachers alike for wearing black, even though technically it is half of the school colors. We use this argument practically daily.

"What's the deal with the dumbass squad today?" says Andy loudly, giving a group of cheerleaders in grass skirts the finger.

"Spirit Week," Mandy and I say in unison with the enthusiasm of a wake.

"Oh, piss off! I hate Spirit Week!" moans Andy, rolling his eyes in aggravation.

It's a double whammy this year. Midterms are next week and this week is Homecoming. We like sports about as much as a poke in the eye, but around here — it's a religion. If you're not a jock or a cheerleader, you're nothing. I apply myself to my classes in an effort to be eligible for scholarships that don't involve any kind of ball. We're all pretty good artists, so we figure we're all in the running for local and college scholarships for creative and artistic types like us. We have to take the SATs next year. I am freaking out because my father has made it plain that if I don't do better than Brett, I am seriously screwed. He will take away my tape player and I will not be allowed to leave the house until I go to college. He is totally serious too. When I got a C in math last year, I was grounded for one month with no phone, no TV, no radio, and no tape player. All I could do was go to school, come home and study. It didn't help at all. It just made me more nervous, which is why I have severe test anxiety. I am seriously contemplating getting drunk before taking the various college entrance exams, at least then I'll be relaxed.

The day is passing pretty painlessly, until lunch. Max, Andy and I all have Algebra/Trig with Miss Fitch right before lunch. I am so lost in there. She expects us to learn through osmosis. She refuses to answer questions. Her response is always, "Read your book and learn it." I got a D minus on the last two tests and am failing miserably. I study for two or three hours each night and I have gone to all of the other math teachers for help. No one can teach me and I can't figure out which one of us is the stupid one. I can't just memorize this stuff. It doesn't stick! I have to understand it. Anyway, by the time we leave that class I am tearing down the hall to my locker making one hell of a mess out of my eyeliner sobbing my heart out. If I get a D, I am totally dead. My father won't just be pissed, he'll break me into little pieces and scatter me like confetti. Max and Andy catch up with me, "Kiera, you'll be okay. We'll help you. You can totally do this stuff."

"I suck!! I am so screwed! I fucking hate her! I can never get a straight answer — ever!" I yell in frustration throwing my books forcefully into the bottom of my locker. People look over at us and clear the hall when they see my distress. I guess they think I'll kick anyone who is in my path. Screw it, let them think what they want. At least if some of them are afraid of me, they'll leave me alone. I bet if I was someone else, it'd matter and they'd ask me what's wrong. I slide down the wall, sit on the floor, bury my face in my arms, and bawl. My friends huddle around me trying to calm me down and reassure me.

Mandy comes swooping down the hall when she sees me, "Kiera? What's going on? Are you OK?" She bends down and grabs my arm trying to pull me to my feet. Max and Andy join her in her efforts.

"She's really sucking it in Algebra/Trig and Miss Bitch won't help her, as usual. I don't know why she has such a vendetta against Kiera!" says Andy, shaking his head and patting me on the back.

"Yeah, it was vicious today. Kiera isn't getting this section and Fitch sent her to the board and made her stay there the whole hour working this one problem, and the bitch wouldn't let her sit down until she got it right," snarls Max, "She was up there the entire fucking hour. I mean, even the Poms felt bad for her."

"I'm going to get her if Kiera gets her ass kicked for the shitty grades because Miss Bitch Fitch couldn't be bothered to TEACH!" screams Mandy stomping her feet in rage.

We all start laughing, partially because Mandy is all of five feet three inches and Miss Fitch is five feet ten, but also because we know that Mandy is entirely capable of doing some serious damage to someone's reality. She's small, but really fierce. I am so lucky she's my friend; lord knows, I'd hate to have her for an enemy.

She slaps at us and flaps her hand irritably, "Screw you guys. You know I can and will do her harm if it comes down to it."

"I have no doubt," I chuckle, wiping the tears off my face.

Mandy reaches over with a clean tissue and helps me to get my mangled mess of eyeliner under control. Then we head to lunch. We don't eat much because the slime they provide isn't what we consider food. Besides, with an upcoming trip to Chicago, I need to save my money for Wax Trax and the cover charge for the club Mandy mentioned.

"So, what's the story with this nightclub your cousin was talking about?" I ask as we intimidate people sitting at our table into leaving hastily. Max towers over some little sophomores like a total eclipse, and they take off like insects fleeing when you flick on a light. We laugh at their frightened departure and plunk down in the chairs. Rumors can work wonders for gaining a little space around here.

"Sandy went weekend before last and called to tell me about it, she thought I'd love the alternative room. It's a club called Medusa's. They have hard core shows there and several rooms with different music. She said they played Siouxsie and Depeche Mode and all kinds of good stuff in the red room," Mandy says, her face glowing with excitement.

"Cool. How much is the cover?" asks Max, his mouth full of peanut butter sandwich.

"I think she said it's five. We can meet her there," Mandy tells him, with a disgusted look at his horrible table manners.

I nibble a granola bar from the partially eaten box I keep in my bag. I always have to eat and run, though sometimes it ends up being more running and less eating.

"I can't wait to shake it for all the ladies!" drawls Andy in a fake British accent as he shakes around in his chair, nearly falling over in his exuberance.

"Ooooo, yeah, baby!" squeals Mandy laughing.

We hear the menacing click of heels stop right behind us, and turn around to find out what we're in trouble for this time. Mrs. Starling has walked up to our table after seeing Andy's chair boogie, and with nostrils flaring — she is not amused.

"What seems to be the problem, Mr. Sherwood?" she asks Andy, looking down at us with pure disdain. C'mon lady. We're kids.

"Nothing, Mrs. Starling. I was just dancing for my friends," Andy says looking at the floor. We all avoid eye contact because he is doing his fake apologetic thing that we all know is complete bullshit. Max has his left hand over his mouth and is concentrating on the ceiling like he's thinking about the terrible things we've been doing. In reality, he is suppressing laughter so that we don't get in trouble.

"In your seat?" she asks, eyebrows raised. You'd think he said he was jacking off under the table, instead of dancing in a chair.

"Yeah. I was being goofy. Sorry. I know you hate that. It won't happen again," Andy says sadly, looking at his shoes.

Mandy and I are almost crying from trying not to laugh. It isn't like Andy was hurting anyone or anything, except maybe Mrs. Starling's sensibilities. She needs to get a sense of humor, and a life — and maybe even a new holiday sweater!

"You would do well to behave yourself, Mr. Sherwood. You and I can be either friends or adversaries. The choice is entirely yours," she sniffs.

"Oh, Mrs. Starling, I would love to be your friend," responds Andy with a soppy grin.

"That's better," Mrs. Starling says, seeming to buy the huge pile of horse poop Andy has concocted. "Tomorrow is Hippy Day so be sure you have something planned, won't you?" she grins cheerfully, clicking away in her Stride Rite low-heeled, beige pumps.

We are all holding our breath until she leaves the cafeteria. Max slyly looks up and around to see if the coast is clear. Mandy and I are shaking and crying with laughter.

"All set to be her bestest fwend?" she giggles, gasping for air and wiping her eyes.

"Now that was my best performance yet," replies Andy with a puckish twinkle and a thumbs up.

Meanwhile Max is falling out of his chair, gasping for breath while he laughs with us, "Dude, she can't be that freaking dense!"

"No, I'm just that convincing!" boasts Andy with a huge, cheesy grin, doing his best romance novel hero pose.

"OK," I say wiping my eyes before settling into my chair. I fold my hands on the table, "Back to the game plan for this weekend. It's the only one before midterms."

"Well, see if you can stay over on Saturday night and go home on Sunday," suggests Mandy.

"It's worth a shot," I say nodding.

The guys look at each other and then us, "Righteous!" they exclaim.

So it's a done deal, if I can stay at Mandy's. I won't be telling anyone we're going to Chicago. They think I'm too young. They allowed Brett to go see Mötley Crüe and Guns N' Roses, and he's only one year older. It's a total double standard because I'm a girl. So, I sneak out sometimes. It isn't like I'm getting knocked up in someone's back seat. I'm going to buy records and go dancing. We don't drink, smoke, or have sex, so I don't see the big deal. I don't feel bad about lying to my parents since they have always lied to me. My parents seem completely incapable of following through on anything, except for punishments. Those are guaranteed and consistent.

The week flies by as we trudge through piles of homework, quizzes — and the usual insults and nastiness from our supposed peers. Around Wednesday, I broker a deal with my mother that if I can stay Mandy's on Saturday, I'll do the laundry and ironing on Sunday. I hate ironing, but it's my one bargaining chip — I trashed one of my father's shirts accidentally on purpose, so he doesn't assign ironing to me as one of my many chores anymore. My mother hates doing anything resembling work, so she was less then pleased with this arrangement, as it meant she had to iron his shirts once a week — or else.

I am getting really excited as the week comes to an end. We've never gone to an actual nightclub before, because we don't do fake I.D.'s and there hasn't been an after-hours club before now. It'll be extremely late, but none of us gives a crap. It'll be like dipping our pinkie toes in the pool of "the real world." High school is so far removed from reality, and we live in the middle of a cornfield. We are as isolated from reality as you can get. I am curious about what happens out there, I think we all are. It's Friday and we are all bouncing off the walls.

"Miss Graves, would you like to go to the board and solve the equation I just went over?" asks Miss Fitch. So much for my daydream. Now I have to go to the board. Why does this woman seem to hate my guts? Why?

"Not really," I mutter as I stand up.

"What did you say?" she snarls, whirling around from the board to face me as I slouch to where she has written an equation that I have no prayer of completing in this century.

"Nothing," I grumble looking at the floor, and hunching over as I cross my arms. This woman takes such vicious pleasure in humiliating me. I have no idea why. I suppose it might have something to do with her looking like a creature out of a horror novel. She has craggy features and a nose that puts the Wicked Witch of the West's to shame. She is 5'10", skinny, and has the frizziest, super long hair that flies around behind her when she stands in front of the heater. She wears a uniform of beige chinos and a buttoned-down shirt every day. She never wears make up or color of any kind. If she wasn't mean as hell, the kids wouldn't all call her "Miss Bitch." She is mean to every student that crosses her threshold and she seems to get off on making cheerleaders cry.

"Now, Miss Graves, I am not hard of hearing," she replies with a sardonic smile, "I distinctly heard you say something to me. Please repeat your answer?" She folds her arms looking triumphant as I cringe in front of the entire class. No one is amused by her nastiness, even though most of the people in here hate my guts. Max and Andy are looking at me, horrified. I look at them and am overtaken by rage so intense, I am about to lose control. Max catches my eye and nods. He knows what I am about to do. Whatever happens, I'm going to pay for it so I am not going to hold back. This time I am going to hit back.

"I said that I didn't really want to come up here because your refusal or inability to answer any of my questions prevents me from answering yours," I say clearly as I glare fixedly at her god-awful, ugly face.

"Excuse me?" Miss Fitch huffs, shocked that a student dares to defend themselves. I swear I could almost see steam coming out of her ears.

"You just said you aren't hard of hearing, so I am sure you heard me quite well," I say smiling at her. In my head, I am tying her to her desk and dousing it with kerosene. Max tosses a match and we laugh, exiting the room to the sound of her pleading and screams.

"You will receive an F for today Miss Graves. I suggest you watch your mouth the next time I call you to the board. I am sure your parents will be very interested to hear what you had to say in my class today" she says in a deadly tone. I return to my seat, shoulders back and head held high. All the fluff balls have their mouths hanging open at my confrontation with Miss Fitch. Her words ring in my ears, and I am in the grip of fear so intense that I can't breathe. This may be the final straw.

"What are you all looking at? Open your books to page four hundred and eleven…" she barks, pacing up and down the rows like an SS officer. Behind her, Max gives her the finger and I hold my breath so I don't laugh. Andy is choking a few desks away, because he witnessed this exchange and couldn't quite control himself. He is coughing to cover his laughter and I slide him the tiniest wink. The bell rings and we are free from the evil empire of the most supreme math bitch.

"What the hell is her major malfunction?" demands Max as we head down the hall.

"She has hated me ever since the first day. I don't know why," I respond, "I wish she would just leave me the hell alone though. This humiliation crap that she does really pisses me off."

"Don't worry, we'll fix her," says Andy with a wicked grin, "I know how to get in the system and I can change your grades, no problem. They'll never figure it out until it's too late."

"OK, except they'll kill us when they do figure it out. Let's meditate on a good prank for Miss Fitch and let her know she needs to back off," I say, putting on my best brave face.

"It's your funeral," replies Andy. He knows full well what my abysmal grades will get me — a serious ass kicking from Daddyshit. I am sure it won't be the last one. I have to have as much fun as possible this weekend, because I probably won't see daylight until sometime after May.

We go to lunch and conspire with Mandy about getting even with Miss Fitch. My friends and I have an extreme dislike for bullies. We couldn't care less about most things, but bullying is a guarantee of having trouble with us. My friends are dying to get my father for all the times he's beaten me black, blue, purple, and green, but they can't figure out how to not get caught. Max keyed my father's car once when he saw it parked in the mall parking lot. My father was super pissed. I still laugh about it.

The day ends without any further fireworks and we all make a break for it. We don't want anything screwing up our plans. The guys head off, walking quickly to Max's. Mandy drops me off and we arrange for her to pick me up early tomorrow, 10 a.m. I am psyched. I enter the house as quietly as I humanly can. I don't hear any noise at all. I tiptoe upstairs to my room and put my stuff away. I pull out my weekend bag and begin to pack. I have my headphones on while I choose my wardrobe and various other necessities.

I listen to New Order wail — asking how it feels to treat him that way the person does.

I have everything tidied up and packed in short order. I am sitting on by bed studying. Suddenly, my door is kicked open with such force, the doorknob is embedded in the wall. I jump about two feet straight up and scoot as far away as I can until I'm squished into the corner. My father enters the room with such fury that with one look I know today is the day I will die. He snatches my hair brush off of my dresser, snaps it in half like it was a toothpick, and throws it aside. I almost pee.

"WHO DO YOU THINK YOU ARE YOU STUPID BITCH?" he roars coming at me like a charging bull.

I curl up into a ball with my back against the wall.

"What are you talking about?" I whimper, "I don't understand."

He grabs me by my upper arms which I have clutched around my knees. I don't uncurl, so I am hanging from his grip like a Christmas ornament.

"I am talking about Miss Fitch and your algebra grades, YOU LITTLE SHIT!" he screams in my face, "STAND UP!"

I remain in a ball. If I uncurl, he will beat me worse than if I can protect my abdomen. I cry and whimper for him to stop. Through my tears, I see my mother standing at the door watching, with a taunting smile. My father drops me like a sack of laundry and I try to scoot away. He kicks me in the head really hard. That's the last thing I remember. Living here is like living in a house that is burning down, and the windows and doors have been nailed shut.

· Five ·

October 17, 1987
B.F.E. Indiana

Jerking into consciousness, I curl into a ball on my bed. There is blood on the wall and pillow. It appears that after kicking me in the head and knocking me out, instead of taking me to a hospital, they put me on my bed. It's 1 a.m. In a few more hours Mandy will be here to get me. I just have to hang on until she gets here. I sink back into unconsciousness, my head throbbing. The day will come when he won't be able to hurt me anymore.

Someone is gently shaking me awake. I flinch, startled, trying to focus on who it is.

"Holy shit, Kiera," whispers Mandy. "What happened to you?"

I groan as I sit up. "Help me get my stuff and get out of here. I'll tell you in the car," I whisper grimacing as I stand up. I feel as if I was beaten from head to toe with a baseball bat. For all I know, maybe I was. My stomach is a knot of fear and panic. I swallow hard, trying to control the nausea that's threatening to surge forward like a wave of toxic waste. She glances at the broken hair brush on the floor and looks at me in horror.

"You can't come back here after this, Kiera," she says, her eyes burning with anger.

"He was mad about my algebra grade and apparently he heard about what happened in class. I have no idea how," I explain, trying to think of what I need to take with me.

We collect some clothes, toiletries and some precious mixed tapes into a duffel bag. I am moving slowly, pain shooting through my body. Glancing at Mandy, I see her hands are shaking as she packs my backpack with my school stuff. She sniffs, and wipes her wet face with the back of her hand, smearing her eyeliner.

"We are going to the hospital," she says, her voice breaking as tears splash down her face. We slowly and silently make our way out of the house. Brett had let Mandy in on his way out to play basketball. We get in the car and Mandy carefully backs out. She is worried. I am just trying to figure out if I actually need medical attention, or if I can just suck it up.

She pulls up to the emergency room entrance and I hesitate. "They are going to kill me if I go in there," I argue.

"The reason you're here is because that asshole already tried. Your mother will take care of it, right?"

I raise my eyebrow and look at her skeptically. "Did you already forget the wonder of Dana?" "Okay.. well, what about your grandparents?" Her confidence that someone will intervene on my behalf kills me. This false hope feels like a brick wall between us that I keep banging my head against. I shrug, anxious to just get this over with. She parks the car and helps me figure out the paperwork. I am scared because this is a small town and my parents will know very soon about me going to the hospital. I know their rules. If you tell, you pay.

I am led back and into a tiny, blue-curtained "room", one of ten in the emergency room. I undress and put on the gown as I have been instructed. The doctor scowls as I relate what happened. As I am being taken to have x-rays done, Mandy goes to call Max and Andy. She gets back just as I am wheeled back into my little cubicle room.

"The boys are coming. They'll be here in about ten minutes. Where the hell was your mom or your brother?" she exclaims, furious that I was left in my room in such a sorry state.

"Mom stood in the doorway watching, at least at the point where he lifted me off the bed," I tell her. I start to cry miserably. I never know how to answer these questions. I can't fathom what makes them act like this. I don't get it either. Mother always tells me, "I don't have the time to worry about hurt feelings" but the thing is, if you don't do what she wants, it's capital offense. She has never behaved in any way that resembles nurturing toward me. I think she's always resented me — pissed off that she was pregnant even though they didn't plan it. That's how they all treat me. It's like I am an intruder on their family and I should be paying rent.

Mandy sits next to me on the hospital gurney bed thing and hugs me. I can't seem to control the flow of tears that flood my eyes, soaking my hospital gown and Mandy's Wax Trax Records t-shirt.

"This is ridiculous. There's got to be a way to get you out of there," she soothes, lightly rubbing my back.

The curtained wall suddenly opens and Max and Andy are standing there. I feel so pathetic and embarrassed. I'm black, blue, green and purple all over. I must look even worse in this hospital gown that's ten sizes too big. They come into the tiny room, Max hunches over so he doesn't get clocked by the lights and various instruments that are hanging at the ready. The expression of shock and horror on his face tells me everything.

"What the hell happened?" Andy asks, outrage contorting his usual happy-go-lucky face. He scowls, frowns and mutters a string of threats mixed with language that would make George Carlin blush. Max lurks in a corner resembling a large, pissed-off vulture looking for a fight.

"Her dad again," replies Mandy.

"Beautiful," snarls Andy. Max looks over with a menacing expression. I can tell he'd like to tear my father apart limb from limb. I would not protest one bit at this point. My head is still killing me, but I really want to go to Chicago. I just want to have some fun and pretend I have a different life. At least for a few hours.

The doctor swoops into the small, crowded room and states, "Well, you are really lucky. You might have a slight concussion, but everything looks OK. Do you want me to bring our police officer in to file the report?"

I stiffen and my heart races. Unless they lock him up forever, I am screwed. "No, that's OK," I mumble shaking my head. I sniff and wipe my tears. "They can't help me," I sigh in despair.

"Miss Graves, I am sure they can if you fill out a report," says the doctor frowning in frustration.

"Kiera, you've got to stand up for yourself and stop letting him do this to you," Mandy says.

"Letting him? Letting him do this to me? Is that what you really think? Do you not understand how much worse it is when I fight back at all?" I explode, pulling away from her.

"No, I know," she pleads. "It's just- there's got to be a way to help you. I can't just sit here and do nothing."

"I'm just trying to get through this alive," I explain, hardening myself to the pain, brushing aside all my feelings. "I'm glad I'm OK, but I'm going to just get dressed and go."

Everyone leaves the curtained room as I change back into real clothes. I clomp into the hallway and sign out. My parents are going to be SO pissed at me for this bill. If he beats me a little harder next time, the police will have him for murder. I am determined not to be just another statistic. I wasn't put on this earth to be my brother or father's punching bag, or my mother's live-in maid. There has to be a better place out there in the world for me.

The automatic doors of the E.R. slide open and a blast of cold outside air hits us like a slap. We walk to Mandy's car in the cold, gray of noon in the fall in Northern Indiana. The murky sky is spitting rain, making the day that much more enjoyable.

"So...Do you feel up to going?" asks Max.

"Are you sure?" asks Andy, looking at my beaten, bruised face. "Maybe you should stay home and get some rest."

" Do you really think they would let me get some rest?" I ask him, my voice dripping with sarcasm.

My friends nod, defeated. They know as well as I do that I'm screwed.

"Dude, I so need this. Let's get out of here!" I respond with a grim half smile.

The mood has lightened and we are all glad I can go without doing myself serious injury. I will be taking it easy on the dance floor though. No pogo-ing for Kiera tonight. We are taking Mandy's car because Max's Lincoln conked out last week and he is still working on getting it fixed. Max is sitting in the front seat because he is so tall. Andy and

I are sitting in the back and singing along with Depeche Mode at the top of our lungs. Mandy keeps her eyes on the road as she and Max join in with us, "Everything counts in large amounts…"

We are all bobbing with the music. Mandy makes killer mixed tapes. This one is mainly Depeche Mode, The Cure, and The Smiths. We converse about which records we're each hoping to purchase at Wax Trax. Skinny Puppy, Ministry, Cocteau Twins, PiL…so much great music and so little cash flow. I keep thinking that will be the cool part of entering adulthood. I can live in my own place, eat whatever I want, and buy records until the cows come home. I wouldn't run myself into debt for my albums, however tempting the thought may be. I plan to move away from cows and cornfields. We drive past Gary, which is a complete dead zone. Most steel towns are, though. Gary always looks so run down and gray with trash and junked cars laying around, smoke painting the sky beige and making an awful stench. Driving past here in the fall when it's cold, drizzly and gray is even more depressing. This is why I think education is a really good idea. I don't want to work in a factory or some kind of plant. There was some kind of plant out near us and it shut down. Now it's a ruin that nobody wants, an eyesore with broken windows and lots of square footage that's of no use to anyone except birds, squirrels, and stray, feral cats.

We wind our way toward the city, eventually hitting some gridlock. It doesn't matter what time of year, if it's daytime, there's a traffic jam somewhere along the way. That's what music is for though. We sing along with Robert Smith about a strange girl who comes from another world.

Andy makes a face at me and I laugh. My head still hurts though, so I try not to. It's only rough having friends who are as hilarious as Mandy and Andy when you're in pain. Max has his humorous, animated moments for sure, as do I — but we tend to be the "quiet ones." We tend to lurk off to one side, observing goings on and people, while Mandy and Andy are the life of the party, entertaining everyone with hilarious anecdotes.

We zoom off the highway onto our exit and head for Lincoln Ave. There's a restaurant next door to Wax Trax where we often pig out before spending almost all of our money on records. I love their soup and croissants. Mandy finds a parking place on a side street and squeezes into it. She has become supremely talented at parallel parking since we began venturing into Chicago. We pause for a moment, while Mandy helps me dab makeup on the worst of the bruises. It'll be dark soon enough, and I am relying on the night to give me the camouflage I need. We pile out of the small vehicle and stretch like a gang of alley cats getting ready for a nightly prowl.

"Dude, I am starving to death!" exclaims Andy.

We nod in agreement, and head for the restaurant. His exclamation is funny because Andy eats *all* the time, and eats such large amounts of food that he puts the football team to shame. He never gains an ounce though. Andy insists that it's because of his naturally springy, borderline hyperactive nature. I would tend to agree. Being around Andy is like being around one of those little rubber superball things that when you bounce it, it goes nuts and bounces all over the room like an over-excited comet. He makes the rest of us look like we're in a coma.

We slide into a booth and quickly order our soups, sandwiches and tea. We need to warm up a bit before traipsing all over the north side of the city. The food arrives quickly and we demolish it like a pack of trolls who haven't eaten in a month. People are looking at us like we're from another planet. Maybe because Mandy has blue streaks in her hair and a Wax Trax Records t-shirt, or possibly because Andy is sporting a violently green shirt that clashes painfully with his red hair. Maybe it's Max with his tall, skinny build draped in a black trench coat looking like Bela himself. Maybe it's me also draped in black, looking like someone has beat the snot out of me with this cut on my head. I'm in no mood for the judgmental, "you're weird" thing that some people do. Everyone in the whole world isn't going to look just like *you.* There is an older woman sitting with her two kids across the aisle from us. She is openly staring at us with a disgusted expression on her face. I look right back at her, cross my arms, and don't look away. Mandy starts giggling and elbows Andy, who sees what I'm doing. It turns into a group staring contest until we both stick out our tongues, and make goofy faces at this rude, obnoxious woman. Max spits the water he just sipped all over himself, laughing and choking. The woman grabs her kids and rushes to pay her bill, glaring at us like we threatened to eat them. Just because we don't like Laura Ashley, doesn't mean that there is *anything* wrong with us. I don't see why blue hair or unusual clothing is so offensive. Granted, some of Andy's shirts are so bright that you see spots sometimes... None of us understand the mentality of the "moral majority" crowd of fuckwits who are so narrow-minded that they think absolutely *every* one else should be, think, talk and dress just like them. Plus, I trust a guy with a Mohawk way more than I trust some dildo in a suit. At least then, with people who show their personality, you know exactly who you're dealing with, more or less. It's the normal-looking people who you've got to watch.

"OK, kids. Ready to go next door?" asks Mandy practically slobbering.

"YEAH!" we respond a little too loudly for our subdued restaurant surroundings. We gather our things and pay our tab. A blast of cold air hits our faces as we exit the cozy warmth of the restaurant and clomp to Wax Trax, the greatest record store — ever. The black door is a welcome sight. The walls are black and there is a beat-up photo booth against the wall. There are rows and rows of records in bins that seem to go on forever. Hard core punk, reggae, ska, every 4AD artist on the planet, every alternative record you can think of is here. I am always overwhelmed because I have so few dollars and love so many bands. There are huge posters hanging from the ceiling of Bauhaus, David Bowie, the Cocteau Twins, and The Cure. Mandy and I go straight for the bin where the Cocteau Twins are. The boys go and forage through the industrial section.

Mandy and I are trying to get our hands on every Cocteau Twins EP, which is turning out to be a bit of a challenge, mainly because we are so poor. We rifle through the available vinyl and stand there for a while, debating. I decide on "The Spanglemaker" and "Peppermint Pig." I have no idea what they sound like and have no qualms whatsoever about spending $32 on these records. All of their music is gorgeous. Elizabeth has the most beautiful voice on earth. Mandy chooses "Love's Easy Tears". Then we go to look at the pile of Siouxsie and the Banshees that is currently available. We gasp and drool. It's so hard to narrow it down. I wish I didn't have to budget! Siouxsie's voice is awesome. I just wouldn't call it beautiful. To me the word "beautiful" sounds fragile and lacy. Siouxsie has a strong, powerful voice that penetrates and howls with such emotion that you feel it down to your toenails. Mandy finally chooses "Hyæna" and we scurry upstairs to look around. Earrings, necklaces, dominatrix-looking dresses and skirts, and of course, band t-shirts. Mandy and I can't afford any more than our records, but we love to look. We hear heavy footsteps clomping up to meet us. I see Andy's spiked crop of bright red hair over the top of the low wall making its way up.

"So what'd you guys get?" asks Mandy bouncing slightly on the balls of her feet in excitement.

"Well, I heard this song downstairs and had to get the record. It's called 'That Total Age' and the band is Nitzer Ebb. It's hard industrial, I'll tape it for you tomorrow, Kiera," replies Max. He knows I love hard industrial music. "They finally had the new Skinny Puppy, so I got that too," he says with a huge grin.

"What about you Andy?" Mandy queries, turning to face Andy who is going through all the t-shirts enthusiastically.

"I got a new copy of 'Good For Your Soul' because I wore my old one out and it sounds like total crap at this point. And, I *finally* picked up 'Special Beat Service' since I've been dying to get it for ages and they finally had a copy here. Woo hoo!" he answers as he skanks around us maniacally. He's our little skate punk skankin' fool. He's so hyper, he needs the physical outlet for all of those hormones and male energy. Mandy and I chipped in and bought him a new board last year for his birthday. We painted it all up for him with a Dia de Los Muertos skull and stuff.

"If we're all paid up, we need to get out of here before we go nuts," I say. We could literally clean this place out if we had the cash. We have some impulse control, but c'mon, we're teenagers. Mandy and I head to the register downstairs to cough up for our record selections. The surly, pierced clerk looks at us with supreme disdain because we are so excited about our new stash. We don't have the capacity to "play it cool" — we're giant geeks. I can't help myself. When I am listening to this music, my whole body and mind are transported to a better place. All of these musicians express what is in my head. It's like they know me, and they write these songs to be there with me. To hold my hand. To stay with me in the darkest places when everyone else has left, and I am alone and afraid. The music stays with me, always. It is the only thing I can count on when everyone and everything else turns to ash.

We tumble out of the store and onto the street like a gang of alley cats looking for a screw, howling and laughing and being generally unruly. We tramp to the car and hide our bags under a bunch of folders and crap littering the trunk of Mandy's car. She keeps it filthy on purpose as a theft deterrent. So far, it has worked really well. We help her keep it clean, but cluttered. The Escort is in pretty good shape overall, we just don't want anyone stealing it or our stuff. We head over to Bizarre Bazaar, which is just like its name. You can get hats, t-shirts, tobacco accessories, jewelry and various other bits and pieces. Mandy and I start trying on hats. She models a gray fedora and flips the brim down.

"I used to totally love John Taylor," she says laughing at herself in the mirror.

"Oh yeah! I did too, remember? We used to sit there and drool over his posters," I reminisce with a smile. "He is still a tasty treat, don't you think?" I ask her as I don a black bowler hat. I have a huge head, so it is perched on my head like some kind of weird mushroom. Mandy gets a load of this and is guffawing loudly enough that people actually give her dirty looks. She wipes her eyes and finds a black beret that suits her to a "T". So very beatnik and cool.

"Yeah, he is one damn fine looking specimen of man. But I know who you really like," she replies with a wicked smile. She knows I am a huge Oingo Boingo freak and worship at the altar of Danny Elfman. Now if I could just see them live I'd be in heaven, but since Boingo doesn't exactly tour in B.F.E. Indiana, I will have to make do with making tapes over at Andy's. We all share our purchases with each other because none of us are well-to-do. We buy as soon as we can, but while we wait on allowances and meager earnings, we borrow. Mandy makes her purchase and we wander around looking for the boys who are perusing weird belt buckles and bolo ties. Max is checking out a scorpion forever frozen in plastic that is the clasp of a bolo tie.

"So, whaddya think, girls?" he says holding it up with a cheesy grin, wiggling his eyebrows like a game show host.

"I think if you were a retiree in Las Vegas it'd be perfect for you. Other than that, I'd have to say, put it back you big goob," I reply.

Max swats at me playfully and laughs. He hangs the tie back on its hook and we make our way around the bazaar. I feel like my friends make up for the shittiness of my family and all the crap that seems to come dumping on my head in my daily life. I love them more than I can express. They are the answers to my childhood prayers.

We are pretty well done window shopping and are antsy to go out to Medusa's. It's not nearly late enough, so we head to a nearby Thai place. The food is fabulous, as well as inexpensive. They give you heaping portions, so we always stuff ourselves. Mandy and I order Thai chicken with spinach and garlic. It literally takes us an hour and a half to eat it all. We have some Thai coffee, which seems to be legalized speed. Finally, we're ready to go and make our way back to where the car is parked. Mandy and Max go over a map to ensure that we know where we're going. You do not want to mess around and get lost in the middle of the night in Chicago. We cruise side streets and circle around to find a parking spot. We see people gathered outside of a three story building on the corner, and my innards explode with excitement. We find a spot about a block or so away and scramble out of the car. Fueled by Thai coffee and excitement, we hurry up to the line that has formed and stand in a cluster chatting about the neighborhood. Belmont seems to be where the bohemians and freaks hang out. There's a place called The Alley that we are all dying to check out next time. We saw it on the way here. It looks like a Goth and punk supply store. Andy is in the market for a leather jacket. He's kind of small standing next to Max and needs a little extra to help him look as fierce as he really is. It's a guy thing. He's not your typical boy, but he doesn't want anyone thinking he's "normal".

Max is looking over the gathering crowd like a vulture on a limb. He and I have a really good sense of people just by looking at them. It's that whole intuitive/sixth sense thing. He looks down at me with his large green eyes and smiles. "I bet you're going to burn a hole in the floor, aren't you?" he ponders aloud.

"Hmmm. Hadn't really thought about it, but I hope to have the opportunity. I have some aggression I need to release," I reply.

There are some skinheads ahead of us and then a cluster of mods ahead of them. Behind us are various Italian guys in suits and a small group of Rastafarians. I can already tell that this is my kind of place. I love when all different kinds of people can be in close proximity to each other, not get into any kind of argument, and just have fun.

Apparently, from what we overhear, there is a live music room in addition to the various dance floors. The band tonight is rumored to be a local reggae band. I have no idea. I just want to get in there and soak it all up. We steadily approach the door as the bouncers check I.D.s and take cash. It is after hours, so we just have to be sixteen. Mandy turns around to look at me and flashes a huge grin as she steps up to show her I.D. Her cheeks are pink from the chilly air and excitement. She takes her I.D. back from the huge, bald, leather-clad bouncer and proceeds ahead to the door. We file through as quickly as they allow us, the bouncer giving me an approving nod. Weirdo. You're fifteen years older than me. Gross!

Mandy, Max and Andy have forked over their cover and I gladly fork over a fiver into the waiting palm of the skinny girl with black hair and a long purple, velvet dress who is taking cover charges. She smiles at us with black lipsticked lips as we make our ascent. We've never been to a nightclub before, so we're all very curious about what we'll see tonight. The stairs are covered in deep red carpet and the banisters are wood. The black painted walls have a trashed out look that adds a Gothic feel to the entryway. Four stories up hangs a dusty chandelier casting a dim light over the stairs. We locate a coat check and check our coats in so that we don't become sweaty beasts the second we start to dance.

Suddenly, there is someone squealing loudly in my ear, "Maandeee! Hi!" An extremely drunk girl with short, black, spiky hair comes lunging at Mandy and knocks her into the wall.

"Sandra?…Oh shit," says Mandy, pushing her cousin out of her face.

"Sorry," apologizes a tall, skinny boy who skitters up to support Mandy's cousin, Sandra, who we were supposed to meet tonight. "We went to a party first and she had waaaaay too much Merlot," he chuckles as Sandra begins to assault Max and Andy.

"Wait…no…WAIT! Who are you?" Sandra slurs, hanging from the front of Max's shirt, "Are you dating my cousin? You'd better be nice…"

Sandra's emaciated friend carefully detaches her claws from Max's shirt and ushers her toward the stairs to get her outside, "We'll probably see you next time around…"

Mandy rolls her eyes, completely aggravated by her cousin's drunkenness, "You'd think she'd at least try to be in decent shape since we were coming. Idiot."

"Well, at least she didn't throw up on us the second we got here," I point out, trying to find the positive.

"Ick, good point," Mandy shudders.

The first room we come to is a small, low-ceilinged blue room with a strobe light. It is clear that whoever said the band tonight would be playing reggae was full of crap. Indecipherable hardcore punk music emanates from within and we see about fifty skinheads in a mass thrashing the hell out of each other. A pair of jack boots and their occupant come flying toward us and we swiftly make our way onward and upward, avoiding death by mosh pit. We find a trendy bar area and a main dance floor. As we proceed, we discover another bar upstairs and balconies that overlook the dance floor so that you can sit upstairs on the red velvet couches and watch people on the main dance floor. They are playing some pop electronic stuff that I don't recognize. Nothing thrilling, so we move onward and upward to a red room. This room is on the top floor. It has hardwood floors, high ceilings, red walls and a projector showing videos. There is a bar along one wall and a red painted plywood box in the middle of the dance floor for people to dance on like a stage. The walls vibrate with the volume of the music. A familiar intro begins and we squeal in delight as we scurry onto the floor. The bells ringing and then the drums, and Siouxsie's voice howling how you are running out of time.

I am enthralled by the experience of feeling the music while I am dancing and seeing the video. I look over at Max who has part of Siouxsie projected across his face. He smiles and we laugh. Andy and Mandy are jamming out and keeping some space open as the place begins to fill. I am being somewhat mellow so that my head doesn't start throbbing. I feel really alive for the first time in my life. I feel like I am real. Most of the time, I feel like I am in a dream…like I am living with a transparent wall that separates me from the rest of the world. Just now I felt like I was really here, just for a split second. As I try to grasp the feeling so I can reproduce it, the moment passes and it all slips away from me like smoke on a windy day. I wonder if that is what most people feel like all the time?

There is some guy is checking me out. Wait, there is some guy checking me out?! I cast a glance around to see if there is someone else nearby who has their gaze. Nope. Definitely me. I flip my hair over my face and hide behind it. I can feel molten heat creeping into my face. The guy is walking toward me. I'm starting to panic and want to run. He's tall, about 6 feet, with dark hair and he's wearing a Black Flag t-shirt with ripped up black jeans. Super cute, and I don't know how to talk to him.

"Hi," he yells over the music which is now "Behind the Wheel."

"Hi," I say back, from beneath a curtain of hair. I look around to my friends for help. Boys never talk to me. I am always too something. Too weird. Too ugly. Too smart. Whatever.

"I'm Chris," he hollers and holds out his hand for me to shake.

"Kiera," I reply and reach for his hand. He takes it and kisses the back of my hand like I am a lady of old. I am very interested. A tall, very cute guy who likes punk and has nice manners? Oooooo. Très yummy. I smile and blush, while slowly withdrawing my hand from his, savoring the kiss. He has lovely lips, along with everything else.

"Hey!" Mandy steps over to us and tugs lightly on my shirt. "I'm Kiera's friend, Mandy. How about we seek some refreshments after all this dancing?" She smiles at me and we exchange a whole conversation with one look -omigodcanyoubelievethisisfinallyhappeningandheis-SOCUTE-! She leads the way to the bar where we each order water and wander over to a vacant red velvet couch. He sits really close to me and I am squirming.

"So, what side of town are you guys from?" Chris asks, taking a long drink from his red plastic cup.

"Uh, well, we're actually from out of town," I respond. I wonder if he's going to think I am some kind of hilljack if I say I'm from Indiana and then he won't like me and he'll bolt. But maybe that wouldn't be the worst thing because I don't know if I can deal with this. Crap. What am I doing?

Mandy sees me squirming, looking like someone put slugs in my underwear and raises her right eyebrow at me asking a silent, "What's your problem?". I make a face and quickly smile at him so he doesn't think I'm not interested.

"We're from Butt Fuck Egypt, Indiana," I say in an exaggerated hillbilly accent.

Chris laughs, almost spitting water out of his nose. He manages to swallow, still laughing as he turns toward me. "I guess you're less than thrilled about that, huh?"

"You might say that," I reply, wishing a hole would appear in the floor right now and swallow me up. I'm such a dork. I can't even talk.

"So, where are you from?" Mandy chimes in during the stretch of awkward silence that threatens to go on forever.

"I live near here," he responds turning to face Mandy. He leans back into the sofa and stretches.

Geez. This guy is so gorgeous. He is tall, thin, and just my type. Mandy knows this. His face is almost pretty, but he has a rough, slightly scruffy air, which makes him undeniably masculine. Why is he talking to me? Mandy is the outgoing one.

"So do you live with parents or roommates or what?" asks Mandy.

"My parents. They are both corporate lawyers and we live a few blocks away from here. I live on the top floor. It's small and I stay out of their way with this arrangement," he answers, leaning forward.

"I know the feeling," I offer.

"Yeah?" He turns his head and looks at me. His face is about six inches from mine and he has these really intense green eyes that take my breath away. I realize I am holding my breath and I let it out slowly and gulp some air. I don't know how to do this. God, I suck.

"Yeah, see that bloody bump on her head?" says Mandy. "That came from her dad."

"What the fuck?" scowls Chris. I am embarrassed by Mandy's directness in volunteering this particular information right at the moment. Heat rushes to my face and I look at my shoes. Great, thanks. Now I can't even pretend to be normal. I wish there was a rock I crawl under right now.

"Hey," he says reaching out to touch my face lightly, "anyone who treats you like that needs a reality check. Nobody deserves that, no matter what, you know?" The gorgeous green eyes look at me and I feel something entirely new. It's like a tickle right in the middle of my chest. It's like that goofy feeling you get on an elevator when it stops really quick and bounces.

"Let me give you my number," Chris says getting up quickly and striding to the bar.

"Dude, he is into you big time," squeaks Mandy plopping down next to me.

"Really? You think so? Jesus Christ though Mandy! He's so..." I say, desperately gesturing, trying to find the words. I am fully feeling my awkward dorkiness. What do I do now?

"Here he comes. Don't be a chicken, Kiera. He seems nice. Let's at least find out if he is, OK? You gotta start sometime," says Mandy scootching over to make space next to me for him.

"Start what?" I ask as he comes striding back.

"Trusting people," she says with a wink.

I roll my eyes at her. Chris sits down close to me and hands me a matchbook with his number scrawled within.

"Here's my number and address," he says as he leans toward me. I almost snatch it out of his hand, trying to cover how much my hands are shaking. I'm starting to sweat, praying the lighting is terrible and he doesn't notice.

Mandy springs up and tears off to head off the boys who are making their way toward us. I feel like I can't breathe. I try to smile. I've flirted with boys, but never had a real boyfriend. I've also never really kissed anyone other than the little boy I had a crush on in kindergarten. I kissed his cheek before he moved away. Such a trollop, I know.

Chris touches my hair and I feel myself start to shake. I try to relax and think about soothing things like the ocean or night skies. He is leaning toward me and looking right into my eyes. I don't think I've ever had anyone this close to my face except when I'm being screamed at or that one time when Mandy helped get cat fur out of my eye. Long story. Oh my gawd! He's going to kiss me! I really hope my breath isn't terrible. I really hope I'm not a crappy kisser. I also hope he isn't a crappy kisser. He puts his hand on the back of my neck and I feel his soft lips on mine. This one touch makes my blood sing. I feel like the perfect girl. I feel like the cosmos has just burst out right through me. We separate and smile at each other.

"Well, what year are you in school?" asks Chris clasping my hand in his. Strong hands. Mmm.

"Junior. One more crappy year," I say, my thoughts racing. Please don't let my hands be sweaty.

"Same as me," he says with a really devilish smile. "We'll write each other, stay in touch, and then see what happens," This guy is so gorgeous, but doesn't act like he knows it.

"Cool," I say, trying to quell my nervousness. "Let's go dance some more before this place closes."

"I'd rather watch, if that's OK," he says.

"Sure, but I gotta warn you. I love to dance," I say, boldly pulling him toward my friends who have been watching us the whole time.

Everyone introduces themselves quickly and we head for the red room once again. We scurry onto the floor as we hear the strains of "Addiction" begin, and Ogre growls about being desperate and deranged, talking in his sleep again.

I am in heaven. Mandy and Andy are close by and we are whirling ourselves silly. Max is hanging with Chris against the wall, watching the crowd. I try not to think about them looking at me. I am really self-conscious and know it.

I am moving smoothly over the floor. There are fewer people up here because the "see and be seen crowd" is downstairs. I like it up here where it's more low key, and I can be off the radar.

The DJ starts mixing in something familiar that we can't quite recognize. Mandy and I look at each other quizzically and then Max comes gliding out onto the floor like a large, black sting ray. The beat gets harder and we are punching it out.

"This is the song I heard in Wax Trax today!" yells Max over the music as we get into a groove. "This band is Nitzer Ebb!"

"They're awesome!" I yell back, grinning.

Mandy and I have this dance that is almost like martial arts, but it isn't. We just make up stuff. This song is a hard industrial song, so it goes well. The DJ finishes mixing and the song comes blasting at us, a man shouting about gold, lies, guns and joining in a chant.

We are ecstatic and sweating. Some people think industrial is neo-Nazi music. We are not fucking Nazis. We just love industrial music. My head is starting to ache and the club is starting to wind down. It's 2 a.m. and time to bail out and go home. We walk over to where Chris is leaning against a low wall, a lock of hair hanging across his forehead. I blush horribly when he looks at me, like he wants to kiss me again. Like I'm dessert, and he has a sweet tooth.

"Well, I'm glad we met. We gotta go. It's a long boring drive home," I say as he reaches for my hand. I smile shyly and rub his hand with my thumb.

"Let me walk you out," he says. My heart skips a beat as we slowly head to the coat check counter.

We all go to retrieve our coats, except Max who always wears his. Mandy leads us down the stairs and out the door into the cold night. We are exhilarated and buzzing with adrenaline. It was even better than we thought it would be. My friends walk ahead of Chris and me, laughing and screwing around on our way to the car. I am quietly happy. I have no idea what the hell to say to Chris. I sneak looks at his face. This is unbelievable.

"So, can I have your phone number too?" he asks, looking at the ground.

"Oh! Sure, if we can dig a pen out of somewhere in the car. I am sure we have one…" I respond, feeling like a big dope. I'm so afraid of messing this up, that it'll disappear into the night air like everything else always seems to.

He smiles and we continue walking in silence, enjoying the glitter of snow caught by the freezing wind. The streetlights make bright pools of light in the white snow, like spotlights. It looks like a perfect Christmas postcard out here.

We reach the car more quickly than should be possible. The walk to Medusa's seemed like miles. Mandy and the boys pile into the car. I knock on the roof, "Hey you guys! Help me! I need a pen!" They dive into the various piles of stuff within and shortly there are three hands poking out of the open door with pens and some index cards. I take them and yell my thanks into the car over the music now emanating from it. Using the roof as a desk, I write my name, phone number, and Mandy's address and phone number on the card.

"Here, this way if you don't hear from me, you can find out what's going on," I say, worried that I won't get messages and he'll think I'm blowing him off. "If you call my house, I'd be deader than dead, so call Mandy's and she'll get me in touch with you."

He leans me against the car gently and holds my head with one hand, "I look forward to talking to you and reading your letters," he says as he leans forward. Each second has slowed down to a crawl and my heart feels like it's going to jump out of my chest it is beating so hard and fast. I can't breathe! I am afraid. No male has ever been allowed to touch me like this or be this close to me and I hardly know this guy. But, there's something in his eyes that tells me he is okay. I feel it inside. He is safe enough for this. Safe enough for where I am right now with my friends nearby and watching, cheering me on silently. I catch a glimpse of Mandy peeking in the rear view mirror, watching us, and Max has the visor flipped down and is watching in that mirror. I feel really self-conscious with everyone looking at us and then…Chris slides in and kisses me so hard. I actually start sliding down a little. I feel all fizzy and stupid. Chris holds me up with a sly grin.

"Um, well, see you when I see you and I'll write you before that. Probably tomorrow, actually," I mutter, blushing and grinning despite myself. I kiss him quickly on the lips and fumble into the car. I feel absolutely drunk as hell and I haven't had a drop. We drive off waving and he waves back as he walks up the street. My friends are slugging me on the shoulder and hollering and whooping…

"Kiera's got a boyfriend! Kiera's got a boyfriend!…"

"Awww…shut it," I retort with a smile.

"We chatted a bit while you guys were on the floor," murmurs Max.

"Yeah? I saw you over there. So, what do you think?" I ask, searching my friend's face for any reservations.

"He seems really cool," responds Max. He turns in the seat so he can see me, "I'm happy for you Kiera. It's about time you had a date." He smiles and turns back around.

Andy is bouncing in his seat next to me like a really hyper muppet. "Dude! He totally kissed you! It's about time too. Sixteen and never been kissed — a total crime. Those lips were made for kissing!" he exclaims making a kissy face at me. I play slap at him and we laugh.

We all crack up and Mandy turns up the music. Siouxsie wails about following the footsteps of a rag doll dance and being entraced, being spellbound.

We drop the boys off at Max's, then we head to Mandy's to crash. I lay on the trundle bed, exhausted and waiting for sleep as Mandy snores softly. It's hard to register that after everything, I could have a night like this. I feel like a totally different person outside of this place. It seems like anything is possible when I get out and be in the world beyond this tiny sphere of bullcrap. The faint flicker returns to my chest, a tiny, glowing ball of possibility.

· Six ·

October 18, 1987
B.F.E. Indiana

I am shaken awake. My eyes are glued shut with mascara and eye liner. I blink a couple of times and groan. My head is still sore from being whacked by my father. Someone is in my face. Instinctively, I jerk away. "It's your Mom on the phone!" Mandy says, shoving the receiver into my hand. Shit.

"Hello?" I croak.

"Where the hell are you?" my mother shrieks in my ear.

"I'm at Mandy's, remember?" I respond, frowning at the receiver.

"Oh… Well, your father wants you home, so pull it together and come home right now," she barks.

"What's the big deal?" I ask, pulling on pants and throwing my stuff together .

"The garage needs to be cleaned out and he wants it done today," she tells me.

"But I just cleaned it last month," I say, in feeble protest.

"Don't you talk to me in that tone, Kiera. I work very hard to keep things nice between you and your father," she says.

"I see. So, is that why I have a concussion? Because of your hard work?" I snap, knowing full well as soon as the words fall out of my mouth that I will pay for it.

"You little shit! Get your ass home now! We will talk when you get here."

I hang up the phone and try not to cry on my way to the shower. Mandy pats my back and tells me it will be alright. It won't be. I am so screwed. I take off my clothes in the bathroom, and wash the gunk off my face and the gel out of my hair. I scrub hard in the hot water trying to remove this invisible mark. Some kind of stain only visible to predators; cruel people who need someone to terrorize and harm. No dice. I emerge to the smell of coffee and sausage.

"Thanks," I say, knowing what lies ahead.

"Don't mention it. So, what's up her ass?" asks Mandy.

"Um, her head because she is still married to that fucker," I rage. "Mostly, she wants her resident servant back."

Mandy rolls her eyes in frustration, "Why the hell doesn't Brett ever have to lift a finger around that house?"

"That would be the $10,000 question, wouldn't it?" I mutter as I stab a piece of sausage viciously with my fork. I consume the food as quickly as possible because I don't know when my next meal will be . I've already thrown all my crap into my bag, with one exception. I am leaving my records here.

"Can you keep these for me until the coast is clear?"

We head out to the car, "No problem," she responds.

We silently make our way to my house.

Morrissey sings about how that joke isn't funny anymore. How it's too close to home and too near the bone. Tears stream down my face as I look out the window. I feel so miserable that I really wish I had succeeded when I tried to kill myself. Those damn pills didn't stay down. I want this to end. It's one long nightmare, day after day. Pain and despair consume me and I can't seem to find a way out. They chip away at me every single day.

I wipe my face on my sleeve as we pull into the driveway of the house where I live. "See you tomorrow," I say, feeling like a big, fat liar. Nothing is guaranteed. Not around here.

"Hang on, Kiera. We've only got one more year, after this," Mandy tries to assure me.

"I've got all my claws dug in, and if that doesn't do it, I don't know what will," I reply extracting myself, and my stuff from her car.

"Think about Chris and all the fun we had, and how much more fun we are going to have," pleads Mandy. She knows I am close to the edge. "If he touches you again, we're going to take you away from there whether they like it or not. Forget their dumbass Christian ideals of 'keeping the family together.' I am not going to watch you get beaten up anymore," she sniffles, as two tears glide down her face like little jewels. She viciously wipes them away, and stares at the steering wheel.

"I appreciate the thought," I say trying to convince myself more than her that I have a chance at all of making it one more day. "I better hurry."

As if on cue, my mother sticks her head out the front door. "Get in here!"

"Bye," I say. I shut the car door and shuffle into the house, dawdling a bit and waving at Mandy who flies backwards out of the driveway, almost hitting the mailbox.

I am greeted by a sharp slap across my face. "Who told you that you could go to the hospital?" screeches my mother. She shakes her finger in my face like people do when they are scolding a dog. I roll my eyes and she draws back her hand. "Don't you roll your eyes at me," she snarls. I give her a dark, hate filled glare, and ignore the stinging pain. I drag myself inside and upstairs. I throw my bag into the closet. The tiny flicker in my chest has gone out and has been replaced with a weight so heavy, I can't breathe.

"WHERE THE HELL HAVE YOU BEEN?" my father yells as I exit my room to come downstairs and receive my orders.

"At Mandy's. I got permission, remember?" I whimper.

"GET YOUR WORTHLESS ASS OUTSIDE AND CLEAN THE GARAGE — NOW!!" he yells about four inches away from my face. I can smell the scotch on his breath. He smells like scotch, aftershave and newspapers. My stomach clenches and I want to throw up.

I slump the rest of the way downstairs and out to the garage. I wonder what Max and Andy are doing right now. Probably playing Frogger over at Mandy's while she does homework. I wonder if Chris will really call. I stuff these thoughts away. No sense in crying over spilled milk. I begin moving all the shelves and various stuff outside so that I can sweep the floor. This is the only way to clean the garage and not get clobbered. I am almost through moving stuff when he comes flying out the door.

"Did you tell anyone?" he grips my arm like a vise, "DID YOU TELL ANYONE ELSE YOU WORTHLESS LITTLE SHIT?"

"No! Please let go…you're hurting my arm," I plead. He throws my arm as if it were a bug that bit him. He turns around with an expression I've never seen before. I stay rooted to where I am standing as if I were chained. I'm afraid to move, breathe, or speak. He goes to the shelves outside and grabs something from it. He turns toward me with a cold, vacant expression, "You're going to pay for what you did. You didn't have our permission to go anywhere." He flicks the bull whip and it unravels with a sinister "snick" on the concrete floor.

"But I did, I asked Mom ahead of time and everything!" I say looking around wildly for an escape route. Standing with my back to a wall, he is in front of the open garage door. I am cornered.

He walks toward me smiling maliciously as he whirls the whip around his head. It comes around and makes a loud CRACK as it hits me right in the chest. I scramble to my right and try to think.

"You're so stupid. I'm not talking about you going to your friend's house. You shouldn't have gone to the hospital, Kiera. We can't afford that kind of expense," he snarls closing in on his quarry.

"You gave me a concussion, dad. You kicked me in the head," I say evenly, trying to reason with him.

He laughs and speaks so calmly, my flesh crawls. "I did no such thing, you little liar. You fell."

"I fell when you dropped me on the floor and then you kicked me in the head," I reply, still looking for a way out, a distraction. Anything.

CRACK!

The whip catches me right in the face and blood shoots all over the floor as the whip continues its journey. Inertia.

Adrenaline screams through me as I dodge around him and run out of the garage. Running as fast as I can toward the subdivision behind our house, I feel him right on my heels. I trip on a giant log in the well worn path. I catch myself on my hands before I smash face first into the log. Searing pain wraps around my throat. I am choking, gagging… gasping for air as I claw hopelessly at the leather wrapped around my neck. With the whip looped around my neck like a leash, he drags me back to the house. Dragged on the ground through the backyard, I thrash against him as hard as I can to free myself. His eyes gleam with sick satisfaction as we get closer to the house, and I black-out.

· Seven ·

I startle awake and look at the clock. It is 11 P.M. It has been over seven hours since my father attacked me. He has always been sadistic, but this is a whole new low. There is a PB&J sandwich sitting on my nightstand and a glass of water. There is also a note.

Kiera-
See what happens when I don't work to keep things nice between you and your dad? Be more careful next time.
— M

I have to figure out how what to do. Now. But what? And how? My head feels like it's on fire. I stifle my tears, eat my sandwich, and drink some water. I have to keep going. I can't give up. He isn't going to win. Someday, I will be free from him. Sadly, I know I also have to get away from my mother. I have to focus. I have to come up with a plan.

Eventually, pain and sadness overwhelm me and I am all cried out. I wince as I lay down to go to sleep. I check my alarm clock and lay on my back, trying not to move. I take a deep breath, then another. It feels cool and soothing. I slip into sleep and dream of being on my back on a bed and there is a man hurting me…intense burning pain between my legs like I have been slashed with a knife then everything goes black. I wake up in a cold sweat yet again. I rub the sore spot on my throat where the whip caught me. A tear leaks out of my eye, absorbed by my pillow. Afraid of what lies ahead, sleep visits me fitfully and I am on edge.

I can't believe that it is me I am looking at in the mirror the next day when I get up. I have a huge bruise across my throat and a gash across my face in addition to a bloody bump on my head. There is a black bruise that surrounds the gash made by the whip. I look like hell on a pogo stick. Brett comes in the bathroom, "Hey fuckface, get out of the way... JESUS KIERA!"

"Shhhh! Shut up!" I flap at him. If they see me, they'll keep me at home for sure.

"What happened to you? Mom and Dad said the shelves fell on you..." says Brett.

"No. Our father did this," I whisper as an ice cold fury awakens inside of me like a serpent in my chest.

"No way. The shelves fell on you, you just don't remember," fumbles Brett.

Furious, I look him directly in the eye and tell him, "No, he beat me with a whip and then strangled me with it." He looks away, turns, and thunders downstairs to go to school.

I snatch my bag from my room and head out.

"Kiera," says my mother from the door.

"What?" I snap, all my patience for her completely used up.

"Where are you going?" she asks in that fake sweet tone of voice that makes me want to slap her.

"Uh — to school, since today is Monday," I say, my voice dripping in sarcasm and rage. Steady girl, I think. I breathe through my nose and try to be calm.

"Watch it..." she snarls, advancing on me as if to slap me.

"No, *you* watch it. You pathetic excuse for a human, letting him do this to your *own daughter*," I say, disgust spilling from me easily like pus from an infected wound.

She glares at me and then draws her hand back to slap me. I catch her wrist and grip it tightly, "Don't ever try and do that again or you'll be sorry," I whisper an inch away from her face.

She sees the look in my eye and draws back, suddenly afraid.

I haul ass downstairs and out the door. I start walking up the street to meet Mandy. I don't know if I am being followed or not. I don't care anymore. The freezing cold makes the pain even worse, as I walk quickly toward the main road. I make it about halfway before Mandy comes zooming up in the Escort. She is instantly horrified when she sees me. "What did he do to your face?" she screams as she leans across and opens the passenger's side door for me.

"He decided that I was taking too long to sweep out the garage and that because I didn't have permission to go to the hospital, I deserved to be beaten with a bull whip that he keeps in the garage," I say tonelessly as I throw myself and my bag into the car. "Step on it, please. Mommy Dearest is after me to keep everything hush hush," I tell her, rolling my eyes.

"WHAT?" yells Mandy, throwing it in reverse, turning the car around. "Dude, Max and Andy are going to freak out. You look like you were beaten with a bat," she says.

"Well it definitely didn't tickle," I say, settling back into the seat. I'm starting to feel a tiny bit better just being in the car with Mandy. I tell her to stop at the convenience store for food.

"God Kiera, I'm so sorry. I just thought—I don't know what I thought," Mandy sobs, and pulls over next to an empty corn field. She leans her head on the steering wheel and just bawls. Tears run down my face.

"It's not your fault. Nobody can stop him. They never have," I sigh in resignation. "It's not your fault that my family is so fucked up."

"I know," she sniffs miserably. "But you would just think that your grandparents or somebody in your family would get of their asses and *do* something to get you out of there. It's insane! Someone needs to stop him!"

She's right. I am so pissed I can't see straight. I have no idea what I'm going to do, but I know I am done being their punching bag, maid and resident doormat. Being born into this family isn't my fault. I haven't done anything wrong and do not deserve to be tortured. It's too bad there is no way to hold my relatives' feet to the fire and force them to do right by me. One of these days, things will change. In one year, I graduate.

From the speakers, New Order sings, asking what do they get out of this, that they always try and always miss.

Mandy and I talk through different scenarios on what to do on our way to school. She pulls in the back parking lot and we trudge in, uncertain what is going to happen next. We're both worried.

"Promise that you won't let them lock me up in some psych ward," I say grabbing her shoulder, terrified of the repercussions of walking into my own school. When they see, someone will notice and ask questions and then…there will be consequences. Probably for me, less for my parents. That's how it works in right-wing fuck nut Indiana.

"If they even try it, we will have the story plastered in every newspaper in the region. Don't worry," says Mandy. I know she and the guys will do anything they can to protect me. I just don't know what they can actually do to stop Peter Graves.

We tromp into the school and are quickly greeted by Max and Andy. "Hey you guys….Kiera! WHAT THE FUCK?" exclaims Andy. Mrs. Starling minces over and begins shaking her finger at Andy for yelling obscenities in the hallway and is about to assign him with detention when she turns and sees me.

"Jesus!" she exclaims. "Kiera! Who did this to you? What happened to your throat?" She grabs my elbow and steers me toward the nearest faculty office. My friends trail behind us solemnly and scoot in before Mrs. Starling can protest.

"Kiera, I know this must be difficult, but you need to tell me what happened," she says standing in front of me and holding my shoulders.

I've been trying to tell you, I think as I sit with my mind racing a million miles an hour going over the various choices. The outcome for each one is a different ring of hell. There is no way for me to win in this predicament. It is very easy to predict the outcome of this. I'll tell. I'll get in trouble. I'll pay the price and he'll get off scot free. This is the way is has always been and apparently, always will be.

My friends peer anxiously at me over her left shoulder, giving me encouraging nods and Andy flashes a "thumbs up." I take a deep breath and look at the floor.

"It was my father," I tell her.

"Your father hit you?" Mrs. Starling asks me, her voice going up several octaves in the realization of what this meant. The Vice Principal of the middle school is a warped, abusive dick. She is an educator. This could be very complicated for her. I study my shoelaces and will myself not to start crying. I feel so hopeless and helpless. My heart sinks into my belly like I swallowed a stone.

"Yes. He beat me and strangled me with a bull whip," I say, staring at my shoes as if they are the key to my salvation.

"Mrs. Starling, he beats her up all the time," chimes in Mandy.

"We had to take her to the hospital on Saturday because he kicked her in the head and gave her a concussion," say Max and Andy in unison.

"WHAT?" shrieks Mrs. Starling despite her demeanor of always being calm and in control. "Well, I am going to call your mother…"

"She already knows and didn't do anything about it except probably help him carry me to my room," I say, choking back a flood of bitter tears.

"But…I…she," blusters Mrs. Starling, the horrific realization registering in her fluffy little head. I am surprised to see her concern lining her face "OK. We will figure this out. You three need to go to class and I am going to talk with the Principal."

Max folds his arms across his chest, "Lady, we're not going anywhere." My friends are clustered in front of the door and she has to get past them to get to the office. She realizes that she is outnumbered and that these kids are not going to budge without a bulldozer.

"Fine, you can stay here for now. I must insist that you return to your classes as soon as possible for your own educational benefit!" she demands as she pushes past them to the door and rushes down the hall toward the main office.

"We're not leaving you alone, Kiera," says Max coming over and giving me a gentle hug. I sniff and look up at him. He winces at seeing my wounds. "I don't get why that asshole does this to you."

"Neither do I. I have to figure out how to get through the next year," I mumble.

"We're going to help you," says Mandy coming over and sitting next to me on the desk where I am perched. She drapes her arm over my shoulder and hugs me. "You're my best friend and I'm not about to throw you to the wolves."

"Thanks," I say and the tears just erupt like Mauna Loa. I cover my face with my hands. It hurts to cry because it makes the cuts sting, and the bruise on my face is still really tender. It just makes me feel worse. We sit there huddled together as I am lost in a storm of tears. We wait in tense silence to hear the click of footsteps coming closer telling us that decisions have been made, for better or worse. The adults around here are more like ostriches than people. Everyone lives in denial of the horrible things that go on here and everywhere in the world. Most of these people will never leave this forsaken town. They are born here and they die here. They are not interested in what goes on "out there." It doesn't matter as long as their little bubble isn't ruptured.

Twenty minutes pass and we hear heavy footsteps in the hall that echo off the lockers and tile floor. The door opens and Mrs. Starling has returned with reinforcements: Mr. Wick, the school principal, and, to my shock and horror — Miss Fitch. They enter the room in a flurry and hurriedly close the door behind them, like they are keeping a vicious animal contained. Mr. Wick and Miss Fitch get a load of me and their mouths drop open like a couple of fish. They quickly recover, Mr. Wick straightening his tie and jacket as though the act of doing so would magically straighten out this situation.

"OK, Kiera...what happened to your face?" Miss Fitch asks gently as she comes over and pats my shoulder, her eyes full of concern. I recoil from her touch and glare at the adults. "I'm the high school's liaison with the police and Sheriff's department," she tells me, aware that I'm not happy with this latest development. My friends and I exchange a look of total disbelief at the rather extreme string of bad luck I seem to be having. The Universe seems to have a really warped sense of humor.

"I was clearing out the garage so I could sweep it out when my father came out and yelled at me for going to the hospital the day before to take care of the concussion he gave me after he kicked me in the head," I say pointing to the now healing bloody lump on my head. There is a sharp intake of breath and Mr. Wick shakes his head as if to purge it of the things he is hearing. "He picked up a bull whip that he keeps in the garage and told me that we couldn't afford the hospital bill, and that I was a liar about how I got the lump on my head. He said I fell. My mother tried to keep me home from school today and they told my brother that shelves fell on me, and that I don't remember how I ended up like this," the truth spills from my lips like poison. This truth is so ugly that even I have a hard time with it, but the fact remains — it happened to me. I want to make this violence stop. NOW.

"Why does he have a bull whip?" says Mrs. Starling, her eyes wide with fear.

"You'd have to ask him. I have no earthly idea," I respond with disgust. He's so twisted, it's anyone's guess what he's done with that thing.

"Alright, for now, is there somewhere else you can stay?" asks Mr. Wick turning to look at my friends who are standing in front of the door in a clump. They visibly relax. They were, like I was, afraid that I would be carted off somewhere against my will.

"Kiera can stay at my house any time. Mom always says that Kiera is family," volunteers Mandy.

"OK, I am going to drive you to your house right now so that you can get some of your things and then we will drop them off at Mandy's. We will get something more concretely figured out, in time, but for now I think this will do," Miss Fitch declares. "So, Mandy and Kiera…you two come with me. Max and Andy, you guys can go to class at this point. Now, everyone in this room, I do not want any of you discussing this situation or plan with anyone outside of this room right now. We need to keep Kiera safe," Miss Fitch says with a slight edge to her voice.

I could kiss her on the lips I am so relieved. Holy guacamole! I am actually getting help! It doesn't seem possible. I am feeling still very on my guard and skeptical, I have to admit. The chance of this staying quiet is so minimal it's ridiculous. No one stays out of other people's business when it comes to gossip. They only stay out of your business if you are screaming for help on their front lawn. Mandy grabs my hand for a second to letting me know she's with me, no matter what. We shuffle down the hallway toward the parking lot and wave over our shoulders at Max and Andy who are shuffling to class, whispering with their heads together. They wave back and we all set off.

It takes my mother a while to answer the door because she was still in bed, sleeping off last night's drunk. She rips open the door, "Can I help you?" she snarls, blinking like a possum in headlights in the hazy afternoon light. "Oh, Miss Fitch, I can explain...you see Kiera is really clumsy and she..."

"I am well aware of what the situation is, Mrs. Graves," interrupts Miss Fitch as we force our way past my mother who is in her robe, looking quite disheveled.

Mandy and I scoot upstairs while my mother and Miss Fitch continue their verbal sparring. I think my mother has just met her match. Mandy instinctively knows what to do. We grab two bags out of the closet and each start filling one. I get my stuff out of the bathroom and we finish in about three minutes. We run back downstairs, flying for the front door we almost make it out when my mother grabs the back of my jacket. I am jerked backwards like a puppet with strings attached to my back. I wrestle from her grip, agitated, angry and ready for whatever comes next. "Where do you think you're going, young lady?" she growls, knowing that it will be her ass on the line if I make my escape.

"None of your business," I respond. Mandy has come up behind me and is scratching her eye with her middle finger. I start to smile and then hold my breath. Laughing right now would be so inappropriate it's not funny.

Miss Fitch wrenches me from my mother's grasp and stands squarely between us. "Mrs. Graves, you have just given me all the evidence I need to take this child away from you. I suggest you and your husband reconsider your behavior immediately and seek counseling."

My mother lunges at her, "Who the hell do you think you are? WHO THE HELL DO YOU THINK YOU ARE?" She continues screaming as Mandy and I take off and get into Miss Fitch's car. We lock all the doors except the driver's side door. My heart is pounding and I feel like I am about to have a fit of the giggles. Mandy and I look at each other and then back at where my mother and Miss Fitch are having it out. "Go to HELL! She's MY daughter! You just wait until I call my husband! You'll never work in this town again!" My mother screams as she chases Miss Fitch down the sidewalk looking like a loon in her robe with her bed head hair, shaking her fists in fury.

"Call anyone you want! We have called the police and are filing a report against you and your husband!" Miss Fitch hollers back as she runs for the car. She slides in, locks her door and we fly backwards out of the driveway, like skeet out of a skeet shooter and zoom away. Mandy turns around in the backseat and gives my mother and the house the finger.

"Jesus Christ, Kiera! Why didn't you ever come to anyone with this before now?" exclaims Miss Fitch in disbelief of what just happened at the house of Graves.

"Because practically everyone in this town hates my guts, except for Mandy, her mom, Max and Andy," I reply.

"I don't hate you," she says sadly. She is just now figuring out the equation. I think she might have even figured out she is already a part of it. I've never seen anyone go up against my mother like that. She was totally fearless. I never thought I'd see the day, especially with this woman! Life can be so crazy. I hope she's ready for what's next. It's all very predictable, yet not. Just wait, you'll see. Some alpha male fuckwit at the police station will support my father and then the whole thing will fall apart. People say I am too cynical. I say I am just realistic. Nobody around here gives a flying one about what is happening anywhere in the world *unless it affects them.*

We drive to Mandy's and deposit my things in a closet in the basement for extra safe keeping. While I use the bathroom, Mandy makes a quick call to Chris to tell him not to send anything to my house and that we'll explain the whole story later. He will probably be very confused when he gets his messages after school, but it's very important that any info about my life doesn't end up in enemy hands or they will have more bargaining chips they could use for blackmailing me. I have to hide my journals really well so that Mommy Dearest won't read them for entertainment. We depart for school and realize that it is lunch time, so Miss Fitch takes us to Pizza Hut. Mandy and I get a veggie pizza and cokes. I feel like someone has run me through a clothes wringer eighteen billion times and then beaten me over the head with a bat for an hour. Mostly, I'm scared out of my mind, and I can't believe I have to trust *these* people. It's all so bizarre.

"How long has this been going on, Kiera?" asks Miss Fitch as we dive in to our lunch. I never actually got to eat the granola bar from the gas station, so I am dying of hunger.

"As long as I can remember. The reason I've never loved my father is because I've always been so afraid of him. He yells at anyone for anything and me for everything, even if I've been gone for two weeks and just got home," I say, through a mouthful of pizza.

"It's true. We dropped her off after we were at camp for two weeks and he met her in the driveway and was just screaming at her 'get your ass in the house right now and straighten it up before I knock your teeth down your throat.' Mom and I have always been terrified for Kiera and we try to help whenever we can," says Mandy. She takes a huge bite of pizza and wrestles with a long string of cheese.

"What about the rest of your family? Don't they know what's going on?" asks Miss Fitch, making the same assumptions that everyone else does. She is examining me as I answer, looking for any sign that I am lying. I have gotten used to grown ups treating me like this, but it doesn't suck any less.

"I have no idea how they couldn't be aware, since they have all witnessed his behavior. But they kind of live in a vacuum, so anything is possible," I reply in my usual sarcastic tone. "I gave up a long time ago, because trying to tell them when something is wrong is like talking to a frog. It never occurred to me to ask anyone at school. I mean, if your family isn't going to help you, who the hell is?"

"Plenty of people, Kiera," says Miss Fitch with a hint of steel in her voice.

She watches me wolf down pizza and I see it dawn on her, "Kiera, do they feed you regularly?" I cringe, and feel heat rising up to my ears. God I hate explaining this.

"Well, it's sort of hit-or-miss. If there is some chore that they want done and it takes too long and I miss lunch or dinner, too bad for me. This morning, I ran out of the house without breakfast because my mother was trying to make me stay home so that no one would see these bruises," I say, and I take a huge bite out of my third piece of pizza. I realize I am chowing down like a starved hyena, so I slow down.

"She had to eat lunch in the bathroom a couple weeks ago because her psycho mom didn't want her to take any breaks from raking their yard and then her dad beat the crap out of her for disobeying her mom," volunteers Mandy. I feel an uncomfortable twinge. It'd be nice if she'd use a little discretion, even if she's trying to help.

"What about your brother? Where is he while this is going on?" asks Miss Fitch, irritation at my relatives rising as she susses out the situation.

"Not sure. Probably playing basketball, riding his three-wheeler with his friends, or drinking and crashing cars," I say rolling my eyes. "Why don't you ask him? I'd be interested to know what he thinks about hearing me scream."

We finish lunch and Miss Fitch pays the bill. "Thanks, Miss Fitch," I say looking at my shoes. "Don't mention it, Kiera," she says, looking at me for a second like she wants to say something, but it passes.

We get back to the school, and the bell rings. I start to head for art class, but Miss Fitch wants me to go with her. Mandy looks at me quizzically and I shrug. She hesistates, then wanders down the hall to go to class looking back at me as I go the opposite direction with Miss Fitch. I'm totally annoyed that I'm missing art class, missing seeing Max and Andy. Now I'll be behind on my drawing. Growl.

I follow Miss Fitch wondering what we're doing. I break out into a cold sweat and feel panicky. I touch Miss Fitch's shoulder and stop her. "Where are we going and what's going to happen?" I ask her. My mouth is so dry, I can't believe any sound came out when I spoke.

"We are going to Mr. Wick's office to meet with your parents," she says, her jaw set.

I back away from her, crossing my arms over my chest. "Whose idea was this?" I ask, backing away from her.

"It's the law, Kiera. We have to do a mediation or we can't do anything for you," she says, cajoling me to continue walking with her. "I will be right there. Nothing is going to happen to you."

Ha. I look at my shoes and scuff them on the floor making small black marks. I've heard that before, my mother used to tell me she wouldn't let anything happen to me. That went so well. I am scared to death. He is in there and he knows that they know. This is a nightmare. He is going to tear me limb from limb the second he sees me. I'm shaking and feel really nauseous. We slowly make our way into the office waiting room where the secretary smiles and says, "They are ready for you, go on in."

We enter the room and my parents are sitting in chairs in front of the desk. They look at me with steely, strained smiles.

"Kiera, honey, now you don't remember because the shelves fell on you," begins my mother, a threat in her voice. *You must obey me, Kiera. Because I said so.*

"Then how do you explain this bruise across my throat where he strangled me with the whip?" I say, much to my surprise. My heart is pounding so hard I can hardly hear myself. I stand by the door, refusing to sit down.

"Brad, I am sure you can appreciate how important discipline is to a young girl Kiera's age," says in my father with a cheesy game show host grin as he addresses Mr. Wick. I am certain that because my father is an Assistant Principal at the middle school, he thinks that Mr. Wick is his ace in the hole. I am silently praying that Mr. Wick has bigger balls than it would appear.

"Yes, Peter, I am very aware of how important discipline is for *everyone* in their lives," says Mr. Wick lacing his fingers and leaning forward on the desk with a cool expression.

My father's face contorts in rage, "She is a liar. She lies to everyone about everything. SHE JUST CAN'T STOP LYING!!" His voice has reached the decibel level that he usually reserves for telling me what a pile of worthless shit I am. Mr. Wick and Miss Fitch are both taken aback and Miss Fitch actually scoots back against the windows.

Mr. Wick stands up at this point and calmly addresses my father, "Mr. Graves, you are so far out of line that I have no way to measure it. We have filed police reports about this incident and we are going to take *every* legal action necessary to ensure Kiera's safety. Now you may leave or I can have you escorted out." I had to shut my mouth because at some point during Mr. Wick's declaration, it dropped open. Miss Fitch has slowly inched over and pulled me toward the windows, behind the desk. Mr. Wick and my father stare each other down for what feels like an eternity. Her hands are sweaty and trembling. She steps in front of me as the frozen room suddenly thaws.

My father leans over and gets right in Mr. Wick's face, "You'll pay for this, Brad. No one tells me what to do. No one." He punctuates the last words by jabbing Mr. Wick in the chest with his finger.

"That is assault, Peter, and you are going to jail. Detective Jones!" yells Mr. Wick.

A man in uniform steps into the office and my mother looks around in panic.

"You have the right to remain silent. Everything you say can and will be held against you in a court of law…" the police officer reads my father his rights, handcuffing him as my father's face has turns an unnatural shade of beet red. He is swearing a blue streak and screaming murderous threats as two police officers haul him out of Principal Wick's office. It seems to all happen in slow motion. My mother is incoherent and clutching at them to stop them from taking him to jail. They are both yelling at me. I can't understand a thing they're screeching as I stand mutely in the corner watching it all play out. As my father is unceremoniously stuffed into a waiting police car, Mr. Wick details his account of events to an officer. It all feels like a dream. I shut my eyes for a moment and squeeze them tight. Then I open them. Nope. I am actually standing here watching my father get hauled off to jail for assaulting the principal of my high school! Now everyone knows I am telling the truth — that he is a psychotic sociopath. Asshole.

Mr. Wick comes back in after seeing the officers out, and looks at me from across his desk. "How did you know?" I ask.

"Peter is a very angry man who is bigger than me. I was not about to try to remove you from his home without the police at the ready," he says with a grim smile, looking at me over his glasses.

"I can't tell you how much I appreciate what you did," I say smiling back.

"Keep being one of our prized students, Kiera. That's all I need you to do," he replies and flops into his chair, exhausted. "Oh, your mother has been told that unless they both want to spend the night in jail that they need to stay at least 50 feet away from you for the next week while we get this sorted out," he tells me with an air of defiance. "My own parents were a couple of real pieces of work. I know what it's like trying to make a life for yourself when you've got a couple of tons of crud hanging onto you with everything they've got," he offers with a wink. "They won't get away with anything while I am still here, so you go on to your friends and relax for once," he smiles as he shoos me out of the office.

I am stunned. This is a Mr. Wick that I don't think anyone knew existed, especially me. Well, I guess that just proves that anything really *is* possible. So there! I am grinning as I step out of his office. I can't help it! I feel like I can breathe for the first time since I can remember. Mandy, Max and Andy are huddled in a corner in the front of the school office, waiting for me to emerge. They audibly gasp in relief when they see me come out grinning ear to ear. I run over and jump onto them, mashing them in a sloppy, sprawling hug. "Did you see what happened?" I ask, excited to share the news.

"We saw your mom getting read the riot act by those cops, but we just got here," Max tells me looking anxious and totally baffled.

"Mr. Wick *rules*," I tell them. "He totally stood up against my father and didn't fall for their bullshit. I am astounded at the apparent giant balls that he must possess, because my father actually threatened him. Big mistake! Mr. Wick had the police waiting, just in case, and they hauled Peter off to jail!" I giggle and jump up and down. My friends look at each other and me in complete shock and then join me in jumping up and down and whooping. The secretary gives us a dirty look and points to the door sternly. We smile at her, wave, and skip outside the front door for a momentary celebration.

Crap. I have just realized that next hour is English with Mrs. Starling. We are booking it to class because the bell is going to ring. They all have Worley for Bio and will get screwed. I slide into the room just as the bell rings. This is going to be one very long hour. Some of my classmates are staring at me and whispering behind their hands.

"Kelli, stop talking and turn around please," chirps Mrs. Starling, smiling at the class. I flip my hair over my face and slide down into my seat until my chin is nearly level with the desk. I want to disappear. I am bruised, tear-stained, and probably still a little bloody in spots since I haven't had time to look in a mirror, or think about anything. I scribble in my notebook as Mrs. Starling drones on about something or other. I vaguely hear her give a writing assignment, and remind us about an upcoming test. I scrawl the dates in my notebook. It's hard to imagine the future. Everything feels so far away, like there's an invisible curtain between me and the rest of the world.

After an agonizingly long hour of class, the bell finally rings and I fly down the hallway to Mandy's locker. My friends arrive breathlessly and we make our way through the throngs of students to the parking lot and pile into Mandy's Escort.

Andy leans between the seats and shoves a tape into the stereo, and Danny Elfman wails how about he isn't the same man he was before, and hasn't lost his perception.

We all sing along, "I haven't lost my protection…"

The boys bounce along with the music, the car groans in protest as we come to a stoplight. Mandy gives Andy a withering look to cut it out, he gives her a toothy grin and stops. She pulls into the driveway and we all pile out.

"So, what's it feel like to get out of prison?" Andy says smiling at me as he closes the car door.

"The best word I can come up with is exhilarating," I respond, with an exhausted half-smile.

We troop inside and immediately remove our shoes. Mandy's Mom is so cool about us hanging out, so we always as responsible as possible. We clean our messes up and try not to make any major ones. We grab some snacks and drinks on our way down to the basement. My head is buzzing. I still can't believe this is really happening! Some people know the truth, which makes me a little safer. So I guess airing some of my family's dirty little secrets is worth the embarrassment. I'll take being fodder for the rumor mill over no one knowing what goes on at Chez Graves.

My mom is probably bailing my father out right now. The cops here have already been acquainted with us with the devil-worshipping nonsense that ended with death threats. That whole mess coincided with Brett getting drunk, and wrecking mom's car last year. He didn't even do community service because my parents "hired a good lawyer". My parents didn't ground him, even though he's wrecked a total of three cars so far. I'm just glad he hasn't killed anyone — yet. That turd didn't fall very far from the asshole. I suspect it'd be a different situation altogether if they were white trash, instead of "upper middle-class" as our father likes to say.

Mandy slips a tape into the stereo and we all collapse onto the couch, chairs and floor. "So, what the bleeding hell happened today?" Andy squawks through a mouthful of chips.

Depeche Mode laments about pain, asking if it will be returned, singing about strange love.

Mandy and I take turns telling the boys about the events of the day. Talk about a jam packed, super crazy ride on the looney wagon. I get so tired of the whole thing sometimes. It gets so boring, but people can't fathom why I am the way I am if they have no idea what's happening. They just think I'm being bitchy. Miss Fitch is probably going to be singing a different tune after all this mess. I don't think she'd believe me if she hadn't seen it herself. It seems like even when people see with their own eyeballs what's going on, they don't believe it. I don't know what other evidence my relatives need, but I can't afford to live in denial. I really wish all this crap would just stop.

"WHAT?!" Max yells, jumping to his feet and flinging Cheetos all over the place. He paces over to the desk and back again with lightning speed, his hands clenched into fists. He is beyond upset. Mandy apparently just got to the strangling part.

I get up and go over to him, "Dude, listen, the good news is that I'm here and I'm okay and things are going to change now." Max throws his arms around me and shocks us all by breaking down and sobbing. I've gotten so used to the circumstances of my life, I forget how hard it is for my friends. I'm so accustomed to my family telling me to sit there and take it, I just do it. It's not even me most of the time. It's like it's all happening to someone else, because this can't possibly be my life. I am stunned by his emotional response. My always ultra cool and aloof friend lost his cool, and it's my fault. I hug Max really tight and tell him, "Don't you ever worry Max. I'm fine," Mandy and Andy both come over and join the huddle.

Andy slaps Max on the back and hoots, "Kiera is waaaay too stubborn to go and die on us. Besides, do you really think she'd let him win?"

"You make a good point there," sniffs Max smiling at me. "You're my little sister and I just can't imagine not having you around. I mean, I don't know where we're all going to end up with college and everything, but I know I want to be friends with you guys no matter what."

"I'll still kick your ass on my board when we're eighty-seven, don't worry," says Andy as he jumps on Max's back and they go flying around the room knocking things over and play wrestling. Eventually Max gets Andy in a headlock and Andy squeaks, "Uncle." Max never waits for Andy's face to turn red. He makes sure Andy can breathe.

"So how does this work?" Mandy asks turning to me. "Does Mom have to sign stuff or something?"

"I have no idea. They said the police are filling out paperwork and we'll take it from there. They don't make it easy. You know, the whole 'keep the family together' line of bullshit," I grumble. "I can't thank you guys enough for helping me out. I honestly feel like if I were to stay there, he would chop me into pieces one of these days," I shiver as a flash of a man standing over me goes through my head. Weird.

We all sit there discussing the different possibilities and scenarios until the phone rings.

"Hello?" Mandy answers, "Hi Mom. Yeah…yep. She's here now. OK. She's OK, I think. Yeah. You got it. Thanks Mom. I love you," she hangs up the phone and grins. "Word travels quick. She wanted to make sure you are OK, Kiera and that you have your stuff. I'll tell her later about the visit to your house to get it. She'll be just thrilled with that stunt your mom pulled," she snickers.

"Yeah, we're all so tickled with my drunk-ass mother's antics," I say, wanting to just drop the whole subject. I want to talk about the future, and where I want to be. "Where do you guys want to apply?" I ask looking around the room. Everybody is squirming and fidgetty. We need to get on the ball with thinking about this stuff. I just want to be somewhere warm and as far away from Indiana as I can get. Fuck cornfields and Bible-beating Jesus freaks. I'm done.

"I dunno. Maybe out West somewhere?" says Mandy, her legs propped up on the back of the couch as she bounces a green super ball off of the wall and catches it. She was originally thinking about N.Y.U. but she decided that the prospect of getting mugged was a little much and has been reconsidering her options.

"Screw California. I do not want to live where tectonic plates do the rumba every six months," quips Max.

"I'll second that!" says Andy at the same time as me. We laugh and he flings himself onto the couch next to Mandy and me.

"What about Arizona? It's sunny and they have some decent schools there," I offer.

"We'll have to go to the library and peruse those college ratings books and see what the deal is," says Mandy. "For now, we need to focus on keeping you breathing, and in one piece," she says, sitting up and whipping the super ball at Max.

The doorbell rings and we tense up looking at each other fearfully. "You guys stay here. I'll deal with this," says Mandy as she gets up and plods upstairs to see who is rapping at the door. Max stealthily follows her and monitors the goings on. Mandy is fierce, but she is tiny. Max is not tiny and can throw people a good distance if provoked. He thunders back down the stairs looking relieved and says, "You'll want to go up…"

"Kiiiiiiiiera! C'mere for a sec!" interrupts Mandy hollering down the stairs. I am puzzled. Max smiles at me and pats my back. I make a noise to question him and he flaps a hand at me impatiently, shooing me upstairs. I trudge up the stairs and blink like a mole who has surfaced from a hole into a sunny day. As my eyes adjust, I hear a boy's voice nearby, "Holy shit Kiera! What the hell happened?"

Chris is standing in the living room. Mandy grins and steps around me to return to the basement and the guys. "See you in a bit," she whispers, smiling widely at me as she disappears down the stairs.

"Chris! Hi! What are you doing here? I mean…" I bluster and blather.

"I got home from school and Mandy had left me this weird message. I just got in my car and drove straight here," Chris explains coming over to inspect my wounds. His face is tense and worried. His eyes darken when he looks at the ugly black and purple bruises spread across my neck. "Your father did this to you?" he says quietly.

"Yes," I reply looking at my shoes. I feel my face burning. I hate this. Even though I didn't do anything wrong, I feel bad. My eyes flood and I blink back the tears. Even when he isn't in the same room as me, my father has always made my life so goddamn difficult.

Chris gently touches my chin and lifts my face up his, which is full of concern and a shadow of steely anger. "I know we just met and everything, but there's something about you. I really like you, Kiera. I'm not going to be easy for anyone, including your father, to get rid of," he says with a grim smile that lets me know he's serious. His lips brush mine. A spark of electric current runs through me, energizing me. I feel his breath on my face and neck. I put my arms around his neck and, he responds by pulling me close. I feel his body pressed against mine. I am breathless in his arms, thinking about things I've never considered before. My aching, beaten body relaxes and I feel like I am melting into him like chocolate on a hot day. I hear raucous peals of laughter echoing up the stairs and reluctantly come back to reality.

"We should probably go down to the basement and join my friends, huh?" I say, feeling shy and embarrassed. I look up at Chris. He smiles at me and takes my hand, "Yeah, it would be the most polite thing to do. Besides, I want to hear the whole story," he says. Urgh. The whole ugly thing. All I know is– I'm not doing it. We tromp downstairs and flop on the couch that has been left conveniently vacant except for Mandy. She pats the space next to her and motions for me to sit by her.

"So…who wants to tell me about what's going on?" asks Chris looking around the room at my friends.

Robert Smith purrs from the stereo about all the faces and all the voices blurring.

I sit mutely squirming in my seat. I feel like I want to drop into a hole and disappear.

"I'll do it," says Mandy, taking a deep breath and rubbing her face with both hands. She relates the whole story to Chris, catching Max and Andy up on the details as well. I am grateful to not have to go through it again. It seems so surreal so much of the time. Is it possible that this really is my life? I really had to live through all of that today? Long, warped, crazy, incomprehensible day.

As Mandy details our lunch with Miss Fitch, Robert Smith wails from the stereo in the background about someone crying for a girl who died many years before. Everyone's jaws drop at the developments, and what the plan is so far.

Everyone, including me, is shocked that Miss Fitch is now an ally. I don't know if she has really changed her opinion of me, if the torture during class will end, or if she's just putting on a show. I don't think Mandy's Mom can really do much. My parents aren't about to let someone else have custody of me. That'd be like losing property. Not going to happen. No one understands my world. This veil of lies and abuse that separates me from the world is as strong as steel. I am screaming and no one can hear me.

The Cure sings about dreaming where all the other people dance.

It is a dream. I have to keep dreaming. I have to let myself believe that it is possible to have a life of my own or I will just shrivel up and die. I have to believe that this boy really does like me, that my friends are really my friends, and that, somehow, the adults who have my fate and future in their hands will find a way to help me get OUT of this dire situation at last. This kind of suffering just can't be my fate.

"So your mom is cool with Kiera staying here for a while?" Chris inquires, the concern clear in his voice. I can tell he trusts adults as much as I do.

"Oh yeah. She has been trying to Kiera out of that hell hole for a long time. She thinks her parents are..." Mandy hesitates and looks at me.

"Go ahead– anyone who has witnessed them in their full glory knows they are total..." "Assholes..." Mandy interrupts finishing both of our sentences. I swear the girl can read my mind.

"Max and I stay away from them altogether because we don't want to go to jail. Our parents would murder us if we pound on Peter Graves for smacking Kiera around and get hauled to the clink," volunteers Andy with a wicked smile that makes you think for a second that maybe he isn't all there.

"Trust me, if I ever see Peter anywhere by himself in the distant future, like after I've left this pathetic excuse of a town — he'll be one sorry motherfucker," intones Max, cracking his knuckles like a gangster in a movie.

"Thanks Max, but I wouldn't want you to waste your time and energy on him. He will get what he deserves one day. What comes around goes around," I say. I just want to crawl into bed. I am so tired I can hardly keep my eyes open.

"Hallelujah and amen to that!" Andy exclaims while flailing his arms around.

"Now don't start speaking in tongues," says Max shoving Andy lightly with an elbow.

Andy hisses like a cat and starts dancing around the room. He pulls Max's shirt over his head so that Max is temporarily disabled and takes off up the stairs. Max regains his composure and bolts up after Andy. We hear howling and loud thumping. Mandy and I are laughing so hard we are crying. The boys have plowed into something upstairs and it sounds like they have knocked over every pot and pan in the kitchen. There is a very loud thud and an audible, "Ow. Dude you're really squishing me". We all go up to see who and what is being maimed. Around the cabinets we see Max's butt sitting on Andy's head which is mashed against the green linoleum floor. His face is beet red and he is looking quite uncomfortable.

"Max, get off before he suffocates!" Mandy demands. "What the hell did you guys break?"

Max stands up, stretches, touches the ceiling and smiles, "Don't worry, no harm done."

"Not to you maybe. Geez you weigh as much as a baby elephant!" exclaims Andy, rubbing the linoleum imprint on his face. Max glares at him in false offense before breaking into a wide grin.

"OK, I'm sorry. I'm just kidding..." says Andy, holding up his hands in surrender, unwilling to do a second round of wrestling with Max.

"When will your mom get home?" I ask Mandy.

"Tonight she'll be late because of an important case they're doing tomorrow," responds Mandy with a roll of her vivid green eyes. "We need to eat some dinner. Hey, Chris — you staying for dinner?" adds Mandy. I am grateful for her suggestion. More time with this very cute boy is just what the doctor ordered.

"Yeah, sure," he says putting a hand on my waist. I flinch because I am not used to being touched like that. I'd love to get used to it. What I am used to is getting the shit knocked out of me. I much prefer to be touched nicely. And it is very nice being touched by Chris. Sheesh. I feel heat crawling into my face.

"OK. Everyone up for pizza?"

She receives a rousing "Yes!" from the boys who seem to never stop eating or growing.

"C'mon," she says grabbing my hand and dragging me into the kitchen, "We'll make the salad."

"Ewwwwwwww," we hear from Max and Andy who have flopped down on the living room floor and are introducing Chris to the Atari.

"Piss off! You don't have to have any!" yells Mandy right back. "You'd think a little roughage kills boys or makes their wieners fall off," she mutters in annoyance.

We finish making the salad in record time. Grabbing the phone book from a kitchen shelf, we go to the living room where the boys are playing a fierce round of Frogger. *poing*poing*poing*

"What do we want on the pizza?" Mandy asks, standing in front of the screen to get their undivided attention.

"I'm up for anything but anchovies," says Chris, making a face.

"How about sausage, mushroom and olive?" I suggest.

"Oooo! Yeah!" says Andy as he wrestles with the joystick, his eyes glued to the TV screen.

Mandy and I order the pizza and clear the large, dark, wooden kitchen table so we can sit and eat. There is quite a rumpus in the other room and we hear Andy holler, "No fair!" Chris comes and joins us in the kitchen.

"Those guys are *way* too competitive for me," he says as he comes over to stand near me. His dark hair falls into his face as he looks at me and smiles. My heart flutters in my chest. Wow. I try not to blush and fail miserably.

"Pizza should be here any second," says Mandy, looking for any excuse to leave the room. "I'll go wait by the door so it doesn't get cold," she glances at me and mouths "go on!"

"So, uh…what are your friends like?" I ask, pulling out a chair so I can sit down and steady myself. He makes me feel like I am made of Jell-o. It's really ridiculous, but I can't help it. *You* try staying cool when he's looking at you with *that* smile on *those* lips.

He flips his hair back and sits down next to me. I feel like I am having the best dream. This beautiful, sweet boy is talking to me. I'm used to being called a dog and a freak at school. No guy has ever given me the time of day. This is entirely new territory, and I wish I knew what I was doing the teeniest bit.

"My two best friends have been my friends since we were about five. We go to the Andrew's Academy and it's the kind of place where you have to figure out in a hurry who your friends are and who are *not*," he says. I can tell he's like me. Doesn't quite fit into a category, so he gets crap from people.

"No offense, but that's kinda everywhere," I say.

"Yeah, but this place is mainly a bunch of kids who have the best nannies and whose rich parents buy them everything. They are crappy parents and the kids turn out to be crappy people who do coke and get drunk every weekend, and buy their book reports or beat up nerds and steal theirs. It's really cutthroat," he says.

"So it's a private school," I looking at my shoes. I am so *not* a debutante. God, people around here think I'm a snob because I'm literate in more than one language and know how to spell properly. I don't eat trailer trash cuisine like SpaghettiOs. If I'm eating junk, it usually involves chocolate.

"Yeah. But, I'm not like them. I've watched my parents and I'm not like them either," Chris glowers and turns to look out the window. "My parents have money and I live really well, but I'm not some spoiled little shithead. I go to school with plenty of those," he says, turning toward me, searching my face with his green eyes. To trust or not to trust, to judge or not to judge. I know the worried expression on his face only too well. Usually, I am the one who has it. People see me as "weird" or "strange" and avoid me. The friends I have have been my friends since I can remember and no additions. The neighborhood kids have always been afraid of my family, not just me. They see how I'm treated and hear my parents yelling. I don't blame them for steering clear. It's rough to be treated so badly by the people who are supposed to love you *and* be shunned by everyone else, too.

I slide to the edge of my chair and lean over to him, "Chris, I don't think you're a shithead of any variety and if my friends did, they would have said so by now," I say with my special brand of sarcastic humor. "You're the first guy to ever...." I pause, totally embarrassed. Blabbermouth. "Mandy is the pretty one with the great personality. I'm the wall flower who holds people's coats or delivers messages. I've always just been sort of nothing in particular. I am invisible girl," I say with a painful laugh. "I think this is the most I've ever said to a guy besides Max or Andy, like...ever."

He laughs and shakes his head with a wide grin, "I can't believe nobody out here ever paid you any attention. Have you seen how long your legs are?" he gives me a look up and down, smiling a wicked smile. My face floods with heat as I squirm in his gaze. It has always been made clear to me, by everyone around me that I am not considered a "babe". I have been reminded on a daily basis how ugly, stupid, and worthless they all think I am. There has always been someone around to cut me down. I am not a blonde cheerleader princess who who gets nothing but love and support from her family and community. I am the reject.

This unexpected affection from this sweet boy is the best confusion I've ever experienced. Chris leans over and just touches my lips with his. I can smell his scent and feel his breath. He smells sweet and spicy, like a rare variety of cinnamon.

"Dinner!" hollers Mandy as the doorbell rings, announcing the arrival of the pizza. Chris and I separate to see if Mandy needs any help. Max and Andy clatter into the kitchen and thunk down at the table. I get up to help Mandy with salad, dressings and plates. The boys are ravenous and dive in to the food without so much as a nod. Mandy whacks Andy in the back of the head and demands, "Hey shitheads, how about a thank you?"

"Geez, sorry. THANK YOU MANDEEEEEEEEEEEE!" howls Andy madly as he grabs two slices of pizza and begins to devour them like a starving canine.

"Thanks," says Max, smiling as he reaches for the Italian dressing.

"Merci beaucoup," I say grinning at my best friend.

"You're off the hook, Kiera. You helped me with everything, it's just these boys who need to learn manners. Oh, thank you, Chris," she says sitting down in the chair that Chris has pulled out for her. She looks at me and twitches her eyebrow to let me know he just scored points with her. She and I are big on manners. That's why we usually go for who everyone else calls geeks. We think they rule. Smart and clean, with good manners and the ability to carry on a conversation that doesn't involve a ball, a puck, or punching people.

"You're very welcome and thanks for dinner. You are quite the hostess," says Chris as he sits down next to me again.

"So, Chris...your friends? We didn't meet anyone the other night and we are all so curious since you've met us," says Mandy. She really likes him, and doesn't want to make him feel like she's giving him the third degree. I can tell.

"My friend Victoria was with me that night, but she left early because her girlfriend dumped her. It was horrible. She told me to stay because she could see that I really wanted to meet you," Chris responds as he looks over at me with a warm smile. "She is a crack-up under normal circumstances, but at the moment she is pissed at the world. I've known her forever. She's the sister I always wanted," he says, a smile spreading across his face.

"So...dumped by her girlfriend? She's gay?" asks Andy trying to get up to speed.

"Wow, you're a quick one, Andy," snaps Mandy, rolling her eyes. Sometimes Andy blurts stuff out, and we all wish he'd stop talking. I try to catch his eye to get him to shut up.

"Yeah, she is. No problem with that, right?" he looks around the table at my friends daring them to say something stupid.

"No, hell no! I am just always interested in meeting pretty Bettys. Obviously, if she's not into guys, she'll be immune to my charms," says Andy with a goofy French accent like Inspector Clouseau.

We all laugh. Max rolls his eyes in mock disgust and shakes his head, "Dude, most girls are immune to *your* charms."

"Victoria is way cool. You guys will love her," says Chris visibly relaxing. "John has been my best friend since I don't know when. He is the smartest guy and knows everything about computers."

"Oooh!" Mandy exclaims. "Does he have a girlfriend?"

"Nope. He's unattached…" says Chris.

"Got a picture?" interrupts Mandy.

"Mandy loves geeks. The nerdier, the better," say Max and Andy in unison. They grin at each other and continue plowing through pizza.

Chris looks at me like, I-can't-believe-these-two-where-did-you-find-them? I shrug with a smile and continue eating my dinner. Mandy is bouncing off the walls with this discovery of a geek that has no girl-friend who she hasn't met, because intelligent life forms around here are few and far between. There are a couple, but after the one tight-assed jerk who dumped her for not being Catholic, she gave up on dating in this town. I've never even tried. I barely have the energy to do all the housework, yard work and homework — let alone juggle a boyfriend. This has been a piece of cake so far though. I guess we'll see how it goes. I admit I am suspicious that a boy this smart, cool and gorgeous doesn't have a girlfriend. Maybe he'll volunteer the info and I won't have to ask.

· Eight ·

October 19, 1987
B.F.E. Indiana

"So when was your last relationship?" Lucky me, all I have to do is wait for Mandy to ask and clear the air on the subject of Chris's last girlfriend.

Chris squirms in his chair, "Anyone need a drink?" He gets up, refills his glass from the kitchen tap, and returns to his chair. Awkward silence engulfs the room, but we wait. My friends and I are all interested in what the deal is. He looks at me for help, and I raise my eyebrow a smidge to let him know I'm listening too.

"Um....OK. About eight months ago, I got dumped by a girl I was dating for about a year. It turns out she only liked me for my parents' cars and bank accounts. She didn't really like me at all," he says looking at his shoes and turning beet red.

"What's her name?" says Mandy.

"Tamara," responds Chris.

"She sounds like a bitch," says Mandy, with a little more venom than most people would expect. Chris looks at me quizzically, shocked by Mandy's forthrightness.

"Mandy hates cheerleader poof balls who only care about the surface and she hates people who beat up nerds," I deadpan, proud of my friend. What she lacks in physical size, she makes up for with a huge vocabulary. She can reduce practically anyone into tears with her verbal lashings. She is only vicious when provoked, kind of like a cobra. "I should have known she was all wrong for me. John and Vic hated her from the first day," says Chris. Regret hangs on his words like a stubborn stain.

"Yeah, well…live and learn. Besides, everyone makes mistakes like that," says Max, avoiding eye contact with Mandy. I can tell he's thinking of when he had that crush on her.

I look at the clock on the wall and realize how late it is and that Mandy's mom isn't home yet. "Dude, where's your mom?" I ask Mandy.

"That's a good question," says Mandy following my gaze to the clock. She crosses the room to the phone and dials. "The machine picked up," she says frowning as she hangs up the receiver. Headlights reflect off a window in the living room as a car squeals into the driveway. A car door slams, and Mandy runs to the door. "Mom! We just tried to call. Is everything okay?"

"Where's Kiera?" Mrs. Goebel asks, rushing in and locking the door behind her. She grabs my arm and starts ushering me to her bedroom.

"No, whatever it is, tell me now," I say, stopping her dead in her tracks. My heart cranks back up to full throttle because I know whatever's coming has to be bad.

"We need to get you out of here," she says. "My boss told me everything that's going on. They can't stop your father with a piece of paper and he is really angry. Your parents stopped by my job tonight and made it clear that they are about to make your life a living hell. Like that would be a change. We need somewhere to put you until I can get things sorted out," she adds pacing the floor and glancing out the window fearfully. "There were people in my office, so they couldn't do much. But here in the middle of the night, I'm just don't know."

I do. She's right to be afraid. I should have known better than to think I could be safe. I should have known this would happen. Nothing in this world can stop Peter Graves. I run down the hall, grab my coat and backpack, heading out the back door before I can think of where to hide. I have to get out of here. I'm so angry, I can't contain it in my skinny, five feet eight inch frame. My breath shakes, and I shiver in the cold night air. I'm so afraid, I can't breathe. I stand, turning on the spot, trying to think. If I hesitate, it's going to cost everybody. I have to hurry.

"Kiera, wait!" Mandy and Max come running out of the house to where I am standing, paralyzed in fear. "Where are you going?"

"I don't know. I'm not about to stay here so he can beat up you guys or your mom. I'd just die if anything happens to any of you guys," I choke on the last word as fear overwhelms me. I'm crying so hard I can't see. I can hardly breathe. I hear my friends talking to me, but it all seems so far away. I am going over my options, but can't seem to find a good one. I have to decide quickly. I have to find one that works. My instincts scream to keep moving, to run, to hide. I have to go right now. There are arms around me and voices, "Kiera, you're going to be alright. We're here and we'll figure it out," my friends are saying to me, trying to persuade me to stay.

I shake my head, pushing them away from me. "I wish you could. I really do. But none of you can stop him. If jail doesn't stop him, nothing will. He's going to kill me if he finds me." I sniff and wipe my face on my sleeve, turning to leave.

"Kiera," says a voice nearby.

I freeze in my tracks, my insides turning to ice as I slowly turn to look at the man. It is my father, standing there smiling at me, beckoning me with his hand "You need to come home now." I lose all control and shake, convulsing like a trapped rodent.

"Miss Fitch said I should stay here," I barely whisper, my breath making puffy clouds in the freezing night air. I can't breathe. Shit. If I can't get out of this, I am dead. My feet seem to be encased in cement, and I am rooted on the spot.

"There has been a change of plan," he says lethally, coming over and clamping my arm in a death grip. His fingers dig into my flesh, searing pain shooting through my arm. I hear Mandy's mom arguing with my mother right behind me as he hauls me off like a sack of potatoes. It's all in slow motion, each second drags on forever. I am screaming and thrashing with everything I've got. I fight like an animal in a trap — screaming, kicking, and writhing. He tightens his grip and I hear a sickening crunch. I feel nothing. My entire being is concentrating on finding an escape route.

"SHE IS STAYING HERE! YOU CRAZY BITCH! THAT'S IT, I AM CALLING THE POLICE!" Mrs. Goebel and my mother are wrestling at the back door, nearly tearing the screen door right off its hinges.

"She is OUR daughter and we are taking her home. Those damn people have no right to interfere in family matters," I hear my mother snarl.

"IF YOUR HUSBAND IS KICKING YOUR DAUGHTER IN THE HEAD THEN THEY SURE AS HELL DO!" yells Mrs. Goebel, as she tries to shut the door on my mother, who slaps her across the face. The sound echoes across the yard in the freezing night air. Unknown to her, Mandy already has the police on the line and they are on their way. Max, Andy, and Chris barricade the gate to the front yard that my father is trying to drag me through. Peter Graves elbows Andy right in the chops and shoves Max roughly out of his way. Chris steps between my father and the gate. "You're not taking her anywhere." "Get out of my way you little punk," my father rages, shoving me through the gate with one hand and pushing Chris with the other. Chris lunges forward and punches him in the face. My father is bent forward for a moment. Chris staggers backwards, shaking his hand in pain. We all realize at the same time, I have been released from my father's grip. We look at each other, and they yell, "RUN!!" Like a starting pistol, their voices spur me into action and I take off. I only make it to the sidewalk before five cop cars come screeching up. I stop short, drop my backpack on the ground, and put my hands on my head. I am standing in the front yard, the headlights of three cops cars shining on me like a giant spotlight. I am out of breath and shaking like an epileptic. I wonder if they can hear my teeth chattering. I close my eyes, silently praying to myself that he isn't right behind me.

I hear cussing behind me as my father continues pursuit, "You little bitch. I'm going to make you pay for this."

The cop hears him and turns to tell him, "Sir, put your hands on your head and come out here where I can see you."

"Nonsense," says my father. "I am the assistant principal at the middle school and this is my daughter," he tells the officer, who is quickly losing patience. The officer unclicks the safety and points his gun at my father.

This particular police officer is the rare, but much appreciated, good kind of good ol' boy. He's country as hell and doesn't take shit from anybody. He isn't interested in who has what title; he is interested in getting down to brass tacks.

"Sir, I don't give a damn if you're the King of England. Put your hands on your head NOW," says the officer creeping toward him, weapon in hand. "I am telling you for the last time, PUT YOUR HANDS ON YOUR HEAD SIR." I hear a loud click that echoes in the cold air. I close my eyes and hold my breath.

My father, rendered helpless for the first time in his life, grudgingly obliges and mutters obscenities under his breath. "You got something to say?" says the officer angrily, which shuts my father up probably for the first time in his life. The officer holsters his weapon and handcuffs my father, who ends up face down in Mandy's front yard. Everything seems to speed up for a moment, as I stand, frozen in the front yard trying to catch my breath and form a coherent thought.

Max, Andy, Chris, Mandy and Mrs. Goebel are talking to various officers. It dawns on me that Chris must think I am a fucking loon. This is my family. A bunch of nutball criminals. So much for that one, I guess. Not exactly anyone's idea of a first date. I look around slowly to see what is going on. Mandy and her mom come out of the house accompanied by an officer and point at my father, "That's him right there!"

The very large police man walks over to my father and says, "Weren't you just bailed out?"

My father splutters from his prone position on the grass, "I have every right to take my daughter home..."

"Not if the school fears for her safety in your care. Since you have decided to disregard a court order, I will personally supervise this case," says the officer to my father, squatting down and leaning into his face.

"Is that a threat?" asks my father, struggling to roll over and sit up.

"No sir. That's a fact," says the massive wall of human being. He turns to me and says gently, "You're Kiera, aren't you?"

"Yes sir," I say, snuffling back tears. I'm so embarrassed. I have never talked to a police officer in my life and I avoid it for the obvious reason that if you are talking to an officer of the law, you have probably screwed up in some major way. In this case, I feel nothing but love toward this man. He is going to make my father play by the rules, which I guarantee has never happened before.

"I'm Sergeant Tidwell, I believe you are friends with my nephew?" he says with a warm smile. "You can take your hands off your head now, darlin'." We all relax. I knew Max had somebody or other in the police, but we'd never met, because like I said — if you're meeting cops, it's usually in circumstances like this.

Sergeant Tidwell is a little under six feet tall, and huge. He has an enormous handlebar moustache and is wearing a straw cowboy hat and beat up brown leather cowboy boots. I've never seen a man this big and broad, except on TV when the Bears game is on. He smiles at me to let me know he's on my side, and saunters over to where Max is still standing in suspended animation.

"Max! What in the hell happened here, boy?" asks Sergeant Tidwell in a southern drawl that sounds just like my Granddaddy. We all walk back into the house and officers take statements from everyone. Off in the dining room, I see Chris talking to an officer and looking grave. So gorgeous. I wish I could have gotten to know him better. Maybe we can be friends. I am in a daze. There is screaming coming from outside as my mother is handcuffed and my parents are stuffed into a couple of squad cars. I am mechanically going over everything from the weekend until right now. The officers are visibly shaken and angered by what has taken place.

"OK, Miss. We've got all the information we need. If you need anything, Sarge says that you are to call him directly. Here is his card." The young man who cornered Peter Graves hands me a business card with embossed gold writing on it. SERGEANT MILO TIDWELL. Boy, I sure would hate to ever get on then wrong side of this guy. He is sweet as can be, but I can tell he hunts criminals down to the ends of the earth and he's got a chip with my father's name on it now. He looks like a bulldog that is about to tear into a chew toy he is so mad.

"Thank you. Uh, can you tell me what is happening?" I feel timid around these officers, and don't want to interrupt, or worse — get on their nerves.

"We are taking your parents to jail. We are going to call the judge who saw your father earlier today and wake him up, which probably won't please him any more than the news we're about to deliver. Based on Sarge's recommendations, we are going to put them in jail for at least a couple of days for their complete disregard of a court order, disturbing the peace, being uncooperative with the administrators and counselors who are trying to ensure your safety," explains the young officer. I feel my body relax a little and breathe deeply. Tonight I will sleep so much better.

"Thank you, sir," I say as I get up and cross the room to gather with my friends and Mandy's mom.

Suddenly, I am aware of throbbing pain in my arm. It becomes intense. "Kiera, are you OK?" Mandy asks, worried and pale. "You just got really white. What's the deal?"

"I heard my arm crunch when he was trying to drag me through the back gate. I think he hurt me," I say. The room starts to spin, and I collapse onto a nearby chair. I am seeing stars.

Max runs out the door and talks quickly with his uncle. Sergeant Tidwell bursts into the room crosses to me. "Let me see what you've got here, young lady," he says gently as he touches my arm. I wince and gasp at the shot of searing pain that runs up my arm. My eyes tear and I am nauseous. "Come with me, we're going on a little trip," he says, his face concerned. He reassures me with a smile, and carefully helps me to his squad car. Everyone in the room is ready to go. "I can't fit all of you in my vehicle, so you all be careful driving over to the hospital," he says. "You'd better come with me too, Andy." Andy has blood trickling from his mouth, his jaw swelling spectacularly. Chris's hand has swollen and is turning fun shades of black and blue.

"I can't believe this," I mumble.

"I can. Your dad's a total dick, Kiera. It's not your fault your parents are completely insane," sneers Andy, holding a washcloth to his face. "The difference is that now the big lie is out in the open and they have nowhere to hide."

"That's true," I respond, focusing on not barfing all over the car. My body is so battered and worn out that I feel like I have been run over several times by a truck. My brain feels like someone is dribbling it against my skull like a basketball.

After what feels like an eternity, we pull up to the emergency room. Chris, Max, Mandy and her mom park Mrs. Goebel's Volvo wagon as

Andy and I get out of the squad car The automatic doors of the ER swoosh open as we enter, and the staff immediately take note of our escort. We get the express check-in since we are with the Sergeant. The doctor who is seeing us is the same doctor I had the last time we were here. He looks at me in surprise. "Weren't you just here a few days ago?" he says, looking over my should at Andy and Sarge .

"Yeah. It's my arm this time and the police are involved as you can see," I smile gratefully at Sergeant Tidwell who gently pats my shoulder. I wince.

"I bet the natives are restless, so I better go and head them off so that you aren't dealing with a pack of animals in here," says Sarge with a wink as he disappears down the corridor, his boots clunking loudly against the polished tile floor.

The doctor carefully examines my arm and set up x-rays to come to me. "We're not busy and you look like you've seen the business end of a steamroller," he says, shaking his head in disgust. He examines Andy and Chris, and scrawls orders for x-rays for them, too. We are quite the trio. Bruised, bleeding, defiant, and totally pissed off.

"I'm sorry about this you guys..." I begin, hanging my head.

"No, Kiera. You have nothing to be sorry for. Your parents are pathetic," says Andy. "I am glad we were able to do something about it for once in our lives. Max and I...and Mandy too, we are sick of you getting beat up all the time and nobody doing squat. Sarge is awesome. Your father won't be able to do anything to you or anybody else after this little ambush."

"I hope you're right. It seems like nothing ever works," I sigh, looking at the ceiling.

The radiology tech wheels in and Andy leaves, "I can't watch this." He knows it is going to hurt. I grit my teeth as the tech positions my arm. At least it's my left arm and I can still write and draw without any trouble. I always try to find the bright spot. It helps to keep me sane. Or at least something like it. I have to hold the pose while the tech takes the picture.

"OK, hold still, this'll just take a minute," she says. Then machine clicks and whirrs and I release the pose that is making me want to barf. "OK. Just one more. Hang in there," says the tech lightly patting my shoulder. "Okey-dokey. You're all set. Can you ask your red-headed friend to come in here?" she asks.

"Sure," I wander out and jerk my thumb over my shoulder as Andy looks up at me from a chair in the corridor.

"We can go home soon, Kiera. Hang on," he grips my shoulder as he hurries by. I nearly pass out from the pain in my arm, and gingerly sit in a chair.

Chris takes over Andy's chair as he waits for his turn to get checked out. "I only wish I'd hit the bastard hard enough to really mess him up," Chris grumbles to the floor.

I sit holding as still as I can. My body is in such pain and I don't want to cry. I feel so miserable. How could my mother *help* him attack me *and* my friends? My stomach surges at the thought. I try to focus on the wall opposite me. Just look at the wall. Nothing exists but the wall. The doctor comes down the hallway briskly.

"I have some good news and some bad news," he says with a grim smile. "The good news is that I have some pain medication for you and a note excusing you from school for a few days. The bad news is that your arm is fractured in a couple of places," he sighs, shaking his head. "I am going to have the nurse give you a dose of the pain meds now so you won't need any until tomorrow. You need to rest, relax, and give your body the time it needs to heal," he gently explains as he pats my shoulder so lightly that I barely feel it. I nod, barely coherent and totally numb.

"Is Mandy here? Is Mrs. Goebel here? I don't know how to get the prescription without my parents," I say, my voice shaking, a tear sliding down my cheek.

"I can help you with that. We have a pharmacy here that is still open. I'll have a chat with Mrs. Goebel, we'll get everything all squared away for you. Don't worry about a thing," he assures me before walking down the hall to take care of business.

"Thanks," I say hanging my head. I stare at my shoes and the floor. I feel like such a burden. I feel like I am such a fuck up with these god-awful people who are my parents. They are probably sitting in jail right now fuming and railing about what a horrid bitch their daughter is . Meanwhile, I'm scared, injured, and want my Mommy — but since she's the enemy, I can't have her.

The nurse comes and gives me two cups, one with a pill and one with water. "This will help, honey. You've got a lot of damage in there," she says with a bland smile. How weird. I take the pill, pop it in my mouth and gulp down the water. My mouth is dry and I realize how parched I am. I want to go to bed.

"They will make you a little sleepy, so don't worry if you start feeling groggy," she says, handing paperwork to Chris and Andy. "The doctor and Mrs. Goebel are getting your prescription now."

I feel like such a parasite, but I have no money of my own, so what am I supposed to do? The sound of heavy boots on the tile floor gets my attention. I see Mandy coming down the hallway toward me. She looks worried and really angry.

"Kiera? Are you OK? Did they give you something for the pain yet? Nurse? Is she OK? Are you doing a cast?" she fires one question after another.

"He fractured my arm in two places, which hurts like hell. Other than that I'm peachy," I tell her with a half-hearted attempt at humor.

"Where's Andy?" she says looking around.

Hearing her voice, Andy pops his head from around the curtain, "Fancy meeting a girl like you in a place like this?" he says, imitating Groucho Marx.

Mandy smiles, "So what's the deal with your peanut head?"

"He thumped me pretty good, so they are giving me some happy pills like Kiera, but just for a couple of days. I am to stay in bed and do nothing. Concussions blow, dude. Luckily, my jaw is fine, just a little bruised," he says flopping down into a chair next to me and wincing. "Ooh. I'd better be a little more chill," he observes aloud.

"This I'll have to take pictures of," says Mandy. "Andy hasn't been still since conception!"

I smile weakly and am starting to feel funky. "The pain stuff is kicking in I think. I feel really weird. Can they do my cast now?" I murmur.

I am ushered to a room that is for the specific purpose of making and cutting off casts. The doctor has to "manipulate" my arm before they set it and put on the cast. The last thing I remember is him gripping my arm and pulling.

I wake up from unsettling dreams where there is a dark man chasing me. It is night and raining, and I am running as hard and fast as I can, but he's still behind me…relentlessly pursuing me like a bloodhound. I hear his breath in my ear and I scream, but nothing comes out.

I am covered in cold sweat and my body feels like I have been run over by a Mack truck. My tongue feels like it has been replaced by a piece of carpet. I slowly look around. I am in Mandy's room. She stirs and rolls over.

"Kiera? Are you OK?" She leans down, looking at my face in the dim light of very early morning. She's sleepy and her heart-shaped face is pale.

I try to talk and nothing comes out. I point to my throat and try to swallow.

"You need something to drink? Water?" she asks, reaching for the light on the nightstand.

I nod. She climbs over me on the pull out bed and wanders out to oblige my request. I struggle with my new cast and try to sit up. I feel like there are weights on my arms and legs. Mandy comes scurrying back into the room and hands me a glass of water. I mouth my thanks and drink. The cool water soothes my aching throat. "Thanks," I croak.

"No problem. How are you feeling?" she whispers, worry furrowing her brow.

I stop chugging the water for a moment, "Like I've been run over several times by a bus." My voice sounds like a frog or an old woman who has been smoking for a few decades. I try to clear my throat.

"Well, it's no wonder. You've gotten the crap beaten out of you and the fucker broke your goddamn arm. You passed out when they were putting the cast on," Mandy says as her eyes fill with tears.

"Oh my god this sucks…" I mutter. My throat is ragged and raw. I swallow painfully.

She wipes angry tears from her eyes and flops down onto her bed. "It's so weird that you come from that fucked up family. It's like you inherited every bit of good that either parent had hidden in their genes, because it sure as hell bypassed them," she fumes.

"Tell me about it," I whisper.

"Well, Mom, Chris and I came up with a plan. I think you'll be pleased. Right now, we need to get some more sleep. It's like 5 a.m.," she yawns, rolling over to check on me.

"I couldn't swallow. It's better now," I whisper.

"Good. If you need anything, just give me a good poke," she says snuggling back under the covers. "'Night, Kiera."

Slowly, I lower myself to lie down and go to sleep. Pain and fatigue overwhelm me, and I'm instantly swallowed into unconsciousness. Darkness takes me and I am running. The dark man is here again. I run into an alley and hide behind a box. There is a door and I go through...

· Nine ·

"Kiera…Kiera…" a voice softly calls my name and someone lightly shakes me from my slumber. I open my eyes and see a blur over me. I still feel like total hell. I blink, trying to focus.

The blur sweetly asks, "Kiera? Are you hungry at all?" It's Mandy. She puts her arms around me, helping me as I struggle to sit up.

I try to answer and make no sound. I reach for the half empty glass and hold up my index finger telling her to hang on a sec. I swallow some water and attempt to clear my throat, which is so raw it feels like someone sanded it while I was sleeping. It hurts like hell. Why does my throat hurt so much?

"Yeah, I know I should eat something," I whisper. "Why is my throat so messed up?" I whisper in frustration.

"When your psychofuck father was dragging you off, you were fighting tooth and nail and screaming like I've never heard in my life," she says.

"Oh," I mouth silently. We sit in silence for a moment while I register this information. I was really fighting hard. That must be why I feel so shitty. It feels like it was all something horrible I saw on TV. I know it happened, but it just can't be my life. I slowly stand up with Mandy's assistance so that I don't get dizzy, fall over, and break something else. I get some clothes on, which is sort of challenging with my new cast. I can't fit it through a t-shirt very well, so it looks like I'll have to wear button up shirts for a while.

I fumble into the hall to the kitchen and flop down into a chair, when I am startled by a male voice softly calling my name. Chris is here. Wait a sec. What day is it?

"Her voice is gone," Mandy tells Chris as she piles a plate with sausage and hash browns. She brings me the plate and a cup of tea. Earl Grey. My favorite. Have I mentioned how much I love Mandy? She sees my confusion at Chris still being here and takes a minute to explain, "Chris stayed over on the couch in the basement after talking with his parents last night, because we have a plan."

"Don't try to talk. But, it's going to be OK," he reassures me, a look of concern shadowing his face. He comes over to gently touch my shoulder. I look at them both, completely baffled.

"What about your parents? What about school?" I whisper in a panic.

"I called my parents last night and told them everything. They can be pretty cool sometimes. We want you to come and stay with us for a couple days so that you can relax," he says, his beautiful green eyes hopeful and pleading with me to say yes. This whole thing is so crazy. I feel like I'm running out of options, but I don't have much time to think anything over.

"OK," I whisper. "Are you sure?"

"Absolutely. I don't want you to be here alone when Mandy goes to school," Chris says, he and Mandy exchanging a dark, angry glance.

"Good point," I whisper.

I start in on breakfast and start feeling a little better. I know I need more pain meds, but I want to be awake for a bit before succumbing to sleep and returning to the chase. The dark man and the chase will have to wait. I eat quietly while Mandy and Chris watch TV in the living room. I finish eating, rinse my dishes, and put them into the dishwasher. As I shuffle off to take a shower, Mandy catches up with me in the hall.

"Hey, I'm going to sit outside the door so that if you need help, you can throw something at me and I'll come give you a hand," she quips.

"Actually, I could use an arm and a hand…" I joke. "How the hell do I take a shower with this thing anyway?"

We assemble a sort of shower cap for my cast with a trash bag and rubber band. I am irritated, frustrated, and fed up with my family. If my grandparents would just step in on my behalf, instead of always standing by their son, I wouldn't be in this predicament.

I climb into the powder blue tub and let the hot water rush over my face and head, trying to let it dissolve my anger and frustration. I think I would shrivel down to nothing if I waited for *that* to happen. My eyes stinging with shampoo, I struggle to wash myself with one hand. It takes forever, and I'm not thrilled with this new set of difficulties. Finally rinsing the last bit of soap off my beaten body, I turn off the water. Drying myself off, I get a load of my reflection in the full length mirror. I look awful. Covered with black, blue, and greenish-yellow bruises, I look like I've been creamed by a Mack truck. It's amazing that the damage wasn't worse, but I'm stunned by my ragged reflection. I've always been thin, but am so skinny at this point — you can count my bones. I look more birdlike than human. I don't recognize myself anymore. Shaking off the overwhelming shame, I escape the bathroom mirrors as I fumble into the hall where Mandy is playing solitaire on the floor. She follows me into her room while I get dressed. I'm going to be with Chris for several days and I have no idea how I'm going to manage hygiene while I'm there. I guess he'll have to get used to it if I start to smell because I am not taking a shower with him outside the door. No way Jose. I'm open-minded, not an exhibitionist. I guess this is where my "Midwestern values" kick in. The other concern is — the last thing I need is to fall and break something else, so I guess I'll just be super stinky girl.

"Chris is a really good guy. You know I wouldn't send you off with some total freak," says Mandy with a serious, yet worried expression.

I nod. "I will feel better for a minute if they don't know where I am," I whisper. "I don't want to be drugged, out of it, and have to fight my asshole father again." I am furious that I haven't heard from any of my relatives. I guess I should be used to it by now, but it really pisses me off that none of them bothered to see if I'm okay — or not.

"Well, from what I understand, your parents are still in jail," says Mandy with a wicked grin.

"Holy shit," I mouth. Right now it seems like there isn't anywhere far enough away from them for me to be safe. When they do finally resurface, they will likely take out their displeasure on me with a vengeance. That seems to be the only thing I can definitely count on.

"If they touch a hair on your head, Sarge is going to make them pay through the nose. He and Mom had a long talk," she laughs. "Chris's parents are pressing charges, too. Against both of them, not just Peter. They are fucking pissed. Your parents messed with the wrong kid and the Sullivans are out for blood.

"I should be so lucky," I whisper. "Oh god, do you know if the Sullivans are mad at me?" I know technically it isn't my fault, but I feel so responsible. I feel like I'm always apologizing to someone for something that my parents or brother has done. Even though it isn't my fault, people seem to think that I have some kind of magical control over them because we're related. Not so. But explain that to everyone else.

"Well, what Chris told me is that they hired a lawyer and they are going after your father in criminal and civil court," Mandy says, clearly enjoying the fate that my parents are being served.

"Holy crap," I whisper because my throat is still so ragged. "He is going to be furious. They deserve everything they get though."

"That's for sure," Mandy agrees. "Mr. and Mrs. Sullivan have more money than anyone in this town has ever seen" my friend giggles. "Their lawyer is going to tear whoever represents your parents a new butthole."

I snicker a little, but feel so embarrassed and ashamed of my family. I finally meet a cute guy and then everything hits the fan and splatters. What his parents must think of me? I wish I could just be someone else sometimes.

I'm finally dressed after some flailing and swearing while trying to button Mandy's shirt that she's letting me borrow. I get my stuff packed up and am ready to go. We go out to collect Chris so that he and I can hit the road. I am excited to escape this miserable town and my insane parents.

"Chris has your meds and the instructions. We figured if he keeps track, then you can't forget and O.D. by accident," Mandy explains.

"Probably a good idea," I nod. "That stuff makes me really loopy. I've totally lost track of time already," I whisper.

Mandy sees us out to Chris's car, a forest green Volvo. She hugs me gingerly and we say good bye. It's weird going to Chicago without her. Granted, I don't think I'll be doing anything fun, but it's still weird. Chris and I get in the car and head out of cowtown.

"Are you up for some tunes?" asks Chris, popping in a cassette at a low volume. "I'm really glad I could do something to help. I was so goddamn mad last night. I can't believe your family."

"Yeah, it's a mess. I'm sorry you were here to witness this," I try to say over the sound of the car. "I hope you're feeling better. I'm so sorry about everything. Thanks for saving my ass."

"It's not your fault, Kiera. Insane people do crazy stuff. We'll go hang out, watch movies and order take out. It'll be fun. If you need anything, you just say the word," he says, glancing at me. Oh my god, those eyes.

"So you're not afraid of me because of what happened?" I hoarsely croak, looking at my shoes, a hot flush of humiliation burning my face. "I figured you'd run away screaming after last night. And, I wouldn't blame you."

"It's not your fault that your family should be in a psych ward, Kiera," Chris tells me. "I haven't even had a chance to really get to know you and your friends. I'm not about to let a little thing like psychotic parents stop me," he grins, trying to make light of the situation.

"Most people don't want to deal with me because I'm not the happiest person in the world," I tell Chris, searching his face for a reaction.

"Who would be if they had to deal with the same stuff you're dealing with? Umm…*nobody*!" Chris responds. "I'm hoping I can con-tribute to reasons for you to be happier," he says, with a wicked smile.

He seems to be sincere and thoughtful. Cute, smart and really super nice? All in one guy? And he wants to hang out with me? I must be taking some good drugs. He turns up the stereo just enough to hear it better over the bumping of the toll road, Depeche Mode croons how the little girl can drive anywhere, do what she wants, and they don't care.

I feel like I am in a dream. We drive along the highway, listening to "Music for the Masses" by Depeche Mode. I am exhausted and beaten up in every sense. Chris is finally relaxing a little since the scene last night. I think he's the cat's meow. We wind through overpasses and underpasses on the long asphalt serpent. If you look straight down out of the window, it looks almost like a conveyor belt running beneath the car. I drift in and out of consciousness as the engine lulls me into a drowsy haze. Chris smiles at me, "You can lean on my shoulder if you want to. I don't care if you drool on me," he laughs.

I smile groggily and drift off again. I hope this is really who he is. There are people who seem so normal that are walking nightmares, and heaven knows, I've had more than my share of dealing with that *particular* brand of weird shit just from being in my family. I want only kind and sane people to enter my life from here on out. Just because I was born into a nightmare, doesn't mean it has to stay that way.

I am roused awake by the car shutting off. We have pulled into a garage that is behind a huge, limestone house. I blink and try to stretch without causing myself pain. Chris comes around and opens the door for me. Chivalry isn't completely dead! It makes me smile that this really masculine, punk, guy is so romantic and gentlemanly. He carries my bag for me, too.

"Well, here is Chez Sullivan," Chris says sheepishly, opening the door. I desperately try not to stand there like a gaping idiot. I shut my mouth and slowly make my way up the few steps and into the massive house. I have never *seen*, let alone been inside of, a house this big and gorgeous. We walk through the giant, gourmet kitchen to the stairs. I have never seen a kitchen this enormous in my life. This room is bigger than the living room and kitchen combined at my house. It has *two* ovens, a gigantic restaurant-type stove, a massive butcher block island, and a huge refrigerator that hums in greeting as we cross through to a hallway. The hardwood floors gleam and the banister glows. Everything is spotless. The high ceilings are framed by crown molding and the gleaming windows line up like long, tall eyes, peering into the bleak Chicago evening.

I have to keep closing my mouth, because it keeps dropping open in awe of this absolutely amazing house. We ascend the stairs to the second floor with more stairs to go. Chris offers to carry me, but I decline. I feel like crap, but I am not up for playing the damsel in distress to the hilt. That is not my style. I ask for help if and *only* if I actually need it. As we walk around to the third floor staircase, I see a painting that catches my attention — my jaw hits the floor and bounces a few times.

"Chris?" I whisper, "Is this…" I stammer and swallow, "Is this a Van Gogh?"

"Uh…yeah," he blushes and fidgets, scuffing his feet on the worn hardwood floor. "My dad got that for my mom for their tenth anniversary or something. I'd never have a party here because if anyone messed it up, I would be in deep trouble," he says.

"Uh, yeah, no kidding!" I whisper, my eyes popping almost out of my head.

"Yeah, I mean, I agree…it's just…" he hesitates and shakes his hair out of his eyes, "I wish my parents wouldn't always be so showy about their money. It'd be cooler if they were more generous toward people," he says. "That's all."

"Well, most people wouldn't mind having problems like that," I whisper, rolling my eyes. Oh the drama of the well-to-do.

We ascend the final staircase and enter his living space. It's like an apartment, but it's so cool that I feel way out of my element. The whole floor has been made into one large room, divided by an old brick wall. Directly in front of us, there is an entertainment center surrounded by large, purple velvet couches and red throw pillows. There is an enormous Bauhaus poster on the wall behind the entertainment center that takes up a tad of the space on the wall in this open, high-ceilinged room. To my left is a kitchen with a bar and stools. There is also a large, wooden table and chairs sort of floating near the kitchen and bar area. There are photos and sketch pads strewn across the table. At the end of the room are two huge windows with black velvet draped on either side, like sentinels guarding an entrance. On the other side of the wall is his bedroom. I assume there is a bathroom somewhere, but I don't plan on asking until I need it.

"So, what do you think?" Chris says spreading his arms and gesturing around like a game show model.

"It's incredible," I whisper, still taking it all in. "Your parents let you live up here like this?" I say, stunned at his gigantic, ultra-cool living quarters.

"They prefer me to be out of sight, because then I am also out of mind," he says, disappointment clouding his beautiful face.

"Well, that sucks, but I have to say, I'd rather be ignored than have people beating the daylights out of me all the time," I say quietly as I shuffle toward his bed. I'm dying for a nap.

"Can't imagine why you feel like that!" he retorts sarcastically, bringing my bag into his bedroom. I collapse onto his bed, a huge, king-sized, carved wooden structure with dark red velvet curtains hanging around the bed that can be drawn. The carvings look like Celtic knotwork and run through the whole thing. I am amazed at this room and his sweetness. Most rich boys are real shitheads. He doesn't act at all like these frat boy types, or my brother's friends. It's like he's a dork who doesn't realize how gorgeous he is. How weird.

"You need to eat and take your meds," he says like a little mother hen.

"OK mommy," I say, laughing.

"If you weren't in bad shape, I would kick your ass," he says with a wicked grin. "But for now…" and he grabs my leg and starts untying my boot. I am flailing weakly and laughing.

"Don't you dare tickle me!" I squeal, kicking at him.

"Re-lax. I am not going to tickle you. Keep that up and you'll hurt yourself, though," he says. He slides my boots off my feet and I notice he, too, is sock-footed. "My parents prefer to not have a herd of elephants overhead and I don't mind because then they don't bug me," he shrugs.

"Got it," I respond, yawning.

"So, what do you want for dinner?" he asks while walking to retrieve what appears to be a basket.

"Something super normal because I feel awful," I moan. Always nice to be in pain and really nauseous around a brand new boyfriend. This whole situation is beyond me.

We peruse his basket full of menus and choose a steakhouse that he and his family apparently eat from all the time. He phones in the order and then sits near me on the bed.

"OK, what movies do you like?" he asks quietly as he strokes my hair.

"I couldn't care less as long as it's not horror. My dreams suck bad enough," I say. I try to be easy to please and not high maintenance. I hate being around picky-ass, bitchy-ass people who won't eat anything but macaroni and cheese or hamburgers. Today I am eating super normal so I don't blow chunks all over Chris's velvet couch or bed spread. If I was feeling healthy, I'd be up for just about anything. I figure being open-minded includes food, too. As Chris reels off a list of movies he owns, I find myself falling asleep. I must be really ill. I am lying on the bed of gorgeous boy who is taking care of *me* and I have no energy to spare for thinking of things to do with him, and to him.

"Just pick something funny and I'll love it," I say with a sleepy smile.

"Have you seen 'Desperately Seeking Susan'?" Chris asks from the other room, as a handful of videos tumble onto him and the floor.

"We keep meaning to rent that, but haven't yet. Is it good?"

"It's good enough to be brain candy for an invalid," he says smiling. "I'm going to go downstairs and wait for our delivery. The bathroom is through the door to the right of the kitchen if you need it," he informs me.

"Cool," I murmur in an exhausted haze.

"I'll be right back," he says as he heads downstairs to get our food.

"Hey, Chris?" I call out, my voice breaking.

He pops his head around the corner, "Yeeeeees?"

"Thanks," I croak.

"You're welcome, Kiera," he says seriously. "I'll be right back."

I hear him thumping downstairs and decide to haul myself into the loo for a pee while he's gone. I'm trying to keep the bodily functions to myself as much as possible. It ruins the romance when you fart and belch in front of your beau. Things happen, but I try to be a lady. It's a little something my Grandma taught me. I stumble to the door and am again, floored. The giant bathroom has a shower *and* a claw-footed tub. It is all blue, gold, and white with classic ceramic fixtures. I've never seen a really beautiful bathroom. You know, I bet having money beats the hell out of being poor. It's a different set of problems than the ones I have now. I hope at some point, I get to find out what having that particular set of problems is like. I lock the door and pee. After scrubbing my hands, I slink back to the bed just as Chris thunders upstairs with our meal. The smell makes my stomach growl. No turning green and wanting to hurl at the smell of food. Always good.

"Kiera?" Chris calls to me as he unloads two bags onto the coffee table in front of his TV.

"Yep? I'm coming, I'm coming…" I respond shuffling over to meet him.

"Dude, no way am I getting food on this couch," I say as I slide onto the floor to sit cross-legged in front of the coffee table.

Chris loads the tape into the VCR and we dig into our salads. I begin to feel more relaxed by the minute, which speaks volumes about Chris. If Chris was a total wanker, I would have sensed it by now. My bullshit detector is pretty sensitive. I suddenly realize how hungry I am and snarf down my salad like a starving giraffe. This movie is the perfect choice, and I start to relax.

"Have I already said 'thank you' for everything you're doing for me?" I ask smiling at him.

"I think you've mentioned something like that, yeah," he replies with a wink. "You need to hurry up and finish so you can take your meds," he says, like an overbearing nanny.

"I know, I know," I concede. "All things considered, things are actually starting to look up and it's mostly because of you," I say before digging into my baked potato.

"Anything for a friend," he says seriously, looking at me from under his long, thick lashes.

My heart does a little rumba and I blush a little. If you could see this guy, you would understand. I look like something out of a horror movie with my cast and bruises and he is undeterred.

We eat our steak and potato dinners until we are stuffed. Despite his protestations that I take it easy, I put leftovers into containers in his fridge, which takes forever because of my cast. I am amazed at how clean the inside of the appliance is. "So, do you clean your fridge out every week? I am shocked by the lack of bachelor pad goo," I laugh.

Chris comes up behind me and lightly places his arms around my waist. "I have a housekeeper that comes in once a week and cleans everything," he purrs in my ear. My whole body is hot all of a sudden and I feel like I am going to melt into a puddle on the floor. Maybe I am feeling better enough to accept some affection from my incredibly cute boyfriend… His breath tickles my neck. I feel a little claustrophobic and wiggle loose from his grasp to turn around and face him.

"Must be nice," I sigh. He kisses me and I feel like everything inside of me is collapsing in onto pillows. Like walls tumbling down in slow motion.

"It's a perk of having rich parents who don't have time for you," he says with a shrug. "Time for your meds. Mandy said she'd have my head if I don't take good care of you, so I'm going to be a pain. She's small, but I believe her!" He laughs, brushing his hair back and stretching.

"OK. Should we write down when I'm taking them so we don't forget?" I ask. I suck at remembering what time I did something or other because my days all blend into one big, miserable blob. You go to school, you work, you clean, you get thrashed, you go to bed, and you start all over, day after day. Whee.

"That's actually a really good idea. Then when Mandy asks, I can tell her in detail and she won't get pissy. I'd rather we get along, since she's your best friend," he cracks.

"You're pretty smart for a guy," I crack back. "Most guys don't think she's big enough to be a problem. Every single one that has tried to mess with her has been very, very sorry. It's ridiculous how boys underestimate girls. Mandy never backs down from them. "You should be safe, as long as you aren't a total jerk to anyone she cares about," I say looking around the room for dramatic effect. He's actually worried about making a good impression with my friends. How cool is that?

We go into the bedroom and he rifles through my bag and produces a bottle of pills. My body is starting to feel like a bunch of tiny gnomes are attacking me with teeny jackhammers so I'm ready for the medication to numb the pain again. I hate taking medicine. I can't help it. My mother is such a pill-popping kook. Booze and pills, the perfect suburban housewife diet. I do *not* want to be like *that.* I sullenly get my water glass and refill it. Chris has ferreted out a notebook to write down when I take medication.

I grimace at the pill he puts in my hand, "Oh goody," I sigh. He raises an eyebrow at me and I chuck the pill in my mouth and guzzle the water. P-tooey! I don't get people who do drugs. This stuff tastes like shit and taking medicine sucks.

"Good. Now we need to get you ready for bed before that kicks in," he says like a nanny overseeing a cranky, petulant child. Some people would give me lip for allowing Chris to be pushy. But, I like having him to lean on. Whenever I've been sick, I've been on my own. My mother isn't exactly maternal and couldn't care less what happens to me. When I get sick it's all about how inconvenient it is for her. She's not worried about her kid, her nose is out of joint because she's minus her maid, cook and laundress. Mandy has always done what she could when I've been under the weather, especially lately. I'm used to being on my own. But I can't say I'd mind having someone in my corner sometimes.

I shuffle off to the bathroom and change into a raggedy "Sex Pistols" t-shirt and sweatpants. I am not one of those girls who "lets it all hang out." Maybe it's a Midwestern thing, I don't know. All I know is that I am totally cool with the kissing (yes!!) and snuggling, but everything else is a no go. Because, as Mandy says, "It's a no go, cuz I'm a no ho." I brush my cruddy teeth, and wash up a little. This way he won't gag if he kisses me. I may be thrashed to smithereens, but I would still like to be somewhat presentable. I put my toiletries in my bag and shuffle to the bed. Groggily, I climb under the covers and try to relax. Chris lies next to me on top of the covers, and we cuddle. He kisses me so gently, I surrender to his warmth. I feel his strong body pressing against mine, and feel protected in his embrace like I've never felt before. His kisses seem to banish all the pain and sadness from my heart. I feel the pain draining out of my body, and cannot resist as sleepiness overwhelms me. Chris's face is swimming in a blur, over me.

"Goodnight, Kiera. I'll be right here if you need me," he strokes my head gently and kisses my forehead. I sink quickly into blackness.

I am five years old and lying on my parents' bed because my father tells me to. He looks over his shoulder toward the door. I am confused. Did I do something wrong and he's going to punish me? I can't remember doing anything. I am scared though, because he is very big and very mean, and I am very small and my mother is out of town. He is whispering to me to be quiet and he removes my underwear. I don't understand why he is doing this. He closes the bedroom door. I am so scared I can't breathe. He starts hurting me. Burning, searing pain between my legs as I scream, he slaps my face really hard, but I don't stop. He grabs his pillow and shoves it over my face to make me stop screaming. I scream and fight with all my five-year-old might and eventually sink into blackness. "Am I dead?" I think to myself in the blackness. When I open my eyes, he is there. "If you ever tell anyone about this, I will kill you. Do you understand?" I nod, terrified. I stay quiet so he won't try to kill me again. I wish Mommy was back from her trip. I wish I was with her instead of lying here on their bed.

I am sitting up in a bed, covered in sweat and I am still screaming. A loud, long, horror movie scream that pierces the darkness. I don't know where I am.

"Kiera! Kiera! What is it?" Chris asks, fumbling in the dark for the lightswitch on his bedside lamp. "Kiera! You're at my house. You're safe here. Nothing's going to hurt you," he says, brushing my sweaty hair off of my forehead.

My mind slides into the present with an almost audible clunk. Now it's all starting to make sense. All the fragments in my memory have assembled themselves into one picture. I remember going to the hospital for a bladder infection and my mother and my doctor explaining it away by saying it was caused by bubble bath. Now I know why I have never been able to sleep. Now I understand my innate, visceral fear of my father. I was such a good little kid. I was so quiet. A little bookworm from the moment I could read. I would always play quietly in my room by myself, drawing pictures, reading books, and creating a beautiful fantasy world where I could be safe.

"Kiera?" asks Chris softly, gathering me into his lap, like a little kid. "What happened? Are you okay? Was it a bad dream?"

I nod, unable to articulate and I sob miserably. Snot runs down my face. He hands me a wad of tissues, and I cover my face. I sit in silence, shaking as he holds me in his lap, rubbing my back.

White hot rage engulfs me in an inferno that I have never before experienced. I literally feel like I'm on fire. I shake uncontrollably. Right now, I want to kill them all. Reaching for my glass on the nightstand, I try to swallow some water. Choking on my words, I stammer and struggle to speak.

"It's OK. You don't have to talk right now if you don't want to," says Chris peering at me with those big, green eyes. He wants to help me. He is afraid for me, not of me. I can feel it.

I feel like the life has been sucked out of me and I have no skin. The pain is palpable. I drag in another breath. I hang my head and just bawl. My father really is evil. Pure and undiluted evil. I hate him like I have never hated anyone before.

"I can't say anything...I can't tell...I know what he'll do..." I whisper, terrified that he'll know if I tell. At least if I stay quiet for now, I have a shot of making it out of Indiana alive.

"Whatever it is, don't worry, Kiera. You're going to be okay," Chris says finitely.

I want to believe him, but I know how this works. If I tell, I could blow my chance to escape. "The system" is broken and no one is interested in fixing it. To hell with it. Once I am eighteen, these assholes are never going to see me again. All I have to do is survive until then. From here on out, I will not make it easy for them. I have been a quiet servant who pretty much just stood there and took what was dished out. I've never had a choice about what happens to me. I am going to fight, and in the end no matter how long it takes, I'm going to win.

"I am not going to sit here and get the shit kicked out of me every other day anymore. I might not be able to get my mother and brother to tell the truth, but I am sure as hell not going to sit here and be their punching bag for the rest of my life. I'd rather die," I rage, wiping my face.

"I'll talk to Mom and see what she and Dad are going to do," replies Chris. "Are you OK?" he asks, brushing my hair out of my face so he can see me.

"Yeah. It's a long story," I tell him, stalling. "I can't really talk about it right now."

It's surprising that even after a realization like this, I feel so safe here, with Chris. Like an electric shock it dawns on me...that's the reason *why* my brain regurgitated the information that it had been trying to remind me of all this time. I feel safe. For the first time that I can remember, I really do feel safe, and it's all because of Chris. I relax into Chris and he lays me on the bed, pulling the covers up around me.

"Stay with me for a little while?" I implore.

"Whatever you want, Kiera. You tell me what you need," he says, climbing over and lying next to me.

He strokes my head, and then we lie in his bed holding hands. We talk about the coming day, breakfast choices, and movie choices. He tells me about his grandfather who used to own a jewelry store and was a genius with math. This grandfather loved clocks and watches, and he collected them. The shop was full of ticking clocks and watches. Some of them were really old, but had rude mechanisms that were porno-graphic. They would laugh and laugh on the hour, every hour. I drift off to the shop in my sleep. Cuckoo clocks and grandfather clocks and chimes. Koo-koo...koo-koo...koo-koo.... Yeah, well...we can't all be perfect.

· Ten ·

Dirty light comes in through the windows. I roll over and gingerly stretch. I am still in a lot of pain. I look at the clock and blink trying to focus on the blue digital numbers. It's noon. I hear shallow breathing next to me and roll over to face Chris, who is still asleep, completely dressed. His arms are crossed as if he wants to be sure not to touch me in my sleep. I don't know if anyone has ever been so careful with me, not to hurt me. Maybe I'll have to keep him. I scooch over and gently kiss his cheek.

He startles awake and blinks at me groggily, "Wha? Huh? Oh, hi," he smiles and stretches. He is long and stretched full length, looking like a huge cat. "Did you sleep OK?" he asks.

"Surprisingly, I did," I say smiling at him shyly.

"Cool," he responds. "What do you want for breakfast?" We are avoiding speaking too close to each other's faces so nobody gets a blast of morning breath.

"Waffles and some Earl Grey?" I say, half joking because I don't expect he has these things, but it sounds good. I shuffle off to the bathroom to pee and clean up a bit.

"Coming right up," he says springing from the bed and heading for his kitchen. He looks so good just rolling out of bed, I can't imagine how good he must look all gussied up. How did I get so lucky?

We have a leisurely breakfast and discuss music in depth. We are both huge fans of Wax Trax, the big difference being that he can make pilgrimages any time he likes because he lives nearby and has money. He is surprisingly sweet for someone with his background and financial status. I keep my answers pretty short, as usual. I prefer to hear other people's stories. It's so much easier than telling mine. We finish waffles that he had in his freezer and the tea he pinched from his parents' pantry. "Mom loves Earl Grey, especially for when they have company, so we always have some laying around," he explains.

You see, in Indiana if you were to request Earl Grey tea, you would be met with a blank stare followed by, "What in tarnation are you askin' fer?". It isn't like the *entire* state is a bunch of fat, stupid redneck hillbullies. It's just the majority. You try and find a cluster of people who aren't gun-toting, truck-driving, country-music-listening, rude, "yew ain't frum here ar yew", ignorant hillbullies in Indiana. I dare you. That's why there are so many trucks with the bumper stickers that say "Kill 'em all and let God sort 'em out."

Chris shows me his guitars and amp, and I tell him how Max and Andy are trying to get a band together, and that Max would love to check out his equipment sometime. "That would be cool to get something together with those guys," he grins. He then shyly shows me some of his artwork, which I immediately fall in love with.

"Chris! These are awesome!" I squeal as I leaf through drawing after drawing. They are charcoal studies of Chicago streets, graphite sketches of punks on Belmont and a really beautiful and sensitive drawing of an old, homeless woman sleeping on a bench. He is struggling with some of his shading techniques, so I show him some ways of crosshatching in his sketch book. I can see the light bulb pop on over his head, and am gratified that I can help him overcome his frustration.

He blushes at my gushing praise of his talent then pulls me to the couch. He sits next to me, and looks at me expectantly, hesitantly and I know what those big green eyes are searching for.

"OK, so now I have to explain, don't I?" I murmur.

"No, you don't have to. I just want to understand what's going on," he says, gently taking my hand.

I launch into an explanation about how I have never been very successful at sleeping for the duration of a whole night, how I have always had these weird fragmented memories and dreams and that one of the reasons for this has been made clear. "…sorry I can't really go into it, but that's the gist," I tell him. I can't look at him. I just want to get out of there in one piece.

"You might go back to Indiana, but you're *not* going back to that house with those people," he says in a deadly serious voice.

"Yeah…well, the jury is still out on that one. We'll see how many strings they have pulled when I get back," I snort. I try not to think about what is likely to be a predictable outcome.

The next two days are like a really good dream. I sleep in the huge four poster bed and am entertained with conversation about books we've read (Poe, Vonnegut, Millay, Browning, Shakespeare, Molière…), music we like (Dead Kennedys, PiL, Sex Pistols, Black Flag, Skinny Puppy…), concerts he's been to (pine pine pine! I want to go toooo!), places we'd like to visit (Paris, London, Australia)… well, you get the picture. I find that he is very funny and witty and that we have a really good time together. I'm relieved that we have put recent events out of our minds temporarily and are able to just hang out and get better acquainted.

He runs a bath for me in the huge clawed foot bathtub and sits outside the door in case I have trouble. We spend plenty of time making out on the bed, on his couch, until he has to go outside for a walk to cool off. We order take out Chinese and Italian, and watch Monty Python on cable while trying not to shoot food through our noses. If you've ever watched any Monty Python, you could see how that would be a challenge to watch while having dinner. We climb on his roof to stargaze, all bundled up in blankets and pillows on a huge wooden chaise lounge. The cold, crisp October night air makes the night clear and perfect for seeing the sky. Lit candles are scattered all over the rooftop creating a beautiful, romantic rooftop sanctuary. We dance, talk, cuddle and kiss for hours on end. He has a small portable stereo playing a mixed tape as we sway, wrapped in an embrace.

Robert Smith purrs that he never thought this day would would or tonight would be this close to him.

I look up into Chris's smiling face and wish I could stay here forever, on this candlelit rooftop. He kisses me and I seem to melt right into him. I feel connected not just to him, but the whole city. This must be what home feels like.

It seems so impossible that this is happening to me, the Queen of Dorks and Outcasts…but it is. It feels so unreal, like it's happening to someone else and I'm watching from the sidelines. Every time I think about leaving, I get sulky and ornery, and Chris is starting to catch on.

"You can come back anytime you want," he says, trying to soothe my jangling nerves.

I inhale the cold night air and wrap my arms around his neck, clinging tightly. I don't want to go back. He hold me tight for a long time. I close my eyes and let myself sink into his warmth, breathing in his scent, listening to his heartbeat.

We go back to his room and Chris hands me my medication. I gulp it down, hang my head, and start to cry out of sheer frustration. He reaches out to hold me and I surrender. I lay my head on his chest as tears roll down my cheeks. He quietly comforts me as I face an unknown future. I'll have to thank Mandy when we get home. I wouldn't have responded to Chris if she hadn't pushed just a little.

We hear a light knock on his door as it opens, a voice calls from the other room, "Chris? Honey? Where are you two?" A tall woman with ash blonde hair, swiftly glides into the room, frowning. "Oh, you must be that poor dear from Indiana, Cassie is it?" She says extending her hand and her face shifting from annoyance to pity.

"It's Kiera, Mom," says Chris, turning pink. "Kiera, this is my mother, Lydia Sullivan," he says shifting uncomfortably.

Lydia Sullivan is impeccably dressed in Ralph Lauren, her hair perfectly coiffed, her house perfectly kept and her life perfectly organized. Chris is uncomfortable talking about his parents because they don't really get along, which I told him is normal for every teenager, really. She was born into money, married money, and really loves money. It isn't that she's actually a bad person, she's just really clueless about reality as most people experience it.

"Pleased to meet you, Mrs. Sullivan," I wipe my tears on my sleeve and shake her slender hand. She has a firm grip.

"Is everything all right?" she says with a wan smile, looking me over carefully.

Chapter Ten

"I am so sorry about everything," I stammer. "I'm so frustrated with this pickle I'm in," my voice shakes and I swallow hard, trying to regain control. I'm so embarrassed. I am beaten, bruised, and raggedy in front of this immaculate woman. I feel even less human.

"Yes, Chris told me everything. I am so sorry. Our attorney has assured me that we are pursuing every avenue available. Your parents clearly need to be taught a lesson. Nobody messes with my son," Lydia declares, a chilling fury hardening her beautiful face. "Our son has excellent taste in friends, so I have no doubt that you are a diamond in the rough," Chris's mother says, looking me over appraisingly.

"I am so grateful for your hospitality and assistance. I slept well for the first time that I can remember and was feeling good until...." My eyes well up and I blink back the tears. "I have to go back tomorrow and I'm scared. I don't want to go back to my house. If he's there, he's going to kill me..."

"Well, our attorney and the police are involved now, so you should be in good hands," she says stiffly, looking uncomfortable.

"Thanks for everything, Mrs. Sullivan. I hope the next time I see you, it's under more pleasant circumstances," I say calmly.

"I trust it will be, dear," she says with a quick smile. "Chris, a moment please?" she says turning to her son, beckoning him to follow her into the hallway, her expensive pumps clicking against the hardwood floor.

After I pack and check to make sure my things are where they should be and not strewn around, I lie down and slip into a hazy dream. I am being forced to walk down a dark alley by myself. A large, wolfish dog comes running after me and attacks me. It chews up my hands as I fight to hold it off and keep it from devouring my face. My blood is everywhere as I struggle with the ferocious animal. I am screaming for help.

"Kiera! Wake up..." My eyes snap open and I find myself sitting up in Chris's bed.

Chris looks at me with a worried expression. "You were yelling for help really loud. Are you OK?"

"I don't want to go back there," I say, trying to calm myself after yet another nightmare. "What time is it?"

"You've got about an hour before we have to get up," he whispers, pulling me to him gently.

"Screw it, I'm not going back into that dream if I can help it," I say, laying my head on his shoulder and curling around him.

· Eleven ·

October 23, 1987

We speed along the highway to Indiana, home of gray skies and closed minds. Morrissey croons how he wants to be taken out tonight…because he wants to see people and he wants to see life.

I stare glumly out the window as we drive in silence back to BFE. Whatever I did right, to attract this super sweet, gorgeous guy, I hope I can keep doing it. Most people don't want to deal with the drama that has attached itself to me. That's why I've never even tried to have a boyfriend. Who the hell would be willing to deal the mountain of baggage that I can't get rid of because I'm related to it?

Tears splash down my face as I listen to Morrissey sing about not wanting to be dropped home, because it isn't his, and he is unwelcome. I was never wanted, but the thing is that they won't leave me alone either. Apathy and indifference are sometimes worse than violence, but in my case, I'll take apathy instead. When I think of someone treating a child of mine the way I've been treated, a searing rage burns through me. I feel like I would crush the abuser's throat with my bare hands and watch the life drain from his eyes. Love isn't a belt, beating you down. It isn't a muzzle of fear that keeps you silent and alone. Love is safe. It lifts you up and lets you shine.

Time seems to have sped up and we are pulling into Mandy's driveway. My face is swollen and my mouth is dry. I have been crying the whole way. Chris turns off the ignition and hangs his head. Taking a deep breath, he turns to me, a pained look on his handsome face.

"You are going to be OK. Mom said you can come and stay any time, and don't be shy about calling for help," he says gently wiping my tears with his hand.

"Really? I was afraid she'd hate me because I was a beaten up, ragamuffin girl when she came around last night," I said in surprise.

"Mom can be incredibly cool at times. She usually comes through in a pinch," he says with a grin.

He reaches over and pulls me toward him, encircling me in his leather-jacket-clad-arms. "You will get through this. Besides, Mom, Dad, and their attorney are about to get serious with his sorry ass," he laughs with confidence I wish I could absorb through my skin. He leans over and gives me with a kiss that re-energizes my soul, like a bright beam of sunlight that warms me through. I wish I could stay with him and never go back.

"Thanks so much for everything, Chris. You are the sweetest guy I've ever known, and I hope I always know you, no matter what," I say, reluctantly letting go of his hand I've been clutching.

"You will," he says looking at me intently. He slides out of the drivers' seat, and comes around to open my door for me.

Mandy hears the clatter, opens the front door and comes running out as Chris scoops my bags out of his trunk. "Can I help?" She throws herself at me and hugs me. "How are you doing? Is your arm feeling better? I am so glad to see you. Max has been inconsolable and Andy has been depressed. Everyone is worried about you, and Mom is in a major twist," she rattles off like a machine gun, giving me no time to respond to any of her questions.

I smile at this enthusiastic greeting from my friend. It just feels good to be missed because they love me, not because they want something from me. "We'll have to call the guys later and hang out," I sigh, flopping onto the living room couch. Mandy takes my stuff from Chris and hauls it into her room with a groan.

Chris sits next to me on the couch, "I've gotta get back, but call me if you need anything. I mean it." I feel heat creep into my face. Being a charity case is humiliating.

"OK, I will," I say quietly, staring at the floor. He searches my face to detect whether I will or not and begins to protest. "I *promise*," I say with a smile, looking up at him. He scoops my hair out of my face and envelops me in a passionate kiss that revs my heart and makes me start to sweat. I feel like I have melted into a pool on Mandy's couch. We stand up and I throw my arms around him. I am afraid and I don't want him to leave.

"I'm here, Kiera. You just call me if you need me and I'll come as quickly as I can without wrapping myself around a guardrail," he says, attempting to lighten my mood.

"Geez Louise! I would really rather not think about something like *that*!" I squawk, slapping at his arm.

He backs out of Mandy's house. "That's why I *don't* speed!" he says cringing against the onslaught of playful slaps I aim at his arm, which is well protected by his leather jacket. He gets in his car and takes off. I watch the tail lights disappear at the corner and turn around to find Mandy perched on the couch looking like a cat that has just had a mighty fine snack of some kind of contraband.

"You have to tell me *every* detail of the last three days!"

I smile dreamily, and launch into a condensed version. I know she's curious to find out how far Chris got with me, but there are some things a lady keeps to herself.

"I wish I could find a guy that romantic," she grouses, knowing full well the pickins around here is *real* slim.

"You will. I don't know where or how, but you will." I try not be discouraging. I can tell she's a little envious that I have a boyfriend and she doesn't. It's weird. I'm thrown off guard that she doesn't seem to be able to be happy for me, so I keep my new found happiness to myself.

We do homework, make a frozen pizza for dinner and go over notes for French class. When it's time for bed, we don't joke around the way we used to. I feel like I've overstayed my welcome as I lay down on the trundle bed, and curl up with the well-worn blankets and chenille bedspread.

"G'night Kiera," Mandy says, rolling over toward me.

"'Night." I say, closing my eyes. I lay there and think about Chris, and the last few days we spent together. I drift off to sleep dreaming of Chris, the candlelit rooftop, and starry sky.

· Twelve ·

Saturday, October 24, 1987
Mandy's house

"Kiera, have you called your house yet since you got back?" Mrs. Goebel asks, placing a hand lightly on my shoulder. She has just come home after being at the office. I can tell there's something off as she sits next to me at the kitchen table where we've been playing crazy eights.

My heart plummets to my knees. "No. Why?" I say stonily. Instantly withdrawing inside myself, her voice becomes a distant echo.

"Since your father is an assistant principal and has such a good reputation for being a so-called 'upstanding pillar of the community,' they let him out and dropped the charges. Your parents had to pay a fine, but their attorney got them out of the jam they were in. They want you to come home" Her voice breaks, and a tear slides down her cheek as she looks away.

I can't feel a thing. I'd rather die than go back there. It seems like everything is in vain. Are there are no consequences? Is it because he's white? Is it because he has money? I can't accept that "social stature" overrides the crimes he has committed. My mind races as I go over each scenario, trying to find one that ends well for me. I stare at the worn, shag carpet and let my brain process the information. Like a skipping record, I keep starting over at the beginning, trying to find a solution that ends well, hitting a brick wall, a snag, and starting over again.

"Kiera?" says Andy in an almost whisper. Andy, Max and Mandy are all looking at me with big, scared eyes. Andy covers his face with a hand and starts to cry. I don't know how to make everything OK for them, especially when I can't make anything OK for myself.

"It's nobody's fault but his," I say. "I just have to keep breathing, right?" All my hope and confidence draining away in a whirlpool of overwhelming fear. I pull Mrs. Goebel into her bedroom and shut the door behind us as Mandy turns around and heads back to the kitchen.

"Can you help me make a run for it?," I whisper.

"Oh Kiera honey, I'm so sorry," she says, hanging her head, reaching out to grasp my hand and give it a motherly squeeze. "I think we've held them off for as long as we can right now."

"I'm so scared," I whimper, covering my face my my hands. "He's going to do something really bad, I just know it."

"We're going to get you through this," she says, taking me into her arms. Leaning down to rest my forehead on her shoulder, I take deep breath and try to believe her. But I don't.

I wipe my face and we head back to the kitchen. I put on a brave face, like I know what I'm doing and sit down next to Max.

"I'm so sorry. My uncle is so pissed off, you should have seen him. Steam was coming out of his ears and he hollered so loud at the judge that the people two doors down came in to see what the racket was," Max tells me, trying to boost my confidence. "If your father ever touches you again, he'd better hope my uncle doesn't answer the call. Milo Tidwell can't stand a bad guy getting off the hook because he's well connected."

Andy sniffs and looks at me with swollen eyes, "It's so hard for me to see you like this. I wish I could do something to stop him."

"Thanks," I say, putting my arm over his shoulders and squeezing him. "I'm so sorry for all of this," I say, my heart breaking that my friends are in such distress because of me. My favorite human superball sniffling back tears, my best friend pale and trembling.

We sit in silence for several minutes. My options have run out and I have to be practical. I plan to write a letter and give it to Mandy's

Mom to keep it safe and only open it in case the worst happens. For now, I've got to keep plodding through this mess.

"We'll see how long he's off the hook after the Sullivan's lawyer gets through with him," I bluff, trying to bolster my friends and maybe even myself.

Mandy grins, "Yeah, I don't think he's out of the woods yet. From what Chris told me, they're just getting warmed up."

All the false bravado and brave talk seems to do the trick. Soon, we're all laughing, and return to our card game. Eventually we stop long enough to demolish some food that Mandy's Mom orders from the Foo Dog. We play Donkey Kong, until it gets late and the boys have to go home. I sense Mandy's Mom looking at me as we get ready for bed, she tries to smile reassuringly, but isn't quite convincing. I keep doing what I've always done — just act like everything is normal.

The dim light of another gray, northern Indiana autumn morning dribbles in through the curtained window. I roll onto my back and sigh. Staring at the ceiling, I try to reconcile the fact that shortly, I will be heading back to the house where my sibling and parents are. Every part of me is resisting and I don't want to get up. I turn over to see if Mandy is awake and find her looking at me.

"Hey," she says with a yawn. "Want some food before you return to your cell?"

"Yeah, I guess I'd better eat something now. Who knows what they're going to do," I mutter.

At this point my friends have given up the idealistic attitude that maybe my family will change and have become resigned to reality, just like me. I am angry that because of all this, my friends are suffering too. I bet this is why most people avoid me. It isn't just because of how I look. It's the thing they can't put their finger on, but they know there is something wrong with the picture. Some people are civil to me, but won't socialize with me. That's how I know I'm right. I have good test scores and good grades. It isn't like I'm a vandal or anything. I'm used to being treated like crap, so it usually rolls right off. But today that I pray no one starts in on me. Today I feel like I have no skin and that nothing can protect me from the certain pain that waits for me in my parents' house. I feel like a walking, bleeding wound that leaves a trail wherever I go.

I scrub myself in the shower and throw on some junky clothes. They'll probably make me clean the whole house with a toothpick or something, and it'll save time if I'm prepared. I flop down at the kitchen table and Mandy brings me a stack of blueberry pancakes and sausages. She has a tin of real maple syrup, too. I pile food onto a plate and being snarfing.

The doorbell rings and I freeze in midbite. The color has drained from Mandy's face and she speeds to answer the door. I hear a cacophony, and hear Max and Andy goofing around, "Jesus Mandy! It's us!"

"Put me DOOOOWWWWWWWNN!" Mandy is hollering and flailing as Max carries her into the kitchen over his shoulder. He is grinning and poking her in the butt with his index finger.

"I thought you were the Pillsbury dough boy," he laughs, putting her down and raising his arms to shield the many blows coming from our petite friend. Mandy slaps Max lightly around the head and shoulders.

"You shithead! I'm on the rag and I could've squirted blood everywhere like a jelly donut!" she screams, smacking him hard on his arm.

Andy starts making puking noises and gestures over the sink, "Blaaaarrrgh! Thanks for the visual, Mandy."

I laugh so hard, tears are streaming down my face. I can never stay down in the dumps very long with these guys as my friends. We have an abundance of silly, which I adore. Andy hands me a box of tissues, "Hey there, girlie, don't forget to swallow" he quips.

"Don't even go there asshole," Mandy laughs and flings a pancake at his head. It lands like a weird beret on the top of his head and he walks around the kitchen modeling it. Mince mince mince, "…and this season in Paree we have this lovely blueberry confection that is fashion and a healthy snack…" Andy narrates in a mock TV announcer's voice.

Max and I are laughing our butts off. We start pointing at each other and laughing, until he farts. I get up quickly and run into the living room, squealing, "EEEEEWWW! You dropped a bomb!" Mandy and Andy are right behind me.

"Fuck, Dude…what the hell did you eat last night?" says Andy, sounding duck-like as he pinches his nostrils shut against the noxious fumes that have escaped Max.

"Same…as…you!" Max replies still laughing and gasping for air.

"Well. Go in there and crack a window so Kiera can eat her breakfast, and keep it down," says Mandy pushing him into the kitchen.

Soon, it is safe to re-enter the kitchen and I snarf down my breakfast. Andy and Max "help" eating the pancakes so that Mandy doesn't have a lot of clean up. "You should really think about culinary school. You're awesome, dude," says Max thickly through stuffed cheeks.

"Only if I can't write for somebody good after college," she grins.

Too soon, it is time to head out. I have to call my parents' house.

It feels like an hour between each ring. My mother answers, like everything is normal.

"Um, I'm coming back shortly and wanted to check in before I got there and make sure everything's cool," I say, fighting to keep the anger out of my voice.

"Sure, Kiera! You come on home now," she says, dangerously sweet.

"K. See you in a little while," I say and hang up the phone.

Come on home. Like anywhere that they are is home for me. Home is supposed to be somewhere safe that you can go and relax, and not be scared shitless every single second of every day that someone is going to strangle you in your sleep or beat you to such a bloody pulp that you have to have a closed casket. I just can't give up the dream of having my own apartment somewhere warm and far, far away from here. I'd be able to put posters on the walls, eat what ever I want. I can sleep in peace. To get there, I just have to keep going. Just somehow find a way to get through this. Just never give up.

We pile into Mandy's car and slowly drive to my parents' house. Morrissey croons in the background, begging to get what he wants for the first time, and that the life he's had can turn a good man bad.

"Mom says this is total bullshit. She's getting in touch with Chris's parents and their attorney," Mandy says as we drive through a desolate area that is nothing more than chopped down cornstalks in clumps of dirt. Dead. Dead gray sky. Fucking Indiana.

"Cool. Listen, thank her for me, will you? I don't know if I'll be able to call anyone," I say. I am terrified about what my future holds, and how hard they will lock me down.

"If they don't let you take any phone calls, we'll just show up, Kiera," says Max, his face angry and defiant.

"For sure, dude. Screw them. We're not going to sit here and let them do whatever they want to you," Andy says nodding. "They need to know that we're watching them."

"Thanks you guys," I say, dubious that anyone can do more than Sargeant Tidwell.

We turn onto my street and my heart drops into my shoes. My father is outside raking. He hears the car, and turns to smile and wave with a big, fake toothy grin. Like he's Mr. Rogers or Ward Cleaver. I swallow hard so I don't barf all over Mandy's car.

"You OK?" she says, touching my arm. "You look green."

I press my lips together and nod, blinking hard to stave off the tears of frustration that prick my eyes. My father is walking over to the car to chat with us? Fuck.

We all pile out of the car and I begin to haul myself and my bag into the house.

"Hi guys!" my father chirps, like he's greeting old friends. "Did you have a good time?"

Like we have just returned from a dance or something. I slink into the house as everyone glares at him with pure hate. He continues his little charade, "We sure missed Kiera the last few days," I can hear him say as I pause at the door to hear the exchange.

"Well, you'd better get used to it because I am going to make sure that she doesn't get stuck with your abusive ass any fucking longer you asshole!" Mandy says furiously as she whirls to face my father.

I hear him launch into a diatribe about what a liar I am as I close the door behind me and skitter upstairs. I fling myself into my room and lock the door. I drag my dresser in front of the door and wait. I unlock my window, just in case. My heart is pounding so hard I think it might pop right out of my ribcage. I hear him thundering into the house and up the stairs.

"Kiera!" *WHAM*WHAM*WHAM* He is pounding on my door and then tries to open it.

"WHAT THE HELL IS THIS? MOVE THIS GODDAMN DRESSER KIERA!"

As he tries to force his way into the room, I hear a quiet voice next to him in the hallway. "Peter, now remember what the judge said…" my mother murmurs softly.

I hear him exhale loudly like a bull preparing to gore a bullfighter. "Dinner is in half an hour. If you want any, you had better come down then," he informs me and walks downstairs to yell at the television. There is always a game on and lucky for me, he has someplace else to vent, at least until I have to come down for dinner.

I am shaking as I put my dirty clothes in my hamper and get my school stuff ready. I know Mandy was just trying to defend me, but I'm worried. Her going off on my father was like pouring gasoline onto flames. The thing is, I'll be the one who gets burned beyond recognition, not her. I jump out of my skin at a light tapping sound from my door, before realizing it's my mother, trying to open it. She merely succeeds in banging it into the dresser.

"Kiera, c'mon now. Open the door," she says patronizingly. "I want to talk to you."

She is thirty sheets to the wind, and I wish I could just walk out of here. The window option looks really good right about now.

I stomp over and shove the dresser out of the way. "What?" I snap, my patience gone.

"Watch it, Kiera," she says, narrowing her eyes at me, her features pulling into in a drunken snarl.

"Your father aaahndzh I are guh-ing out for zhinner duh-night, zoh clean itd up after you ahhndzh Brett eat," she slurs.

"Fine."

"How abouddt 'Thankssj Mom'?" she prods.

"Thanks," I says tonelessly. I can't believe she expects me to be grateful to her for anything.

She looks at me sourly and stalks out. Whatever. If it was her arm instead of mine, we wouldn't still be here. She can't be bothered to work, so she stays for the money. It's easier to be a parasite. That's her world. I plan to keep working, and make a life for myself.

I shove the dresser back in front of the door and do homework until I hear the garage door hum and clang its way up and their car zoom out of the driveway.

Dinner is uneventful since Brett takes over the remote and is absorbed in some game. I snarf down my food until I am full and speedily clean the kitchen. I know I will be in trouble for something when they get home, because they always get drunk when they go out. Then they fight on the way home. You know, add alcohol and watch the fun. At least this way, if he comes after me, it'll be for nothing and he'll get thrown in jail again. Ha ha ha.

I return to my room and continue doing homework until I hear the car pull in, followed by yelling, slamming of cars doors. Brett runs up the stairs and into his room, locking the door. I sit, waiting. I hear the garage door slam open and hit the wall, as my parents enter the house fighting. I take my set of car keys and put them in my bag, ready to run for it.

My father yells, "KIIIIEEEERRRAA!!!"

"No Peter! PETER, NO!" I hear my mother pleading. They are flat out yelling at each other. I know if I don't answer, he'll tear me apart when he gets up here.

"What?" I yell from the top of the stairs.

"GET YOUR FAT ASS DOWN HERE NOW!"

I grab my bag and run down the stairs. I leave the bag just out of sight around the corner as I walk into the kitchen.

He's a rabid, snarling animal coming at me as I enter the room. He's completely out of control and I know I am going to die. He grabs my throat, slamming me into the wall. He strangles me, his eyes glowing with the insane rage and pleasure of a psychopath. I kick, try to scratch... anything to get free. I see my mother over his shoulder, watching silently. Everything is getting fuzzy and I am seeing spots. Can't breathe! Everything is in slow motion. Then...

I am five years old and he is smothering me with a pillow.

MOMMY! MOMMY! MOMMY! HELP ME! WHERE ARE YOU? HELP ME! HELP ME!

I fight with all of my five year old might. I fiercely shake my head from side to side and kick, trying to get free.

NOOOOOOO! MAKE IT STOP! STOP IT STOP IT STOP IT...

I gasp for air and everything starts to close in, when he lets go to belt me really hard. I fall to the floor and he hits the wall instead of my face. I drag in a large breath and reach around the corner, snatch my bag and run. He is right on my heels.

My father's face is right in mine. I am lying on their bed.

"If you ever tell anyone about this, I will kill you," he says. I smell the Rolling Rock on his breath. I smell his aftershave.

"Do you understand?" he commands, still pinning me to the bed.

I slowly nod my head.

I snap more fully into the present and am running breathlessly. I make it to the car and fumble with the key in the lock. My sweaty, shaking hands take too long and he is on me. Five year old me turns to face him and freezes. My brain is replaying all the old images and I can barely tell where I am, much less what's happening. He picks me up and throws me. My body slams really hard into the driver's side door, and back into the present. There is a muffled tinkle as the window cracks. I gasp for air and flail, scrambling to get out of his reach. He violently pries the keys out of my hand, leaving a long gash in my palm. I have finally have my breath back now, allowing me to start screaming bloody murder for the whole world to hear.

"YOU FUCKING BASTARD! I HATE YOU! LEAVE ME ALONE! STOP IT! STOP THIS! AAAAAAAAAAUUUUUUUGGGGGHHH-HH!" I see porch lights flick on in front of all the houses all down the street. I keep screaming and screaming because I want to draw out as many witnesses as possible. Out of the corner of my eye, I see the garage door going up. He doesn't.

WHAM

I see stars. He smacks me across my face so hard that my right ear is ringing so loudly that I can no longer hear out of it.

"GET BACK IN THE HOUSE NOW!"

"FUCK YOOOOOOOOOOOOOOUUUUU!!" I scream.

He starts after me and I run for it. He grabs hold of my hair and I fall onto the cement driveway like I have hung my neck on a clothes-line. My head hits the pavement with a melon-like thunk. I scramble to get up, to get away from him. I'm like an overturned beetle scrabbling for purchase on the ground.

Meanwhile, my mother and brother see the whole thing from the garage. They stand there gawking, doing and saying absolutely nothing.

I gasp for air and pick myself up off the ground before he can get in a kick. I scurry away from him, toward my mother, who is looking at us in horror and disgust.

"SEE WHAT HE DID?" I yell at her, showing her my hand, which is dripping blood all over the floor of the garage. Plop. Plop. She is horrified, not that I am hurt, but that they got caught. Now the whole neighborhood will know the truth.

My father is wearing the expression of a two year old who got caught breaking his toys on purpose. "She's a liar," he sulks. "She's lying."

I run into the house and grab the other set of keys off the key rack. I hear them thundering through the house yelling. I keep moving, and slip out the front door. I keep running. Instead of slow motion, everything speeds up, and I am in hyper-drive. I get into the car and I fly out of the driveway. I have it floored. I don't look at the speedometer. I pray to get pulled over so I can tell the police what happened. The blood from my hand is making the steering wheel slippery. I wipe it on my pants while frantically looking for something to sop up the blood. I am driving all over the road as I get on the toll road. I have to stop looking in the rearview mirror before I hit something. I drive until I get to a rest stop, and stop holding my breath. Digging change out of the side pocket in the car, I scramble to a payphone in the foggy, freezing night air. Automatically, I dial the number, "Mandy? You gotta call the police for me. I ran for it. He's going to kill me," I say, my words coming out in spasms because I can't seem to catch my breath. I am gasping for air and shaking, I swallow and look around, "I gotta go…call the police and tell them what happened. I'll call you again when I get farther away," I say, rushing to get away and hide. "Tell them to go to the house and look for my blood in the driveway," I plead. "I'll call you soon," I hang up on her yelling at me, asking me where I was at the moment and where I planned to go. I'm in a blind panic. I don't want to die like this. Please help me!

Still shaking, I take a deep breath, wipe my face on my sleeve. Pink Floyd continues to play on the radio station, telling me to run, run, run.

After what seems like an eternity on the highway, I finally reach the familiar corner store and I pray to whatever deity is out there that Chris answers his phone. It seems to ring forever.

"Hello?"

"Chris? Uh, hi…listen, I know it's kind of soon, but I need help…again," it all comes out in a gush of snot, panic and tears. People walking by look at me as if I were a serial killer. I feel so pathetic.

"Kiera? Where are you?" he says, taking control of the situation, trying to calm me down.

"At the corner store pay phone, by your house," I sniff, my hands shaking.

Click.

I am worried. Is he mad? Will he be OK with me just showing up? I get a load of myself in a reflection of the front window. Now I know why everyone is looking at me funny. I look like I have been dragged behind a trash truck for few miles. I have blood all over me and more bruises than I can count. My cast is filthy and spattered with blood. I see Chris through the window.

He stops for one second and his face goes white. He runs in and gently takes me into his arms.

"Kiera! Jesus! What happened?" he whispers in horror at what he is seeing.

"Where is all the blood coming from?" he says, panicked, searching my head for a cut.

I hold out my hand, which is still bleeding. "He sliced it open when he tried to take the keys from me," I whimper like an injured animal.

"Please don't make me go back there," I sob into his shoulder, soaking his shirt with tears and blood. My knees try to buckle as we exit the store, and he holds me up.

"You don't have to go anywhere," he says, smoothing my hair. "But, we need to take pictures," he suggests and leads me toward his house.

I sigh heavily, nodding. "I'm so sorry you got dragged into this, but I'm so glad you're here."

"We're going to help you, Kiera" he says, gently taking my good arm and leading me to his house, where we call the police and arrange to meet them at the nearest emergency room. Lydia Sullivan greets us at the door of Chris's house. She is on the phone with their attorney, her beautiful face stern with a cold fury I've never seen before. Peter Graves is going down the hard way. I am not thrilled with going to the hospital *again* and filling out *another* police report, but this is the only way I know to try and get out. I will live in my car if I have to, but I'm not going back to that house.

· **Thirteen** ·

October 28, 1987
B.F.E. Indiana

I didn't call my mother until Sunday. I couldn't figure out how to run away for good without my psychotic parents calling the police to report me as a runaway, or something else totally shitty happening — so I'm following the Sullivan's plan and I'm heading back once things are in place. The deal that has been brokered is that my mother is filing for divorce. Apparently, she was plotting to file for divorce anyway, but this way the Sullivan's high power attorney is paid for, she's off the hook, and Peter gets what's coming to him. They won't press charges against her in criminal or civil court as long as she agreed to petition for full custody of me, and move out of the house immediately. I didn't believe it was really going to happen until we arrived in front of the apartment and she handed me the key.

Now I'm sitting in our little apartment that Mom got in town. It's a two bedroom on the top floor, so there's nobody walking around over me like a herd of elephants. My room is a horrible shade of bright yellow. I am slowly but surely covering it with my artwork, concert flyers I snagged off of telephone poles in Chicago, and cool photographs from different magazines. My small collection of belongings is in milk crates in the closet, since Mom has taken my bedroom furniture for her room. I don't even care that I sleep on a mattress on the floor. It is the most beautiful place I have ever seen, warts and all. I feel reborn.

I have to wear my cast for another six weeks, but everyone in town knows exactly how I got it. Everyone knows about Chris's parents and their attorney ripping my father a new one, and he is being treated like he has the plague. It's a bitter pill for a power hungry climber like my father to choke on. Nothing stays a secret in a small town, unless you tell absolutely no one and take it to your grave. Pretty hard to keep his bright orange community service jumpsuit a secret while he's out there along Taylor Road, picking up trash with the rest of the inmates. So I feel pretty good about the state of things.

My brother is all pissed off for god knows what reason. It isn't like he loved hearing them scream at each other. Maybe he enjoyed watching me getting beaten half to death every other day, I have no idea. He graduates this year and is going off to some private college in Illinois. I will probably always wonder why my parents aren't shocked when their beloved son comes home drunk — again. All I know is that finding him passed out in the driver's seat of the car will no longer be my problem. He is living with my father out in the boonies, which means they are nowhere near me. That is the only part of the equation I care about right now.

I'm stoked to be in town near my friends. Senior year is going to kick ass! Mandy's only about five blocks away while Max is about ten blocks the other direction. Maybe I can actually have them over and cook dinner or we can hang out here sometimes. The only drawback at this point is that I still have to live under the same roof as my mother, who seems to be permanently stuck in a state of non-reality. I have one more year to go. But it won't be half as bad as when I was stuck living with my whole family. One of them is far easier to manage than three. Besides, she passes out around nine o'clock every night, so I'll be free as a bird after that, more or less.

To my complete shock and amazement, she's starting a job as a secretary at the school corporation on Monday. Brett's best friend's mom got her in. I hope she can keep it together long enough for me to graduate. She has plenty of money from her parents. She loves to spend it only on herself, mainly on stuff she doesn't really need. This whole "responsible parent" thing has always thrown a wrench in her works. She and my father have always moaned about how expensive it is to have kids. She should have used a condom if she didn't want to deal with parenting. Her whole life is one big drama on her very own stage in her very own spotlight, and *everything* that *everyone* says, does or thinks has something to do with her. After all, she is the center of the Universe, right? I suspect her need for constant attention is why she took this job in the first place. The only thing that would make sense is for her to be attempting to climb the very limited social ladder around here. Now that she's divorcing my father, any number of horrifying ideas spring to mind, and I just don't want to think about it.

I'm just laying here on my ugly beige carpet, looking at the dirty ceiling, listening to one whole side of the new Love and Rockets album that Max let me borrow. They're singing about when you're down it's a long way up, and there's no new tale to tell.

I feel like I just might get a clean slate this time.

I feel like I've got one foot out the door. One more piddly year, and I'm outta here.

November 10, 1987

Since the court said I had to go see a therapist to determine how much damage my father has done and to "help me cope," my mother has to cough up the cash for therapy. It hardly endears her to me when she whines the whole drive to the office building in the next town over. I just want to slap the expression off of her face when she bitterly chews her lower lip, while writing out the check and handing it to the receptionist.

I sit in a dark, paneled waiting room with threadbare, stained beige carpet that makes me nauseous just looking at it. It's cold, dead and gray outside. I am contemplating whether to tell this guy the truth, or lie. I wonder if this doctor can help me at all. A miniscule flicker of hope glimmers inside me as I listen to my Walkman while contemplating my grim surroundings.

Danny Elfman howls through my headphones that someone else makes the rules, if you walk on four legs and break the law; you're in the house of pain.

A weird, gnome-looking dude comes out of the office and says, "Kiera?" He extends his hand. I am leery. He has these beady little eyes. He's rumpled and very short, and his proportions are so odd that it is disconcerting. He looks like a reflection in a funhouse mirror.

"What are you listening to?" the shrink asks. "Can I listen?"

"Sure…" I lift the headphones from my head and hold them up.

He leans in, "The house of pain, huh? Interesting."

There's something too intimate the way he looks into my eyes, standing way too close to me. I wrap my jacket around myself tightly and hunch over.

"I'm Dr. Samuel. Shall we?" He motions for me to go into his office.

His smile makes my skin crawl and I hesitate at the door, looking over my shoulder to the empty waiting room. My mother won't be back to pick me up for forty-five minutes and the receptionist just left, turning off the lights in the office. It's 5:00 P.M. and most of the people who work in this building are on their way home. I really don't want to be alone in a room with this guy.

I walk in and stuff my Walkman in my bag. Perching lightly on the edge of the ugly, orange-cat-puke-colored chairs, I watch him get behind his massive, heavy walnut desk. The hulking desk is so enormous that it takes up most of the space in the room and resembles a judge's bench. It is sitting up on a platform, due to his diminutive stature, no doubt, so that he can peer down at his clients.

The room is dark, has dark paneling, no windows and a large, disturbing painting of old ships being tossed on a stormy sea. His taste in décor is like something out of a bad seventies movie. There is one bizarre pod-looking lamp in the corner that emits a weak, orange-ish light, making the whole experience even more surreal. For some reason, the overhead fluorescent lights are turned off. I don't know if it's to make you relax or what, but it has the opposite effect, and my palms start to sweat.

"So, Kiera, I understand you've been having some problems…" says Dr. Samuel leaning forward slightly. "Why don't you tell me what's been going on?"

"Well, this cast and all these bruises aren't because I'm on the football team," I say, launching into the condensed version of my life's story. I stop short as Dr. Samuel walks around the desk and is stands in front of me. He leans forward and touches my necklace, making me squirm.

"Well, I can make things very easy for you or very hard," he says putting his face in mine, a reptilian leer stealing across his lopsided features.

My blood is pounding in my ears and my heart almost jumps out of my chest. I must be losing my mind, because this isn't possible. I feel the heat burning my face as I scoot back in my chair, away from his ugly, bearded, evil, gnome-like face.

"What do you mean?" I say, incredulously.

He stands directly in front of me so that his crotch is right in front of my face and leans over into my face, "I think you know exactly what I mean," he whispers, touching my hair. He starts to try and grab my shoulders, and I jump straight up, nearly head-butting him.

"GET THE HELL AWAY FROM ME!" I scream, grabbing my bag and bolting for the door.

He steps between me and his office door, barring the way. "KIERA! Lower your voice. Like I was saying, this can be hard or easy," he says evilly, narrowing his eyes. "I can help you with this situation or you can try and figure out what to do after I've made my report."

I am face to face with this warped, little man. As short as he is, I tower over him menacingly, "FUCK YOU. Move out of my way, NOW."

His already contorted face twists in rage, "Who did you think they are going to believe, you stupid little bitch? You or me?" I push past him, throwing open the office door, which smashes into the wall behind me, making a huge dent. I am hyperventilating; hot tears of humiliation splash down my cheeks as I run down the fire escape stairs. Charging through the exit like I'm on fire, I keep running as fast as I can.

What a stupid fuck. I am a good foot taller than him, and even with a cast and all my injuries, I could mop the floor with his disgusting, teeny little power-tripping ass. We'll see who's going to do what to whom when it's all said and done. I am going to TELL. I am going to tell Miss Fitch, since she set this whole thing up, and I am going to tell Sergeant Tidwell. My hope then they'll be arm wrestling to see who gets to break this twisted little weeble in half.

I am thinking and plotting what damage I am going to cause in Dr. Samuel's world as I book it across the parking lot in the cold rain. When I am out of sight behind a tree, I fumble for my Walkman, and flip over the tape.

Jello screams about a well paid scientist who always talks in facts and knows how to prove himself right.

I stomp through deep, freezing cold puddles on the flooded sidewalk. I stop and let out one scream of rage at the relentlessly gray sky that persists spewing this icy curtain of water, soaking me through.. Since when in the fucking hell do therapists try and take advantage of teenage clients who are clearly already screwed? I am totally fed up with old, white men. I am going to start retaliating and they had better all watch out for me. I've had it with this whole wad of horseshit.

I have walked about a half-mile up road, toward the direction of the mall, where I know my mother has been consoling herself by buying crap she doesn't need. A car comes screeching up, and I jump about ten feet back, ready to beat the hell out of whoever is inside. The passenger side door flings open and my mother yells, "Kiera! What the hell are you doing? Get in the car, you stupid girl!"

I throw myself in, close the door and buckle my belt while she berates me for a) leaving early and b) getting soaking wet. I remain silent until she shuts up, which takes a while. I focus on the rhythm of the windshield wipers.

*squeak*squoak*squeak*squoak*squeak*squaok*

As soon as she is finished with her lecture on "reasons why it's bad to make a mess in her car," I tell her what happened and that there is no way in hell I am going back.

"WHAT!?" she says, almost rear ending the car in front of us at a stop sign.

"He tried to make me do what he wanted me to do — whatever that was going to be, so I told him to fuck off and I left," I tell her looking at my shoes.

"Are you sure he didn't mean something else?"

"He kept touching me and made it clear by sticking his crotch in my face exactly what he had in mind," I snarl.

"Surely not, Kiera," says my mother matter-of-factly. "He's a doctor, for pity's sake. He's highly recommended, Kiera. You must have misunderstood," she says like it's the end of the discussion.

"HE TRIED TO RAPE ME!"

"Watch your tone of voice with me, young lady or you will be very sorry!" my mother snarls.

"How could you possibly think I made it up?" I seethe. My anger and disdain for her swallows me whole, and I withdraw into it, protecting myself from her coldness, and complete inability to detect the truth. She says nothing, and keeps her eyes on the road. We reach town and she stops the car in front of Mandy's.

"Get out," she orders, reaching across me to open my door. I am stunned, once again by her utter indifference, but quickly shake it off. It's just typical Dana.

I fling myself out of the car into the continuing downpour. "I'll be by later to get my stuff," I shout, slamming the door as hard as I can. She lives her life like an ostrich and always has. I can't think of anyone who is more in denial than she is. The prom queen would *never* have married an abusive asshole who beats her kids and raped her daughter. The perfect little cheerleader would *never* get a divorce and end up working some crappy little job in a crappy little town. No. Not her. Her life remains blissfully free from facts.

I trudge up the steps as Mandy peeks out the front door and throws it open realizing it's me walking through the deluge to her house. I am completely drenched and water runs off of me, pooling at my feet on her front porch. I feel like I'm frozen solid.

"Holy shit Kiera! What the hell is going on?" she says ushering me inside and taking my bag from my shoulder, as I create a small pond in the entryway of her house.

"You wouldn't believe me if I told you.," I groan. "Mom didn't."

I have left a tiny river behind me on my way to the bathtub to remove my heavy, wet clothes. I wrestle them off, and pile them on the powder blue linoleum floor. Naked and shivering, I turn on the hot water and let it run over my head and body. I lean my forehead against the wall. It feels like what he did is never coming off, like a bloodstain. Mandy hands me a towel and then gives me some privacy to dry off. I press the clean, rough towel into my face, smelling the fabric softener that always makes me think of this house, and my body starts to relax. Climbing into the dry, warm clothes she lets me borrow, I tell her the whole story while we sit on her bed. Her mouth is open the entire time I am talking and she sputters a couple of times in incredulous fury.

"Your mother is *the* stupidest fuck on the face of planet Earth," Mandy explodes in frustration.

"Tell me about it," I grouse, curling into a ball on my best friend's bed. I'm so glad to be here, not in that apartment with *her*. "I want to talk to Miss Fitch and see what the options are of nailing this asshole," I say, gritting my teeth. "I want to call Sargeant Tidwell too."

Mandy brightens, "That's an *awesome* idea, Kiera! Ooooo! They are going to be majorly pissed that the courts have been using a pervert to assess clients. They'll both want Dr. Pervert's head on a post."

"Hey, what time will your mom be home? I need to find a ride to go get some of my stuff from the apartment before my mother sets it on fire or throws it away," I ask.

Just then a door closes and Mrs. Goebel yells, "Mandy? I'm home!"

Mandy and I look at each other and smile, "Perfect timing" we say in unison, and climb off the bed to go talk to her.

"Kiera! Hi honey! Are you OK? What's going on?" Mrs. Goebel asks, concerned that I have shown up so soon after the court-required counseling session.

"I'm OK, but I need to get my stuff before Mom burns it," I say. "If I could just not have anything else shitty happen to me today, that would be great."

"We'll fill you in on the way," says Mandy, grabbing our jackets and turning her Mother around by her shoulders so that we are all walking toward the garage.

Mrs. Goebel looks at us with concern and confusion as we pile into the front seat of the car and Mandy launches into the latest installment of "Kiera's crappy life". I'm so sick of this ongoing bullshit that I could just throw up. My head hurts and I'm so exhausted that I feel like I've just run twenty miles.

"WHAT?!" Mrs. Goebel screeches, as she narrowly avoids nailing a street light.

Mandy has gotten to the super icky part of this afternoon's installment of the story. Being a real Mom, Mrs. Goebel reacts appropriately.

We pull into the parking lot of the run-down, old apartment complex and I prepare myself to deal with my mother.

"I'll be right back," I say plunging into the cold wet night.

"Wait! I'm coming with you!" says Mandy, sliding out of the car right behind me.

We run inside and plod up the stairs to the apartment. I unlock the door and we slip inside, trying not to disturb the beast. We make it to my room when my mother peers in.

"What the hell are you doing?" she slurs, narrowing her eyes at me.

"Getting my stuff," I say, throwing things into a duffel bag while Mandy is busy grabbing my crate of records and my tape case.

"You're not allowed," my mother informs me.

"You dumped me off at Mandy's, so that's where I'll be and I'm taking my stuff," I tell her, ready for a fight.

"You little bitch! How dare you leave me here by myself after everything I've done for you!"

"Really? I told you what that psycho shrink tried to do and you didn't believe me! You dumped me like a bag of trash over at Mandy's house," I snarl as I finish throwing the rest of the important stuff into the bag. I hitch it onto my shoulder to head out and she blocks the door. "Get out of my way," I say calmly.

"You aren't going anywhere young lady, so you can just put that bag down right now," she replies, sprawling to cover the whole doorway.

I look at Mandy and she knows exactly what I'm thinking. We walk quickly toward my mother and don't stop, smashing into her with our shoulders, the duffel, and the crate, knocking her flat. I don't stop. I just keep walking and Mandy is right behind me. We pull the door shut and lock it despite my mother's incoherent yelling and protests. In a blur, we scramble down the stairs and out into the freezing torrents of rain that continue to drench this miserable little cow town. We put my stuff in the back seat and throw ourselves into the front seat just in time. Mrs. Goebel hits the gas just as my mother makes it to the door and pokes her head out.

We head back to Mandy's and call in a delivery from The Foo Dog. Mrs. Goebel is on the phone with her friend and co-worker, Hazel Dunway, who knows everything about everyone and has an uncanny ability to pull all the right strings. It isn't just that she's well connected;

it's that she knows practically all the skeletons in everyone's closets intimately since she is the administrative assistant for Mr. Broker, one of the head assholes of the law firm. She has worked for him for thirty years and has job security because she knows all of *his* dirty laundry, too. No one wants to get on her bad side. The really funny thing is that she looks like someone's grandma. She's a healthy sixty-one and wears colorful outfits that defy the stereotype of legal secretary big time. Mandy and I have always thought of her as being pretty cool. We haven't talked to her much personally except for "hello", "yes, please" and "yes, ma'am". She's not mean or anything, we just don't want to be on the receiving end of her wrath if we ever do something stupid and cross her the wrong way.

I pick up the phone and dial the number Miss Fitch gave me a while back. I am startled when she actually answers. I summarize what has just happened, and she practically hangs up on me so I can call Sargeant Tidwell, who gets quite pissed. I have to keep holding the phone away from my ear, he is yelling so loud. "GODDAMMIT, I TOLD JUDGE THORNTON THREE YEARS AGO THAT THERE WAS SOMETHING WRONG WITH THAT GUY!" Mandy is turning purple laughing her head off on the couch, listening to his diatribe. The doorbell rings just as I finish the conversation, and Mandy runs to the door, grabbing a wad of bills from the coffee table.

She opens the door for the soggy college student laden with many bags of food, "Your total is twenty-four eighteen." He hands her the bags and takes the money.

"Keep the change, dude," she says and waves, shutting the door.

We troop into the kitchen to lay out our feast. Mrs. Goebel joins us as we unload the bags of food. They look at me expectantly.

"Well, it appears that my parents are in deep shit, pardon my French," I say, piling food onto a plate and flopping into the nearest chair.

"What's the latest?" Mandy asks, piling her plate with heaps of Mongolian beef, Chinese veggies, rice, egg rolls and crab Rangoon.

"Apparently, there have been numerous complaints over the years. Sarge told Judge Thornton a long time ago that Dr. Samuel was a pervert and that he needed to find a new psychologist. The judge didn't do it. Sarge never got wind until now. He is going to the judge's house right now to read him the riot act. Man, I sure would hate to be in his shoes," I laugh, chowing down on an egg roll.

"Oooooo! What's he going to do?"

"I don't really know, but it won't be pretty. I have a feeling when it comes to scumbag assholes like Dr. Samuel, he has a really short fuse and an even bigger stick," I grin through a bite of veggies.

"Hazel is going to track down all of the prior complaints and make copies for us. She said she'll probably drop by later," says Mandy's Mom with a smile.

My insides feel all lit up like the Fourth of July even though it's a cold, miserable November night. This is one man who is about to find out what happens when you misuse your personal power. Too bad for him. I start to feel more calm and relaxed as we continue to devour our dinner. Once we're stuffed like animals in a taxidermy shop, Mandy and I head to the basement to listen to records and brainstorm.

"Dude, we need to go on a trip to Chicago and go to Medusa's. You need some fun and a trip that doesn't involve hiding from your shitsack parents," says Mandy. "How's Chris?" she adds with a smile.

"I'm all for a trip to go dancing as soon as I feel better. My body has really had enough of the being beaten on thing," I say. "Chris is so romantic and sweet. He's a really good artist. You guys would love his stuff," I tell her, relaxing in the darkened room. "Treasure" is playing in the background and we have lit candles that are scattered around the room. It makes me remember the special candlelit night with Chris. I want to see him again as soon as possible.

"Max and Andy are worried about what the divorce might cause your parents to do," she tells me, looking at the floor.

"Yeah, but so far — so good, right?" I say sadly. "And they aren't finished with Peter yet, so we'll see."

"We're all going to help you Kiera. You won't be alone," Mandy assures me, flicking my knee and smiling.

I throw a pillow at her and she throws it back. We laugh and whip pillows at each other. She uses my cast to her full advantage and throttles me pretty good, so we pause.

"So...did you meet his friend John yet?" she slyly asks me with a telling smile.

"Not yet, you little tart," I laugh.

She makes a fake, pouty face like she's insulted and we laugh our butts off.

The doorbell rings, the front door opens, and a woman's heels click into the entryway. We hear Ms. Dunway's voice mingled with Mrs. Goebel's. We look at each other and grin. *This* is going to be *good.* We drop the pillows and stealthily creep up the stairs to eavesdrop. We are totally busted at the top of the stairs and try to act like we weren't sneaking around. Mandy and her Mom exchange a look, and we head into the kitchen. As we sit down at the kitchen table, Hazel dumps a giant stack of folders and paper onto it. Our eyes almost pop out of our heads.

"I've copied everything, and gotten in touch with Sargeant Tidwell. I also understand you had a good chat with my niece?" Ms. Dunway says, brushing a few raindrops off of her thick, beige trenchcoat.

"Sorry, who?" I ask, completely confused.

"Margaret Fitch, dear."

· Fourteen ·

I'm back at school and for the last couple of days, the rumors have been swirling relentlessly. People are so stupid. They whisper right of front of my face, like I'm suddenly blind and deaf. From the little bits I have heard, a news station in the next county over got wind of this business and did a story about Dr. Perv and Judge Thornton. That's why everyone is chattering like a flock of birds. News travels fast around here. That's how it is in a small town.

Apparently Dr. Samuel has been doing this sexual extortion for years. His abuses were a factor in a suicide of one of the law firm partner's daughters about fifteen years ago. The very same law firm that Mrs. Goebel and Ms. Dunway work for. The court didn't do squat about it because the law firm didn't want their good reputation ruined. The family was somehow "persuaded" to relocate and that was that.

I love Hazel Dunway. She knows absolutely *everything* about *everyone*. She was at the funeral and she knew all of the information that was hushed up and covered up. The partners bribed, paid off, threatened, and relocated everyone involved in the whole scandal. They made the foolish mistake of thinking that Ms. Dunway would keep quiet because she's a loyal and faithful employee. She was the one who made all the travel arrangements for that poor family. Biding her time with a filing cabinet full of faxes, receipts and the only paper trail that exists; she is now using it to save another innocent victim. I am over the moon that I helped nail this guy, and this crooked Judge. I was starting to lose all hope that the good guys even *can* win in this town.

I am sitting in US History class, zoning out and thinking about everything that's been happening when an obnoxious voice slaps me in the head, "Kiera?… KIERA! Get up here, *now*," orders Mr. Worley

I walk up to the front of the class and stand there, defiant. I can't believe this asshole is substituting for Mr. Deiter. I've had way too much going on, and am behind in reading and outlining the chapters we're on.

"Miss Graves, the chapter please…summarize," Mr. Worley sneers, rolling a piece of chalk in his palm.

I turn to face him and glare at him, "I have absolutely no idea."

"Well, if you did your homework, you would understand this chapter, Miss Graves. You haven't handed in the last three assignments. Is your social life interfering with your schoolwork?" he insinuates. He couldn't be more wrong thinking that I am a nogoodnik, wasteoid who screws off and doesn't bother with paltry things like *grades*. His face is triumphant as he attempts to cut me down in front of the class.

"I've been a little busy with my parents' divorce, the court case surrounding my father after he tried to kill me, and the latest issue of a perverted shrink," I spit angrily, watching Mr. Worley's face blister with indignation.

Mandy and Andy give me a standing ovation whistling and clapping, "Yeah! Kieeeeeeera! Wooo! Encore! Bravo! Bravo!" I curtsy and bow slightly.

"Sit down this minute and be quiet!" They sit hastily, snickering. The teacher we have christened "Mr. Fuckly" blanches and motions for me to return to my seat. I obey, trying restrain myself as Mandy and Andy give him the finger from under their desks. The rest of class is relatively uneventful, other than people continuing to look at me and whisper behind their hands. Mercifully, the bell rings and we troop into the hall to meet up with Max and head to lunch.

"Dude! You have cast iron *balls* telling him off like that for getting on you! That was awesome!" squeals Andy, slugging me in the shoulder.

"Actually, I have a vagina, not balls...so, no..." I respond, laughing.

Mandy drapes her arm over my shoulders and gives me a squeeze, "You totally rock, Kiera. I love when you rip someone a new one."

"I'm just fed up with these men ordering me around like I'm not even human," I mutter.

"What's so funny you guys?" Max asks as he joins us in line for the joke that is school lunch.

"Kiera tore Mr. Worley a new one," says Andy, laughing.

"You should've seen it. True poetry," Mandy says, holding her hand to her chest dramatically.

They take turns giving Max a blow-by-blow account as we pass on all the deep fried crap on a stick, settling instead for milk and cookies. At least they won't bite back. Max's jaw drops when he hears that I said this standing in front of the whole class. He knows I'm terrified of being in front of people, and that talking in front of people is the eighth ring of hell for me.

"Kiera! That's awesome! You must have been seriously *pissed*. I know you wouldn't have unloaded on him unless he damn near set you on fire," Max says.

"Yeah, not a fan of the whole public humiliation thing," I grumble, shuffling to our table.

It really irks me that anyone would ever think I'm slacking when all I can think about is getting to college, and away from this place. The constant threat of torture or death from my father is definitely a motivating factor, too. Avoiding disembowelment has always been at the top of my list. Imagine that. Speaking of which, I notice Mr. Worley stalking over to our table looking pissy. Oh goody.

"Miss Graves? A moment please?" he says snottily, motioning me to come to one side to chat privately.

"Sure," I say sitting solidly in my chair and not budging one centimeter.

"Over here, please?" he demands through gritted teeth.

"Whatever you want to say, you can say it in front them," I say, glaring at him defiantly.

"Very well. I do not appreciate your attitude problem or sense of humor in history class," he says, like he's chewing through a turd.

"Actually, you're the one with the problem," I retort, knowing full well what is coming.

"You-need-to-learn-to-respect-those-in-authority-young-lady!" Fuckly snarls, losing his composure for an instant.

"I only give my respect to people who *deserve* it," I seethe, throwing him a withering look.

The rage is visible in his pallid cheeks and he actually flexes her fingers like he would like nothing better than wrapping them around my neck and squeezing. He swallows and attempts to regain his reserve as everyone turns around to watch the spectacle. I hold my breath so I don't laugh in his face. Max and Andy are hiding behind folders, snickering and trying to keep their cool.

To my surprise, Worley gives me a yellow-toothed, satified smile, "You will learn about respect today during last hour when you are sitting in detention, Miss Graves." He informs me, handing me the pink detention slip and almost skipping away.

"Fascist," I mutter under my breath.

"At least you get to miss his class," says Andy, absolutely crying with mirth.

"Thank heavens for small favors," I snort, thankful that I don't have to face Mr. Worley again today. I'm not thrilled with the prospect of detention, but it beats good ole Fuckly. Most of the kids in detention are burnouts and fuck-ups, so conversing with any of them is out of the question. What the hell would we talk about? Books? Most of them are borderline literate at best. Music? I'm not a big fan of "G-n_R", or Whitesnake, so that's out. Guess I'll just keep to myself.

Mandy gives me a huge Cheshire cat grin, "Dude, it's nothing short of a miracle that this is your first detention."

I nudge her lightly with my cast and she nudges me back.

We screw around for the rest of lunch and head to art class. Today we are working on my least favorite thing, a still life. There's no budget of course, so it is the same chipped vase, fake flowers, and ceramic figurines we have been drawing for the last two years. They seem to purchase random stuff at a thrift store for the art and theater departments to use. The lack of variety snuffs my enthusiasm like a cigarette in the teacher's lounge. At least when we draw one another it is interesting. I'm not slamming Mrs. Michael; she's very cool and a fabulous teacher. I just think it's total bullshit that the football team just got a new locker room and weights, while the art department budget hasn't gotten jack. If it weren't for artists, everyone would be naked and sitting on the floor.

The hour passes quickly and after the bell, I dawdle along in the hallway to detention. There are no windows and no clock in this small classroom. It's really more of a large janitor's closet. Smells like one, too. Maybe it's just the malodorous stink of the unwashed burnouts who sprawl in the desks around me. The detention monitor surveys the class as the bell rings. His reptilian expression that makes my skin crawl. His blue eyes are cold and soulless. I make a mental note to find out who it is, and not take any of his classes. Jesus, what a kook! He wordlessly takes the seat at the desk and whips out a newspaper. I slide my Walkman out and pop on the tape.

The earphones I have are those little ones that fit into your ears, so my hair covers them and no one can tell what I'm doing unless I turn it way up. I whip out my pen and some paper, and start scrawling a note to Mandy. I doodle along the edges and ramble pointlessly about what a crashing bore the whole day has been and a few ideas on what kind of punishments would be suitable for Worley. We would never *actually* harm another living thing, but it is somewhat satisfying to fantasize about multiple uses for household items. I scrawl a couple of hasty notes for Max and Andy, who I know will be offended if I don't. I ask them about their plans, because I haven't had much time with them and I really want to hang out. I scribble a car taking us to Chicago. All I can think about is getting out of this ridiculous cow town anytime I can manage it. I hear the detention monitor's newspaper rattle and stealthily return my Walkman and headphones to my bag along with the notes. Wouldn't want this sadist getting hold of those. That would probably mean even more detention for Kiera and that would be bad.

Five more minutes. The portly teacher's footsteps are deafening in the silence of this room. His wingtips gleam like they have been polished to perfection, and his heavy military strides resonate against the speckled, whitish-gray, industrial tile floor.

He patrols the aisles like a prison warden. Four more minutes.

I stare blankly at my Literature book that I brought as my "homework." I finished reading the entire book a few weeks ago, and

I can easily discuss any of the assignments, no problem. Too bad I didn't have time to read ahead in US History and Mr. Deiter got jury duty. If Fuckly hadn't been the substitute, I probably would've gotten a little slack this one time.

The teacher in here must have sinus problems because his breathing would give Vader a run for his money. The hair on my neck stands on end as he abruptly stops right next to me.

"Miss Graves?" he says in a quiet but deadly voice.

"Yes sir?" I respond, barely audible. I can see his crotch peripherally, right next to my head.

"Why aren't you working?"

"I am," I respond, working hard to keep the tone of my voice even, eyes fixed on the desk.

You fucking knob. Pick on someone your own I.Q.

Two more minutes.

"You have nothing in front of you but that book," Vader's bastard cousin once-removed wheezes, his cold, blue eyes trying to penetrate my calm exterior.

"Yes, sir. I'm finishing my reading assignment for tomorrow's discussion and quiz," I tell him, staring hard at the desk so that I don't involuntarily roll my eyes.

Wanker.

RRIIIIINNNNNNGGG!

"Saved by the bell, Miss Graves," he says.

I don't respond, grab my stuff, and zoom into the hallway as quickly as I can. These teachers who seem to have some kind of vendetta against me for no good reason really freak me out. I am swallowed up in the flow of students, moving down the corridor toward my locker. It's odd to be surrounded by all these people and feel so completely alone. I see them all laughing and talking like they have no fears, no worries. Nothing is wrong in their worlds. They get allowance, do homework, hang out with friends, and go on vacations. They fit in, cheer the team on, and go shopping with their parents. I bet most of them are loved by their families. I bet they wouldn't be able to get their heads wrapped around my life at all. The concept is so foreign to "normal" people. The only reason my friends understand me is because they've witnessed this stuff for so long, they already get it.

Everyone else just thinks I'm weird. Maybe I am, but I don't see why that's such a scary thing to them.

I look up at a rushing noise in time to see Andy and Max sliding toward me on the dusty floor like they are surfing. They smack into the lockers next to me and receive their respective notes, grinning.

"Hey Kiera! So what are you guys doing later?" asks Max.

"Probably just hanging out at Mandy's," I respond. "That's your invitation right there," I tell them, tapping his note.

"Cool!" says Andy draping his arm over my shoulders. "I haven't given you *nearly* enough shit this week. I am *waaaaaay* under quota," he says, laughing as I give him a noogie on his flaming red head.

We hear a girl's voice echoing up the hallway, "Why can't I get...just one kiss? Why can't I get just one kiss?"

Mandy smiles widely at us and comes pelting down the hall. As she reaches us, she jumps up slightly and body slams Max with as much force as she can muster. They slam into each other all the way down the hall as we make our way out.

The plan for the night is to order from the Foo Dog, play video games, watch TV and hang out. Mandy's mom is *the* coolest and I am grateful for her kindness and generosity. We are in the living room playing Pac-Man when Mrs. Goebel arrives home.

"Hey kids! Has anyone ordered dinner yet?" she says, smiling widely at the collection of riff raff lying around on her living room floor.

"Nope. We were waiting for you so we could get whatever sounds good to you," Mandy tells her, as she gives her a monster hug and a big kiss on her face.

"Ooof! Thanks honey! Let's go ahead and order. I am starving!" she announces, kissing her daughter with a loud smack.

We are all in a good mood. Making some progress can really improve your outlook on life. We order mountains of food and clear off the kitchen table and prepare for our Chinese feast.

"So, there's supposed to be an announcement next week on foreign language programs around the state that we can get college credit for," Mandy tells her mom as she sets silverware on the table with a metallic clatter.

"That should be really interesting," Mrs. Goebel replies.

"How did you hear about it?" I ask her, wondering why she hadn't already told me.

"I heard some of the teachers chatting in the lounge on my way to the restroom," she says grinning wickedly, "I walked by a couple times to catch the whole story, but then they saw me and shut the door."

"You wayr nevayhr very good at survay-lonce," says Andy, mimicking Inspector Clouseau.

Mandy flicks him in the head and sits down, waiting for the doorbell.

"I would loooooove to get out of here for a few weeks!" I moan, every fiber of my being primed for any excuse to escape this place.

"Well, you shouldn't have any problem getting in," Mrs. Goebel says.

"It's the money part I'd have trouble with," I sigh, shaking my head. "My parents will buy fishing boats, fur coats, and a three-wheeler for Brett. When it comes to me, they can never find the money for anything, even if it's important."

Max and Andy look at each other and simultaneously roll their eyes.

"We'll never understand how you came out of that gene pool, Kiera," groans Andy sympathetically.

The doorbell rings and we swarm to the door to pay the delivery guy. We plunk the bags on the table and dig into our piles of food. I steer the conversation toward talking about taking classes at one of the colleges offering honors courses. I would love it! Getting away from my parents *and* getting better at French would be awesome. It goes along with my plans of taking off to Europe at the first opportunity. I figure I'll sign up for foreign exchange at college and study abroad for as long as I am allowed. Then, after I graduate, I can get a job as an artist somewhere and go to Paris whenever I want.

"Don't worry Kiera, we'll help you figure out how to get the money so you get to go," says Max, his cheeks stuffed with egg roll.

"I could have a bake sale!" I giggle.

"You could have a raffle!" says Andy.

Mandy looks at him like he has just snorted moo goo gai pan up his nose, "Dude, a raffle? How very church-y of you!"

"It was *supposed* to be a joke, you ninny!" he says, crossing his arms in a fake hissy fit.

"You're the ninny," she says, sticking out her tongue and grinning.

"OK you guys, that's enough," says Mrs. Goebel, raising an eyebrow. She knows that when things escalate around food, Andy often takes it too far and things get flung around her clean house. Our very own shit-chucking monkey. The phone hanging on the wall of the kitchen rings, and Mandy's Mom answers it. She stretches the phone around the corner so she can hear the caller over our shenanigans. When she hangs up the phone and turns to face us, all the chatter immediately stops. Stunned, she flops into her chair at the table.

"Judge Thornton spilled the story to his connection at the local newspaper. So, tomorrow, the headlining story will expose the corruption and sleaze going on with Judge Thornton, Dr. Samuel and their section of 'the system'."

"Holy crap!" I exclaim, unable to contain my shock at this revelation.

Max, Mandy, Andy and I are all looking at each in amazement with our mouths agape like a school of fish.

"He's also trying to vilify Sargeant Tidwell, and call the minors involved "troublemakers," Mrs. Goebel tells us in a very small voice.

"They're going to drag me into their mess?" I ask, worried about being dragged through the muck — again.

"All they can say is "minors". They can't legally name names. Sarge is going to crawl right up their behinds. Hazel says he has handpicked the judge that will replace Thornton when he steps down," Mrs. Goebel assures me.

"You think he'll resign?" asks Max excitedly, shoveling a forkful of cashew chicken into his mouth.

"If he has any brains in his twisted skull, he will," laughs Mrs. Goebel, "The City Council's office will terminate him if he doesn't vacate on his own. Sarge isn't going to take this kind of character assassination lying down, believe me."

"This is going to get worse, isn't it?" I say, my heart dropping to my knees.

"I don't know, honey. But, we'll all here for you," she says, putting her arm across my shoulders.

· Fifteen ·

November 13, 1987
B.F.E. Indiana

"LOCAL JUDGE DISGRACED ACCEPTING BRIBES FROM AL-
LEGED PEDOPHILE PSYCHOLOGIST".

Shit is going to fly, that's for sure. Mandy scans the article while I
scarf down breakfast. Giggling with delight, her eyes nearly pop out of
her head a couple of times. I take this as a good sign and plan to scan
as much as I can before we rush to school. I figure most of my peers
don't bother reading anything, let alone the local paper, so the likeli-
hood of needing to know the article verbatim is minimal.

"What do you think?" I ask between bites of toast.

"This guy's a real dirt bag," Mandy says with a disgusted expression.
"Milo Tidwell is going to be super pissed."

"I just hope I can stay off the radar," I say.

Everyone around here is related in some way or another. If someone get ratted on, then their nephew-in-law pays the whistle blower or
their car windows a visit with a baseball bat and that's the end of the
story. Not to mention the local rumor mill that operates faster than
anything else around here. I'll pass on the whole kit and caboodle,
thanks.

I skim the article while Mandy piles her stuff into her bag and my
stuff into mine. I am so glad to be a minor so that they can't actually

print my name. Like that'll deter anyone from speculating. The really gross part of this whole thing is that a former partner of the Pratt, Sinn, and Broker law firm had a daughter who was raped by Dr. Samuel during counseling. One day she sent a note to her father's secretary that detailed her appointments with Dr. Samuel, how she told her parents what was happening. They said she was overreacting, that it "couldn't be true." The sixteen year old blonde cheerleader princess took it upon herself to solve the problem for good, by blowing her brains out with a .45 in her daddy's Mercedes. Talk about a big "Fuck you, Daddy."

After their attempt to blow the whistle on these assholes fifteen years ago, this lawyer and his wife were conveniently relocated to Florida never to be heard from again. It would've ruined the law firm, and made the legal system here look like the joke it is. Now Pratt, Sinn and Broker will have to answer for a lot more. That just goes to show you, what comes around really does go around. The truth doesn't stay buried forever.

We look at the clock, realize we're running late, snatch up our stuff, and haul ass. We screech out of her driveway and zoom toward the high school.

"Well, at least today won't be boring," says Mandy as we fly into the parking lot.

Oingo Boingo blasts from the speakers, wailing about biting the big weenie, and wasn't it good?

"I guess. I just hope the preppy parasite squad isn't all upon the latest news," I grumble, hauling my butt out of the car and slinging my bag over my shoulder.

"Are you expecting them to read this early in the morning?" asks Mandy, rolling her eyes in annoyance.

We tromp into the crowded, noisy hallway and make our way to our respective lockers. I'll meet up with Mandy and Andy in first hour French class, until then I try to keep busy and become as invisible as humanly possible. I keep my head down, studying the floor tiles as I plod to my metal box to dump everything I don't need for the first half of the day. I suddenly notice the hush that seems to be following me like a wave down the hall. People are whispering behind their hands and looking at me. What the hell? I feel my face burning. I am used to the "normal" level of being stared at, but this is a new level of weird-ness. Something's up. I intend to find out what.

I haul my heavy, book-laden bag onto my shoulder and slouch to class, flopping into a desk at the back. Andy glides in a moment later and plops into a desk next to me and whispers, "You OK?"

"What the hell is going on, dude? People are staring at me like I've got an arm growing out of my head," I hiss back in frustration.

"Typical gossip from the rumor mill," my red-headed friend tells me. "Fuck 'em all. Just ignore it, don't respond to anything and they can't prove squat."

I nod, and we go into quiet mode for class. Today is going to be a stay quiet, don't make any sudden moves, don't say anything and it'll roll by kind of day. Maybe if I can just keep ducking out of the way, I can make it through unscathed.

We fiddle with our art bins, getting out supplies as the teacher takes attendance. There's no way we're discussing anything here or now. We don't want to give anything away.

Out of nowhere, Miss Fitch appears in the doorway. ""Kiera Graves? Come with me please."

My friends all look at me as I slowly get up to follow her. I have no idea what this is about, but it seems serious, and I'm scared shitless. I slouch down the hallway trying to make eye contact with Miss Fitch, who is studiously avoiding looking at me.

*click*click*click*

Her low heels clack on the tile floor and echo down the hallway. We reach the office and I see my mother and Mrs. Goebel sitting in the waiting area. Mother is reading a romance novel, and doesn't even look up. Mrs. Goebel gives me an encouraging wave as Miss Fitch leads me into the principal's office. Completely stumped, I raise my eye-brows questioningly and sit in the chair closest to the door.

"Ms. Graves, do you know why you are here?" ask Mr. Wick from behind his desk.

"I haven't the foggiest notion," I tell him.

Miss Fitch sits next to me, and rests her hand on my shoulder.

"Sorry if we startled you, Kiera, but we just got word and wanted you to know as soon as possible," Miss Fitch begins. "Your father has been dismissed from his position at the Middle School, resulting from a letter from the Sullivans' attorney.

Panic explodes in my solar plexus, and I start to pant. Miss Fitch takes my hand, and Mr. Wick comes over to squat in front of me.

"You're okay, Kiera. We've got you. From what I understand he is planning to pack up and move to Texas," Mr. Wick reassures me as tears splash down my face. I look from one to the other and try to control my breathing.

"We've all talked with your Mom and she understands the dire consequences if she doesn't keep him away from you. She will be in jail, and the civil suit will be resumed," Miss Fitch tells me. We sit for a few minutes, while I try to collect myself. They murmur reassurances that I want to believe, but after everything he's done to me and gotten away with, it's hard to trust anyone. I sit in stunned silence for a good minute, as the words roll around my skull like pinballs.

"Really?" I finally whisper, looking at Miss Fitch who nods with finality. She gives me detail by delicious detail on the undoing of Peter Graves, and my body starts to unclench. Relief washes over me like sunshine after a long, dark winter.

After reluctantly keeping a lid on it all day, I throw my books into my bag and we flee the beige walls of the institution that is supposed to be one of learning. The sky is a blank, gray slate of misery spitting of freezing rain at us as we slam through the exit to the parking lot. We scurry to Mandy's car, quickly piling in to avoid being chilled to the bone.

The silence is split by the Dead Milkmen wailing about exploits with their bitchin' Camaro that are now in all the papers. Mandy turns up the volume and we thrash around to the music as Mandy drives her small, reliable steed toward her humble abode. The back end bottoms out at the end of the driveway as she screeches into the driveway. We laugh as we tumble out of the car and make a break for the front door.

Mandy fumbles with her house key. "Take off your shoes!" she hollers to everyone as we clamber into the front hall, our shoes squeaking like a bunch of spastic mice. I remove my sodden shoes and retreat to her room to throw my bag under her bed along with my other stuff. I return to the living room and hear a ruckus coming up from the basement, letting me know that my friends have retreated to our usual lair.

I pad downstairs in my socks as my friends wait expectantly for this bombshell of a story that was so top secret Miss Fitch told no one else. Their eyes bug out in shock, as I unravel the whole story.

"NO WAAAAAAAAAY! YOU'RE FULL OF CRAP!" I hear Max bellow.

We whoop, jump up and down and congratulate ourselves on my escape from certain death. We call Chris to share the news and share the celebration.

November 17, 1987
Butt Fuck Egypt, Indiana

The weekend was one long and monotonous blur of cold, gray drizzle, spent doing whatever we could think of to not be bored into a catatonic state. This place is so goddamn dull; I swear that it kills brain cells. It was kinda rough landing back in reality after the revelation that my father is leaving town for good. We mostly hung around Max's watching him and Andy mess around on their guitars. They are actually Max's guitars, but Andy is his fellow "band mate" if you could call the two of them a band. Max is a fabulous bassist. Andy doesn't have enough focus yet to be really good, but he has the personality and charisma of a rock star, so it makes sense.

Anyway, we're slogging our way through another thrilling week in high school. The weather and mindless drones are getting to me, so I'm exuding an extra potent "fuck off and die" vibe. People aren't even trying to say stupid shit to me this week. They are afraid I'll eat their pets, even though I have vegetarian leanings, because in their world, people like me are dangerous. Not the crazy, redneck gun nuts who threaten to kill people they don't like.

Fucking idiots.

Much to everyone's complete shock, Judge Thornton has resigned. His little media "leak" backfired spectacularly, and the City Council is livid. The State Attorney General's Office is now investigating the whole thing since Judge Thornton kept letting well-connected violent criminals out of jail, and has been taking bribes from Dr.-fucked-in-the-head-pedophile-Samuel. I'm so glad he got called on his insane, corrupt bullshit. It'll be on his record and he'll never be a judge again. Sargeant Tidwell packed up Judge Thornton's personal stuff in a box and drove it over to his house in his squad car. A little birdy told me every detail. Ms. Dunway sent unofficial word through Miss Fitch, because blood is thicker around here and we all have to be extra careful right now. I never thought I'd see any reason to take a math class, but this time it's paying off.

I am very interested to know who will be taking his place. This could be either very good or really crappy for me. I won't know until after school when Mandy's mom gets home from work. I do know that my time at their house is running out and I'll have to go back to living with Mommy Dearest soon. I'd rather be doused in kerosene and set on fire, but that doesn't count in warped world. All the little Christian goody-goodies around here think that family is *the* most important thing in the whole world. They don't care about how badly the kids are abused. They only care about appearances. That's part of why my existence offends them. I don't give a flying one about appearances. I care about the truth. It's last hour and I am trying not to grind my teeth down to a nub in Mrs. Starling's class. She has given me another C minus because in her opinion, my journal lacks style. She basically wants everyone to write *exactly* the way she does, or it's wrong. What a dingbat.

I thumb through a copy of e. e. cummings' collected works that I checked out from the library at lunch. Case in point with this guy. I mean, totally free form, right? I like his sense of humor. I chew on my lower lip to try and keep from laughing out loud as I read.

"may I feel said he"

Gee, I wonder what this poem is about...

You'd have to explain it in really small words to people like this one pom pom girl, who's sitting in the back of the class, chattering away like a chipmunk on speed. That girl never shuts her mouth. She's one of the ones who usually can't resist messing with me. But, to her credit, she's picked up on the fact that I may snap her head off at the neck if she does this week. I detest brainless poseur morons as much as I detest poofball cheerleaders because there is, in essence, no difference between the two. Neither thinks independently and neither really thinks at all come to think of it. Sheep following along blindly. Baa. You know, one of these days, they're going to go right over a cliff with the flock.

Mercifully, the bell finally rings and I chuck my book in my bag, zipping out the door into the stream of students.

I slam my locker and stomp toward the exit, death glaring at anyone who crosses my path so that they get out of my way and leave me alone. I plod across the parking lot and plant myself on Mandy's hood so that if she looks out the window for me, she can see me easily. I whip out my headphones and snap on the tape to distract myself.

I smile as The Dead Milkmen snarl about a moron who makes a waste of the gene pool, and whose brain cells have all died. Synchronicity is a beautiful thing. I perch on Mandy's car like a crow on a headstone, bobbing my head to the music. Mandy exits the brick monstrosity of a high school, spots me and gives me huge grin as she bounces over.

November 25, 1987
Butt Fuck Egypt, Indiana

On Sunday, Sarge came over to Mandy's to deliver the news that I had to pack it up and go back "home" with my mother. I've been in a terrible mood needless to say, and to make matters worse, I have three tests to study for and a paper to write. The best part of this week so far is that Peter is being closely watched so that if he tries mess with me again, he goes straight back to jail. So far, so good, I haven't heard a peep. The only news is that Brett is going to crash at his buddy's house until he graduates, then he'll go to Texas to live with our father.

Today I trudge the few blocks home by myself to study and do my homework. Everyone is traveling to different places for Thanksgiving. Mandy, Max and Andy are all going to various relatives' homes for the holiday. I will be here, thankfully. It isn't like my relatives are nice to me. They treat me like something on the bottom of their shoes, because I'm "different". They follow the rules so to speak, and are the biggest bunch of greedy, shallow, ill-mannered jerks I've ever had the displeasure of knowing, aside from the brainless wonders at school. I've always been ashamed of them because they treat people like crap.

It's embarrassing. I don't care if you're a maid or an ambassador to France, you're a human being and deserve to be treated like one. I'm fed up with the whole ball of wax, and as far as I'm concerned they can all go pound sand.

It is a typical cold, gray, nasty and depressing afternoon. Mom will be home in the next couple of hours, so it doesn't look like things will improve. I drag myself up the stairs and into the stale-smelling, small apartment. It's really not that bad. At least we're on the top level so we aren't beneath elephants all day. I throw my bag and books into a crate sitting just inside my room, when the downstairs buzzer sounds. I walk hesitantly to the intercom.

"Kiera! Get down here," I hear a man's voice command.

It's my delusional father. Thankfully, this building is secured by several locks so you can't just come in and knock on the door of the apartment. I breathe deeply to steady myself, but I don't respond. He hits the buzzer several times. I hear my heart pounding in my ears and heat rising in my face. I'm so angry that I am out the door and on my way downstairs before I really take a minute to think about what I am doing.

"WHAT?" I yell at him through the glass.

"Open the door, Kiera," he seethes.

I smirk nastily at him and walk right up to the door, "No."

He then notices the police car parked next to his as the officer inside watches his every move.

Turning an interesting shade of magenta, my father shifts uncomfortably, fidgeting with the collar of his expensive wool winter coat. "I just came by to let you know that Mom and Dad are coming with me to Texas."

"Bullshit," I protest. "They don't have any friends or family there. They've never even visited!"

"I have to leave after I lost my job because of you, and they need to be close, so I'm setting up an auction for their big stuff, and we're moving the rest," he snivels.

My heart drops. "All the furniture from Grandma's family? You're getting rid of it?"

"We have to," he growls.

"No, you don't. And it isn't my fault that you're a violent asshole. That's on you, Dad," I snarl as I turn to go back upstairs.

"They want you to come to Thanksgiving before we go," he yells.

I shake my head with a bitter laugh. As if that would happen. I'm not doing this one more time. Not another birthday, not another Christmas. This whole manipulative chess game is over.

Thanksgiving 1987

I have had to fight tooth and nail to be at home alone on this stupid holiday. Now my grandparents are all pissed off and not speaking to me. The people I've been the closest to my whole life, who I adore have turned their backs on me. Their son is selling off antique family heirlooms that have been passed down for a few centuries. All that history — gone in an instant. I'll never be able to find it all again. I went over to help them pack and they were both exhausted. I've never seen them look so bad. But, they won't stand up to their son, who has arranged this whole clusterfuck of a move, so I don't know what. All I know is that I am sixteen years old, a Junior in high school, and I'm trying to find my way in this crazy, messed up world. It looks even more like I'll be doing it on my own.

They are moving to Texas day after tomorrow. They don't even want to see me if I won't also see their son, so I don't even get to say goodbye. Guilt hangs heavily on me, but I just can't face being his punching bag again. Not even for them. Mom has no sympathy for what I'm going through, and seems to be totally unaware of my world slowly unraveling.

Mom is at some shindig at Olivia Walsh's house, all my friends are with relatives. I'd rather drink elephant piss than go have Thanksgiving dinner with my grandparents, brother and father at the only really nice restaurant in town "Le Maison". So, I'm sitting here by myself eating a Tombstone pizza and going over some notes for the umpteenth time. All I can think about is going back to the library, which has become my second home, and digging through the college guides again. I am obsessed with dotting all my "i's", crossing every "t" and getting myself out of this mess.

· Sixteen ·

We can't get out of cowtown as fast enough. We all rush to finish homework. I scramble around like a maniac doing the endless list of chores mother has required to be done before I can leave. The second I finish, Andy and Mandy grab me and my stuff. We hotfoot it down the stairs, climb into the waiting car, and head for the highway. Max kept the Lincoln warm for us since it is effing freezing out here. Typical Indiana cold, gray, frozen, ugly and depressing winter. This time we cruise to the Windy City in Max's huge, black boat. The glow-in-the-dark skull that dangles from the rearview mirror grins at us toothily as we sing along with the Violent Femmes, Oingo Boingo and Bauhaus. Max has so many tapes in his car, they spill out of the glove compartment and shoe box in the back seat.

In what seems like no time at all, we're at Chris's front door to meet up with him and his friends, and then go to Medusa's for a long-anticipated night of dancing and blowing off all the tension of the last month. Between all the crap with my father, my grandparents, the judge, the shrink, and then mid-year tests and writing papers, I've been feeling like I'm running on a treadmill and getting nowhere fast. I still have this scratchy, icky cast on my arm for now, but other than that, I'm looking good and I'm soooo ready to dance my butt off.

Mandy let me borrow this plaid mini that I love, so I am feeling très cute and am psyched to finally be standing at Chris's house.

Mandy slugs me on the arm, "Ring the damn bell! It's colder than a well digger's out here!"

I press the doorbell, laughing at her exclamation. Indiana has weird country sayings like that. It means colder than a well digger's butt.

The bell doesn't ding, so much as DONG. I can feel its tone vibrating in my teeth. I guess with a house this big, you have to have one hell of a doorbell. We hear feet thundering down the stairs and into the hall, a clickety-clack of the lock being undone and...

"KIERA!!" exclaims Chris sweeping me into his arms and into the house in one motion. Before I can say anything, I am absorbed in a kiss so passionate, the world surrounding us ceases to exist.

He releases me a bit and looks down at me with a wide grin, "Hi!"

I look up shyly hoping he doesn't notice the sheen of sweat on my flushed face, "Hi." I'm not used to this kind greeting — yet. Don't get me wrong, 'cause I'm not complaining.

"OK, break it up you two," says a girl's voice over his shoulder.

Startled, I look over and see a short girl with raven and violet hued spiky hair, jet black lips, purple eye shadow and a black velvet dress.

"You'll have to excuse Vic, she's leery of strangers," Chris says in irritation, raising his eyebrows at Victoria like, would you pleasejustbehaveyourself?

"Excuse yourself for your disgusting display," she says to Chris with a sneer.

"Last time I checked, I didn't need your permission, Victoria," he says. "Don't mind Victoria, she's over-protective and apparently in a mood today."

"Hi! I'm Mandy!" my petite friend declares holding out her hand to introduce herself.

"Victoria," Chris's friend responds, taking just the tips of Mandy's fingers into her grasp, like she's diseased.

"Look, Bride of Frankenstein, if we're all going to hang out, you'll have to chill out," says Andy skipping up to her and Mandy, who is now laughing.

Max stands by the door, observing the scene, trying not to totally crack up at Andy's comment.

"What did you call me?" Victoria snits, turning toward him.

Andy steps right up, his face less than an inch away from hers and says, "Bride of Frankenstein."

"Get it right, it's Dracula's Bride," she says with a deep chuckle, that can't conceal her amusement with Andy's direct but hilarious nature.

"Fine, Drac," says Andy, sticking his elbow out for her, "Shall we head over to Medusa's for dancing and merriment?"

"Who the hell are *you*? Raggedy Andy from Hell?"

I look up at the ceiling and cringe.

"I'm Andy, and I'm not raggedy, but you seem to be on the rag," he says, leaping out of the way as she swats him with a hat she's just taken out of the hall closet.

"Well, you just met Mandy," I say motioning to my best friend who's now standing next to me. "This is Max," I tell Victoria as I motion to the tall, watchful overgrown bat who has not moved from the doorway. "And I believe you've met Andy," I laugh as my flame-haired friend exaggeratedly bows like a cartoony butler.

"We know who you are. Chris hasn't shut up about you since the night you two met," Victoria groans, as she slides on her heavy coat.

"Then you must be John!" exclaims Mandy as she rushes over to a guy who has been lurking, watching us silently from the stairs.

He mutely nods, looking like he wants to disappear into the wall. Pushing his glasses back up his nose, he looks toward Chris in complete panic.

"I warned you..." Chris says to his friend.

"What's that supposed to mean?" demands Mandy, glaring at Chris.

"I only repeated what you told me," he says holding up his hands in surrender.

"That I really like smart guys?" she asks.

"Yep," Chris admits with a smile.

"It's true, you know," Mandy tells John, slyly slipping her arm through his. He shrinks back at first, but then gingerly comes down the last few steps with her gentle coaxing.

John turns bright fuchsia, looks at her incredulously, and snaps his mouth closed. Obviously perplexed and avoiding eye contact with everyone, he wanders over to the closet to get his coat so we can go.

John, Chris's best friend, is about 5'8", with sandy blonde hair, and clear blue eyes that are hidden behind huge glasses that he seems to constantly push back up the bridge of his nose. My heart goes out to him. Never thought I'd meet someone more shy and awkward than me.

Bundled in winter coats, scarves and mittens, we plunge into the cold night. Andy whoops and runs around the group like a very colorful and odd satellite.

"Is he on medication?" asks Chris, laughing at my friend's spastic orbit.

"Nah, probably should be at least some of the time," I reply chuckling at Andy's antics.

I overhear Mandy chattering happily at John who has still not spoken out loud.

"What's the deal with John?" I ask.

"He's never gotten positive attention from a pretty girl, so he's totally freaking out," Chris tells me in an undertone.

"Why?" I ask discreetly, not wanting to overheard.

"Well, I can see that he's not gross and you can see that he's not gross, but the girls at our school can't see it at all," he whispers, shaking his head in disapproval.

"Mandy definitely sees him as something completely different," I tell Chris with a grin. I guess the uptick of living in hillbully cowtown USA is that we've all learned a lot about people. The difference between superficiality and integrity.

"She kicks ass," says Chris with a wide grin as he glances at his best friend who is slowly but surely warming up to Mandy.

The few blocks to the club seem like nothing even in the bitter cold because I'm keeping such great company. We get in the short line and try to find out if there are any bands tonight. That is the one good thing about this weather, it keeps the line short because most people won't wait outside in the arctic temperatures. Chris holds me close to keep me warm and our little group huddles together against the bone-chilling wind that whips through the streets. They don't call it "the Windy City" for nothing. The bouncers do a great job and we are inside in record time. I'm glad because the muscles in my face seem to have stopped working, which is not too cute.

I smile at Mandy over John's shoulder as he politely takes her coat at the coat check. She grins back and silently exclaims, "He's so cute!" at me. I laugh and mouth back "Good!"

Max and Victoria are busy competing for the cranky award at the moment. Waiting impatiently to one side for us, Max eyes John with an expression of loathing and suspicion. Victoria is still giving me the once-over, with a sour expression. I am baffled by her reaction to me, but I have all night to find out what her deal is, so I shrug it off for now and bask in the warmth of Chris's affection.

We troop upstairs and head out to the main floor in a hurry, as we hear the sensuous rhythm of Love and Rockets as they croon about how one day the mirror people will be free, they don't know how to cry and scream inside. Mandy and I are in heaven as we swirl around the floor. Mandy spins and winks at John who is lurking nearby with Max. Andy is grinning like a maniac and pogoing with the beat. The lights catch Chris's face and he smiles at me.

I am struck at this moment by how happy I am to be with my friends, here, right now. I wish I could stay here in this moment forever. I live for happy moments like this, because they seem to be so few and far between. Other people love December and winter because it's a happy time, and they have families who love them and who they love. For me it is a time of loneliness and alienation. I don't know what it's like to have a whole family in your corner.

But, I am lucky. I have my friends.

It is a great night and the DJ is making us really happy. They are playing more real alternative on the main floor tonight, which is not the norm. Typically they play a lot of Euro-dance mixed with industrial and the occasional alternative tune.

Mandy and I head up the stairs to the bar for water, and to catch a breather on the red velvet couches.

"What do you think about John?" she asks me, her face aglow with excitement.

"Well, I haven't been able to talk to him, he seems nice, but I can't *really* tell you until I have a chance to chat with him," I say.

"I know he's quiet, but he has really good manners, right?" she pleads.

"I like him! I do!" I tell my friend to soothe her, "I'm looking forward to talking to him myself is all." They're called "crushes" for a reason, and I don't want her to be crushed.

"Speak of the devil," Mandy purrs, looking over to where John, Chris, Max and Andy have ascended the stairs and are moving to a corner where a couple of long, large, red velvet couches face each other. The large, round table that squats between them is littered with empty cups and a few dirty ashtrays. This corner is very desirable because it allows you to watch the dance floor through a wrought iron balcony railing, but is set back from the main thoroughfare and more conducive to conversation.

We get some extra waters along with our previous order and take them over to the boys. Chris and John stand up when we come over and help us distribute drinks. I am so impressed by their gentlemanly behavior. I used to have a thing for English men because I always figured they had to have better manners than American men. They always sound so cultured and intelligent, even if they aren't. I wouldn't know for sure, because I've never actually met one.

Mandy curls up on a couch cushion next to John and is chatting, trying no doubt to get him to talk about himself. Chris looks over sympathetically and yells over the music, "Dude, give her a break! Just talk!"

John looks mortified for a moment and then, with obvious effort, begins to talk to Mandy, much to her delight. She leans closer and is almost sitting in his lap, which I can tell is making him really nervous.

"Have I told you how beautiful you look tonight?" Chris purrs in my ear.

"Um, not specifically," I answer, looking at my shoes.

"You look amazing," he says, looking at me with those eyes that reveal to me what he's thinking. I feel heat flooding my whole body. This guy makes me sweat. He's looking at me like I'm an ice cream sundae.

"You look really nice, too," I tell him with a grin, plucking his ragged Cramps t-shirt.

"Are you pulling my chain?" Chris gasps in mock horror, grinning wickedly.

He leans over with a wolfish smile and kisses me so intensely that I think my shoes will melt and pool on the floor, adding to the already sticky muck.

"You two! Break it up!" Victoria orders as she saunters up.

"Awwww, shut it you tart," Chris yells back, laughing.

"You're the tart! Look at you!" she scolds, lightly tapping him on the head with her handbag. "Ooo! I see John has a new friend!"

John blushes at Victoria's loud observation and Mandy just keeps right on talking to John as if she hasn't heard a thing. I know she'd probably like to duct tape Victoria's mouth shut at this point because she has finally broken the ice with him — and doesn't want John to freeze back up. Mandy looks over at me with an expression that says, "what's her major malfunction?," and I cover my mouth with my hand to stop myself from cracking up.

Suddenly, a voice pipes up, "Why don't you zip it, Vampira?" We all look at John in shocked silence. He hasn't said two words hardly all night but when he does, it ends up being quite the mouthful. Mandy, Andy and I laugh so hard, I feel like my abdomen is going to split open. I gasp for air through my tears of mirth, hoping that my eyeliner isn't running all over my face.

"Oooo! Serious!" replies Victoria, wiggling her fingers by her face in a taunting gesture.

"Bite me," John replies, grabbing Mandy's hand.

Mandy slides her fishnet-stocking-clad legs across John's lap and grins at Victoria in triumph. Her hand grasped firmly by John who is clearly enjoying Mandy's company, and I can see his confidence blooming.

Just as Victoria is about to sit down next to Andy, a couple of girls come strutting up to our group. Before I know what's happening, the blonde girl sidles past me, putting her narrow ass in my face, and plops herself into Chris's lap.

Chris leaps to his feet, his mouth agape and his face furious, "Screw you, Tamara."

"What's the matter darling?" the fluffy Barbie clone asks with dangerously honeyed tones, as she reaches out to stroke his jaw with her finger.

I have no idea what the hell is going on, so I sit with my mouth hanging open like a giant carp. I can't decide if I should get up, stay still, or what. Then, Victoria hustles past Max toward the blonde girl who is clearly the ex-girlfriend. "You fucking whore, the problem is that you can't keep your mouth or your legs closed for longer than two seconds."

Tamara flips her hair over her shoulder, turning to look at Victoria who is now about an inch away from he face. "Ah, Victor, nice to see you, too. I heard Suze is here tonight, why aren't you with…awww, I forgot, she dumped you last month," Tamara says with a vicious smile.

"Yeah, but at least it wasn't because she caught me with my lips around someone else's genitalia!" Victoria snarls in Tamara's milk white face.

"Whatever," sniffs Tamara, tossing her blonde mane around her bony shoulders.

Meanwhile, Tamara's best friend, an Asian girl, is perched next to John, trying to flirt with him. He carefully removes Mandy's legs from his lap and pats her on the knee as he stands up. "I saw you giving that guy a blow job, Tamara," he says, jerking his leg away from the Asian girl's pursuit. "I saw you screwing that other guy in your car," John states loudly and clearly enough for everyone in the area to hear, "You're a liar and a skank, and you are not going to be with Chris ever again."

Tamara laughs nastily, tossing her blonde hair, "You think you can tell me what to do, geek?"

"No, but I can," growls Chris, as he grabs her arm and drags her past me, "You screwed up big time. Don't ever talk to me or my friends again."

Tamara nods toward me with a nasty look, "So trailer trash is your new fascination? How did she get the cast? A drunken brawl with her 'Mama'?" she and the Asian girl laugh. I feel heat rising in my face, tears of shame threatening to fill my eyes. My feelings turn to ice and I stand up to walk away until they've settled things. The very, very stupid are so easy to predict and I am not about to rise to this fluffy little blonde nitwit. She's not even worth talking to. "Are you going to 'git me'?" Tamara giggles, slipping her arm around Chris's waist.

As the Asian girl slides past John to join Tamara, she tries to kiss him on the lips.

"No!" John stammers, pushing her away in horror.

Tracy stumbles into Tamara as Chris forcefully removes Tamara's hand from touching him. They stumble around like drunken dwarves and I smile.

"Chris, honey, come here so we can finish our conversation with Victoria," I say, smiling at my very adorable, very pissed off boyfriend. I hold out my hand which he immediately accepts with a huge smile, kissing it.

"Don't call him 'honey', trailer trash," Tamara snarls at me, shoving me in the shoulder as I'm sitting back down by Chris.

Touching me in a violent way is always a bad idea.

"Don't touch me again you fucking parasite," I say, dangerously quiet.

"What'cha going to do about it, trailer trash?" she asks, prodding me hard in the chest with her Lee Press-On claws.

"The only person here who's acting like trailer trash would be you. Screwing everything that moves and picking fights with people is sort of the definition of trailer trash — or it was the last time I checked. I guess since you must also be illiterate, I'll cut you some slack," I tell Tamara with a venomous grin.

My friends have all gotten up at this point and are giving me a standing ovation. A bouncer who obviously just witnessed this whole thing is striding toward us.

"Excuse me, sir?" Mandy rushes over to meet the bouncer. "This girl just shoved my friend twice for no reason. We were just sitting here and she walked up and started being a total…pain," she says, catching herself just in time.

"Yeah, I saw the whole thing," the short, muscular, tattooed man growls. "You two are coming with me," he tells Tamara and Tracy.

"I don't think so," sniffs Tamara, tossing her blonde hair in disgust.

"Well I do, girlie," he growls, taking each of them by the elbow and dragging them toward the exit. We hear their squeals of protest all the way to the door.

"I hope she gets banned," snarls Victoria, glaring after them.

It's almost time to go, so we bounce downstairs to the dance floor to catch a few more songs before we have to leave. I am dancing with more concentration than usual, as my mind analyzes what just occurred. I can't imagine Chris dating a bitch like Tamara. How did that happen in the first place? And what was with her little friend and John?

The DJ is playing mostly industrial and we are all totally drenched in sweat. There's nothing like a little Front 242 to work out your aggression. Max is in heaven, flailing around the dance floor. He almost never dances, but he loves industrial so much that he just can't resist. It sounds amazing on the massive sound system. Chris is nearby, moving gracefully. He's one of the best dancers I've ever seen. I've never understood reluctant dancers- especially when they are actually good!

As lights come on, we all shuffle toward the coat check to get our stuff before we go back to Chris's to crash. Victoria is looking around hopefully to catch a glimpse of Suze. I feel a sliver of anger slice through my fatigue. That was so cruel of Tamara to bring up Suze. I can't stand people who are just horrible to everyone because they *enjoy* it.

Chris helps me with my coat as John helps Mandy with hers, and I hear a snippet of their conversation, "…she knew I wanted to date her and she was always mean to me. She just did it because she likes being mean…" I overhear John explaining to Mandy. I turn my head just in time to see John grab Mandy and plant one hell of a kiss on her. She is so surprised that he actually has to hold my petite friend up so she doesn't fall. All that pent up desire to be liked by a girl focused into one kiss will really knock you for a loop.

I smile to myself and begin walking down the stairs with Chris. We share a silent moment where we smile at each other, knowing our best friends are getting along, shall we say, quite well. Andy has again begun his spastic orbit around the group, much to Max's annoyance.

"Dude! You need to stop drinking Coke," he yawns grumpily at the red-headed satellite that bounds past him.

"I haven't had any since ten!" replies Andy as he jumps around us, grinning like a loon.

Max rolls his eyes as he and Victoria continue their conversation, most likely about music.

In no time we reach Chris's house. "OK everyone, be quiet coming in so we don't wake my parents up," Chris says as he unlocks the door.

We tiptoe inside and silently remove our shoes so that we don't sound like a herd of wild elephants stampeding up the stairs. We pad up to Chris's "room," if you can call it that. It's more like an apartment, really.

"Holy crap!" gasps Mandy as we walk in, "This is your *room?*" She rounds on me accusingly, "*This* is where you've been staying?"

"Yeah, I said it was nice…" I shrug, trying to defend myself. She glowers at me once more and skips off to flop down next to John on the couch.

"OK, there are four guest rooms just outside my door on this level," Chris explains. "My parents are pretty cool, but they'll have a conniption if everyone is sleeping in here," he says.

"Cool…Mandy? You and I in a room?" I ask tentatively.

"Absolutely! Then Max and Andy can share one, and Vic and John can each have one," she says with a smile, "Perfect!"

Chris sidles up to me and puts his arms around my waist, "I thought you'd be in here with me again," he whispers in ear, giving me goosebumps. He nuzzles my neck, and as hard as it's getting, I resist.

"No way. I don't need supervision this time, so a guest room it is," I tell him sternly.

Oh god, it is getting tough to be a "good girl," but I really don't want to make that kind of commitment just yet. I mean, that's as close as you can get to another human and I am not going to just whip my clothes off for the first cute guy that shows some interest. I want a real boyfriend. Someone who really loves me the way I am and hopefully gets along with my friends, too. So far, so good. I'm just not there yet, so either he'll wait or he won't.

Max has rifled through Chris's records and put on Bauhaus. John and Mandy are on the couch chatting quietly. Chris and I sit next to them while the rest of the group is splayed on the other couch and an overstuffed chair that Victoria calls her "throne."

Andy asks, "So, who the hell were those girls at the club, anyway?"

"That was my ex and her best pal," mutters Chris disdainfully.

"Lovely girl, if you don't count personality or lack of brains," sneers Max. "How did you end up with *her?*"

"She's the prettiest girl in school and she asked me out last year," mutters Chris as a fierce blush creeps through his neck, ears and face.

"I'd never been on a date or anything before and most of the girls at school hate me because I'm not a jock."

"Is she nice to people at school?" grumbles Max.

"I wasn't really aware of how she treated anyone other than me, because I just wasn't watching what other people were doing. I stay to myself and hang out with Vic and John. I don't go to games or dances or any of that crap," Chris growls defensively.

"I can see that," Andy pipes up. "Who the hell wants to be an athletic supporter?" he says, laughing.

"You suck," Mandy snorts, rolling her eyes.

We all snicker at Andy's stupid pun and the tension between Chris and Max finally breaks.

"Besides, Max, that girl was beee-yooo-tee-ful. I wouldn't have turned her down either and neither would you," says Andy, wiggling his eyebrows at Max like, you-know-what-I-mean?

"Screw you! I wouldn't go out with some girl just because she's pretty," retorts Max, pushing Andy roughly with his shoulder.

"Yeah right, furry palms…." Andy says, jumping up and running away as Max lunges for him.

"Tamara knew she could, so she did," interjects Victoria with a grimace, "and Tracy messed with John's head the whole time because she's a twisted little sadist."

Mandy's head jerks so fast to look at John that it looks like she hurt her neck. "Tracy?" she asks him quietly.

"We never dated. She would just lead me on and flirt with me, and then humiliate me," he replies with a sigh.

"What the hell?" demands Mandy.

"We would end up in the same place because I'm John's friend and she's Tamara's friend, and she would act like she liked me and then make fun of me behind my back or play pranks on me and stuff," John miserably chokes out. It's obvious how badly he's treated at school. It makes me want to thump some people.

"They are both complete bitches," sneers Victoria. "They call me 'the Dyke' at school."

"Lovely," I say sarcastically. "But why are they so mean? They have everything, it isn't like they have to *claw* their way to the top of the pile."

"They just want to remain at the top," sighs Chris.

"Now, why would anyone want to hang around a big stinky pile?" chimes in Andy, who has returned from wrestling around with Max near the kitchen area.

"Chris and Tamara were, like, the royal couple last year until…" Victoria trails off, looking squeamishly at John.

"I was out one night, coming home from an academic competition, and I saw Tamara giving some guy a blow job. I didn't want to, but I told him about it because I didn't want him to catch something from that whore," John tells us venomously. "Of course, she lied and said that it wasn't her."

"I know better than to believe someone else over John," interjects Chris. "He's been my best friend since we were about five, so there's no way he'd screw me over. He has no reason to."

"How long has it been since all of this happened?" asks Mandy.

"February…so, it's been almost one year," replies Chris, who is squirming and desperate to change topics. "I felt like such a dumbass. I should have known better."

"Why is she still chasing you if it's been over for so long?" I ask Chris with a stern look.

"Oh! Oh! Oh! Can I answer this one?" Victoria says loudly, raising her hand.

Chris laughs, shakes his head before nodding at her.

"She is a psychotic, twisted whore who likes to play with boys' heads and she likes keeping trophies," Victoria explains to us. "Her father is a total asshole and her mother is the original ice queen, so she comes by it honestly, I guess. She's just mean and shallow because that's what she was taught to be. That's what her parents and that whole crowd expect from her, so she's just fulfilling her pre-destiny."

"Chris was just something for her to play with," John says, fury darkening his innocent face. "She doesn't give a crap about anyone or anything, except maybe money."

"Well, she better stay away from Kiera, because if she fools with her again, I am going to personally thrash her within an inch of her life," seethes Mandy.

"I'll help," says Max with flash of a wicked grin.

"I'm just glad Chris found someone cool who has awesome friends this time," interjects John with a sly wink to Mandy. In return, she leans over and gives him a big kiss. He blushes from the tips of his ears all the way down his neck.

"OK everyone, I'm done for and am going to drag my ass to bed," I say groggily. The adrenaline has definitely worn off and I am feeling ragged. It is now 2:30 a.m. anyhow, so it really is time to catch some z's.

"Allow me!" says Chris, scooping me off the couch and carrying me toward the door.

I giggle sleepily as I drape my arms around Chris's neck. I haven't been carried like this since my Granddaddy carried me up to bed when I was little. Chris sets me down in front of the first guest room door. "This one has a half bath so you guys don't have to deal with Max and Andy," he tells me with a knowing grin.

"Awesome. Well, g'night," I whisper. He crushes me into a red hot, brain melting kiss and I awkwardly turn, and bumble into the door. He sure knows how to make a girl all squishy. I wash up before I collapse into bed. Despite the blonde vacant one and her sidekick showing up, we had a great night. I sink into the pillows with a smile, slowly drifting into a deep, sweet and serene sleep like I haven't had since I don't know when.

· Seventeen ·

December 6, 1987
Chicago

I roll over languidly stretching as wide as I can with this gnarly cast still on my arm. Just a couple more weeks! I roll out of bed and throw some rumpled clothes, run a brush through my hair, and pad to the door to go see if Chris is up yet. I'm guessing he probably is, since the tiny clock in the guest room was showing that it's one o'clock in the afternoon.

"You asshole! Get back here!" I hear Victoria hollering at someone through Chris's door.

I wander in to find Andy bolting across the room holding something over his head and Victoria chasing after him. Max is draped across one of the couches and Chris is in the kitchen making a pot of coffee. Something smells fabulous.

Chris sees me and greets me with a wide grin, "Hiya gorgeous! Want some breakfast?"

"Dude, you must have had some funny herbs today to call me gorgeous at the moment," I reply as a flush creeps into my face and neck.

"Nope, no drugs. You're just gorgeous. Toast? Sausage? Cinnamon rolls? Coffee?" He offers with gestures like the models on "The Price is Right."

"That would be what smells so good!" I exclaim, grabbing a plate and loading it with sausage and rolls as Chris hands me a cup of coffee.

"Milk and sugar, just the way you like it," he says with a wolfish grin, raising one eyebrow like, do-I-get-a-smooch-for-this-or-what? I give him a peck on the cheek as I glide past him to inhale some food. I'm starving and have beast breath more than likely, so that's all the smooching I'm up for at the red hot second.

"Kiera! Saaaave me!" howls Andy from Chris's bed where he has been cornered by Victoria who is sitting on top of him, giving him noogies.

"What are they doing?" I ask Chris as he sits down next to me at his table.

"Andy went through her purse and stole her tampons, apparently, and today would be not the day to do that," Chris tells me in a low voice so that Victoria doesn't hear him.

"I see."

"KIIIEERA! HELP!"

"Dude, you need to learn how to play more nicely with others," I tell Andy after I swallow a bite delicious cinnamon roll.

"You can say that again," murmurs Max from the couch. "Isn't Mandy getting up?"

"She was still out when I got up. Do you think she'd want us to wake her up?"

"Hard to say with her, but I'd guess that she'll be mad if we let her sleep too much longer. She hates missing anything," Max replies, stretching his long, lanky frame as he settles in to watch "The Young Ones" on cable.

Just then the door opens and a ruffled looking John shuffles in and heads toward the food and coffee. "Morning, or afternoon everybody..." he murmurs sleepily. His hair sticks up in back like a cockatoo, and he scratches his head absently.

"Hi John," I say with a smile, gesturing at the vacant chair next to me, hopeful he'll sit next to me so we can chat and become more familiar with each other.

He shuffles over and plops into the chair, "Hi," he says shyly.

"I have to say, you have great taste in girls," I say with a big smile.

"Thanks..." comes the muffled reply as he finishes chewing a bite. "I really like Mandy. She's not like the girls at our school."

"What are the girls at your school like?" I ask John to try and figure out what the deal is with the people who go to the Andrew's Academy.

"Most of them are total snobs and are really plastic. You know, cheerleader types," he grumbles, hunching over his plate and taking a bite of sausage.

"So they aren't very nice, I guess?" I say more as a statement than a question.

"No. They're really mean," he stammers. "You and Mandy are so cool. I'm glad you guys decided to go to Medusa's that one night. Max and Andy are cool, too. Max said he plays guitar," John says in a rush. He then stuffs a huge bite of cinnamon roll in his mouth and concentrates on his mug like he's trying to make it levitate. He's the only person I've met who is more uncomfortable around people than me. I didn't think that was even possible.

"Do you play an instrument?"

"I'm...uh...learning to play bass," he tells me with a shrug.

"Cool! I always wanted to learn, but things just never worked out," I confide. "I think I like keyboards better anyway because I already know how to play...you know piano lessons forever ago..."

"I had violin lessons instead because my parents let me choose," he tells me.

"Wow, that's awesome that they let you pick. Was it hard?" I continue the conversation with John while we eat and when I have finished, it occurs to me that Mandy is going to kill us if I don't go get her about now.

"I'm going to go and rouse Sleeping Beauty before she gets pissed that we let her sleep all day," I say, standing up and wandering into the hallway to fetch our snoozing comrade.

I flop down on her bed, "Hey, time to get up, dude."

"Urrrgghh," she responds, pulling the covers over her head.

"It's like, 2:30 in the afternoon, Mandy, and we've all had breakfast," I tell my friend.

Mandy sits straight up in a panic, "What?! Why didn't you wake me up when you got up?"

"Because you were totally out!" I try and defend myself. "Besides, you need your beauty sleep," I say, dodging as she whacks me over the head with her pillow.

"You should talk! Look at you, scruffy!"

"Screw you! We're all scruffy today, dear heart..." I challenge, raising my cast to block her blows with the pillow. "No fair attacking an invalid!" I call, running from the room.

"Maybe mentally invalid!" she yells, running after me.

"Oy! 'Ooose making all the racket?" says Andy poking his head out the door, using a voice like Vyvyan from "The Young Ones." He is bowled over as we come running into Chris's room, and makes a rude hand gesture.

Mandy gives him the finger over her shoulder as she enters the kitchen area to get herself some food. She greets John by blowing him a kiss and smiling like a cat that's just caught a plump mouse.

"Glad to see you finally broke loose from your confinement," I say to Andy, who's now sitting next to Max on the couch.

"Yeah, I gave her plugs back to her," he informs me with a wicked grin.

Victoria, who is reclining on the other couch grabs a throw pillow and whips it at his head, "Piss off!"

Before we know it, we are packing up and heading home. Everyone dawdles as we collect ourselves and our stuff. Nobody is in a hurry to get back, but pile into Max's car for the journey back to Butt Fuck Egypt. Mandy is wrapped around John by the trunk and I am hanging from Chris on the passenger's side as Max and Andy sit in the car waiting for us.

"Thanks for everything, Chris," I say, hugging him tightly.

"You know you're always welcome," he tells me as he squeezes the air out of me.

Andy and Max are getting impatient and are making loud retching noises from inside the car.

"We'll see you guys again really soon," I say. It's tough to leave and go back to a place where we get relentlessly fucked with. Apprehension begins snaking in, stealing my happy glow and I know he can tell.

"I am sure it'll end up being sooner than you think," Chris says, looking into my face.

"Can't wait!" I exclaim, shivering in the freezing cold.

With that, he gives me one last kiss that leaves me sweating even though it must be a wind chill of twenty below.

I look over to Mandy to see if they are done saying goodbye. She has opened her door and is climbing in as Max and Andy start mashing their faces against the window to make goofy faces at us.

I get in the car and look back at Chris, John and Victoria who are smiling and furiously waving goodbye.

I love belonging *somewhere*. And I know I'll be back.

December 15, 1987
The frozen tundra of Butt Fuck Indiana

I got my cast off yesterday! YAY!!!! My arm is kind of smelly and it is paler than the rest of me at the moment, but the doc says I'm all patched up. I am one very happy girl, despite the fact that I'm still in this shitty little cowtown, sitting in Mrs. Starling's class fighting the urge to gouge my eardrums with my pen so that I don't have to listen to anymore goddamn Christmas carols. I fucking *hate* Christmas. That's right, you heard me.

My relatives have never given me something I actually want, let alone an appropriate gift for any occasion. I also hate all holidays that require one to congregate with one's "family" for any purpose, whether it's eating, singing stupid songs, or giving and receiving "gifts". And, it's in the middle of winter. It's mother effing cold up here and I hate being frozen solid until around May. It blows.

"Remember class! Tomorrow, if you wear a Christmas sweater, you get an extra credit point!" Mrs. Starling cries gleefully as the bell rings. We thunder into the hall, moving rapidly to depart the dungeon known as high school.

I'd rather eat toenail clippings than wear some stupid ass sweater. Thankfully I don't own anything that could be construed as "holiday clothing." Anything given to me of that variety has been quickly given to the Salvation Army. Go figure. Glittery crap sewn or glued to anything isn't something I define as attractive.

"How was it today?" Mandy asks me as I come gliding down the hallway to my locker.

"Well, if the Poms could shut the hell up for longer than two seconds, it would have been more tolerable," I glower. "I hate this time of year."

"I know, Grinch, but you'll have to hang in for a few more days," Mandy tells me, patting my shoulder sympathetically.

"Let's get out of here," I respond, swinging my heavy bag over my shoulder.

It takes about five minutes for Mandy to drop me off. "I'll come over later so we can do our homework together," I tell my friend.

"Before or after dinner?" she yells as I get out of her vehicle.

"After. Mom is getting pissy about me never being here, so I have to make an effort," I shout over the freezing wind that's kicking up.

"Then maybe I should come over here to do homework?" queries Mandy.

"Yeah, probably a good idea. But be prepared...." I warn her.

"I know. I'll call you before I come, OK?" Mandy declares before driving off with a final wave.

She hasn't been around my mother very often lately. Mom is usually drunk, which isn't exactly a news flash, but it has gotten worse. She throws herself a pity party every night when she gets home from work. Scotch and Chardonnay are her favorite ways to get the party rolling.

I have about an hour before mother gets home, and an hour or so after that before she's three sheets to the wind. She hates her new job. Everyone she works with is from here, and most of them never went to college. She was head cheerleader in high school, and a sorority girl in college. To her, these people aren't fit to shine her shoes. She is absolutely livid that she has to do something so far beneath her. Yep. That's my mom.

The light on the answering machine is blinking cheerfully at me as I enter our abode. My heart does a jig, maybe Chris called? I always want it to be him.

I dump my bag and coat in my room, and hit "play" on my way to the kitchen to clean up and start cooking.

"Kiera? This is Reverend Holloway. I was wondering if you could stop by tomorrow after school so I can talk with you a few minutes and see how you're doing, call me back and let me know if you can..."

I haven't heard from him since I got thrown out of confirmation class. He always seemed pretty decent. I guess he wants to check on the kid and make sure the divorce hasn't torn me up too badly. Yeah, right. Bee oh oh, aitch oh oh. I pick up the phone and dial the number I've scrawled from the machine.

"Hello? This is Kiera Graves. I was just calling to let you know that dropping by tomorrow after school would be no problem. I should be able to get there by three thirty. Call and let me know if there's a problem, otherwise I'll see you then," I leave a brief message on their machine. I don't really give a crap one way or another. I figure it's no big deal, so I'll just go and avoid further static.

"So, what does he want?" asks Mandy as we go over French vocabulary words for tomorrow's test.

"No clue. I'm guessing it's a 'check on the kid' thing," I reply. "I'm not crazy about going back into that place."

"I know, you're allergic," says Mandy with a grin.

"Yup. I'm allergic to assholes who can't think for themselves at all," I say, flipping my pen at her.

"You must break out in hives every time you have to be around your brother," Mandy giggles, flipping it back.

"Luckily, at the moment, that isn't really an issue because he is living with his buddy and he acts like he doesn't know me at school," I inform Mandy. It is so nice not to have to put up with Brett's crap anymore.

"How handy!" she exclaims. "OK, your turn…"

We continue drilling each other as we go through the vocabulary list and our notes. We have to bone up and make sure we get this stuff if we're going to go to that Honors Program over the summer. We're supposed to get information packets when we come back from Christmas break.

"Is everyone staying in the area for the holidays?" Mandy asks me, cocking one eyebrow.

"No idea. I haven't asked around yet. I'm hoping we can take off to Chicago at least once," I confide.

"John is the sweetest thing!" she gushes. "I think he's going to be more relaxed the next time we visit," she says. She is over the moon crazy about this darling boy. I think it'll all work itself out over time.

"I hope for his sake he is!" I commiserate. "We'll call Chris's this week to see what they're all up to and if our breaks are at the same time."

"Good idea," Mandy nods, looking back at her notes and chewing on her pen cap.

I love the idea of going back to Chris's for more than one day and the group hanging out. We had such a blast last time! Victoria and Max are so alike it's ridiculous. It's like we're all puzzle pieces that fit together perfectly.

I bid adieu to my friend from the apartment building's front door. Tomorrow is another thrilling day at the high school. I can hardly wait.

December 16, 1987
The most boring cowtown in Indiana

Well, I aced the French test, I'm sure of it. Mandy feels good about it, too. We're at lunch, discussing possible plans for the holidays.

"I definitely think that we can sneak off more than once," says Max. "I know I'm getting some money from my grandparents and it has 'Wax Trax' written all over it. Besides, I wore out my 'In God We Trust, Inc.'."

"Again?" demands Andy.

"Well, I bought it second hand, so it wasn't too hard to do," shrugs Max.

"Still working on learning the guitar, eh?" asks Mandy.

Max just looks at her with a "you stupid idiot" expression.

"So, Mandy says you have an appointment with the clergy later," snickers Andy.

"Yeah…whoop-dee-doo," I grumble. "This way he'll shut up and go away. Otherwise he'd keep calling and pissing me off, not to mention what would happen if he woke my mother up."

"I see your point," Andy says, rolling his eyes in disgust. "I can't wait until we graduate and we can get you the hell away from your insane parents."

"Join the club," I respond.

"Don't take any shit from penguin boy," he advises me.

I almost spit milk through my nose and Max thumps me on the back while I choke and sputter.

"Penguin boy?" I roar. "Where'd that come from?"

"Well, doesn't he wear a little black suit with a little white collar or something?" he grins.

"They wear different weirdness at different times," I inform him. "And people think we're odd!"

"Don't be afraid to stand up for yourself, Kiera. I don't like the idea of you being alone with some church dude," says Max. He vividly remembers last year with the whole stupid "Satan scare," when people were being beaten, we were getting daily death threats — and the ministers and cops didn't protect us. Instead, used the situation to bully anyone they thought was "different' in the community.

"Do you really think I'm going to start taking crap from anyone now?" I laugh.

"You know, we could go with you and wait for you," volunteers Mandy.

We're getting together to do homework over at Mandy's because we all have art projects to complete and her basement is sort of the studio for all of us. My mom would kill me if I made a mess in the apartment. That's the thing about art. It usually involves making a mess to some degree.

"Really?" I say, wishing I'd thought of it myself. "That'd be cool because it should only be a few minutes. I'll be in and out, and then we can just go get cracking."

"Done deal," Mandy agrees.

· Eighteen ·

The heavy, wooden door slams shut behind me as I step into the church and the entryway is almost completely dark. With the fluorescent lights turned off, the low ceiling makes me claustrophobic. I take a deep breath to clear my head and shake it off. Bolting down the dungeon-like hallway that leads to the office, I feel like I need a shower after being here. The rust-colored carpet is stained, and dirty white walls need repainting. Luckily, my friends are waiting just outside in the car. I didn't want to torture them by asking them to come and sit in that ugly, dark foyer on the hard, dark wood benches. Right about now though, I'm having second thoughts.

"Kiera! Glad you could make it! Please sit down," the Reverend says with a toothy smile, motioning to the cracked, orange plastic chair facing his desk. Cautiously, I take a seat.

Reverend Holloway is a short, balding man with a snow white fringe of hair that rings his head like Caesar's crown. He has a leprechaun-like quality about him that he accentuates by carrying a shillelagh while walking from the house he and his family live in, to the church. He greets people with a wide, friendly smile, seems like a nice guy. Despite locking horns with him during confirmation class, I'm sure this will be a quick check in, and that will be that.

The window looks out into the small courtyard, which is scattered with dead flowers, dead leaves. A bare tree stands alone and bereft in the middle of it. Behind Reverend Holloway are tall, dark wooden shelves that hold various versions of the Bible, figurines, and small, framed pictures of Christ in various states of crucifixion. I clutch my backpack in front of me like a shield.

"So, how have you been?" he asks me, his demeanor now serious and concerned.

"I'm doing really well, actually, thanks for asking," I reply, hoping that this will be enough to satisfy him. I sit on the edge of my seat and wish for this to be over with. Next time, I'm choosing to take as much flak as people want to dish out, because this sucks.

"Your family has been a part of this church since you first moved here," Reverend Holloway says, clasping his hands on the desk and leaning forward.

"Um, yes, I guess so," I stammer, wondering what that has to do with why I'm here.

"The Bible clearly states God's Law and you are not abiding by these laws, Kiera," he tells me, frowning.

"Pardon?" I'm aghast and confused by this admonishment.

"Your parents created you and you owe everything to them. I have heard that you are not being respectful of your parents, specifically, your father," Reverend Holloway says, piercing me with a judgmental, angry glare.

Rage instantly consumes me. "Some people do not deserve respect," I seethe.

"That isn't for you to say, Kiera. God's Law is clearly written and if you do not abide by it, you are going to hell."

I stand up quickly, the chair flinging backward and falling over. "What does God say about men who beat their children? Do they go to hell?"

"Your father has never laid a finger on you and you know it, you little insolent liar," the minister barks.

"Fuck you! You are both evil!"

I storm out of the office, slamming the door behind me, and shattering the glass. He dodges splinters of glass pursuing me as I break into a run. "KIERA! Get back here! We're not finished talking!" I accidentally slam the front door into the wall as I bolt through it, running to the car.

That went well. Telling me that I'm going to hell for trying to stay alive? Fuck you and fuck your god.

My friends all pop out of the car when they see me running toward them like my ass is on fire. "Kiera? What the hell happened in there?" Mandy asks grabbing my hand and pulling me toward her. "C'mon, get in the car..."

Mandy grinds the car into gear as she sees Reverend Holloway trotting out of the front door. The tires squeal and we haul through a stop sign, heading for Mandy's house.

"He told me I was going to hell for not respecting my father," I tell them. "He actually tried to use the Bible to guilt trip me into kissing and making up with that paternal pile of shit."

"WHAT!!?" Three voices yell at once.

"Yep. He doesn't give a toss about what happens to me. He just wants me to be nice to my *father*," I rage. "I thought the whole point of being a minister was to help people and do good things, not be a total power-tripping asshole." I'm so shocked, and so angry at what has just happened that I burst into tears.

"Well, I guess this is just one more reason not to go to church ever again," shrugs Andy, patting me on the shoulder. "I think people who really believe there is some dude on a cloud that is watching your every move, waiting for you to screw up so he can smite you are completely idiotic."

"That's fucked up that he started yelling at you," adds Max.

"I'm so glad I'm Jewish," sighs Mandy. "The more crap I see with this Christian bullshit, the more I'm glad I wasn't raised into all of that. I mean, picking on a teenager? What adult does that?"

"Apparently plenty of them around here," I growl. "The really ironic thing is that my father never went to church until we moved here, and he was forty. Oh my god, I broke the glass in the office door. My parents are going to kill me!" Furious with myself for being upset, I angrily wipe my eyes on my t-shirt. I just want to punch something.

"Screw the door. Your parents can take a flying one," Mandy mutters. "Why the change? Do you think he suddenly found Jesus?"

"He probably just wanted to look good," I say. "You know, upstanding pillar of the community and all that crap."

Andy yells, "Form of...an ice dildo!"

"Shape of... a baboon's ass!" yells Max.

Apparently referring to my father as an "upstanding pillar" inspired Andy. They begin making up adventures with their "Wonder Twins" spoof while Mandy and I help by making suggestions of what the "Wonder Twins" could do to right the injustice of today.

We specialize in the ridiculous and goofy, even when there is bullshit looming. Having a sense of humor makes things so much easier. I wish that all hard core fundamentalists would get a clue and develop one.

December 23, 1987

"Honey?" My mother calls from her room.

Uh-oh. Whenever I'm "honey" she wants something that I will likely not want to do.

"Coming!" I yell back.

"Could you do the laundry today?" she says. "Olivia is having a party and she asked me to go."

"Who the hell is Olivia?"

"Not that it's any of your beeswax, but Olivia Walsh," she tells me. I try not to roll my eyes at her trying to climb the local social ladder since she somehow fell off the one she was born into. My mother proceeds to launch into the whole story. The Walshes have decided that my mother is interesting and being the former head cheerleader and a debutante — she is going whole hog for this shindig. Olivia Walsh is the town's biggest socialite, if you can be a socialite in a town this goddamn small. She is blonde, prim and a work in progress, so to speak. The woman has had more work done than most of the historic buildings in the county. Anyway, my mother got an invite because Mr. Walsh is on the school board in addition to being CEO of the local appliance plant and President of the Chamber of Commerce. Olivia is the best source of gossip because she's rich and her husband is powerful, which makes her powerful by default. She regularly throws huge parties to gather the "who's who" of the area and swap gossip, make deals, pull strings and show off anything new they've purchased.

"Why don't you do your own laundry?" I grumble, glaring at her.

"Because I'm the mom and you will do what I say," she snaps.

"Fine," I snap right back, "then when I ask to go to Chicago, the answer is 'yes,' isn't it?"

"Sure honey," she says, distractedly, holding earrings up and looking in the mirror to discern which look best.

"You have to at least sort it first," I tell her, stomping off.

"All right, Kiera! Geez..." she mutters.

You would think that I was the parent the way she acts. Last week we had nothing in the fridge to eat and I had to call for pizza because she just sat on the couch, crying. Which I don't get because being nowhere near Peter means no beatings, no yelling, and not thinking every second of every day that you're going to die horribly. I've taken over grocery shopping just to make sure that we have food in the house. Neither of us is here all the time, so I try not to buy a ton of perishables. I'd say I score pretty high on the responsible scale, considering that kids my age aren't supposed to *have* to think about this stuff. She spends her time whining, drinking, sulking and generally being an obnoxious pain in the ass.

She sorts her laundry and I throw a load of our clothes into a waiting basket. Tired and grumbling, I go down to the basement laundry room with a sketch book, a pencil and my Walkman. I toss the dark clothes into a washer and pound on the coin acceptor to force it to accept the quarters. I dump soap in and perch on top of the whooshing washing machine to wait. You can't just leave your laundry. People mess with it if you aren't there the second it's done. I almost killed this woman from the second floor for leaving our wet clothes on a dirty table in here. Five minutes late, and our clothes were covered in crud. Trust me, when nobody is looking out for you, self-reliance and punctuality become habits fast.

I pass the time doodling in my sketch book and listening to The Cocteau Twins. It's stuffy in the tiny, windowless, gray laundry room. There is no ventilation, so doing laundry is not exactly fun. I draw a two-faced monster coming out of a hole in the ground. I sketch the room I'm sitting in, I doodle ideas for paintings, and I draw images that the music creates in my mind. I get so absorbed in my drawing, I hardly notice when the machine finally gets to the spin cycle! I dump the soggy clothes into a dryer with fabric softener and return to working on my crosshatching technique.

A couple hours later, I trudge back upstairs with a basket of clean laundry.

"It's about time!" my ungrateful mother screeches the second I step through the door.

I scream right back at her in my mind. You know, I don't actually *have* to do any of this shit for you. You're actually sort of supposed to take care of me, seeing as how I'm *your* kid. Never mind. One more year and I'll be a memory.

She snatches her clothes out of the basket and continues to fuss and plan her ensemble for the party tomorrow. She'll go and rub elbows with the wealthiest people around, just like when she was a kid. My grandfather, Leo Gold, built himself up from being dirt poor to being a multimillionaire. My mother grew up in the society pages of Louisville, Kentucky. Granddaddy built a big, beautiful house for his family on five acres. When I was little, my mom would drive down with me and my brother in tow. We would stay at Granddaddy and Grandmother's house, a two story classic with the prettiest magnolia tree in the front yard. They were the first ever in our family to have a three car garage and servants. There was an apartment over the garage where their servants stayed. Isn't that weird? Anyway, it explains my mother's allergy to housework, or work in general. She never had to do any chores or housework growing up, and was expected to marry wealthy. So much for that idea, I guess.

Anyway, she, her sister, and her mother were born to shop, not work. So this party tomorrow night is, as Granddaddy would say, right up her alley. I'll just be glad she's out of the house. She said if I clean the whole apartment, then I can go spend the weekend at Mandy's. Course, we'll be going to Chicago and hanging out there, but she doesn't need to know about that. Mandy's mom knows where we're going, and that's good enough for me. Less static is better.

Tomorrow is Christmas Eve and I plan to spend the day cleaning everything from top to bottom so that my dear mother can't find any reason to go psycho. Yippee. My friends are all with family and doing that whole thing, so I'll be here with Mom I guess. I hope the Foo Dog is open. I'm not cooking on top of doing all the laundry *and* cleaning everything. My family sucks at buying gifts for me because they don't know me. They don't bother. They give me gifts for the person they wish I was, rather than who I am. For me, Christmas is a day spent with people I loathe while it is freezing cold outside, icy and snowy, and most of the time, dismally gray. Before they got divorced, I was always the serving girl on holidays. I had to clean all the silver and crystal and then the house and then I got to serve everyone. At least being alone doesn't entail being around a bunch of rude, drunk assholes who get off on ordering me around like Cinderella.

Tomorrow I'll complete my servitude and earn the freedom to go gallivanting around Chicago with my friends. Both sets of my grand-parents usuallysend me money for Christmas, since it fits so nicely into a card. I don't mind. It makes things easy on me, too. I am looking forward to the mail coming to see if things are back to normal between me and my grandparents — or not. I know I won't be able to cash the checks before we go, but I can pay Mandy back without a hitch when we get back. She knows I would never in a trillion years not pay her back. I guess I rely pretty heavily on my friends, but what else am I supposed to do when I don't have anyone else to go to for help?

December 25, 1987
B.F.E.

I think I am going to puke. Olivia Walsh introduced my mother to some guy and he *asked her on a date*. The divorce isn't even final yet! The ink is nowhere near dry and she's dating!

She's been floating around the apartment all day, humming some stupid James Taylor song.

I can understand after being married to the king of all assholes, you might be a little hard up — especially in this teeny town. But give me a break! At least wait until it's final before you start dating a new one. Obviously, she has no taste in anything, especially men.

The good news is, I get to leave tomorrow morning and not come home until Monday! Yahoooo! We should have the dance floor to ourselves because most of the regular Medusa's clientele will probably be in some holiday destination. I couldn't care less. I love the idea of having all the room I can handle and not having to elbow rude little poseur puffballs who just stand on the dance floor, smoking cloves, taking up space and trying to be cool. Besides, I'll get to see Chris, which is always a good thing. I have been working on a painting for him for the last month in between school projects. I hope he likes it.

So, tonight Brett's coming over to "celebrate" Christmas. Whatever. I am cooking our holiday dinner: roast chicken, instant stuffing, mashed potatoes and green beans. For dessert, we're having pumpkin pie. I bought whipped cream because my father never let us have whipped cream on our pie. He controlled everything that passed our lips. We could not use salt on anything — ever. We were not allowed to use condiments either, except for salad dressing. Ranch was unacceptable because it was high fat. He is obsessive about food and taught us that being fat is the worst crime you can commit. All he ever talks about is how fat, ugly and stupid the people are around here. Charming, eh? Anyway, it's nice that now, when I can wrestle some grocery money from my mother, I can actually eat what I want, when and how much I want. The problem, currently, is that I have very little time.

"Don't say anything to Brett about Hank, Kiera," my mother orders, "I will address it."

"I have no plans to ever discuss your dating situation with anyone, ever, for any reason, Mom." I can't for the life of me understand why she thinks her love life should be of any importance to me! I am so disgusted with her acting like a teenager.

"Watch it," she snaps, just as the door bell rings, "I'll get it." She shoots me a warning look and plasters a smile on her face.

She flings open the door and covers Brett with hugs and kisses as he enters the small apartment, scowling and waving her off like a pesky mosquito. "Mom...stop..." he grumbles, taking off his coat and throwing it on the back of the couch.

"Hey," he calls to me from the living room area. The living room, dining room and kitchen are basically one big open space, depending on where you put the furniture. We have the couch facing the sliding glass doors creating the illusion that it is a separate space from the dining room.

"Hey," I call back benignly, nodding at my elder brother who I haven't really seen in about a month. It's kind of lucky, really. Absence doesn't always make the heart grow fonder; in this case, it just gives him fewer opportunities to be a complete asshole to me and my friends.

I set the table earlier the way mother instructed and I'm now placing the food in the center. "Dinner is served," I announce as I sit down on the end, distancing myself from Brett. Let her sit next to her spawn. I sure as hell have nothing to say to him.

"Hey, Kiera, Dad wants you to come to church with us tonight," he tells me, piling his plate with chicken and gravy.

"That's nice." Here I am trying to keep my seething to a minimum and ten minutes in, all hope is lost. I didn't even know he was in town. Fantastic.

"I think you should go. He's our Dad and you haven't seen him in a long time," Brett states with such false authority that I want to clock him over the head with the bowl of green beans I am holding.

"I don't give a flying one what he wants and there is no fucking way I'm going back to that church," I snarl flinging some beans onto my plate and slamming the bowl onto the table. The serving spoon bounces out and clatters to the floor. Nobody moves to pick it up, and mother silently goes to the drawer for a clean spoon.

"Geez...fine, Kiera, whatever..." Brett shrugs as he begins shoveling down the food he has piled on his plate.

"Are Grandma and Grandpa here too? At the Holiday Inn?" I ask, trying to find the silver lining in the middle of this heinous storm.

"Nope." he says, fiddling with his fork and avoiding looking at me.

"Where are they?"

He looks at Mom and they share a knowing look. "They're in their apartment in Texas, Kiera."

"WHAT? He left them alone in a new place with absolutely nobody at Christmas?" I holler, standing up to pace the room. I can't believe this. My poor grandparents all alone down there. They weren't social butterflies here, and they only knew a few people.

"Where is he staying then?" I demand stepping right up to my brother so he can't avoid me.

"Reverend Holloway's house," he tells me, jamming a bite into his mouth. I sit back in my seat, with no intention of speaking at all the rest of the night. It's just unbelievable.

"So, I had a lovely time at Mrs. Walsh's holiday fête last night," Mom says to Brett with a grin.

"Oh, yeah?" he responds. One thing we have in common is our complete apathy about her social life. Right now, I'm worried silly about my grandparents and plan to call them the second Brett leaves.

"She introduced me to a really interesting man," my mother begins.

Oh holy shit, she's doing this now? And she doesn't see it coming. I do.

CLANK

Brett's fork bangs against his plate. "You're dating already?" he exclaims in disbelief.

"Well, Hank hasn't asked me out yet, but I thought..." she back-pedals.

"THE DIVORCE ISN'T EVEN FINAL YET, MOM!" Brett pushes his chair back and leaps to his feet.

"Well, that may be so, but I'm not dead," replies Mom furious that her perfect son isn't backing her up.

"Couldn't you at least wait until it's final?" he storms, grabbing his coat off the back of the couch.

"Brett, I am an adult and I do not have to answer to you," snaps my mother in her holier than thou tone.

"Whatever you say, Mom...I'm outta here," he says shaking his head in disgust and leaving the apartment in a whirl of anger, disbelief and disdain.

"Did you know he was here? Did you know he just left them and took off?" I demand, turning on my mother who is polishing off her Chardonnay.

"I don't remember the details, Kiera. Brett told me he was coming, but I've been busy and forgot to tell you. What can I say?" she shrugs, refilling her wine glass.

"Hank is a really nice man, Kiera. You'll really like him," she says, completely changing the subject.

"Maybe," I tell her, "but you still should have waited longer than a month and a half."

"I didn't ask for your opinion!" She grabs the half full wine bottle, her glass, and flounces to her room in a huff. The door slams, and I am left alone to clean up this mess.

I remain in my seat and finish my dinner, and then proceed to put away all the food. I hear her crying softly in her room. Too bad, I think.

This time, Brett is right. Besides, there isn't anyone around this town who is going to think anything better. That's for certain.

I pick up the phone and dial the number I've worked to memorize. I have to tell them I didn't know, and make sure they're okay. Grandma sounds tired and shaky, but happy to hear my voice. They trade off talking and I stay on the phone with them until they are all talked out. When they ask if I've gotten the card and their check yet, I feel a horrible twinge of guilt. I'd like to give my father a piece of my mind, but it's just not worth it. I am going to stay off the radar for as long as possible. I don't know what I can actually do for my grandparents. They've really stepped in it this time, and being so far away right now when I'm just trying to keep my life from imploding. I don't see how to help them when I can barely help myself.

It's late when I finally finish talking on the phone, but I pad around the apartment cleaning and straightening. I'm making absolutely sure there's nothing my mother can try to use at the last minute to keep me here. It takes hours of listening to The Cocteau Twins to finally unwind. Tomorrow I leave for Chicago with my friends for some fun and I can't wait! I have definitely earned it.

· Nineteen ·

December 26, 1987

I check my watch again. It is 10 A.M. and I'm impatiently waiting at the frosty, glass door of my apartment building for my friends to arrive. They need to get here before my mother wakes up and has a chance to change the rules. She always does that. She'll make a long list of stuff she wants me to do in exchange for permission to do whatever. I complete the list to the letter and then she'll add something on at the last minute. Not this time. I'm getting the hell out of here!

For once, the sun is shining blindingly bright, reflecting off the foot or so of snow on the ground. You can always count on a ton of snow up here. It's called "lake effect." It means Chicago gets five inches and we get ten. Loads of fun to shovel. That's something about living in an apartment that I love. No more shoveling snow, or snow-blowing the driveway.

Slipping on my sunglasses to see something besides glare, I see Mandy pull into the parking lot, the car's exhaust making a small plume. I hoist my bag onto my shoulder and step out into the subzero air that hits me like a smack in the face, taking my breath away. Carefully, I make my way to the car, my boots crunching in the snow and ice that cover the pavement.

"Hurry up before you turn into a statue!" calls Mandy, waving a red-gloved hand at me as she pops the trunk.

"I'm trying not to fall on my butt!" I chatter, chucking my bag into the trunk and hustling around to the passenger's side.

I settle in as Max and Andy greet me from the back seat. Mandy hands me a thermal travel cup, "Coffee?"

"You kick ass," I tell her, gratefully taking the cup and swallowing a sip to thaw out my lips and face.

We take the toll road because there are fewer potholes that could swallow her car. It's frightening how big the holes are on the regular highway. We take turns handing her change. We always give whoever is driving gas money and toll money because that's the way we do things. I don't expect my friends to pay for hauling my ass around.

Max and Mandy are so cool about being the chauffeurs for our little group. But then, they're always there when you need them. Max's Lincoln is out of commission at the moment because he needs new tires. The current ones are bald and he doesn't want to land in a ditch. Brett and I have an ugly, green Buick Skylark that we are supposedly "sharing." I gave up ever even trying to use it because the perfect little golden Prince always gets what he wants, regardless of what is fair to me. So, the option of me driving is a total impossibility at the moment, unless I steal a car. Andy is the youngest and gets his license this upcoming year. We're not sure about getting into a car with our favorite spazmosis behind the wheel — but you gotta take some risks, right?

Danny warbles cheerfully about ain't this the life, baby?

Ain't it though?

The trip goes slower because of all the holiday traffic on the road, but we eventually reach our destination. Mandy parks on the street in front of Chris's house where we are quickly greeted by our host.

"You should park in the driveway because if the plows come through, they might crunch your car," Chris informs Mandy through the driver's side window.

Mandy throws it in reverse, pulls into the freshly snow-blown driveway, and parks her trusty silver steed where Chris guides her. We all pile out of the car and Chris sweeps me into his arms, planting a kiss on me without even saying "hi."

Emerging from a heart revving, passionate kiss, I hear Mandy squeal as John comes shuffling up the driveway to greet us, "Sorry

I'm…" and his words are muffled as she throws her arms around his neck and plants a huge kiss on him. "…late…" John finishes as they part.

"I'm so happy to see you!" Her cheeks are bright pink and her breath makes humid puffs in the freezing cold air.

"I'm happy to see you, too," he responds, still not believing this very pretty girl has a thing for him. Poor guy. He'll learn soon enough that Mandy is really hard to get rid of when she likes you. He guides her toward the house with his arm around her teensy waist.

Max and Andy get our stuff out of the trunk as we all clatter into the house, talking and greeting each other. Victoria is waiting for us just inside the house and greets each of us in turn with a hug, "Hi, you guys! Glad you could make it! Tonight is going to be awesome…"

We climb the stairs, set our bags down in the guest rooms, and then congregate in Chris's room to discuss lunch.

"Pizza?" suggests Andy, foaming at the mouth.

"Yeah!" Mandy and I exclaim simultaneously, "Giordano's!"

"Ooooo…" says Max rubbing his hands together.

"I've got a menu here and we're in delivery range, so let's get a couple," says Chris with a chuckle at our enthusiasm. This pizza is *the* best pizza in Chicago, and you can't get anything even close in Indiana. All we can get is Domino's, which is el-crapola in comparison.

We are ravenous by the time the pizza finally arrives around 1:30 p.m. We've ordered two large, stuffed pizzas. One is sausage and mushroom while the other is spinach and tomatoes. If you've never had Giordano's, I highly recommend the experience. Between bites, we discuss plans for the rest of the day and agree going to Wax Trax is the next thing on our "to do" list. Conversation drifts into family gatherings for the holidays and I listen uncomfortably. I hear stories about drunk uncles telling rude jokes at the dinner table and hijinks ensuing; and stories of dogs getting a hold of ribbon and depositing barf, containing said ribbon, on the pile of coats on someone's bed. I hear stories about groups of relatives who like each other. Family. People who get along, on the whole, and who enjoy time spent together. I can't imagine what that would be like.

In my family, my father's parents, Dale and Lucille Graves, basically raised me. They are out of joint right now since he moved them to

Texas and I didn't magically stop them from complying. When I called them at Christmas, they desperately pleaded for me to be on good terms with my father. I stated, quite loudly and clearly, that hell will freeze over several times before that ever occurs. So, they have gone from doting on me and being my only source of emotional support, to giving me the silent treatment. It really sucks because I love them very much. They used to always tell me what a good girl I was and that I could do anything. Now they are being pissy because I don't talk to their demon spawn and I want to go to school, not babysit them. I don't know what I'm supposed to do, and I don't really have anyone to ask. So it's hard. I feel like I've leaned on Mrs. Goebel and the Sullivans about as hard as anyone can take. I don't want to wear out my welcome, so to speak.

Mom's parents, Leo and Cleo Gold, I mostly get along with...mainly because I've seen them about twenty times total my entire life. Cleo has always hated me, which could be because she hates my father. I think she just detests children. Period. She's got some issues, so I let her nasty comments slide. The woman is perpetually soused and melodramatic. Granddaddy is nice most of the time. He's stern sometimes, but he's never been mean or nasty. Not like the rest of them. Combine my relatives, add alcohol, and you've got one hell of a mess on your hands. I am the favorite target of cruel jokes, being made fun of and humiliated. A whole new breed of scapegoat. This is why I detest them and loathe being around them. Fortunately, anymore, it is few and far between, so no biggie. It isn't like they ever call or write me to say "hi" or see what's going on. The grandparents send birthday and Christmas cards, which is nice, when there isn't any guilt trip enclosed. Family = total insane, warped assholes. Friends = good.

My friends, boyfriend and I bundle up and head out to the taxis that Chris has ordered. There's no way for all of us to fit in one car, and parking in that neighborhood is impossible. Taxi rides in this city are sort of like taking a ride on a roller coaster, especially when it snows — which, it started doing about an hour ago.

"The estrogen mobile! Cool!" declares Mandy, sliding across the slick, black vinyl seat. She grimaces at me as she picks a used wad of chewing gum off of her glove from the grimy, yellow cab. I slide in next to her and Victoria follows me. The boys climb in the other cab.

"I'm not sure I'd want to be in a car with Andy," says Victoria, shaking her head.

"So where you headed?" our cabbie drawls, turning to face us.

"2445 Lincoln Avenue, Wax Trax Records," Mandy says. We are grinning ear to ear, happy to be here and escape cowtown for a weekend.

"You got it," responds our very obviously native Chicagoan cabbie. He is a balding, fifty-something year old man with a large gut, a five o'clock shadow, grimy hands and a thick Chicago accent.

We brace ourselves against the back seat, our feet pressed against the filthy cab front seat as we careen through the streets. A bus nearly slides into us at a stop light and we all squeal in alarm.

"Relax, dolls," our cabbie yells back to us, "I won't let anything happen to such pretty girls."

Mandy shoots me a totally grossed-out look, and we sit in terrified silence until we come to a stop in front of the familiar and very welcome black door. Chris rushes over from the other cab to pay the fare as we hastily exit the cab from Hades.

We congratulate ourselves on making it to our destination in one piece as we enter the store. Andy and Max immediately seize Chris and John, and drag them into the photo booth.

"Get your butt out of my face!…Sorry…OUCH!…Hey!" emanates from the tiny booth as feet and arms flail out of the curtain as the boys get situated within. "Mandy! Hey! Help us out!" hollers Andy as a hand shoots out of the booth holding two dollars.

Mandy and I are dying laughing. She takes the dollar bills from the protruding hand and inserts them into the machine.

We can hear Max cracking up as the flash pops through its four pictures. The boys tumble out, red-faced and laughing. Next, Mandy and I coerce Victoria into the booth after giving Max money to feed the machine. We hoot with laughter as we pass the pictures around the group. I tear off one from each strip to put into my billfold. Andy is fake picking Max's nose in the boys' picture and in the one with the girls, we're all giving the camera the finger and laughing. The photo booth at Wax Trax is becoming a fun tradition.

Mandy and I make our way to the Cocteau Twins bin, as usual. I select "Lullabies" and scurry off to the Siouxsie and the Banshees' bin, only to be shooed away by Andy who is, evidently, lookout for Max. "Go upstairs!" he orders me, flapping his hands at me like I'm a large mosquito that has invaded his space.

"What the hell?" I giggle, taking off upstairs. I think I'll get my very own Skinny Puppy t-shirt instead, since I am guessing they're buying a Siouxsie album for me. I rummage through the rack and find what I have been waiting what seems like forever to buy — a Skinny Puppy "Dig It" t-shirt. I have borrowed Mandy's, and I know she'll always let me borrow it, but I've always wanted my own. I take the shirt from the rack and approach the surly, bespectacled female salesperson who is lurking behind the jewelry display case so I can happily make my purchase. This employee looks at me with such disdain, it's like my very existence offends her.

I wordlessly hand her the shirt and fumble for my cash as she presses the buttons on the cash register with such viciousness, I think that she's just having a terrible day. As my transaction is completed, I hear heavy footsteps ascending the stairs and see Andy and Max coming up to release me from my banishment. "You almost ruined the surprise, Kiera!" Andy exclaims as he socks me lightly in the arm .

Max steps forward to present me with a large, red Wax Trax bag. He and Andy are grinning like idiots, which tells me they got something I'm going to absolutely love.

"Go on…" urges Max, still grinning.

I reach in and pull out Siouxsie and the Banshees' "Juju" and "Tinderbox", as well as PiL's "Album." "HOLY SHIT YOU GUYS!!" I squeal and jump up and down. Now I can listen to "Monitor" over and over and over without worrying that I'm wearing out the tape. I have my *own* copy of "Juju" now!

They are laughing their butts off as I throw my arms around them, hugging them and accidentally banging their heads together. "You're welcome, Kiera. We know you're sick of having to tape everything from us," Max tells me, patting my shoulder.

"You guys kick ASS!" I say so loud, I earn a glare from the nearby, bad tempered salesperson. "I've been *dying* to get my own 'Juju' for eons, but you knew that already. I LOVE that album soooooo much!"

Chris and Mandy come thundering upstairs to see what all the squeaking is about. Chris smiles appreciatively at my exuberance as he gives me a hug. Mandy grins with delight at Max and Andy's very generous gifts. These cost at least fifty bucks, which is a lot of money for kids like us. I have the absolute best friends on earth. Max and Andy are such good guys. I feel sorry for any girl who dates either of them, because Mandy and I will probably be relentlessly protective of our guys. They are so sensitive and thoughtful.

Mandy is now bugging Max and Andy to hand over the bag they have for her, "Uh uh! You have to wait until later Miss Nosy Ass!" Max tells her, holding the bag high above his head.

"No fair!" pouts Mandy

"Oh, all right," Max says, rolling his eyes like a parent handling an impatient child.

Mandy squeals as she pulls "Louder Than Bombs" by The Smiths out of the bag, "Oh my gawd, you guys! Thanks!" She also does a little happy dance and looks at the back of the album rapturously.

"I'll be commandeering your stereo later, Chris," Mandy grins. We have the worst poker faces—ever, and are struggling right now to keep our surprise a secret. I studiously avoid looking at her, and we giggle.

Mandy and I pitched in and got Max and Andy a new amp for their band practice, since one of the amps is fuzzing out and being crappy. It took many odd jobs, but it's worth it. Mandy stashed it in one of her bags, causing Max to wonder aloud, "what is in here? A hacked up dead body?"

To which Mandy replied, "Yep. It's Fred."

Anyway, we are planning to give them their present when we get back. Chris is getting the painting from me and Mandy is getting a dress I found at the Antique Mall that I know she'll love. It's a deep red 1920s flapper dress with fringe all over it. It'll go well with most of her hats, too.

We peruse the posters longingly and then bundle up for the trip home. Outside, the snow has stopped falling, but now it is blowing around in subzero wind that instantaneously makes my face stop working properly. Chris and Max flag down a couple of taxis and we wind our way back to Chris's to get ready for our night out at Medusa's.

Mandy, Victoria, Andy and I all pile into one ice-covered cab and Chris, Max and John climb into the other. Thankfully, our taxi is quite hot inside. After having been lashed by the icy wind and blowing snow, it feels really good. Unfortunately, we sweat the whole way back to Chris's like a pack of very disgruntled sardines. "Why did you bail on the guys?" groans Mandy who is almost sitting on Andy's lap.

"Because they are all so freaking tall that it's even more crowded than being stuffed in here with you guys!" Andy retorts.

Our cabdriver is a friendly, cigar smoking Indian dude named Suresh who tries to flirt with Victoria and almost pulls back a stump. We are all gagging on the cigar smoke in the hot taxi by the time we pull up to the driveway and can't exit the cab fast enough. Suresh is, by definition, a character. He's like an SNL caricature of a Chicago cab driver. He has Christmas lights hanging around the perimeter of the interior and various postcard-sized pictures of Ganesh hanging from the rearview mirror and taped to the dashboard. There is a faint smell of incense and he puffs his cigar as he chats to us about our day, receiving brief replies. Victoria throws him a parting glare as we flee up the driveway to the back door. We remove our shoes just inside the door, laughing about the insanity of the cab ride we just endured.

"What the hell was that guy on?" growls Victoria, shaking a wad of snow out of her short, black boot.

Mandy and I have the giggles and are growing giddier by the minute. Today was so much fun and tonight is going to be awesome. Victoria rolls her eyes at our buoyant mood and chuckles dryly. "You guys are so easily amused," she quips, as we race upstairs with the presents we just got from Max and Andy.

I beat Mandy to the stereo and we decide to play my new PiL.

Johnny Rotten wails farewell to his fair weather friend that no one can depend on.

Mandy and I dance around the coffee table gleefully.

"Bad times…now they must eeeend!" we holler along with Mr. Rotten.

Chris and John watch us in amusement from the couch.

"Dude, we gotta get ready," Mandy realizes, looking at her watch.

I look at her wrist and gasp. It is already six o'clock!

"Hey! What do you want for dinner?" Chris asks as we skitter across the floor toward the door to change clothes and get pretty.

"Chinese!" we yell back in perfect unison.

We retreat to our guest room and I pull Mandy's present out of my bag, "Merry Christmas, Mandy," I say smiling enormously as I hand her the soft package.

"What did you do?" asks Mandy, accepting the parcel. She rips it open and gasps, "Oh Kiera! It's gorgeous! Where did you find it?" she squeals holding the dress over her front and running into the bathroom to look at herself in the mirror with her new dress.

"I saw it at the antique mall and it just jumped into my hands," I grin at my friend who is jumping up and down.

"This is SO awesome! I am totally wearing it tonight!" she exclaims, hugging me.

I love when I get to give my friends presents that they really like. It's so cool. Joy is my drug of choice, for sure.

"OK, your turn," she says, handing me a small, gift wrapped box.

I open it carefully and slowly, causing Mandy to lose patience and yell, "Hurry up! Rip it!"

I extract the box from the wrapping and open it. Inside there is a beautiful, antique silver locket. There is an enormous lump in my throat and I am overwhelmed with emotion. I swallow hard. "Wow, this is so beautiful."

My friend looks at me, shocked at my reaction, "Do you like it?" she asks, worried.

"I love it! It's the nicest thing anyone has ever given me!" I exclaim, bursting into tears and throwing my arms around her. I

"Well…. Open it!" she grins, wiping a tear off my cheek with her thumb.

I pop it open and inside the locket is a picture of her on one side and me on the other.

"Together forever!" she says, hugging me.

"We'd better be!" I laugh, squeezing her in a giant hug.

I wipe my face and work on de-puffing after crying. Mandy swishes around the room in her new fringy dress.

"Want to give Max and Andy theirs next?" I ask Mandy as I pull on my socks.

"You know it!" she grins. We are so excited that we pulled this off. It's one of our last Christmases together, so we wanted to do something extra special for our closest friends.

We go back into Chris's room and get Victoria and Chris to cover the boys' eyes while we carry in the large, battered-looking gift for the guys.

"OK you guys, this is for both of you, from us," Mandy tells them.

"Dude! You didn't!" hollers Andy, as he and Max zip over to demolish the wrapping.

"HOLY CRAP!" whoops Max, "I can't believe you guys!"

Mandy and I are then picked up and squeezed within an inch of our lives as the boys exuberantly thank us for the guitar amp.

"Nice one," Chris says appreciatively, checking out the amplifier. "Hey, who gave you that?" he inquires, lightly touching the locket now hanging around my neck.

"Mandy," I tell him with an enormous grin, holding the locket with one hand.

"I like your dress," says John coming in from being stationed downstairs to get our dinner. Victoria rushes over to help him because he's so weighed down by the many bags of Chinese food and his face turning pink from the strain of carrying everything and not dropping it.

"Thanks! I just looooooove it! Kiera just gave it to me!" She twirls around, making the fringe swirl.

"Great choice," nods John, checking out his very cute girlfriend as he and Victoria set the bags on the kitchen counter.

"I'm glad you like it, too," I respond, giggling with pleasure that our gifts are all so well received and appreciated. My friends are so cool.

"Oh! I almost forgot! Do you want yours now or later?" asks Chris with a wicked grin.

"I'll get yours and then we can trade," I tell him, running to get his painting. I did a painting of two people sitting under a tree in moonlight. It turned out pretty well, considering it all came out of my head. I've never painted from a live model, since our school art program is so underfunded. I couldn't afford models and have to be conservative with the paint, because it's expensive. I figured he'd like this better than me going out and buying a "thing" since he can go out buy anything he wants.

I return and apprehensively hand it to him. "I hope it's OK," I stammer.

He hands me a largish box and begins to unwrap his gift. I am watching him, holding my breath. His eyes get really big.

"Is it OK?" I ask him timidly, afraid that he hates it.

"Kiera, I had no idea you were this talented, I mean...I did...I'm just blown away!" he says, setting it against the wall and rushing to hug me.

"Really? It's OK?" I stutter.

"It's waaaay better than OK, Kiera. It's awesome," Chris tells me, and I can see in his eyes that he really means it. "I'll be right back," he says and runs into his bedroom. He comes back holding a hammer and what looks like a box of nails.

"Hey, Max! Help me out, would ya?" Chris calls loudly, over the din of Max and Andy screwing around on borrowed guitars on their new amp.

"Sure!" calls Max, loping over to Chris.

Max holds the painting up on the wall over the television and Chris makes some marks before nailing a picture hanger into the wall. Chris proudly hangs his new painting and steps back to admire it, "What do you think, Max?"

"I think you have really good taste in art," he replies, winking at me and going back over to Andy.

"Alright, your turn," says Chris, "Go on, open it."

I'm still holding the box he handed me and sit down to open it.

"Oh my GOD! Chris!!" I squeak, my heart beating a million miles an hour.

Inside the box is the most gorgeous, deep red velvet dress that anyone could dream of. I pull it out and hold it in front of me.

"Try it on and see if it fits. I wasn't sure, so..." blushes Chris.

Mandy screams when she see me holding the dress. Grabbing my hand, she scurries with me into Chris's bathroom to help me try it on. It fits like a glove and I look like someone else completely. I feel like Sophia Loren. I walk out to show Chris and blush furiously as his jaw drops and Max drops a guitar with a resounding CLANG as it hits the floor.

"Wow," says Chris, still openly gaping at me.

"Who are you and what did you do with Kiera?" hollers Max from the other side of the room.

"This thing fits like it was tailored just for me," I say, turning around.

"You can say that again!" giggles Mandy, nodding appreciatively.

"I definitely did something right this time," mumbles Chris, still gaping at me, "You look incredible."

"Thanks," I respond, feeling the intense blush working its way up my back and into my face. I feel like I must match the dress as badly as I am blushing.

"So, uh... I know it's kind of early to ask about this, but I was wondering if we could go to prom?" stammers Chris.

"With this dress in my closet? I have to say yes!" I beam, giving Chris a huge kiss that leaves both of us a little loopy.

Mandy squeals at this suggestion and we begin plotting a takeover of the lame cowtown prom.

I stagger off to change back into my regular clothes, Mandy trailing behind me.

"That boy really likes you," says Mandy, matter-of-factly. "Can you imagine their faces when we walk into prom with our guys?:

"That would be classic," I tell her, grinning like a loon. "Isn't Chris the sweetest?"

"He's very sweet," she nods. "Although, John gives him some competition there."

"I couldn't be happier!" I tell my friend. It is so exciting and the best kismet that we are dating two best friends. Absolutely adorable guys!

I am breathless from all the excitement as I slip on my fishnet stockings and a long black skirt. Mandy finishes her makeup in the bathroom.

"Hey, did you bring something for John?" I ask, trying to remember if she already told me.

"I found a neat vest that I'm giving him," she replies, rummaging through her giant, endless bag and fishing out a rumpled package. "It's black with paisley lining. You'll see," she grins, motioning for me to come with her.

We slip back into Chris's room and she sidles up to John and sets the package in his lap, giving him a kiss on the cheek. John's ears turn bright red.

"Gee, thanks," he mutters as he unwraps his gift. He kind of bumbles nervously, which is cute because he obviously likes Mandy an awful lot. She thinks he's the cat's meow, so she is very patient and supportive.

"Oh wow, Mandy…this is too cool," he grins, immediately putting it on over his white, buttoned down collar shirt. He digs around in his front pocket and produces a beautiful gold bracelet that he hands to Mandy, "Sorry, I didn't have time to wrap it…"

She gleefully muffles his apology with a kiss and he turns, if possible, even redder. Mandy holds out her hand and he carefully slides the bracelet onto her tiny wrist.

"Ooh! Thank you John! It's just perfect!" she beams.

Chris disappears for a moment before coming in with a large box and drops it on Victoria's lap, turning her sour expression to complete surprise. "Go on, Vic— it's from all of us," he tells her, giving me a sly wink. We didn't think about accidentally leaving Victoria out. Luckily, Chris has yet again saved the day.

She quickly demolishes the wrapping and with a delighted gasp, pulls out a gorgeous deep purple velvet cloak.

"Where in the world did you find this?" Victoria asks, whirling the cloak around her shoulders.

"I'll never tell," Chris replies with a wicked grin.

We are all shocked when Victoria hugs each of us in turn, "Thank you so much, you guys!" I am glad the ice has finally thawed and we are all on even ground.

Chris elbows Andy and Max in the ribs, "C'mon, let's have some dinner before it's stone cold."

After the last of the crab Rangoon has been devoured, we begin our short, but bitterly cold journey to Medusa's. We have to walk carefully, because everything is covered in ice. It's too easy to have a grand wipeout and bruise the hell out of yourself when it's like this. We end up walking along in the road where car tires have worn the ice away and there are stripes of frozen asphalt to follow. Andy is quieter and more sedate than usual because he doesn't want to get a concussion and land in the E.R. He tends to land on his head, rather than on his butt like everyone else. He says it's because, "I don't have a butt!"

Which no one can really debate. He is so skinny, none of us think it's possible for anything to be back there.

We reach the building and are pleasantly surprised at the total lack of a line. We get our I.D.'s checked and waltz right into the club, grinning like a bunch of fools.

"Dude! That has *never* happened, like, *ever!*" exclaims Andy in disbelief.

"Let's hurry up and check our coats in so we can go make our requests early!" says Mandy, hustling everyone along up the stairs.

She and I quickly get our coats checked in and scurry up to the DJ booth to make requests on behalf of our group. We are stunned to see that there are only a couple of handfuls of people on the main dance floor, bobbing cautiously to some electronic song that we cannot identify. We look at each other in amazement and wait to catch the eye of the DJ who has a huge, blue Mohawk.

"Can I help you?" he asks, smiling at us.

"Yes!" replies Mandy with a big grin, " Could you please play some Nitzer Ebb, some Cure, some Smiths, some Depeche Mode and some Siouxsie for us?"

"Will you dance if play those songs?" he asks, skeptically raising an eyebrow.

"You can bet on it!" Mandy giving him a playful shimmy in her new fringed dress.

"Then, you've got it," he responds, grinning at my petite friend's enthusiasm.

We fly down the stairs to the main floor as Max, Andy and Chris wander in. We see John and Victoria hanging around at the perimeter, looking to see who's here tonight.

Mandy, the boys, and I are wearing a hole in the floor as we stomp, flail and thrash around to Nitzer Ebb, Ministry and other industrial artists whom we plan to identify by asking the DJ at the end of the night. For now, we enjoy his selections and are drenched in sweat in a fairly short time. It's sooooooo great to have this much room to dance!

I notice two figures in the balcony watching our group and catch Mandy's eye. She looks up, shrugs, and continues dancing. I am watchful of our observers as we stomp our way around the floor.

One of the classic favorites comes through the speakers and Mandy and I fall into our boogie as Ministry howls about letting their teeny minds think that they're dealing with someone who is over the brink. Chris and the boys exit the floor in search of water and seating, since we are all totally soaked and in need of a short respite. We shortly join them on a few large, red velvet couches near the bar.

"Hey, did you guys notice the people watching us from upstairs?" I ask the group.

"Yeah, I saw 'em. I have no clue who they are. I think they're girls though," says Andy with a shrug. Wiping sweat from his forehead with his sleeve, he guzzles water from a plastic cup.

Victoria saunters over to join us and John sits next to Mandy. "I guess I'll be joining you when you're ready to go back out," she informs the group.

"Oh! Thank you for gracing us with your mystical presence, O Empress of Night!" declares Andy.

"Shut the fuck up, moron," she says, lightly slapping his shoulder and grinning.

"As you wish, O royal one," he mocks with a bow.

"I'll give you a royal one, carrot head," she growls good-naturedly.

"OK, you two, break it up," sighs Max.

Andy spends half his time around Victoria apologizing for taking his extremely sarcastic sense of humor too far and Max is bored with the whole thing.

"Shall we?" says Mandy brightly, popping up off the couch like a jack in the box springing from a box.

"Let's," I say, hooking my arm in hers. We skip to the dance floor just as we hear the pulsating rhythm of "Monitor" issuing from the giant speakers.

We grin at each other as Siouxsie howls to sit back and enjoy the real McCoy.

Everyone in the place is grooving on the floor because anyone with one quarter of a brain loves this song. Victoria is thoroughly enjoying herself and John is nervously optimistic as he stiffly jerks to the beat.

Siouxsie screams as we stomp and twirl to the band's excellence.

I feel the back of my neck prickle and turn to see that the two observers have returned to the balcony. "Hey! Victoria! Do you know who that is up there?" I holler over the music to my new friend, who is not pleased with being interrupted during the rapture of whirling around a nearly deserted dance floor to Siouxsie and the Banshees.

"Who?" she asks, squinting to see what or whom I am referring to.

I jerk my head in the general direction and she walks toward them to better identify who has been so interested in our little group.

"It's a couple of girls. I think they're checking out your boys," Victoria informs me, cackling.

"Do you know them at all?" I question, wanting to better establish identity and motivation, especially after the run-in with Tamara and Tracy.

"I think it's a couple of chicks from Suze's school, but I can go check," she tells me, rolling her eyes and sliding across the floor to determine who is peering over the balcony railing at us instead of dancing.

"I was right, it's a couple of girls from St. Joseph's," Victoria grumbles, "What a couple of airheads."

"Why don't they come over and say hello instead of peering at us from the balcony?" I giggle, surprised that anyone who goes to Medusa's would be intimidated by our little group of weirdos.

"Who cares?" Victoria tells me, getting back into her groove.

Mandy and I burst into gales of laughter and return to dancing energetically to Love and Rockets singing about giving love in every sense, and being raised up so high that all the cavemen fade away.

Yes, please.

Mandy and I whirl happily around, grinning. I watch my friends dancing together and feel so happy, I could pop.

What a great night.

Suddenly, the house lights come on and we shuffle toward the door of the nearly empty nightclub. We are all damp with sweat and none of us are looking forward to the icy night air hitting us.

Chris helps me get my coat on and John helps Mandy with hers. We look at each other and smile. Tonight was so perfect and so much fun. It's the kind of night that stays with you even after it's over. It's the kind of feeling you want to replicate as often as possible.

We thunder down the staircase and brace ourselves for the shock of cold when we step outside. We scurry toward Chris's house as quickly as possible. A cruel, icy wind chases us, forcing our heads down and erasing all possibility of conversation along the way.

John, Mandy, Victoria and I all head upstairs to collapse into bed. We sneak in soundlessly, hightail it sock-footed upstairs before we burst out laughing and disturb Chris's parents. We fling ourselves on the beds and gasp for air, laughing hysterically. We are high as kites on adrenaline and pure, undiluted joy. We see John shake his head and go to his room wearing a puzzled expression of, "I'll never understand these girls", which makes us laugh even harder.

"Duuuuuude! We have prom dates!" exclaims Mandy gleefully.

"Oh my god. Tonight was awesome!" I say, dragging my butt toward the bathroom to wash my face.

"Sheer perfection," she agrees, sprawling on the bed.

I agree, nodding sleepily.

We hear the boys padding over to the door as I dry my face.

I cross the room to Chris and wrap my arms around his waist, snuggling his thin but muscular boy body. "Thanks for a wonderful day and night," I sigh, breathing deeply the wonderful scent of eau de Chris.

"You're welcome," he responds, lightly squeezing me. "I'm beat, time for sleep."

"Me too," I yawn. "Oooo. 'Scuse me."

"See you tomorrow," he says, lifting my face in his hand.

He kisses me goodnight with a kiss that is like chocolate and honey all rolled in one and I wander off to bed feeling drunk, happy and so grateful to be exactly where I am on this night...which is an entirely new and unfamiliar feeling, but I like it.

· Twenty ·

January 3, 1988

"What?" I say shaking the static out of my head like a wet dog flapping its ears.

I know Mom is talking to me, but somehow I can't hear her. "What?"

"Your Grandpa has a brain tumor..." she's talking and talking and it doesn't make any sense. I try to read her lips.

"He passed out and your Grandma picked him up, I don't know what she was thinking..."

I have to go. I have to pack. I grab a duffle bag from my closet and start shoving things in, ignoring my shaking hands, fast forwarding through the screaming panic that floods my mind. In two steps I snatch up the phone, dialing before I can comprehend the toxic pellets that spill from my mother's mouth. "They're already at the hospital and he'll have surgery in the morning."

Defeated, I set the phone down. There's a keening that fills the apartment, like a puppy whining for its mother. She stands looking at me coldly, "I can talk to my travel agent if you want."

I realize I am making this sorrowful whimper. "Yes, please."

From that moment my world stands still. The packing, phone calls, a plane ticket, Mandy and her Mom taking me to the airport.

Arriving to a warm, humid blast of air as I glide through the automatic doors and land with a clunk in the backseat of a taxi.

"St. Anne's Hospital, please," I tell the driver, fishing sunglasses out of my backpack and rubbing my eyes.

I've been so worried ever since he moved them down here and then left them all alone at Christmas. It's ironic that his parents were the one who took care of me. It's all so complicated. I adore them, hate him, and they want us to be best friends. Just forget about the part where he beat the crap out of me.

Like a jackhammer in the back of my brain is the same litany, please let him be okay...please let him be okay...please let him be okay...please...

Bargaining with God that I'll slurp as much shit as required when I get home if he just lets my Grandpa be alive. I'll join the choir you son of a bitch, just let him be okay. Okay, I'm sorry. Just please fix this, I bargain in my head.

I throw some bills at the taxi driver and rocket through the automatic doors, dodging people left and right as I speed toward the help desk. "Dale Graves, please?"

"I'm sorry, only immediate family is allowed in the ICU," snips the short, dumpy troll.

"I'm his granddaughter, does that count?"

"Down the hall to your left, get a pass at the double doors," the helmet haired, mousy woman says robotically.

I can't even spare the brain cells to lash out at this idiot woman who has chosen to make my already very difficult day even worse. Reaching the double doors, a nurse hands me a visitor tag and guides me down the curtained corridor until I see the giant white pleather purse that my Grandma has carried for a trillion years sitting on the floor. Ominous beeping of various monitors and medical equipment sets me on edge, as I take a deep and shaky breath.

Peeking around the curtain, I see my Grandpa in the bed with tubes, wires and his face is black and blue. I spin right back around so they won't see me lose it. Grandma shuffles out from behind the curtain and stands beside me, "He's going to be okay," she whispers.

"I'm sorry, it's just...I tried to call and I got here as soon as I could, and I'm sorry..." it all comes out in a flood of tears as I hug her like I'm clinging to her for dear life. She pats me softly, comforting me as she always has. It was their bed I sprawled in when I had chickenpox, and they waited on me hand and foot. I was their baby girl.

"Why is his face so bruised?" I'm so scared to see him like this. My Grandpa has never been seen in his pajamas, let alone a hospital gown.

"They had to go up his nose to get the tumor out," she says, her eyes magnified by her thick glasses so she looks like a small, fluffy owl. "It's not cancer."

I sit abruptly on a nearby chair. The relief hits me like a two by four to the chest. He is saved. Okay God, I owe you one.

We creep back into his curtained room and I slip my hand into his. "I love you Grandpa." I lightly rub his hand with my thumb, grateful to feel his warm hand, grateful to see him breathe. These big hands have always held mine. Gentle hands that never hit belonging to a gentle man who almost never yells. He's the very best Grandpa, and has always been number one.

Grandma looks on with a loving smile. I can tell she feels better with me here.

"I'll find someplace to get Chinese, since he doesn't like it anyway, might as well," I whisper, trying to think of something to get our minds off of the ICU. She brightens, and I head off to hunt down a phone book. I only have a couple of days here, but it's better than nothing. I'm so happy he's alive, I could light this whole town!

That night, we sit at the table in my grandparents' apartment. There are still some boxes stacked against the wall, not yet unpacked.

"Sorry about this mess," Grandma apologizes, chowing down on the Chinese take out like she hasn't eaten in weeks. "Grandpa and I just haven't quite gotten to everything yet."

"Don't worry about it," I say, trying to force myself to smile. The doorbell rings, and I get up, "Don't worry, I'll tell them you don't want any." I joke.

I open the door and I am face to face with Peter Graves. Without thinking, I slam the door in his face. Backing toward my grandmother, I am speechless as my father enters the apartment.

"Have you been to see Dad?" he asks, his eyes flashing with anger.

"Yes," I respond, trying to stay calm. My heart is racing. He is looking at me like he wants to throw me through the wall.

My Grandma sits, watching, then it dawns on me — his showing up here was planned. I act like everything is fine and sit back down in my chair.

"It isn't just a tumor," he begins to tell us. "Dad has Alzheimer's..." I sink back into myself as I listen my my father explain my Grandpa's diagnosis. It all seems like a bad nightmare, and I just want to wake up.

January 5, 1988

Grasping his hand, I look into my Grandpa's blue eyes that sparkle with recognition. "What's a girl like you doing in a place like this?" he croaks.

I battle to smile as a wave of despair crashes onto me. "To see you mon cher. I have to go catch a plane. I can't miss too much school right now," I explain slowly, kissing his hand and hugging it to my face. I am distraught that I have to leave them like this. Their son, who can't be bothered to help them unpack, has left them alone to manage through my Grandpa's crisis. I don't know what he's doing, and haven't asked.

"No, you go, study hard," he says, patting my head. "You have to get into a good college, Kiera. You're a good girl."

I turn my face away so he won't see me crying. I wipe the snot on my sleeve and plaster a smile on as I tell my grandparents goodbye. I gently hug him and kiss his face. Turning to my Grandma, I can see she's still in shock. I hug her, and promise to call her every night. And I will.

I quickly chat with the nurse, giving her my home phone number. She tells me I'm a minor, so she won't be using it. I tell her it's just in case, and to please look after my beloved Grandma and Grandpa. She just gives me a sad smile as I press the button for the double doors of the ICU to open. I collapse into a waiting cab and cry all the way to the airport.

· **Twenty-One** ·

March 8, 1988
B.F.E. Indiana

Today, I wake up and I am seventeen years old, totally depressed. My mother didn't even wish me "Happy Birthday" this morning before school. My grandparents aren't here, and they've never missed a birthday. I'm going to pretend that I don't care (even though I do) because tonight Mandy and the rest of my friends are up to something. I know it'll be cool. I wonder if Mom just completely forgot. I haven't seen much of her since Hank showed up in December. She spends all her time over at his house and almost never comes home. I've even started asking Mandy to drive me to the school corporation's administration building after school once a week so I can get money for food, soap, cleaning supplies, paper products and laundry. I mean, I'm still a minor and I think I should have the bare minimum covered. Her lack of responsibility shouldn't be my problem. Unfortunately, at this stage of the game it is, which doesn't thrill me.

The good news is, that despite the fright he gave us in January, that my Grandpa is recovering well. I have called and talked with Grandma everyday, and done what I can. The phone bill might be part of what's contributing to my mother's malaise. I can never tell.

Smiling broadly, my friend pulls up in her Escort to take us to school. "Happy Birthday, Kiera!" Mandy hollers as I open the car door.

"Thanks," I respond, climbing in and shutting the door.

"Nice ensemble," she grins, knowing I have been in a permanent bad mood since Grandpa was in the hospital.

I went full-on get-the-hell-away-from-me-you-hayseed today. I spiked my hair, all ten inches of it, and streaked it with blue stuff that L'Oreal makes. I'm wearing my Docs, fishnets, a purple miniskirt, my black Skinny Puppy "Dig It" t-shirt and a Salvation Army bought men's suit coat that I love. I have several pins on it that amuse me. One reads "fuck off" backwards, I have one Dead Kennedys logo pin, one Boingo pin and various pins that my grandmother gave me a few years ago that I wear all the time. Between the pins and the Docs, you can hear me coming down the hall. I like it that way.

"Ready for the quiz?" Mandy asks, raising her eyebrow. She's very competitive and hates that I do better than her much of time in French class. I study everyday and she doesn't. It's that simple.

"You betcha," I grin.

I dump unnecessary stuff into my locker and slide into my seat just as the bell rings.

"What the hell?" I hear someone behind me snarl.

I turn around and find myself looking at a cheerleader, Pom pom, dipshit extraordinaire.

"What did you do to your hair?" she asks me with disgust, like I have dog shit in it instead of hairspray.

"Fuck you, airhead," I growl, turning back around in my seat.

Miss Pom Pom raises her hand, "Monsieur Green, I can't see the board because of Kiera's hair…"

"En français, mademoiselle, en français," he says looking up from his desk, with a smile.

"Elle hair ay in the way, Monsieur," she says, making everyone giggle.

"Si je peux te voir, ce n'est pas vrai," Monsieur Green informs her. I could swear I saw a millisecond of smirk.

"What? What did you say?" she asks, looking around the room to see if her friends know.

"He said, 'if I can see you, that is not true'," Mandy tells her loudly. "Which means you need to shut up about Kiera's hair, dingbat."

The whole class roars with laughter, and Miss Poofball slouches in her desk, sulking.

"D'accord classe, maintenant, nous faisons un quiz..." Monsieur Green tells the class.

I smile to myself knowing that not only did pom pom poofball fail to screw with me, my score will ruin the curve for her. Ha ha. I hate these brainless little sheep who actually think that they are so great that everyone should be *just like them*. Bite me.

I finish the quiz in record time and watch Monsieur Green smile as he grades it and hands it back to me before Miss Pom Pom even finishes hers. A plus. One hundred percent correct, plus bonus questions.

I always do well in this, but it always feels like you can win if it's your birthday.

I plod through the day until lunch and am delighted and embarrassed to find decorations at our table along with Max and Andy standing next to it, grinning like fools. I don't like the whole birthday humiliation thing that some people like doing. I am praying that this is the extent of their craziness in public, because they know I'll kill them if they start singing.

"HAPPY BIRTHDAY, KIERA!" they say together, very loudly, making a few people look around.

"Thanks, you guys," I laugh, sitting down to think about what to eat.

"No line for you today, we have something for you," Andy tells me with a sweeping motion to his left.

I look and see Mandy and her mom walking toward us with a pizza box.

"Dude! This is awesome!" I am grinning ear to ear. It's so great to have something good happen to cheer you up after all the bad.

I stand up to hug everyone, "You guys rule! Thanks a lot Mrs. Goebel. I really appreciate the actual food."

She laughs, "You're welcome Kiera, I'll see you tonight." And with hugs all around and a kiss on Mandy's cheek, she departs for her office.

We happily devour the pizza and chat about Spring Break, which is next week. We're throwing around ideas and talking about prom.

There was something going on among the three of them, but I can't put my finger on it. The thing is, I love good surprises and wouldn't want to ruin anything they're planning for tonight just because Andy can't keep a straight face to save his life. You can't play cards with him because he can't bluff or keep a straight face at all. And if it's Old Maid, he laughs like an imbecile every time he gets the Old Maid. I admit that his honesty to a fault is part of the reason I just love him to bits. Mandy is a good secret keeper. She only lies when it's for something important and I always know when she lying. Max isn't great at keeping secrets only because he's not always aware of when he needs to keep information to himself. His saving grace is that he is really quiet and he observes more than he talks.

Before I realize it, we have drifted through fifth and sixth hour and it is time to leave the beige, brick monstrosity known as the high school! Yes! I hope if there's birthday cake, that chocolate is involved. I chuck my books into my locker and meet Mandy by the door to the parking lot. Max and Andy are suspiciously nervous.

"The boys need a ride, do you mind?" Mandy says in what is supposed to be an offhand way, but I can tell something is going on.

"No, of course not," I say, smiling at them like I have no idea what's going on.

They smile at each other and we all head across the parking lot and pile into the car. I am always surprised that the tires don't just give way under the small car with all of us in it. I am herded into the front seat and soon after, I am blindfolded.

"Don't flatten my hair or I'll kill you," I giggle.

"Would we mess up such a lovely hairdo?" says Andy, a smile in his voice.

"We had to do it, or the surprise would be ruined," Mandy tells me.

"Surprise?" I ask.

"You'll see when we get there," Max tells me, barely stifling a laugh.

It must be a good one if he's all giddy. Nervous and excited, I am guided out of the car, and steered into what I assume is a house, and then deposited into a chair.

"OK, ready?" asks Mandy.

I nod uncertainly.

Mandy carefully unties the blindfold and I see Chris, John, and Victoria standing in Mandy's living room smiling at me.

"HAPPY BIRTHDAY, KIERA!" they say together at a pretty good volume, making me jump.

"Oh my god, you guys!" I laugh, getting up to hug everyone. "I've never had more than three people celebrating my birthday before. This looks like an actual birthday party!"

Chris wraps his arms around my scrawny waist, "I like your hair," he says, kissing me lightly on the lips.

"I'm so psyched to see you, sugar!" I squeal, throwing my arms around his neck and wrapping my legs around him so that I'm hanging on him like a monkey.

I set my feet back on the floor, realizing with slight embarrassment that I may have just mooned everyone.

"I'm glad to see you, too, pretty," Chris purrs with a wide smile. My insides melt and pool in my boots. I'm ready for some quality time with him in a dark corner downstairs.

"Well, shall we get to the fun part?" asks Andy rubbing his hands together.

"The cake?" I ask, making everyone laugh.

"I was thinking presents," says Andy, chuckling.

"Not until Mom gets home, she wants to be here," scolds Mandy.

My eyes fill so fast I can't stop the tears that spill onto my jacket.

"Kiera? What's wrong?" Mandy asks, swiftly taking me from Chris and steering me into her room, Max and Andy in our wake.

"I'm sorry…" I gasp through sobs that I can't seem to control, "It's just that my own mother didn't even say 'Happy Birthday' and my grandparents have never missed my birthday," I wail, throwing my arms around Mandy's neck and bawling.

"Oh Kiera, I'm sorry," she says softly, hugging me as I soak her jacket. Max and Andy stand close and are touching my shoulders, letting me know they are there.

"I just don't get it!" I sob in frustration.

Max, drops down on his knees so he can talk to me. "We're here and we love you."

"Yeah," says Andy coming down next to Max. "It's not your fault that your mom is off doing whatever and your Dad took off with your grandparents."

Chris, John and Victoria come over to the huddle. "We're all behind you, girl," says Victoria, which means the world to me. I finally feel like we're officially friends.

"You're right guys," I say dejectedly. "I'm sorry about this. It's just so overwhelming sometimes."

"We're almost done with this year, then it's just one more year and we're outta here!" Mandy says, hugging me tightly.

"Yeah, I know. It just sucks right now. But you know what? Today is my birthday and we're going to have fun!" I say with false bravado.

Mandy and I go into the bathroom to repair my ruined eye make up and rejoin our friends in the living room.

"They're going to think I'm a complete jerk," I tell her. I'm so ashamed of being weak, overwhelmed, and emotional.

"Nah, I already explained everything to them. Everybody knows what the deal is with your family, so don't worry," Mandy says, soothing my face with a cool washcloth.

"I'm just tired of it," I sigh miserably. "I want to be done with this shitty little town and shitty little family, and I want to go be somewhere else where nobody knows me and I can get a do-over."

"Just one more year," Mandy says, sympathetically patting my arm as we go out to join the group.

Everyone looks up, concerned expressions on their faces. "Sorry everybody...Anyway, so what's this I hear about cake?" I say with a wan smile.

Everybody laughs and Andy says, "You have a one track mind..."

"So you do you...." I retort, lightly slugging his arm as I come over and squeeze myself between him and Max on the brown plaid sofa that takes up half of the living room.

We begin a game of charades, which with Max and Andy, is always fun.

"A water buffalo?..." Andy hollers out as John is miming what looks like a spout of water.

"No, you dumbass..." quips Max in false criticism, "it's obviously an elephant."

John nods in relief and sits down to watch Andy take his turn.

Andy pulls a card out of the pile and grins wickedly.

Uh oh.

"Hi everybody!" Mandy's mom calls out loudly as she comes in.

"Hi, Mrs. Goebel" we say in unison, Mandy getting up to give her Mom a hug and kiss.

"Happy Birthday, Kiera!" Mrs. Goebel says, coming over to hug me.

"Thanks," I respond, gratefully receiving a hug from her.

"Let's have some dinner before it gets late and you're all starving," she says, going into the kitchen and picking up the phone, "the usual, Kiera?"

"Better make it double with this many people, though," I grin.

She is sort of the den mother to the pack and is usually here when we order from the Foo Dog. She also knows that the boys eat like a couple of starved hyenas. She nods at me with a broad smile and waves me over to her, "Help me pick out a few extra things, too."

We pore over the menu that I have extracted from the kitchen drawer and select three more dishes to go with the usual pile of food that we order.

This is my idea of a great time. I love this more than almost anything, except maybe going to Medusa's and Wax Trax. Being with cool people and having great food — there's nothing better! I'm very lucky.

We go back into the living room to find that everyone has moved into the basement to play records and hang out. Mandy and I pad down the stairs in our socks and I am privately pleased to see several presents on the miraculously clean table. Usually the table is strewn with bits of chips and paint brushes, scraps of paper from homework or art projects and other miscellaneous crap.

"Hey you guys, I'm so glad to see you!" I say, walking up to Chris and John who are in deep conversation with Max and Andy about the evolution of punk music.

"...don't forget about Iggy Pop, I mean, c'mon!" says Andy in frustration.

"Thanks for coming to celebrate my birthday, you guys," I say.

"Aren't you going to open your presents?" John asks me shyly, casting an eye to the table and brightly wrapped packages.

"Not yet," says Max. "We're saving the best for last," he says, winking at me.

Then, as if on cue, we hear the doorbell ring and we trundle up the stairs to help carry the masses of food into the kitchen. Mrs. Goebel smiles as we form a human chain and pass the bags of food down the line and into the kitchen.

"Thanks for everything, Mrs. Goebel. This is the best birthday I think I've ever had!" I exclaim, hugging her in gratitude.

"You're welcome, honey, I'm so glad to help. You deserve it!" she says, giving me a big hug in return. Mandy, Mrs. Goebel and I walk into the kitchen to find that Max and Andy have gotten everything laid out and ready to go.

We have dinner buffet style, everyone piling egg rolls, crab Rangoon, pot stickers, sweet and sour pork, phoenix and dragon, and other scrumptious delights onto plates. I pile my plate high and sit in the place saved for me between Chris and Mandy.

"Howdy stranger," says Chris impishly.

"Hi," I respond, leaning over to give him a kiss on the lips before I get beast breath. "I'm so happy you're here."

"Me too," he grins, lingering to sneak another kiss. "I have so much fun every time I see you."

Victoria mimes gagging herself with her finger, so we dig into our food. I startle a little as he puts his hand on my thigh and my eyes get big as it slides up. I elbow him and squeeze my legs together, and his hand slides back toward my knees. I feel like my body is aflame. And now I have to try and concentrate on food?

We launch into the story of this morning with the cheerleader dingbat and her snit about my hairstyle. The really hilarious thing is that the poofballs spike their bangs up higher than we do most of the time. We call it "the claw" because it looks like they have a clawed hand sticking out of the front of their foreheads. Everyone laughs at the anecdote and seems to be having a great time. Most of the cheerleaders and poms wear these stupid-ass, enormous bows in their hair. I've fantasized a million times about walking up behind them and chopping them out after they've been mean to me or my friends. But I stick to verbal defense because with their lack of brain power, it just isn't that hard to make their microscopic brains liquefy.

We demolish the majority of the food, wrap up the remainder, and put it in the fridge. When I spy the cake, I am quickly ushered back into the basement for presents. This is so much fun for me! My mother didn't even give me a card and I'm hoping not to hear from my father. Mandy puts on "Black Celebration" and sits next to me on the red velour couch, as John perches on the arm by her. Chris is sitting on my other side. Max, Victoria, and Andy are sitting across the table from us on the floor. Mrs. Goebel stands behind them, smiling knowingly. They are all expectant and excited, so much so that I am very curious at this point and eager to get this show on the road.

"This one first," says Andy, pulling a long cylinder from the table and handing it to me.

I smile widely at my friends. It looks like a large poster. I quickly pull off the red wrapping paper and pull out a COCTEAU TWINS POSTER!!

"Oh my god, you guys!!" I scream, leaping to me feet and almost overturning the large coffee table as I reach to embrace my friends.

Everyone is laughing and smiling at my obvious pleasure of receiving this gift.

Since December, Max and Andy have been working a lot to earn money for gas and for college. Mandy and I have been spending more time together without them, by default. Max is finally getting the hang of driving his large, black Continental in the snow. Therefore, Mandy and I plan to get him to drive the next time we all go to the Windy City because Mandy's Escort groans under the weight of the four of us, let alone trying to stuff anyone or anything else in with us. The trunk of his car is so big you could fit four bodies in there with no problem!

"OK spaz, sit down and open these or we'll be here all night and we'll never get to the cake," chuckles Mandy.

"Oh…right…Sorry," I mutter, carefully laying my new poster on top of the TV and returning to my seat.

"OK, this one next," Chris says as he hands me a large box.

I look at him curiously and begin undoing the deep violet wrapping paper.

"C'mon, rip it!" yells Andy, gesturing wildly with his hands.

Chris laughs and nods at me, "Well, go on…"

I'm shy about this because if Chris keeps getting extravagant presents for me every holiday, I'm never going to catch up or even come close. I have no prospects for getting my hands on a lot of money unless I inherit a bunch from an unknown relative, or I rob a bank, so…it looks pretty dismal until I can get a part-time job someplace.

I lift the lid of the box, pulling out a very pretty, purple sundress. "Oh, Chris! It's gorgeous! Thank you!" I say, smiling and burying my face in his neck as I hug him.

"You're welcome, Kiera," he says, giving me a light kiss.

"Alright, now this one," says Mandy, handing me another big box.

I tear the paper and underneath, on the box lid I see the dead dude smiley that Mandy and my little band of kooks draw on notes and folders and things as sort of our mark. Now I know who this one is from and I smile, nudging her, "What did you do?" I lift the lid and pull out a very cute pair of dark green pin-striped shorts, a black short-sleeved shirt and a belt. "This is so cool! Where did you find the shorts?" I squeal.

"Esprit," she shrugs, grinning at me.

"This one, this one!" yells Andy, thrusting a large box at me.

"OK!" I laugh, taking the box and tearing off the violently orange paper, knowing full well it's from Andy.

I lift the lid off the box and pull out the cutest tie-dye t-shirt and skirt I've ever seen. It's green with blue and purple tie-dye on the sides. "Where on earth did you find these? This is so cool!" I exclaim, jumping up and holding them up to see how they'll fit.

"Bizarre Bazaar," Andy informs me with a smug grin, fully enjoying my reaction to his gift.

"OK, now this one," says Max, handing me a box.

I smile at my serious friend and gratefully take the box. I pull off the comics he has used as wrapping paper and lift the lid of the box. "Oh, Max!" I yell, lifting a pair of earrings out of the box that look like small brass charms. One is a snowflake, one is a mask, and one is a faery. "These are so beautiful!" I gasp, blinking away tears. I am so overwhelmed by my friends' generosity and that they know me so well.

"Keep going," he tells me, smiling.

I pull another pair of earrings out of the box that are like silver charms, a skull, a cat, a witch, and a bat.

"Keep going," he nods, urging me to open the next box.

I pull a beautiful moonstone pendant on a silver chain out and everyone oohs and ahhs.

"This is gorgeous!" I squeal, motioning for Mandy to help me put it on.

"A little token from me to you," John says, smiling at Mandy and I as she fastens the clasp. Then Chris hands me a card and you could cut the tension in the room with a knife.

"Shut up!" Max shushes, flinging his hand over Andy's mouth. "Don't say anything!"

I look around at my friends quizzically and open the envelope, pull out a funny birthday card, and a check? Pay to the order of Kiera Graves, Eight Hundred and Fifty Dollars and no one hundredths cents. I hear buzzing in my ears and can't breathe. What the hell?

"She's going to faint...Kiera, breathe honey," I faintly hear Mrs. Goebel saying as I turn to look at Mandy, in a dream-like state.

"I don't understand," I mutter dizzily.

"The Honors French program," Mandy reminds me. "We took some liberties, I hope you won't mind..."

"Oh...I..." I swallow painfully as my throat tightens.

Chris sits next to me, holding my hands. "Mandy kinda snagged some of your artwork and gave it me. Mom has a friend who has an art gallery, so over the holidays, your stuff sold out and this is the check."

I stare at him, then look around at my friends who are all nodding, smiling at me, knowing any second my brain will accept this is real.

"An art gallery?? Are you serious? How did you?...When?" I throw my arms around Chris's neck, nearly strangling him. "I'm writing a thank you note to your parents tonight. Can you please thank them for me too when you see them? Oh my god? She did that for *me*?"

Suddenly, it fully dawns on me that not only did my artwork sell out, I get to escape this shithole town for six whole weeks with two of my best friends. "YOU GUYS!" I yell. "I GET TO GOOOOOOO!" I holler, jumping up and down all over the place, Mandy and Andy standing up and joining me, "YAAAAAY!" we yell. We stop to catch our breath.

"You've got a few more to go before we're ready for cake," giggles Mrs. Goebel.

"OK, I'll get cracking, I'm ready for dessert!" I say glowing with happiness. Despite everything, this is turning out to be the best birthday ever.

I open the card attached to a box and inside it says:

Kiera -
Sorry it took me so long. I'm glad you found
Chris.
Happy Birthday you big weirdo!
Love,
The Empress of all Bitches, Victoria

I tear the deep red wrapping paper off the box and lift the lid. It's a very cool, black, porkpie hat that fits me perfectly! Immediately I put in on, and go hug Victoria who seems to be having a good time in spite of being in cowtown.

"HAPPY BIRTHDAY TO YOOOOOOU!!!!" everyone sings loudly at me.

"WOOOOOO!" I scream, jumping up and down some more and doing an impromptu conga line around the basement with my friends. "C'est bon ca! Nous allons cette ete..." we chant as we conga around the bean bag chairs.

We go by Mrs. Goebel, each of us giving her a kiss on the cheek as we go by, "Merci, Mrs. Goebel!"

"You're all so welcome," she says, smiling at her fan club. "Anyone for cake?"

"Yeah!" Mandy and I yell at the same time as we tear off to the kitchen, everyone else trailing behind us.

"You're the birthday girl, so you have to go sit down," says Mandy, shooing me away.

Everyone except Mandy and her Mom gathers around me at the kitchen table, until they come slowly toward us holding a fabulous three-layer, chocolate overdose cake that has seventeen candles on it.

"Happy Birthday to yoooou..."

I am so happy and love my friends so much!

"Happy Birthday to yooooo..."

"Happy Birthday dear Kiera...Happy Birthday to yooooou!"

I look down at the cake to blow out the candles and almost choke with laughter at what is written on it:

Happy Fucking Birthday Kiera

We're all cracking up as I take another breath and blow out the candles.

The thing is, my wish already came true.

Chris and I have swollen lips from so much smooching in a bean bag we dragged off into a corner. Mandy and I get the giggles, and it pisses Vic off to no end. But, if there was ever someone you'd want as your friend, it's her. She's a little rough around the edges, but if you're her friend, she'll stick by you no matter what. Our fierce, badass ice queen — all wrapped up in crushed velvet.

Mandy and John are very cute together, too. She still gets frustrated sometimes when he clams up, but they have devised a signal (her poking him really hard) to let him know when he's doing it. She's always been so open with everyone about everything — so it drives her insane when she feels like she doesn't know what is going on with John. All I know is that every time he looks at Mandy, you can see that he's head over heels. His quiet adoration of my best friend is everything I wished for her.

As far as Chris and I? So much of the time, I can't get anyone to hear me and I am invisible. He makes me feel like I'm not a hopeless case. I feel safe and comfortable with him. And I'm less crabby when he's around. He's my friend, and my sweetheart — which is so cool. I love that it doesn't matter to him if my hair is all messy or my makeup comes off while I'm dancing. He doesn't criticize me. That's major for me. So, he is great for my confidence and self-esteem. It feels so good to be heard and not be invisible. But not with him and not with my friends.

Tonight has been incredible for me. I feel like my world is opening up, making these new, awesome friends outside of our miniscule sphere in Bubbaland.

We see them out for the drive home, knowing we'll see them again soon.

I feel like we'll always be together, in some way.

· Twenty-Two ·

Thursday afternoon
May 1988
Cowtown

As I'm putting away the dishes, the front door lock clicks open, making me jump. She's home really early. She's completely soaking wet — fully dressed .

"What the heck is going on?" I ask, scowling at her as she leaves a puddle in front of the door.

"I went swimming at Hank's," Mom tells me nonchalantly leaving soggy footsteps all the way down the hall. I put down the plate I'm holding and wander after her, trying to figure out what in the name of creation is happening.

You have to understand, this is the woman who has never left the house without a full face of makeup in her life. She doesn't get her face wet, and certainly not her hair. Nobody ever touches her hair except the hairdresser. Hank's house is in the middle of the subdivision, and it's 3:30 in the afternoon. The fence around the pool is chain link, and her underwear is completely transparent.

"Why didn't he give you a towel to use for gods' sakes?" She strips off her dripping wet clothes, piling them on the floor in a heap.

"Oh Kiera, one day when you're a grown up, you'll understand," she patronizes, stepping into the bathroom for a shower.

I sincerely doubt, if I live to be one hundred and twenty, that I will ever understand half of the crazy shit my mother does. Shaking my head, I wander back to the kitchen, snap on my headphones and finish unloading the dishwasher. I slam some cereal bowls into the cabinet. Brett is about to graduate, I'm trying to figure out where to go to college and what to do with my life; and my mother has disappeared into mist. It isn't like she's been around much for me anyway, but I always thought she'd show up. I don't know what I'm supposed to do since none of the adults I'm related to are available, or acting like grown-ups. Make no mistake, whatever is going on here — I'm staying the hell out of it unless I am dragged.

May 21, 1988
Cowtown

I am so nervous that I am starting to sweat even though it's about 60 degrees outside. Normally, I am cold so much that Chris calls me "lizard girl." We are getting ready to go to prom! Victoria, Mandy and I get our hair done at the salon Mandy's Mom goes to. I've never had my hair professionally done for anything before in my life. I have a French braid with some ribbon that matches the gorgeous red velvet dress that Chris gave me for Christmas. Mandy has her hair in an elegant French twist. Victoria has a bob, so she just had them do her usual style. We get dressed at Mandy's house, listening to The Smiths and Depeche Mode. We help each other with makeup, do our nails and chit-chat about our plans for the evening.

What a surprise we have in store. The prom queen will not be expecting this pack of nobodies to even be there. Mandy and I look at each other and giggle when we see the huge, black stretch limo pull into the driveway. You have to understand, for us this is super glamorous. There are no limos in cowtown. This is the company that Chris's parents use all the time, and probably have frequent user miles or something crazy. I feel the prettiest I've ever felt, which is solidified as Chris's jaw drops while exiting the limo.

He abruptly closes his mouth and comes over to me, "Wow, you look so amazing," he says, taking my hand.

"Thanks," I demure, "You look awesome, yourself."

And boy does he ever! He looks good enough to eat in his black tuxedo with black tie and cummerbund. His thick, dark hair falls into his eyes as he fumbles with a small plastic box.

"I hope this is alright," he stammers, holding out a corsage for me.

I gasp at the lovely arrangement of red roses that match the dress perfectly, "Chris! They're gorgeous!" I exclaim, as I let him slip the corsage onto my wrist. I know darn well his mother has orchestrated this whole thing. Mrs. Lydia Sullivan is turning out to be one of the greatest women I've ever met.

I look over to Mandy to see how she's doing and am stunned. After struggling with the slippery upholstery, John emerges looking like a young Gene Kelly in his tuxedo without his glasses! Mandy is jumping up and down and squealing, "You look so awesome, honey! I love your contacts!!" She leaps onto him, knocking him backwards into the open limo door.

Chris, Victoria and I laugh uproariously and give them a few minutes alone, before we walk over to the feet sticking out of the car.

John's face is covered in lipstick kiss prints and Mandy is grinning at us over her shoulder, "What, you want to join us or something?"

"Scoot over, tart," quips Victoria, hiking the skirt of her black satin dress up so she can climb into the car. She looks absolutely fabulous wearing a black satin dress that fits her like a glove, with long, black satin gloves, and black satin pumps. She looks like a starlet from old Hollywood. Chris was sweet and also got her a wrist corsage, of course. I'm so happy she's crashing prom! She's just the kick in the pants this town has earned.

Chris and I pile in after Vic and we caterwaul along with The Cure on the way to Le Maison where Chris and John made reservations. I look at Chris and smile as we all sing along with Robert about kissing from his feet to where his head begins

I can think of a few other places I'd like to kiss. It's so hard not to think these things when I am sitting next to the most gorgeous, sweet, and intelligent guy I've ever known. He's so beautiful. Inside and out. Purr.

We pull up to the restaurant, which is the only "nice" one in town. I feel intimidated as the patrons all gawk at us on our way to our table, or rather, tables. The staff have pushed two tables together in a corner by the kitchen door. Mandy and I exchange a look of holy-crap-dude-can-you-believe-this? Half the law firm of Sinn, Pratt and Broker is in here tonight along with a few other prom goers. Victoria gives one gawping table two black satin gloved fingers up as we settle in. Victoria sits between the two couples like a den mother watching over her brood, and helps us not to trash our clothes before we actually get to the prom.

"Mandy, watch it there," Victoria points out as Mandy nearly knocks over her water glass while gesturing animatedly in a conversation with John.

"Thanks, Vic," says Mandy, catching herself and the glass just in time.

Mandy is wearing the prettiest tea-length, strapless, midnight blue satin dress, accented by long, white satin gloves and white pumps. It really suits her beautiful, pale skin. She looks like her mom's prom picture, actually. John followed Chris's example and got a wrist corsage, in white roses instead of red. John is still kind of in awe of his good luck in having Mandy for his girlfriend. At one point while she was in the ladies' room, he asks me, "Do you think she really likes me, for real?"

"Dude, if you don't know by now that Mandy is completely nuts about you, then I just don't know what," I reply, causing him to blush and stammer.

"How did I get so lucky?"

"Because you're a nice guy, John. Nice guys don't always finish last," I tell him.

It's true. If geeks would stop drooling over cheerleaders and check out the pretty, smart girls, they'd definitely be pleasantly surprised. Only very stupid girls don't know how great geeks are. Besides, who do you want to marry, the smart, successful guy or the brainless muscle-bound guy? Duh. No-brainer. But then, that *is* the problem.

John is gazing at his date with complete adoration and she is thoroughly enjoying his face sans spectacles. Victoria seems amused watching them in their little cloud of mutual affection.

"I love Max and Andy, but I'm so glad they're not here," says Mandy.

I look at her in shock, "How come?"

"Because they have the manners of starving orangutans," she giggles.

"I see your point," I respond, looking around the restaurant.

Andy and Max are the coolest guys to be friends with and we love them dearly, but the truth is — you can't take them anywhere. I am hoping they'll grow out of it, or maybe they'll get girlfriends who can help train them a bit. Max isn't as bad as Andy. Andy just can't seem to refrain from belching or speak in an "indoor" voice, so going to a restaurant with him can be an experience. They are used to him at the Foo Dog, and don't care because we are good tippers.

Dinner is coming to an end sooner than I would prefer. We order chocolate mousse cake for dessert and I'm thinking about how I wish I could suspend time during fabulous moments like this. I wish I could make time slow down or pause for just a little while.

Chris takes my hand and kisses it, "I can't wait to take you to the dance."

"Thanks," I say, leaning over to kiss his luscious lips. I don't give a crap about public displays of affection. As long as I'm not being disgusting, who cares? I mean, Chris is gorgeous...like, flat out, drool and slobber gorgeous. I'm terrified that I won't live up to his expectations. I'm worried about what's going to happen when we arrive. I quickly shove these stressful thoughts out of my head and take a deep breath.

"What's wrong," Chris asks me, his green eyes searching my face.

"Nothing, sugar. I'm just a little nervous," I say, smiling at him.

"Why are you nervous?" he asks, leaning over and touching his forehead to mine. "You have nothing to worry about. You look beautiful and you're with me."

"Yes, I am," I respond, winking at him slyly.

"OK you two, knock it off before everybody barfs," groans Victoria. "Same for you!" she barks, swatting John with her handbag.

John had just finished feeding a bite of cake to Mandy who was giggling and making suggestive movements with her mouth, making John turn deep red. We notice that most of the patrons in the dining room are still staring openly at us, and seem to have sticks up their butts. Heaven forbid some kids have fun in this town.

We thank John and Chris for dinner and glide out to the car under all the watchful eyes. We slide into the limo and proceed to the high school gym.

Mandy is positively squirming to get there and is squeezing the hell out of John's hand, much to his discomfort. Victoria sits regally in her seat like a queen reclining on her throne as we discuss music possibilities for the evening.

"I just hope they play *some* decent music," I groan.

"They will, don't worry," winks Victoria.

"How do you know?" I ask, bewildered by her certainty.

"I brought a few friends with me," she grins, reaching into her bag and pulling something out, "I thought I'd persuade the DJ with my friends, the Jacksons," she tells me, showing me a wad of twenty dollar bills she is holding.

"You're kidding!" I gasp.

"Nope. I'm tired of the pep squad always running the show, so I'm going to take over," Victoria tells me haughtily. "Plus, it'll give me something to entertain myself with while you four are playing tonsil hockey."

Mandy and I look at each other and scream with laughter. This is going to be one hell of a night, for certain. Victoria is a pistol. I can't wait to see what happens.

"Don't worry, I'll be on my best behavior. Besides, the DJ is an old friend," Vic tells me, smiling wickedly.

We pull up in front of the school by the gym entrance and pile out of the limo. Mandy and I exchange anxious looks and take a deep breath. Everyone outside has turned to see who on earth showed up in a limo. Our group clatters into the entryway which has cardboard palm trees stuck to the walls here and there along with crepe paper that is strung and taped across every available flat surface. Victoria struts into the room ahead of us and immediately heads to the DJ who is stationed on one end. They are playing "Heartbreak Beat" by the Psychedelic Furs and the dance floor is full. This is already looking and sounding way better than I expected.

Chris and John grin at each other as they lead us across the room to an empty table with a card on it that says: "reserved Sullivan and

Sutherlin – 5." I take a seat at the small, round table trying to relax and get my bearings. Mandy sits next to me and looks around the gym at the other people, soaking it in. Chris and John depart to get drinks for everyone in our group. We're wired enough, so we're strictly non-caffeinated tonight.

"Wow, it's like they just realized we exist," Mandy mutters in disgust as we watch a cluster of poofballs gathering across the gym. So stealthy, that bunch.

"Aren't they sneaky staring at us and whispering?" I say wryly, grinning at my best friend.

Victoria glides over and sits in her spot across the table from us, "Did you guys bring your dancing shoes?" she asks, with a wicked smile.

"Ooooo! What did you get them to play?" squeals Mandy excitedly.

"It's a surprise," Victoria says raising her eyebrows.

The guys get back just in time because the DJ is playing one of Victoria's "special requests" and we have a ball dancing around to our favorites. About this time, I notice that several tables full of people are looking at us and I catch Chris's attention, "What's with them?"

"They probably want to know where we found such pretty girls," he replies, with a wolfish grin.

"They look like cheerleaders to me," grumbles John. "Just ignore them."

I try desperately to do just that, but you know that feeling you get on the back of your head and neck when people are staring at you? I hate that. I eventually shake it off, knowing that after next year — I never have to see them again.

Chris and I are waltzing to a slow Thompson Twins song when someone runs into us.

"Excuse you," snaps a voice I wish I didn't recognize.

"Fuck you, dingbat. You don't own this school," I snarl at Miss Poofball from french class who has decided to harass me. Because that would be new and different.

"Shut up freak," says her doofy date whose face looks like it has seen the business end of the ugly stick. Chris and I cross the floor away from the hillbullies. I am enveloped in his embrace, in our own little world.

The song ends and we turn to go sit at our table. Everyone is standing around gaping at us like we're from another planet. Geez, this gets old.

"What the hell is going on?" says Victoria, meeting me at the table.

"They don't like "outsiders"," I sigh in frustration.

"What?" Vic asks, her eyes narrowing.

"One of the girls in my french class and her date decided to get all pissy," I say rolling my eyes as Mandy plops into the vacant chair next to me.

"Where's Chris?" demands Victoria.

"I think he and John are getting drinks. Don't worry about it. Happens all the time," I shrug.

"I'm going to give the little tart a piece of my mind," growls Victoria. You can almost see steam coming out of ears like a cartoon. She stomps toward the dance floor and disappears in the gathering crowd.

"Are you OK?" asks Mandy timidly.

"I'm just pissed," I sigh, "I wish that little blonde Barbie doll would fuck off and die."

"I'll second that," John interjects acidly, making me snicker.

Chris and Victoria return to our table laughing their heads off.

"Well, that was fun. How do you guys put up with these morons day after day?" Victoria asks.

"One more year!" Mandy and I exclaim simultaneously, our little group roars with laughter.

"Don't worry, I let 'Little Miss Hot Shit' know that if she even looks at any of us the wrong way tonight that I'll mop up the parking lot with her skanky little ass," Victoria tells us, punching her right hand into her left palm menacingly.

"Well, I'm not about to pick a fight, but I won't take any crap from her," I tell everyone, glaring at the crowd who is still staring at us.

At the first strains of "Halloween" by The Dead Kennedys, we all skitter onto the floor to thrash around as much as one can thrash around in formal wear, and we forget all about the run-in with Little Miss Pom Pom and her date. I am guessing that Victoria must have dropped two hundred bucks getting the DJ to play music that we like because he played plenty of New Order, Depeche Mode and even The

Cocteau Twins, which transports Mandy and me into bliss as we whirl around the gym with our adorable boyfriends. The night is passing by me like a movie on fast forward though. It's all going by so fast it's like I'm trying to hold rushing water in my cupped hands. I try to memorize every detail, to imprint this in my mind. I want to remember the beautiful parts, not just the bitter.

Pink-faced and exhilarated, we climb into the limo at the end of the dance and go for a drive around the park. It is so beautiful at night. Victoria is sitting in front with the driver so that, in her words, "the lovebirds can get it on."

We are, shall we say, enjoying our boyfriends' company until we finally pull up to Mandy's house. Mandy and I roll out of the limo, rumpled, with swollen lips, and we're both grinning like idiots. "Goodnight you two," Vic says good-naturedly, waving at us, "You'll see your loverboys soon enough."

I walk over to the rolled down window of the limo. "Hey, thanks for coming with us tonight. You totally saved the whole prom!" I tell Victoria who waves her hand as if to say- don't mention it.

"Thanks again for everything, Chris, and you too John," I whisper into the open car door, not wanting to disturb the neighbors. They blow us kisses and we float inside, falling into bed and deep and blissful slumber. I am so glad that this Cinderella made it to the ball, and didn't have to ruin everything by having to disappear before midnight.

· Twenty-Three ·

June 3, 1988
cowtown

"I've got to see you before you leave," pleads Chris. It's been two weeks since we've seen each other, and time is short. He knows I'm overloaded with work before we go to Indiana State University for six weeks.

"Nobody has time to drive anywhere right now," I sigh. "We're all going full speed ahead." I feel bad that I can't get there to see him. I know it's not fair, but it's out of my hands.

We hang up, and I am having mixed emotions about everything. Tomorrow is Brett's graduation, so today after spending time at the library researching colleges, I have to run errands, do laundry and clean. I juggle seven bags of groceries up two flights of stairs and collapse inside just as one bag tips over. I jump when there is a knock at the door as I wrestle frozen food into the freezer.

Wiping sweat off my forehead with the back of my hand, I peer through the peephole and see Chris. I throw open the door. He's standing there in an old Devo t-shirt that hangs off of him, showing his lean boy body underneath. I reach my hand around the back of his neck, pulling him inside. Nibbling on his lower lip, I lead him down the hall to my room. He whips his shirt onto the floor and I shove him on the bed, leaping onto him. We kiss and kiss until we finally put ourselves out of our misery.

Now I completely understand why people go crazy. Now I understand what lunatic means. Heavens help me, now I'm hooked, head over heels for this gorgeous boy, and everything he does to me. We spend the whole afternoon together, entwined, in my room. Finally, I have to kiss him goodbye. We're going to write while I'm away, this is going to make it even harder, but I have keep forging ahead — no matter what.

June 4, 1988
B.F.E. Indiana

My mother is all a-dither because her golden boy is graduating today. I'm being dragged along on pain of disembowelment. So needless to say, I've conjured up the most obnoxious outfit I can dream up. I'm resigned to sitting in the bleachers and roasting, but if she's going to be a pain in my ass — she's getting it right back.

Brett is getting a huge stereo as a graduation gift. I didn't bother getting him a card or anything. I can't wait until he leaves for college and I don't have to deal with him and little friends threatening me all the time. He has been accepted to Bradley University, Hank's alma mater coincidentally, so everyone is all smiles. Brett doesn't have a clue what he wants to do with his life, so he's just coasting along and following orders. Nothing new there.

Mandy has volunteered to keep me company so that when other relatives show up, I have someone in my corner. She meets me by the gate where the graduates and their families are streaming in.

"Dressed for the occasion, I see," she says, laughing as she walks up to me.

"Yeah, I figured it was the least I could do," I say savagely. I'm wearing Mandy's old "In God We Trust, Inc." Dead Kennedys t-shirt with baggy, army green shorts and my Docs. I went all out and spiked my hair, adding green streaks here and there. I think it's totally hilarious that so many people have such a hissy fit about something as small and non-violent as hair color. Today it's about getting under the skin of as many people as possible because they get under mine. I show her the bicycle horn I've stowed in the pocket of my shorts, and we set off for the ceremony.

We clomp down the walk and into the bleachers, sitting a few rows behind my mother, Hank, and…my father. Hank and my father are exchanging looks of hatred and loathing. I'm going to enjoy this little battle. I am fairly sure that my father will restrain himself only out of fear of jail, since he's still on probation.

Everyone has taken their seats and we are bored to death within the first two minutes as some local businessman drones on about "responsibility and building your future." Like anyone is going to take this Nazi's advice? Yeah right. Mandy and I pass the time by making fun of people with snarky remarks, and making faces at parents and grandparents who are stupid enough to turn around and stare at us. Then we start going around, sitting behind them, and I honk the horn, making them jump out of their skin. We look around innocently and take off running.

Mandy and I go all the way to the back of the stadium so we can quietly discuss our plans for the rest of the summer. We are all set to go for six whole weeks to attend the Honors French program at Indiana State University! Completing the program is worth two college credits in French. It just can't come soon enough. I know that Terre Haute won't be a huge change from here. It's still the middle of nowhere, Indiana, but at least my family doesn't live there and I can meet people who are not from here. Andy is going, too. We're both hoping he isn't a super spaz so that we don't all get in trouble all the time during class. Mandy assures me that Andy is interested in improving his accent, so he will actually not screw around the whole time. I remain skeptical.

So, until July 10, we'll be working as couriers and gophers at Pratt, Sinn and Broker and painting a fence for Ms. Fitch. I think she overheard us trying to figure out how to finance our academic summer excursion, because she approached us during our fretful discussion and offered us $50 each to paint the picket fence around her house. Of course, we gratefully accepted on the spot. A little sweat and hard work never hurt anyone. Mrs. Sullivan's connection at the art gallery is clamoring for more artwork, so I am drawing and painting every spare moment I have until it's time to go.

So, we are set for the summer. The French program will get us through to August 20, and then it's just a couple of weeks until senior year! I can't wait to finish.

I enviously watch the students parading across the stage. Next year, it'll be us and then we will finally be free! This is one of those times I wish I could do the fast forward thing when time zooms right past. But, that's not how it works…so I'll just keep working and stay focused on getting the hell out of here. I can't imagine staying here in this cruddy, little cowtown, with no ambition to go anywhere or do anything. With my friends, Chris, Mrs. Goebel and the Sullivans backing me up, I feel like I'm going to make it in one piece. Al I have to do is stay focused and remain one step ahead of my parents.

I cannot wait to leave! There is a whole world out there and I am so excited to be this close to stepping out into it. If I stay alive long enough, my diploma will be my one way ticket out of here! Guess I'll keep my fingers crossed.

Hiding under the bleachers after our latest bicycle horn prank, Mandy elbows me. "So are you all packed?"

"You know it! I am far beyond ready to blow this joint."

We grin at each other as my mother, thoroughly embarrassed by our shenanigans, shoos us off. "Go ahead and go, Kiera." My family gathers around Brett in a tense clot among the celebrating graduates. I'm surprised and relieved to be so readily dismissed.

Without waiting for a second invitation, or looking back, we take off for Mandy's car, laughing in the bright summer sun.

Resources dealing with incest and child abuse

United States
http://www.rainn.org/
http://www.cwla.org/
http://www.kidshelp.org/zip.htm
http://www.girlsandboystown.org/home.asp

Indiana
http://www.aardvarc.org/dv/states/inddv.shtml

Illinois
http://www.shelter-inc.org/

Mississippi
http://hopevillagems.org/
http://www.sunshineshelter.org/
http://www.hopehavenshelter.org/about.html

New York
http://www.safehorizon.org/page.php?nav=sb&page=cac_about

Often PTSD goes undiagnosed in child victims of violence and abuse. Below are resources to consider if you or someone you know has experienced violent trauma.

Post Traumatic Stress Disorder (PTSD)

http://www.ncptsd.va.gov/facts/index.html
http://www.nmha.org/reassurance/ptsd.cfm